Angie Hockman is a 2019 RWA
Her professional background includes stints in law, education,
and eco-tourism, but these days you can find her writing swoony,
romantic stories, enjoying the outdoors with her family, or
dreaming of her next travel adventure.

To learn more, visit: **www.angiehockman.com** or follow
Angie on Instagram and Twitter: **@Angie_Hockman**.

Praise for *Shipped*:

'An extraordinary debut. Witty, romantic,
and completely addictive'
Lauren Layne, *New York Times* bestselling author

'*Shipped* is exactly what we all need right now: a rollicking
rom-com with a conscience. Through lush description and
sparkling prose, Angie Hockman takes us on an exhilarating
journey to the Galapagos Islands and straight into the hearts
of her characters. I relished every swoony second I spent reading
this story, and I can't wait to see what Angie comes up with next!'
Kristin Rockaway, author of *She's Faking It*

'*Shipped* is a sweet, sunny getaway of a novel with an
ambitious heroine I liked right away and a hero who's *chef's
kiss* a supportive dreamboat (pun intended). A vicarious
enemies-to-lovers trip to the Galapagos was exactly what I needed
right about now. I stan an environmentally aware romance'
Sarah Hogle, author of *You Deserve Each Other*

'Witty, charming as hell, and layered with real passion
for ecotourism, *Shipped* is a sparkling debut.
The perfect slice of vacation in book form'
Rosie Danan, author of *The Roommate*

'Enchanting, hilarious and a perfectly delightful escape!
I loved every second of this enemies-to-lovers romance.
Henley and Graeme are relatable, swoony, and all-around
driven. The backdrop of the islands will have you
yearning for sunny skies and sandy beaches'
Nina Bocci, *USA Today* bestselling author of
On the Corner of Love and Hate

'Flirty and fun, with a starring couple you'll fall in love
with, *Shipped* is an eco-conscious rom-com with great
characters, lots of laughs, and a stunning location . . . I'm sold!'
Sarah Morgenthaler, author of *The Tourist Attraction*

'Angie Hockman sparkles in this unputdownable
enemies-to-lovers romance!'
Miranda Liasson, author of *Then There was You*

'*Shipped* is the hilarious rom-com we all need right now.
I fell in love with Henley and Graeme, and it was such a
delight to watch them fall for each other. Angie Hockman has
written the perfect escape that's exploding with sexual tension'
Kerry Winfrey, author of *Waiting for Tom Hanks*

'*Shipped* is the most wonderful escape! In this sweet,
enemies-to-lovers rom-com, Angie Hockman seriously
delivers. I can't wait to see what she brings us next!'
Alexa Martin, author of *Intercepted*

'With a sharp, clever voice and so much charm. *Shipped* is a
pitch-perfect romantic comedy. I fell in love with the
Galapagos as Henley and Graeme did, and then I fell for
them as a couple. A lovely, joy-filled romp'
Rachel Lynn Solomon, author of *Today Tonight Tomorrow*

Shipped

ANGIE HOCKMAN

**HEADLINE
ETERNAL**

Published by arrangement with Gallery Books,
an imprint of Simon & Schuster.

First published in Great Britain in 2021
by HEADLINE ETERNAL
An imprint of HEADLINE PUBLISHING GROUP

2

Cataloguing in Publication Data is available from the British Library

ISBN 978 1 4722 8066 4

Offset in 10.8/14.90 pt Adobe Garamond Pro by Jouve (UK), Milton Keynes

Printed and bound in Great Britain by Clays Ltd, Elcograf S.p.A.

Headline's policy is to use papers that are natural, renewable and recyclable
products and made from wood grown in well-managed forests and other
controlled sources. The logging and manufacturing processes are expected
to conform to the environmental regulations of the country of origin.

HEADLINE PUBLISHING GROUP
An Hachette UK Company
Carmelite House
50 Victoria Embankment
London EC4Y 0DZ

www.headlineeternal.com
www.headline.co.uk
www.hachette.co.uk

For my grandma Betty.
And for the little girl who was afraid to fail.

1

Every time I collect my mail from the paint-spattered box in the lobby and see my name printed over and over in bold black ink, I'm reminded that I'm named after a rock star.

Not an endlessly cool rocker like Stevie Nicks, Joan Jett, or Madonna. No, my name is Henley Rose Evans, and my parents consciously named me after the lead singer and drummer of every boomer's favorite easy listening band, the Eagles.

Too bad I'm the furthest thing from a rock star you can find on planet Earth. My landlord barely remembers my name, let alone hordes of screaming fans, and I've trashed precisely zero hotel rooms. I do have dreams though. Big dreams for a shiny, successful career. Just not one that requires me to sing in public.

Tucking my stack of mostly junk mail inside my tote, I huff my way up the carpeted stairs of my downtown Seattle apartment building. By the time I reach my floor, my thighs are burning. I could have taken the ancient matchbox elevator, but I still needed to get my steps in today.

Floorboards creak as I trudge down the hall while the smell of lemon cleaner hangs in the air. My phone buzzes and I pull it from my pocket. It's a text from my sister, Walsh.

I have a big surprise . . . 💣 💥

My stomach drops like a stone chucked off a cliff. Walsh's "surprises" are surprises in the same way that getting hit by a bus is a surprise. I stop to respond, water droplets rolling off my coat and soaking into the patterned green carpet.

> **What's his name?**

> Not a guy. Tell you tomorrow.

> **Pregnant?**

> Hell no.

> **Fired?**

> Ha!

> **Come on what is it**

> Talk soon! 🐢 💜 ✈️ 👖 ☀️

"Motherfu—"

The door beside me opens with a wash of music and laughter. I jolt and my bag slips down the slick fabric of my raincoat to the crook of my elbow, wrenching my arm, and I almost drop my phone. Fumbling, I shove it into my bag.

"Oh," says my neighbor Sophie. Or is it Sophia? Sophie and Sophia moved into 4E last month, and they're both roughly the same height with long, highlighted blond hair and the same generically pretty features. They remind me of Walsh. "Hey, Hannah."

"Henley," I enunciate. A by-product of having a name outside the mainstream? No one ever gets it right.

"Are you just getting home from work?" Sophie/Sophia asks, glancing at the window at the end of the hall. It's well after 8 p.m. and completely dark outside.

"Night class."

"Cool." Looping a slim purse strap over her head, she closes the door behind her and the music and chatter that had filled the hallway is reduced to a dull rumble. "We're having a little get-together. Nothing fancy. I'm headed out for a beer run, but feel free to swing by."

I offer her a genuine smile. "Thanks. Maybe I will."

I won't.

My laptop and strategic management textbook weigh my bag—and my mood—down like a couple of bricks. My temples throb with exhaustion from the long day, and it's not even over yet. I still have the almighty task list to address.

Guilt twinges my gut as I turn the corner, but I brush it away. I like my new neighbors even though they're younger than I am; I'm twenty-eight and they're fresh from undergraduate-ville. We'll just have to hang out some other night. One where I don't have work or classes hovering over my head. So, sometime next century, maybe?

Reaching my apartment, I shove my key into the lock and shoulder open the door. A raspy yowl greets me. I set my bag on the floor and flip on the light.

"Hi, Noodles." I hang my keys on a hook by the door and my coat in the narrow front closet. Noodles the cat saunters into the foyer. He's a long-haired gray tabby with wiry fur that sticks out every which way, no matter how much I brush him, and golden-green eyes that focus in two completely different directions.

One time I googled "What's the opposite of cross-eyed" and the term "divergent strabismus" popped up, which sounds more like a sci-fi novel than a medical condition, but the vet said in his case it's hereditary, so nothing to worry about.

Whatever it's called though, Noodles is one rough-looking cat. Hence his status as the veteran resident of the local animal shelter before I adopted him last summer. I reach down to scratch Noodles under the chin. He croaks a meow like he's been smoking two packs a day for a decade.

"Miss me?"

Silence.

"I see how it is." I head to the kitchen and Noodles trots after me. I feed my smug cat before changing into yoga pants and a Boise State T-shirt. Grabbing a container of leftover quinoa salad from the fridge, I pad across the wood floor with a glass of pinot grigio back to my cozy living room.

Anyone who steps into my one-bedroom Belltown apartment would think I'm a first-rate world traveler—if they didn't know me. Oversized, colorful maps, framed marinescapes, and wildlife portraits are arranged in a collage above my ruby sofa. Along the opposite wall, which I've painted the same jewel-toned shade of reddish pink, stacks of marketing and travel books teeter on a trunk, while a Craigslist armchair squats under the window. It's like *National Geographic* and *Porthole Cruise* magazine had a baby and that baby splatted all over my apartment.

But the truth is: except for a handful of trips to Colorado as a kid and one generic spring break in Cancún when I was nineteen, I've never been outside the Pacific Northwest. No, I'm not a fraud. I'm a marketing manager for a global adventure cruise line.

So all the posters and prints? Office swag. Thanks, Seaquest Adventures, for the cheap decorating.

It's not that I don't *want* to travel. When I took this job three years ago, I had high hopes of seeing the world. Then life happened. Career ambitions. Grad school. Student loans. The vague, persistent headache that is adulting. But mostly my career. It's hard to take time out of the office when you're trying to climb the corporate ladder and make director before the age of thirty.

Setting my dinner and drink on my Ikea coffee table, I plop onto the sofa and yank the elastic band out of my bun. My hair tumbles over my shoulders and I shake it out, massaging the roots to ease my sore scalp. I wish I could turn in right now, just crawl into bed and clock out for the night, but my task list is burning a hole in my to-do app. I won't be able to sleep until everything is checked off, so I might as well get it over with.

Taking a sip of wine, I pull up the list and read the first item.

Task #1: Confirm Graeme posted British Columbia social media content.

I fish my laptop out of my bag and flip it open. Noodles hops up next to me and nestles against my thigh, purring. Thirty seconds later I'm scanning Seaquest Adventures's Twitter feed. I shove a bite of quinoa salad into my mouth and chew. I barely taste it as I scroll. Scanning tweet after tweet, I put down my fork, eyebrows furrowing.

When I reach yesterday's tweets, rage swells inside my chest. I log on to Facebook. Same. Instagram. Same. I squeeze my eyes shut and pinch the bridge of my nose. "*Graeme.*"

He didn't do it. He said he would, but he didn't. So freaking typical of Mr. High-and-Mighty Social Media Guru. I was right to make "confirm social media posts" the number-one item on my to-do list.

I glare at the tiny photo beside Graeme's name, at his strong, smooth chin and short brown hair. I hate to admit it, but the first time I saw his picture, I actually thought the arrogant jerk was handsome. And when we spoke on the phone on his very first day over a year ago, *oof.* I nearly melted. His voice is deep and rich and husky, like a lumberjack dipped in a chocolate fountain.

Then we started working together, and it wasn't two weeks before Graeme The Rotten Troll showed his true colors.

It started when some gem video footage from one of our Costa Rica cruises landed in my in-box. Most of it was typical—guests having fun on a hike, beaming smiles, high energy—but toward the end, the videographer included B-roll showing two capuchin monkeys grooming each other. It was *blink-or-you-miss-it* fast: one monkey appeared to sniff the other monkey's butt, made a sour face, then lost its balance and fell out of a tree. Hilarious, right?

I figured, hey, people love funny animal videos, so let's cut in some other wildlife clips from our cruises, set it to music, add clever captions, and post it on social media with hashtags targeted to boost engagement. I put my halfway-decent video editing skills to good use, and when I had a version I was happy with, I forwarded it to Graeme, our newly minted social media manager, for posting.

And the damn thing went viral.

I didn't know it went viral until the next morning, when our boss, James, pulled it up at our weekly department meeting. More than fifty thousand views and climbing. Post engagement was up 67 percent and our website traffic had shot through the roof.

After the clapping and laughter died down, James boomed his approval in the general direction of the speakerphone where Graeme was dialed in.

"Fabulous, brilliant. See, everyone? This is what ingenuity looks like. Well done, Graeme."

"Well done, Graeme." Not, *"Well done,* Henley."

And what did Graeme say in response to our boss wrongly giving him all the credit? After a few seconds of staticky phone silence, he simply said, "*Thank you.*"

As if that wasn't enough, James decided to smear salt in the wound. "*I wish all of you would take Graeme's initiative,*" he said to the group, then looked directly at me. "*Especially you, Henley. Costa Rica is your region, after all.*"

I know, I know. I probably should have said something right then and there—corrected James on the spot and told him exactly who was responsible for the viral video. But my mouth was too full of shock to do anything except hang open like a drowned fish. And James hates being told he's wrong, especially in front of other people. Once the meeting was over though, it was too late. Going to James at that point would have been like tattling, and who wanted to look petty in front of their boss?

So Graeme got away with it. He got away with swiping the credit and the praise right out from under me.

That *asshole*.

Ever since then, he's used the incident to launch himself to BFF status with our boss. The beginning and ending of every staff meeting is positively packed with testosterone-filled chatter.

How's your son? How was boating last weekend? Did you catch the latest Mariners game? There was enough brownnosing masquerading as bro bonding to make me want to smash the speakerphone into smithereens under my pointiest heels.

Here's the thing: I've worked with Graeme's type before. He might have the whole nice-guy facade down to a science, but I knew the truth. He was a sneaky, entitled user who was willing to do whatever it took to get ahead.

Graeme must have figured out somewhere along the line that I was onto him, because over the past year he's become nothing less than the bane of my professional existence. Anytime I want something done quickly, there's always a reason he can't do it. If I have an idea, he questions it. I send him an email? I get a curt response—never mind a please or thank-you.

Apart from the occasional video conference, I've never actually seen Graeme in person, since he works full time from home. So I like to think that despite his steel-cut jaw and those deep-set eyes, he has spindly arms and legs and cottage cheese breath to match his personality. I picture a short, paunchy Graeme cackling and dancing around a fire pit holding a pitchfork.

Logging in to Outlook, I punch out an email like I'm entering the nuclear codes.

To: GraemeC@sqadventures.com
Cc: JamesW@sqadventures.com
From: HenleyE@sqadventures.com
Subject: Social Media OVERDUE

Graeme,

I noticed that my requested social media posts promoting the airfare deal for all remaining 2019 "Coastal British Columbia & the Inside Passage" departures were not published today. As this deal expires in a week, and none of the September voyages are currently at capacity, I expect to see it marketed robustly on our social media platforms. See the Google Doc I shared last week for content. Please address ASAP.

Thanks,
Henley

Henley R. Evans
Marketing Manager, North and Central America
Seaquest Adventures | www.seaquestadventures.com

As soon as I click send, I snag my phone and tap on the box next to Task #1. A big black line appears, crossing it out. I inhale deeply through my nose and a sense of calm slowly spreads over me.

At least my end of this task is done. For now. Graeme better hop to it and get my shit posted though, like, yesterday.

My muscles relax as I nestle into the soft cushions and stretch out my legs. Crossing my feet at the ankles on the coffee table, I read tasks #2 and #3 on my list:

Task #2: Make student loan payment.

I make a retching noise in my throat and my shoulders tense automatically. I need to double-check my savings account and monthly budget before I drop that behemoth. Reluctantly, I reassign this task for tomorrow. I don't have the emotional energy to deal with it right now.

Task #3: Outline strategic management final paper, due Monday.

That I can do. But just as I'm about to set my laptop aside to grudgingly pull my textbook out of my bag, my in-box dings.

Graeme has replied. Nostrils flaring, I open his email.

To: HenleyE@sqadventures.com
From: GraemeC@sqadventures.com
Subject: Re: Social Media OVERDUE

soon -G

Graeme Crawford-Collins
Social Media Manager
Seaquest Adventures | www.seaquestadventures.com

I blink.

Blink again.

Soon? Is that soon like *right now* soon or *next Tuesday* soon? I scrunch my hand into a fist on top of Noodles. He purrs louder. This is so . . . unacceptable. And not just because he left our boss out of the CC. I grind my teeth until my jaw aches.

Graeme Crawford-Collins. *Graham Cracker-Collins.* I can't let him blow me off again. I won't.

Bookings for Pacific cruises from Alaska to Panama have gone up every single quarter since I joined the company—thanks in large part to my tireless efforts—and I will *not* see my track record ruined because of him. Especially not now, not when there are rumblings that Seaquest Adventures is creating a brand-new director of digital marketing position—one that I would do anything to land.

I'd work overtime. Pursue my master's in business administration at night. Volunteer for extra projects. Oh wait, I already do *all* of those things, so that promotion should have my name plastered all over it. But only if I don't fumble the game-winning pass late in the fourth quarter. I crack my knuckles against my jaw and, with a growl, drain my wine, slam the glass onto the coffee table, and click reply.

Gird your loins, Graeme Crawford-Collins. Because you're about to get a dose of *Henley thunder.*

2

To: GraemeC@sqadventures.com
From: HenleyE@sqadventures.com
Subject: Re: Social Media OVERDUE

To: GraemeC@sqadventures.com
From: HenleyE@sqadventures.com
Subject: Re: Social Media OVERDUE

Graeme,

"Soon" is a relative term. Please define.

Thanks,
Henley

Zing, take that, Graeme!

Okay, so it's not exactly thunder, but it is pretty biting in an understated sort of way. I smirk as I click send. I drum my fingers against my laptop. Chew on my thumbnail. Click refresh on my in-box. Nothing. Just when I figure Graeme has logged off for the night, an email pops up with a ding.

To: HenleyE@sqadventures.com
From: GraemeC@sqadventures.com
Subject: Re: Social Media OVERDUE

Soon, *adverb*
  1. In or after a short time

2. Without undue time lapse
3. When I get to it

-G

I cough in disbelief before fury surges through my veins. Squeezing my laptop in a death grip, I rearrange myself so I'm sitting cross-legged on the couch. Noodles hops down with a discontented meow at being jostled.

The man can't be bothered to send me anything except one-word emails 97 percent of the time, and when he finally does deign to communicate like a normal human being, it's a multipart dictionary definition steeped in sarcasm. A growl works its way up my throat.

To: GraemeC@sqadventures.com
From: HenleyE@sqadventures.com
Subject: Re: Social Media OVERDUE

Graeme,

Get to it now, please.

Thanks,
Henley

Not ten seconds later . . .

To: HenleyE@sqadventures.com
From: GraemeC@sqadventures.com
Subject: Re: Social Media OVERDUE

It might be 8:40 in Seattle, but it's almost midnight here in Michigan. Your posts can wait.

Like hell they can!

To: GraemeC@sqadventures.com
From: HenleyE@sqadventures.com
Subject: Re: Social Media OVERDUE

If you can take the time to reply to my emails, you have time
to post my social media content, at least to Facebook and
Instagram. Save the tweets for tomorrow.

Tweets only stay relevant for about eighteen minutes, so it's
too late in the day for them to reach an effective audience now.

A chat message pops up along the side of my screen.

> You don't have anything better to do
> than email me about work?

My mouth twists into a frown.

> Pot, meet kettle. Don't you have
> anything better to do than respond?

> You didn't answer my question. No fun
> plans for Henley Rose tonight?

I narrow my eyes at the screen. I *hate* it when he calls me Henley Rose. In that blissful first two weeks of his employment, he asked me what the "R" in my email signature stood for, and I made the mistake of telling him. I recall how he drawled my name on the phone, *Henley Rose*, like he had a secret to tell me . . . one that I wanted to hear . . .

Now he reserves the moniker for use on special occasions—aka when it's guaranteed to ensure maximum annoyance.

> No hot boyfriend to keep you busy?

Automatically, I gaze around my empty apartment, as if an imaginary boyfriend is going to pop out of my bedroom holding a dozen tacos and a chocolate cake. Noodles looks up at me from the floor—or rather, one eyeball fastens on the couch while the other checks out the coffee table. He's not impressed.

> I don't need a boyfriend. I'm too busy polishing my collection of knives. Big ones. With sharp, jabby ends.

> I'll take that as a no . . . so you like the big ones then?

> The bigger the better.

> Isn't that what she said?

Whoa, whoa, whoooa. Are we *flirting*? No way. My insides go all twisty and confused and heat flushes across my collarbone. I click on Graeme's contact photo again. His full lips seem to smirk at me, and I have the sudden desire to mash my mouth against his, just to see how it feels. Either that or slap him.

Chewing my bottom lip, I click over to Instagram and type "Graeme Crawford-Collins" in the search bar. Maybe a different picture would show his bad side . . . his slap-worthy side . . .

Nothing comes up. Huh. I try Facebook—he's not on there either. And Twitter makes strike three. A social media manager who isn't on social media? *Weird.*

I shake my head hard once. "What am I doing?" Fumbling with

the touch pad, I close the three incriminating tabs. Good God, I need to get out more. Actually go on a date once in a while—and not with my purple, battery-operated friend that lives in my nightstand. Because if I'm hate-attracted to Graham Cracker-Collins? My sex life is in a baaaad place.

Time to get back to the issue at hand.

> You know, in the time that this delightful conversation has happened, you could have posted my content by now.

> You didn't see the volcano, did you?

> . . . what?

> Volcano. You know, those things that erupt from time to time with molten hot lava?

Yes, I know what a volcano is. Jesus!

> What are you smoking? What volcano?

> Huh. Looks like you didn't read my tweets. I'm disappointed in you, HR. A volcano erupted in Galápagos this evening. Our ship was on the scene and the videographer on board captured some hot footage (pun intended).

I swallow a laugh and force my scowl back into place.

No, I hadn't heard about the volcano. When I'd browsed the

Twitter feed before, I was only looking for mentions of the airfare deal for British Columbia. I'd barely registered anything else. I click over a tab and reread the feed. Yep, there it is. Tweet after tweet about the volcanic eruption in an uninhabited corner of Isabela Island and how our cruise ship witnessed it live—from a safe distance. What a fantastic marketing opportunity. And damn it, Graeme actually boosted the publicity pretty well.

> I prioritized.

I can practically see the shrug.

> Well, prioritize my content next.

I begin typing how the airfare deal expires next week and we need to promote it on social media more, but before I can hit the return button, another message from Graeme pops up.

> I'll post your British Columbia content first thing tomorrow morning. Not that it will make much difference at this point in attracting more September bookings.

> Have fun polishing those big knives.

The bubble next to his contact turns red, indicating that he's offline.

I clamp my molars until my jaw pops. My dentist is going to lecture me about grinding my teeth again, I know it.

"Graeme," I grate.

Who is he to infer that my marketing plan for social media

won't net a few more bookings over the next week? That's just so . . . presumptuous. And *rude*. And so totally wrong.

I snatch my quinoa salad off the coffee table and stuff a bite into my mouth. It tastes like sawdust. Shoving my laptop away, I stomp to the kitchen, toss the quinoa into the trash, and riffle around my fridge. It's slim pickings: three containers of vanilla yogurt, various condiments, and a single mini Babybel cheese. Mental note: add grocery shopping to my weekend task list.

I grab a jar of grape jelly and my last two pieces of bread from an upper cabinet and make myself a peanut butter and jelly sandwich. I slap on the jelly with a bit too much gusto and it splatters across my gray laminate countertop. Graeme's words niggle at my brain. *Not that it will make much difference.* With a huff, I brace my hips against the counter and tear into my PB and J like a bear eating a salmon.

I should start my paper, but Graeme's parting shot has my stomach contracting and my skin itching. There's something I need to do. Polishing off my sandwich in four more bites, I return to my laptop and dig up last year's numbers for British Columbia and cross-reference them with our social media activity.

There was barely an increase in bookings. My social media marketing for these voyages last September hadn't worked as well as I remembered. Even with the airfare promotion, which was my idea, we needed to do something different to get the word out. Something outside the box.

I open a blank Google Doc. After a minute, the ideas trickle in. I start typing. It's after ten when I finish, and I haven't even started outlining my paper yet. If I want to stay on track to meet Monday's due date, I need to at least get that done tonight. I silently curse Graeme as I flop my textbook open on the coffee table and begin brainstorming.

"Rough night?" Christina pops her head over the gray cubicle wall between our desks, catching me rubbing my eyes. It's 9:15 on a Friday morning, and in the hour since I've been here, a gentle murmur of conversation has slowly overtaken the early-morning silence.

As far as offices go, ours is pretty clutch. It takes up the entire top floor of a historic building downtown, and it has high ceilings, exposed brick, and tons of light streaming in from wide, arched windows. Thanks to our proximity to Puget Sound, the scent of clean ocean brine is a permanent fixture in the building, bringing to life the framed cruise ship photos that line the inner hallways.

I tear my gaze away from the email I'm drafting to James's assistant to discuss my idea for a last-minute British Columbia direct call campaign.

"Just busy," I say. "And sleep-deprived. How about you?"

Hopping up to perch on the edge of my desk, Christina crosses her legs, emerald capris hiking higher up her slender calves. "Awful," she says with her usual flair. She flips her long sheet of straight black hair over one shoulder. It stands out starkly against her white eyelet shirt.

Rereading my email one more time, I hit send before settling in to listen to what will likely be a very long-winded, very dramatic story.

"So remember how I was going on a date with that guy from Bumble last night?" she begins.

Only vaguely, but I nod anyway.

"Well it was all going fine until we left the restaurant. There we were, standing on the sidewalk, talking about what to do next, when a cop drives by. And you know what this guy does? Leaps behind the nearest trash can like he's Batman or something. It turned out my date has a warrant out for his arrest."

I sit up straighter. "What did you do?"

She shrugs. "Went home with him. He was pretty cute."

My jaw pops open.

She laughs. "I'm kidding, Henley, geez! I told him I got a migraine and ditched him, of course. But then I met this *other* cute guy . . ."

"All right, well, I'm going to need the full debrief." I prop my elbow on the desk, chin in hand. Not having much of a dating life of my own, I live vicariously through Christina's adventures in dating land.

She slides off my desk. "How about lunch? Waterfront Park?"

I bite my lower lip. I have a lot I need to accomplish today.

"I know you're always 'so busy,'" she says, complete with air quotes. "But come on. We haven't done lunch in weeks."

"I know," I groan. "I'm terrible. Happy hour instead?" I can't remember the last time I went for drinks after work that didn't involve a business school networking event.

"Don't you have class?"

"Not on Fridays. Besides, the summer term ended yesterday and I'm off for the next month before fall classes start."

"Okay, happy hour it is," she says with a grin. "Miller Room?"

"Yes, please."

Catching sight of someone over her shoulder, she turns. "Tory!" she calls with a wave.

Footsteps approach, and a moment later our coworker Tory Hageman appears. Her platinum pixie cut catches the light and I practically squint at its radiance.

Whereas Christina is a year younger than me, Tory is four years older. But unlike Christina and me, Tory actually has her life together in ways that make ours seem hopelessly childish. She's married, for one. And second, she lives in a house. Not an apartment or a condo, but an actual house with grass and a fence and designated guest towels and everything.

"Hey, ladies," Tory says with a grin, hugging a stack of folders to her chest. "What are you two plotting over here?"

"Happy hour at Miller Room after work. You in?" asks Christina.

"Yes, perfect. Count me in. I have news to tell you too. Big news." Her smile widens to the point that I think her round cheeks are going to crack.

"Spill," I say.

She checks her watch. "Can't. I'm late for a meeting, got to run. Oh, and Henley—it looks like that director of digital marketing position is finally happening. I'll give you the details later." She crosses her fingers as she backs away, then turns and bustles toward the conference rooms.

My breath catches in my throat and I use every ounce of willpower not to paste a million-watt smile on my face. Tory is the director of financial planning and analysis, so her office has to approve the budget for any new positions. She undoubtedly has all the tea.

Christina nods after Tory. "It's about time we had a digital director."

I slide a look to Christina. It's no secret that I'm gunning for the new role, but she's been with Seaquest longer than I have . . . what if *she* expects the promotion? We haven't actually talked about it.

Dropping her chin, she puckers her lips. "Oh, come on, Hen. You really think I'm some nineties sitcom version of the friend who gets all catty over her bestie's success? We both know you deserve that promotion. You work harder than anyone else in this entire company. It's kind of pathetic, actually." Winking, she hops off the desk and sidesteps our divider to return to her cube.

My chest fills with warmth. Christina's not just a work friend anymore, she's a *real* friend. And it's not like I have an inexhaustible supply of those. I smile to myself as I pull my phone out of my bag. Tory's whole "big news" thing has reminded me of something. I open Walsh's texts from last night and fire back a reply.

> So what's the surprise?

I drum my fingernails against my cheek. No answer. Undoubtedly, Walsh is revving me up for whatever crazy bit of news she has to share. Either that or she's not awake yet. She's on mountain time in Colorado, so presumably she should be awake, but then again time is a loose concept to Walsh.

My phone buzzes in my hand, making me jump.

> When do you get off work? I'll tell you then.

Well, look who's up.

> Tell me now

> Ugh. Fine. 5:30

> Cool, talk soon!

Crap, I forgot about happy hour. I start typing a reply but my computer dings with two new emails. I click off my phone and open the first. It's from Graeme, a reply to my original message last night.

To: HenleyE@sqadventures.com
Cc: JamesW@sqadventures.com
From: GraemeC@sqadventures.com
Subject: Re: Social Media OVERDUE

done -G

James is back in the loop, and Graeme is back to a monosyllabic caveman. Typical.

I browse our social media pages. They're now filled with tweets and posts of the British Columbia airfare promotion. I suck in a deep breath through my nose. Was it only last night that Graeme and I were joking about the size of my hypothetical knife collection? I'd like to believe it never happened because it's just too weird. But my stomach somersaults, reminding me that it did.

The second unread email draws my eye. It's a calendar invite to meet with James at four o'clock. As I'm clicking to accept the invitation, my desk phone rings. I answer it.

"Evans," I say automatically.

"Hi, Henley, it's Barbara," says James's secretary in her light, airy voice.

Is this about the digital director position? Every speck of hope inside me distills into a pulsing, living thing inside my heart. Aiming for calm, I lean back in my chair and smooth my coral skirt over my knees. "Hey, Barb, how are you? I just got the meeting invite."

"That's what I'm calling about. I know I probably shouldn't

say anything . . ." Her voice is muffled now like she's whispering behind her hand. "But I overheard James talking to Marlen this morning." Marlen is our CEO. The blood freezes in my veins and I don't dare breathe.

"Your four o'clock meeting? It's not just about your British Columbia idea. I overheard Marlen tell James that he wants to consider you for director of digital marketing . . . Henley, you made the short list."

irst thought: I'm on the short list! The *short list*! That director job is as good as mine. *Yes!* Fist pump, high five, get some!

Second thought: Short list . . . what *short list*? I should *be* the list. One name. Me. No one else. *Hulk smash!*

I blink several times and realize that Barbara is still talking. ". . . I can't say any more."

"Who else is on the list?" I ask, voice quiet and urgent. The plastic of the telephone groans under my grip.

"Barbara! Get in here." James's voice booms in the background.

"I'm sure James will fill you in. I-I'd better go."

"Right." I shake my head. "Sorry, yeah. Thanks so much for the heads-up. I really appreciate it."

"You're welcome, honey. I'm pulling for you." *Click.*

I only realize I haven't hung up when an insistent buzzing sounds in my ear. Shaking myself, I stuff the receiver back in the cradle and run my fingers through my hair, pulling slightly.

Okay. This is happening.

And I'm not the only one up for the job. Who else could they be considering for this? Eyeing the occupants of the cubicles across the way, I quickly flip through the possibilities—no, no, nope, unlikely, hells to the no. Not to toot my own horn, but Christina was right. There's really no one else on the marketing team who's in the same league.

If they're looking at an outside candidate, someone who doesn't work for Seaquest Adventures, then I have no idea who that could be. I shrug. *All I can focus on right now is myself.* Once I find out who the other short listers are, *then* I can strategize.

After taking the morning to address some urgent emails and coordinate with the art department on next quarter's Central America mailing, I spend the afternoon preparing for my meeting with James.

I polish my British Columbia proposal, send my updated résumé to HR, and draft talking points for why I'm the strongest choice for the director role. I'm so engrossed in what I'm doing that I barely register when my computer thrums. I glance at the screen, and choke on my iced tea. It splatters down the front of my shirt.

"Shit, shit, double shit," I grate. It's four o'clock. I snag a note-pad, my résumé, phone, and a printed copy of my proposal and launch out of my seat. James is all about punctuality. If you're on time, you're late. Christina raises her eyebrows at me as I jog past her desk, but I don't stop. I scurry down the hall, coughing to clear my stinging throat, and try not to drop anything.

Barbara is sitting at the desk outside James's office. I can hear his trumpeting voice on the other side of the closed door. When she sees me coming, she touches her shoulders in the sign of the cross.

I pause by her desk. "That bad?"

"He just got off the phone with his ex-wife."

I wince.

"*And* he wrote a tuition check to UCLA for Toby today."

I groan. A conversation with his hated ex-wife and dropping serious money on his kid's college tuition? He's going to be in A Mood. Great.

"Thanks for the warning." Straightening my skirt, I cross the final three steps to his door and knock.

Wait. Ack, I forgot something to write with. I lunge toward Barbara's desk.

"Pen?" I ask, scrunching my eyes.

Her hair bounces as she fishes one out of a coffee mug and hands it to me. "Here. Oh, you have a little . . ." She motions at her chest. Crap, the tea. I flick my hair over my shoulders, light brown over white silk, and rearrange it to cover the worst of the spill.

Barbara gives me the thumbs-up, turquoise nails flashing.

"Come in," James barks.

"You're the best," I mouth over my shoulder as I push open the heavy wood door and breach the threshold into his corner office.

"You're late," he says without preamble, nodding at the door. I close it softly behind me, stomach knotting. The pervasive smell of tuna, presumably leftovers from James's lunch, does nothing to quell my nerves.

Infusing my spine with steel, I cross the room to sink into one of the square orange chairs facing his monolithic desk. "Sorry about that." My heart thumps against my ribs as James dips his chin to peer at me over his wire-rimmed glasses.

James Wilcox, chief marketing officer, has buzzed, thinning gray-brown hair, the crinkled, papery skin of a pastry bag even though he's only in his late fifties, and enough self-importance to fill a football stadium.

"Thanks for making time in your schedule to meet with—" I begin, but he cuts me off.

"I have some interesting news for you, Henley." He folds his hands over the stack of papers on his desk, mouth twisting into a frown. I sit there, my own hands clasped in my lap, legs crossed at the ankle, looking what I hope is pleasantly surprised and not dog-panting excited.

"Marlen and I had a meeting this morning, and we both agree it's time to pull the trigger on hiring a director of digital marketing. We're eyeing you for the job."

I smile broadly as every cell of my body exhales at the confirmation. "Oh my goodness, James, that's wonderful news. Thank you, I—"

"Don't thank me yet, sweetheart. You're not the only one up for the promotion." He leans back in his chair with a thud. "We're considering Graeme for the position too."

The world slows. A fly hopscotches across the window behind James, and I imagine I can see every beat of its tiny, transparent wings.

"Graeme . . ." I repeat. My own voice sounds far away. "Graham Cracker—Crawford—Crawlin," I stutter. Oh God, I'm losing my mind. I swallow. *Get a hold of yourself, Henley.* I give myself a mental slap and the world rights itself. "Graeme Crawford-Collins?" I finally manage to get out.

"Oh good, you know his name." James tips his chin and stares down his stubby nose at me. "Graeme has experience in the digital marketing arena, and he's done a bang-up job for us on social media over the past year. He's a strong candidate."

"But he lives in . . . Michigan. Wouldn't it be more beneficial to fill the position with someone from Seattle?"

I hate how halting and unsure my voice has become.

James waves dismissively. "We'll relocate him."

All I can do is stare at the swirling yellow-and-gold pattern of his tie. I've been with the company for three years to Graeme's one. And I've done more than a bang-up job in many more arenas than simply social media, digital marketing included.

And the whole "we'll relocate him." *We will* relocate him. Will. Future tense, definite. My lungs seize. He's going to get the job. I can feel it down to my glitter-painted toes. He's a man, he can banter with James about sports, and his reputation as a stand-out all started with stealing credit for my viral monkey video—of *course* James will pick him. All the talking points I've so carefully crafted about my candidacy crumble into dust on my tongue.

James rises from his seat, all five and a half feet of him. If I stood up right now, I'd have a full two inches on him in my heels. Tugging his pants up by the belt, he saunters around his desk and perches on the edge, one shiny brown loafer dangling.

"You're a good kid, Henley," he says, leaning forward to pat my bare knee. I shift automatically to cross my legs away from him. Lips thinning, he withdraws his hand. "You've been a good sport over the years and you've done top-notch work for us too. Everyone recognizes that. So we want to give you a swinging chance at this."

"Well, isn't that *sporting* of you," I say through a tight smile, trying not to choke on the condescension.

A muffled noise sounds from the desk. I furrow my eyebrows. Was that . . . ? I stare at the telephone. No, it couldn't be. Allowing someone to listen in on speakerphone unannounced would be low, even for James.

Sliding to his feet, he resumes his seat behind the desk. "As part of the selection process, we're sending you and Graeme aboard *Discovery* next month for a cruise." *Discovery* is our ship that sails the Galápagos Islands year-round. "I was surprised to learn that neither of you has been on one of our ships before."

"I toured *Golden Dawn* when it was in port last spring—" I begin.

"But you've never actually been on one of our cruises for a full voyage, correct?"

"Well, with my workload—"

"No excuse. It's like working in a restaurant and never tasting the food. How are you supposed to recommend anything?" He wags his rounded chin with a *tsk*. "Graeme," he barks suddenly. "You still there?"

After a brief pause, a familiar husky voice echoes from the phone on James's desk. "I'm here."

My heart drops to my feet. I was right. Someone was—no *is*—on speakerphone. *Graeme.* And he's been listening to our conversation *this entire goddamned time*. Eavesdropping. Like a rat. That noise I heard? Now I know what it was. It was Graeme. Snickering.

I glare at the black hunk of telephone like I can see Graeme's smug face through its tangle of fiberglass innards. I mentally rewind the conversation. Every patronizing "kid" and "sport" and "sweetheart" strikes me like an arrow through the gut.

"We have two voyages coming up in September with plenty of cabin space," says James. He talks at the phone but tosses a glance my way as he rattles off a series of dates.

Numbly, I swipe open my cell and tap on my calendar app. Fall classes start on September 16, so the second set of dates is out. "I'm available for the first cruise," I say. My muscles clench as I realize it departs in less than two weeks.

"So am I," says Graeme.

Nooooo. No, no, no, no. My chest tightens and heat flushes my neck. No way am I spending a week on a ship with Graeme Crawford-Collins.

"Terrific," says James, marking something down. "Passports current?"

I nod. "Yes."

"Yes, sir," says Graeme.

And heeeere we go. *Sir.* It's already begun. The brownnosing. The one-upmanship. I grind my teeth so hard I could crack a walnut.

"Good," says James firmly. "Now while you're there, I want you both to soak up the experience from the guests' perspective. Our Galápagos numbers are low right now, especially compared to the competition. Figure out how to use digital marketing to change that. When you get back, you'll submit a proposal, which I'll rely on heavily when I decide who will be the new digital marketing director. Got it?"

I nod dumbly, all out of words.

"Got it," Graeme echoes.

"Competition breeds innovation," says James with a sanctimonious nod like he's the Dalai Lama dispensing a nugget of earth-shattering wisdom. "And you two," he says, slapping his desk with a hearty guffaw. "Let's just say I expect top innovation from you."

"I appreciate the opportunity," says Graeme.

"I do too, so much. Thanks for your faith in me, James," I say, pressing my hand against my chest in a show of (in)sincere supplication, for good measure.

James leans forward to talk directly into the speakerphone. "Graeme, thanks for your time. Be sure to call our reservations department to arrange your cruise, today if possible. We'll talk soon." Before Graeme can say goodbye, James lifts and lowers the receiver, effectively ending the call. Settling into his chair, he rests his elbows on the desk and steeples his fingers against his chin. "Now, about your British Columbia idea . . ."

I stumble back to my desk at five, dump my pile of p
to my keyboard, and collapse into my squeaky chair. The o....
quiet, and Christina's not at her desk.

What was supposed to be my big chance, my time to shine, turned out to be a Henley Humiliation Fest followed by half an hour of nitpicking my direct-call idea for British Columbia. To cap it off? As I walked out of his office, James openly perused my tea-splattered boobs and suggested that I might want to start using a straw.

At least he ultimately approved my British Columbia idea—except of course he did, because it's freaking brilliant.

I scrub both palms over my eyes and flop my head against the top of my chair so I'm staring at the exposed ductwork on the ceiling. Sure, I may technically be up for this promotion, but James might as well pat me on the head and hand me a participation ribbon right now. It's obvious Graeme is his favorite.

Graeme. That snake. Listening to our entire conversation and not having the decency to announce himself. How is he even qualified for this promotion? A social media manager making a leap to director of digital marketing? Ridiculous.

Rolling my hands into fists on top of my armrests, I sit up.

I'll show him. I'll show them all. I'll simply have to knock my proposal so far out of the park that they'll need to drive to Canada to find the ball. And Graeme? He can stay in Michigan and rot.

A light on my desk phone catches my eye and my fury recedes a fraction. I have a voice mail. I punch in my code and shove the phone tightly against my ear.

"Henley, it's Graeme."

My lungs inflate like a Macy's Thanksgiving Day Parade balloon.

"I just wanted to say, ah, congratulations." He blows out a breath and mumbles something unintelligible. "I know this is awkward, being up for the same job. And I hope it doesn't get in the way of us working together. I posted your British Columbia content this morning. Let me know if there's anything else I can do for you. I"—he clears his throat—"I'm looking forward to meeting you in person finally. And . . . and that's it."

Just as I think the message is over it keeps going.

"You know what, that's not it. There's something I've been meaning to tell you . . ." He sucks in a deep breath. "You shouldn't let James talk to you like that. It's unprofessional. Take care."

Unprofessional. *Unprofessional?*

The synthesized voice of a woman cuts in. "To delete this message . . ."

I slam the receiver down. Pick it up. Slam it again.

As if I have any choice in how James talks to me. He's our boss. What the hell am I supposed to do? My chest constricts and I slow my runaway breathing. I know what's going on here. Graeme is trying to psych me out. Throw me off my game. Well, guess what, Graeme? It's not working.

In fact, I've learned something. If I want this job, I need to stay a step ahead of the competition. I need to be tireless. I need to crumble that Graham Cracker into *dust*. Setting my jaw, I scoop up my cell phone and enter a new item in my to-do app. Highest priority.

Task #1: Defeat Graeme Crawford-Collins.

I intercept Tory and Christina at the elevator.

"Who's ready for happy hour?" Tory loops her arms around our shoulders. She's five foot nothing on a good day, so she has to stand on tiptoe to do it.

"Me," I say as I push the down button. After the roller coaster of a day I've had, I definitely need a drink. Or ten. My phone buzzes in my bag and I dig it out. It's Walsh. I forgot she was going to call. "Sorry, I have to take this."

The elevator doors open and I file inside behind Tory and Christina. I tap the green accept icon and hold the phone to my ear. "Hello?"

"Henley!" says Walsh in her smooth alto.

"Hey, baby sis, what's up?"

"Not much. Are you leaving work now?" Her tone is light, but there's a tension to it that has my alarm bells jerking awake.

"Just about, I'm in the elevator. So, what's the big surprise?"

Walsh hesitates. "Oh, you know. The usual."

Way too breezy. My chest tightens in warning. "Walsh," I grate.

"I'm moving," she says. I can practically see the overly bright, forced smile she must have plastered on her face. "Surprise!"

I groan. "Again?"

"Boulder was too . . . expensive."

I roll my eyes so hard at the bronzed ceiling I nearly give my eyeballs whiplash. *If she had a full-time job, it wouldn't be so expensive.* "Where to now?" I ask. I try to keep my tone casual, but I'm not sure I'm nailing it. Blood is pounding in my ears. With everything else going on in my life, Walsh couldn't have picked a worse time to pull a Walsh.

She's twenty-four. If you think she'd have her life figured out by now, you'd be wrong.

"That's what I wanted to talk to you about . . ."

The elevator doors rattle open. I look up. And find myself face-to-face with my sister.

"Walsh?" I splutter in disbelief, lowering the phone.

An imaginary engine revs as the Walsh surprise bus crashes into me, running over my stunned body with a double thump.

I throw my arms out, mostly in a what-the-fuck question, but a thread of delight also snakes its way into my heart. As much as she pushes my crazy buttons, Walsh is still my sister.

And she's here, standing not ten feet away, wearing denim cut-offs, strappy sandals, and a rose-colored top that hangs loosely off one shoulder. Her golden blond hair is shorter than it was at Christmas, skimming her shoulders in a wavy lob—must be a new cut since it hasn't shown up on Instagram yet. And she's added muscle to her long, lean legs. But her heart-shaped face and perfectly straight button nose, which is adorned with a delicate crystal piercing, are the same as always.

The elevator dings. Christina clears her throat. Right, the doors are closing and we're all still inside. I shove my fist into the void, tripping the sensor to open, and step into the lobby.

"What are you doing here?" I ask, floating toward Walsh as though I'm on a conveyor belt. My heels clack against the tile floor.

My sister stuffs her phone into her back pocket and I don't miss the flash of strain before she hitches her lips into a beaming grin. In a rush, she bounds forward and throws her arms around my neck. I hug her automatically, still too stunned to fully process.

"What, I need an excuse to visit my big sister?" she murmurs into my hair. And doesn't let go. Her body is tense, and I catch a quiver as she inhales. What's up with her? Leaning away, I study her face. Her expression smooths and now all I see is the same old Walsh. Her cornflower eyes flick between me and something behind me. Oh yeah.

"Introductions," I say, stepping back. "Walsh, this is Tory and Christina. We work together. Guys, this is my sister, Walsh."

Christina sticks out her hand, but before she can blink, Walsh wraps her in a hug. Christina is not a hugger. She stiffens, mouth twisted into a frown, and awkwardly pats Walsh on the back. I snort in amusement. I can't help it.

"Great to meet you," says Walsh.

"Uh-huh," Christina mutters.

Walsh gives Tory a hug in turn, who takes it in stride. "I didn't know Henley had a sister. Visiting from out of town?" She nods toward the row of chairs along the far wall, and for the first time, I notice the two massive purple suitcases pushed innocently against the window, a bulging shoulder bag perched on top.

Those are *not* weekend bags. Those are I've-packed-everything-I-own-in-this-world bags. Walsh said she's moving. Oh no. She's not . . . she couldn't be . . .

My stomach tumbles like clothes in a hot dryer.

"Not exactly visiting," says Walsh, shifting her weight.

Rage simmers in my veins. Walsh has some explaining to do. Now. I ball my hand into a fist around my purse strap and face my coworkers. "Guys, I'm sorry about happy hour, but—"

"Happy hour?" chirps Walsh, a hopeful gleam in her eye.

"Yeah, why don't you join us?" asks Tory. "My wife's coming too, so you won't be the only non–Seaquest Adventurer there."

"Great! But my luggage . . ." She glances around as if a storage locker is going to magically *poof* into existence.

I purse my lips. "Come on. The bar's only a block away. We'll store your suitcases at my desk and come back for them later. Then we can talk." I turn to Christina and Tory and give them a tight smile. "Sorry about this. Meet you there?"

"Sure," says Christina. "See you in a bit."

I march over to the first suitcase and lurch it to a roll.

Walsh trots after me, lugging the other one. "Henley, I'm sorry—"

"Why didn't you tell me you were coming? Or, I don't know, ask me if this was a good time for an extended visit?"

"I needed to leave Boulder. I figured I could stay with you—"

"Of course you did. You just assumed I'd roll out the red carpet because Princess Walsh has arrived. You know what though? I have a life. And my own problems to deal with. I don't have time for your bullshit right now."

Her chin trembles. Goddamn it. I hit the button and the elevator opens.

We pile inside, and I snatch my badge out of my bag and wave it in front of the security sensor before pushing the button for the seventh floor. I blow out a long breath. I don't look at Walsh. "Why didn't you just go to Mom and Dad's?"

"You know why," she says softly.

Some people would call where we grew up in rural Idaho idyllic. There's certainly plenty of nature. But not much else, including people, jobs, or any sort of nuanced appreciation for the wider world. Except for our parents, who relish the quiet of rural living, there's nothing for us there—either one of us.

"And, Henley, I—I need you right now. I need my sister. I'm sorry I didn't tell you I was coming, but I knew you'd be mad and I—" Her words break off like a shard of glass. I jerk my head to look at her. In spite of my frustration, my heart catches in my throat. Big, fat tears are streaking down Walsh's flushed cheeks.

Her face scrunches like a wadded-up napkin and a sob escapes her in a hiccup.

Anger leaves me in a retreating wave. I curl a protective arm around my sister's shoulders as she visibly chokes back tears the rest of the ride up.

When we reach my floor, I shove her bags against the wall by the empty front desk and steer her into the nearest conference room, which is blessedly unoccupied. The automatic ceiling lights flicker on. As soon as the opaque glass door shuts behind us, I gently grasp her by the shoulders. "What's going on?"

Her red-rimmed eyes search my face. "You . . . you were right. I got fired."

"Again?"

"God, why do you have to say it like that? I know I'm a screwup, okay? Not everyone is perfect like you." Turning, she collapses into the nearest office chair, arms sprawled over the armrests.

Of all the days for my baby sister to show up on my doorstep midmeltdown, why did she have to pick today? I slide into the seat next to her and force my jaw to unclench. "I'm not perfect. And you're not a screwup. What happened?"

She lifts and lowers one shoulder. "I missed an appointment I had with a client last week. It was the third time it happened, so Massage Spot gave me the boot."

"Don't you have that calendar app? I showed you how to set reminders so you get notifications. Why aren't you using it?"

"I know, I know. I just forget. I don't know what's wrong with me."

"Why move though? You could always find another job. Weren't you seeing that guy . . . Kevin?"

"Keith." She spits the word the same way you might say "vomit." "He turned out to be an asshole. There's nothing left for me in Boulder. Not anymore."

I blow out a long breath. "Well, good thing I have a pull-out couch. You can stay with me and Noodles until you figure out your next move. And at least now I'll have a built-in cat sitter."

She sits up straighter. "Why do you need a cat sitter? Are you going somewhere?"

"On a work trip, but not for a couple weeks."

"A cruise?"

I shift my weight. "Yeah."

"Where to?"

"The Galápagos."

She tilts her head. "Is that where people have traces of an extinct human species in their DNA? Near Australia?"

"You're thinking Papua New Guinea. No, the Galápagos Islands are off the coast of Ecuador in South America. You know . . . Darwin? Finches? Giant tortoises?"

"Ahhh yes. Okay, got it." She fiddles with the slim gold necklace tucked into her shirt, but then her head snaps up. "Can I come?"

I was afraid of this. "No. It's a work trip. And look, if you're planning on staying in Seattle for any length of time, you need to focus on finding a job. Maybe even two jobs, if you want to make ends meet until you figure out something more permanent."

"We'll see. I still have to finish my yoga training."

I open my mouth to speak. Close it. I desperately want to lecture her about, I don't know, being a halfway credible adult? But then the tear tracks on her cheek stop me and I'm reminded why she's here. She needs me.

I smile and hope it doesn't look too forced. "We'll start job hunting tomorrow."

"Sounds good." She pushes to her feet. Even though her legs are wobbly, she's already regaining some of her old Walsh swagger. "I could sure use that drink now."

Straightening my skirt, I stand with a nod. "Me too."

4

*M*ichelle's pregnant!"

Tory's big news. A piercing collective of squeals and exclamations meets her pronouncement that's quickly swallowed by the bar's noisy chatter.

"Oh my God, you're going to be moms? You're going to be moms! Congratulations!" I jump out of my chair and round the small circular table to give Tory, then Michelle, a squeeze.

Returning to my chair, I swirl the ice cubes around my empty glass. We've been here barely an hour but I'm on my second drink and I already need another one. Christina echoes my congrats. "I had no idea you guys went ahead with the IVF."

"We were going to wait until I made partner at the firm," says Michelle, pushing a tight coil of black hair behind her ear before threading her fingers with Tory's on top of the table. "But we found a donor we liked. We went for it, and it took."

Walsh shoves to her feet. "This calls for a round of shots!" I've never heard a baby announcement met with shots before, but okay.

She turns to me. "Henley, a hand?" I sigh. This must be all part of the fun-loving, crazy Walsh mask she's fastened into place for the evening.

Threading through the crowd to the bar, we squeeze into a

spot next to a raucous mix of young professionals and a pair of older women. All the barstools are occupied, so we stand.

"What's eating you?" asks Walsh as we rest our elbows on the smooth wooden surface, waiting for one of the bartenders to acknowledge our presence.

"What do you mean?" I try to catch the bartender's eye and fail. He's mixing some sort of tiki drink, the bar's specialty.

Walsh gives me a look. "Be real. Something's up with you that has nothing to do with me."

"Doesn't everything have to do with you?"

"Usually. But come on, I know you. Spill."

One of the bartenders comes over—a twentysomething with a flamboyant, nineteenth-century mustache. He lifts two full martini glasses and sets them on the bar in front of us, forearm muscles rippling beneath full-sleeve tattoos. The drinks are yellow-pink and frothy with blueberries floating on top.

"We didn't order these," I say.

"For two pretty ladies? On the house." He looks exclusively at Walsh as he says this and slips a piece of paper across the bar toward her. A name—Miles—is scribbled in blue along with a phone number.

I strain not to roll my eyes.

"Wow, thank you," she croons, flashing him a Cheshire cat grin. Her crystal nose piercing sparkles in the dim light as she studies the number, slips it into her pocket with a shrug, and takes a sip of her drink.

The bartender's eyes smolder as he turns away.

"Hey," I yell after him. "Can we also get a ginger ale, an order of roast beef sliders, nachos, and four shots of—what should we get?" I ask Walsh.

"Something scrumptious. Surprise us," she calls to the bartender.

I push my credit card across the bar. My fingers tense automatically at the thought of the charges I'll see on my next bill. At least a pay raise is on the horizon—hopefully. And besides, I know Tory and Christina will throw a few bucks my way to cover their share.

The bartender takes my card with a nod. "You got it." He winks at Walsh, who openly ogles him as he puts in our food order. Not that I care if she's interested in this guy, but the surge of familiarity over the situation makes my chest ache.

My little sister is objectively beautiful. Me? I'm cute. Not pretty, exactly, but cute. I have startlingly light brown eyes and nicely defined eyebrows—Mom says they have character—but my jaw is too severe and my nose is too sharp, according to conventional beauty standards anyway.

Walsh is soft curves and gentle slopes, while I'm harsh angles.

Rolling waves vs. a rocky shore. Happy-go-lucky charm vs. resting bitch face.

Don't get me wrong. Now that I'm older, I've embraced my looks, but I haven't always. Because ever since we were teenagers, given the choice between me or Walsh, guys choose Walsh. Hands down, every time. And damn it if that doesn't kick my confidence right in the balls. Ovaries? Whatever.

To hell with it. I pull the cocktail over and take a long sip while I stuff my childhood insecurities back inside their mental lockbox. Blueberries and vodka with a tang of lemon bursts on my tongue. "Work's been stressful lately," I tell her.

"Shocker."

"I'm up for a promotion. It's why they're sending me on this Galápagos cruise, and I—"

"What?" she chokes, finally tearing her attention away from the bartender. "Oh my God, Henley, that's great news!"

"But this guy I work with is up for it too."

Narrowing her eyes, she nods. "Hmmm, I see. Competition."

"Exactly. And he's . . . he's . . ." I make a strangled sound. "He's our social media manager. He lives in Michigan. And he's the *worst*. Remember Sean, that guy I used to work with at Prima Health?"

"The one you banged and then he—"

"Bzzzt! We don't need to rehash it. But yeah, this guy— Graeme—he's basically Sean 2.0. But without the banging." I shake my head hard to dispel that nauseating image. "I even had a meeting with our boss today and he listened in on speakerphone, on the sly, to our entire conversation. Then I get a voice mail from him after the fact that's practically psychological warfare."

"You shouldn't take that."

"No, I shouldn't."

"You need to show him what a badass boss bitch you are."

I smack the bar top. "Yes!"

"You should call him."

"Yeah—w-what?"

Walsh waves me on. "Call him. Tell him you're onto him. Let him know he can't intimidate you."

The thought of telling Graeme off has me all jittery like I've guzzled a pot of coffee.

"There are men out there who think they're entitled to everything . . ." She trails off, her expression darkening. I don't think she's talking about Graeme anymore. She tosses her head. "What are this guy's qualifications anyway?"

"I don't know, he has a dick and so does our boss?"

"We can't let the dickholes win."

"Down with the dickholes."

"Cheers to that." She clinks her glass against mine and we both drink. After several gulps, I lick the sugar from my lips. My head's starting to feel pleasantly fuzzy. Like an angora sweater. Or one of those fluffy ponies . . . Sheepland? Shetland?

"What are you waiting for?" Walsh blurts. "Go! Confront him. Now."

The bartender appears and lines up four shot glasses in front of us, filling each one with light green liquid from a shaker. I slide open my phone and a notification from my to-do app pops up.

Task #1: Defeat Graeme Crawford-Collins.

A sense of righteous certainty wraps around my lungs. Pushing away from the bar, I return a second later, snatch the closest shot, and toss its contents into my mouth. Fire burns my throat. "I'll be back," I wheeze.

A noisy bar is perhaps not the best place to make a phone call, especially not when you're firing the opening salvo in a battle against your nemesis, but when I peer out the window, rain splatters coat the glass. Good old Seattle weather. I wind through the crowd to stand at the far edge of the bar, near, but not in, the bathroom—too echoy. This is as good as it's going to get.

"You can do this," I murmur to myself as I wedge a hip against an empty patch of wall and scroll through my contacts. Graeme's name pops up and I glare at it. My chest puffs and heat scorches my neck. Time to nip this—whatever *this* is, this game he's playing—in the bud.

I tap his number. Ringing fills my ear. I notice the leather of my left shoe is pinching my little toe. I wiggle my toes, but the pinch gets worse. With a huff, I crouch and stick a finger inside my shoe, tugging.

"Hello?" Graeme answers.

I bolt upright and nearly lose my balance. My phone slips through my fumbling fingers and I manage to catch it with both hands before it hits the floor. I lift it, intent on returning it to my ear, and freeze.

Graeme's face fills my screen. His eyebrows are raised, his expression expectant.

Oh God, we're FaceTiming. *We're FaceTiming.*

I must have accidentally pressed the FaceTime request icon and he . . . accepted.

Shit.

Graeme's outside, and with the time zone difference, the sky behind him is blooming with the last vestiges of purple twilight. A streetlamp washes a dim golden glow over his face, which is obscured by a scruffy two-week growth of stubble. His eyes blaze at me and his jaw is as unforgiving as a mountain.

It's been weeks since I've seen Graeme in the flesh—er, pixel—since he's opted to keep his camera off for video conferences lately. And this is the best view I've had of him yet. The image is clear and his face isn't too close to the camera. His hair is longer than I remember, and he looks rougher somehow—certainly older than his smooth-faced Outlook picture—but still no older than thirty.

Heat sizzles in my stomach. There's no denying it: Graeme is *hot*. The thick stubble can't hide his magnificent bone structure—the high, wide cheekbones, defined nose, and deep-set eyes.

No, no, no. Don't be distracted by your conniving coworker's ridiculously good looks.

He pivots to sit on a park bench. Rummaging in my purse, I pull out my earbuds with the built-in microphone and stuff them into my ears. "Uh, hi, Graeme, it's Henley," I begin.

His lips crack into a wide smile. "I know. I can see you." Amusement suffuses his voice and it's smooth and satiny like caramel. "What can I do for you?"

"You can stop playing games with me," I snap, jamming my finger at the phone for emphasis.

In front of me, a slightly stunned, barely legal bar patron points to his own narrow chest, eyes widening. "Me?" he mouths.

"No, not you," I mouth back. Rolling my eyes, I motion at the phone. *Hello, can't you see I'm talking here?* I turn my back on him.

Graeme's jaw tightens. "I didn't know we were playing a game."

"Oh, give me a break. You act all innocent, but really you're a manipulative asshole!" Silence. I barrel on, glorying in the renewed vortex of anger churning in my chest. "I got your voice mail. Biggest load of crap I've ever heard after the stunt you pulled today—"

Graeme jerks forward, frowning. "Okay, pump the brakes. What stunt? What are you talking about?"

"You know exactly what I'm talking about."

"You'll have to enlighten me."

"Eavesdropping on my meeting with James?" I grit through clenched teeth.

"You . . . you think I was eavesdropping?" A dog barks somewhere on his end, a series of loud, gruff yips. If it's his, it's probably some obnoxious purebred.

"Yes, I do. Like you do for every meeting, skulking on the phone, letting people forget you're even on the line. Except this time, I wasn't expecting you to be there at all so it was extra shitty."

A crease forms between his eyebrows. "Is that really what you think I do?"

"If the shoe fits."

Graeme brings the phone closer to his face and his eyes flash. Are they blue? Green? It's too difficult to make out in the growing darkness. "How much have you had to drink?"

Busted. Goose bumps rise along my arms.

"What? *Pffff.* None. Nothing. Zip."

"I can hear you're in a bar. Some guy just ordered a Naughty Nellie. Where are you?"

"What do you care?"

He lifts and lowers one shoulder. "I don't. Except who would I argue with about work if you end up floating facedown in the bay?"

I snort. "Your mom." A not-so-attractive feature of my personality: I get dreadfully immature when I'm drunk.

Craaaaap. I'm drunk.

My empty stomach gurgles, suddenly longing for food to soak up the booze sloshing around in there, and my head swims. Graeme stands and makes a sound of frustration halfway between a huff and a growl, and I finally catch a glimpse of what's behind him—headstones.

"Are you in a graveyard?" I blurt.

"It's a good place to walk my dog." Scrubbing a hand across his jaw, he glances away.

Weird. "Okay, Buffy."

"Drink some water. Don't do anything stupid. Well, more stupid than drunk-dialing a coworker. Seriously, not smart. You know," he says, tapping his chin, a mischievous gleam in his eye, "I could go to HR for this."

Human resources at our company is about as useful as square wheels on a bicycle, but ice still fills my veins and my vision nearly doubles. "You wouldn't."

"Wouldn't I?" His smile is tight and unreadable. "See you in the Galápagos."

"See you in hell."

He tips his head back and laughs. After a ripple of movement across the screen, the call ends. I blink. He hung up on me. *He* hung up on *me*? "That *asshole*," I mutter. Ripping my earbuds from my ears, I shove them into my purse.

My heartbeat thunders and my chest rises and falls like a ship pitching on the waves in a storm. That did not go at all the way I planned.

After a quick detour to the bathroom, I return to our table. The cold water I've splashed on my face has done nothing to cool the fire burning in my veins and the heat in my cheeks.

"I just Venmoed you twenty bucks, but let me know if you need more for the food—hey, are you okay?" Christina puts her phone down to peer at me as I sit with a plop.

"I'm fine."

"She's upset over Graeme," says Walsh through a mouthful of nachos. "Did you tell him off?"

"Hold up, what's going on with Graeme?" demands Christina. "I mean, besides the usual bickering."

Time to spill the beans. "We had a meeting with James today, and it turns out we're both up for the new digital marketing director role."

"You are?" Tory blurts at the same time Christina squawks, "Henley! Why didn't you tell us?"

"I just found out not even two hours ago. I was going to tell you, but then I didn't want to steal your thunder." I motion toward Tory and Michelle. "Babies beat promotions."

Tory clucks. "What did James say? What are your next steps?"

I suck in a deep breath. "Well, he's sending me and Graeme on a cruise to the Galápagos in two weeks as part of the selection process. He wants us to come up with a plan for how to boost sales in the region, and, *guys*, I need to kill it. I have to come up with the best marketing idea in Seaquest Adventures history. I don't want there to be even the slightest chance of Graeme getting this promotion over me. And you know how much James loves Graeme," I add darkly.

Tory hisses in a breath through her teeth. "He really does," she says to Michelle, who inclines her chin sympathetically.

"I know what would help," Walsh chimes in. "Moral support. From me, on the cruise. It's practically my sisterly duty." Her tone is light, but there's an edge to it I can't miss.

Tory and Michelle chuckle, but Christina's eyes pop and she holds up both hands, palms out. "Hold up. Brain wave. What if Walsh *did* go on the cruise with you?"

I roll my eyes. "Get serious."

"No, listen, you know how James is always going on about capturing more of the young adult market. Well, what if you brought your own Gen Z along? Someone who's an outsider you can tap for honest feedback to help you brainstorm. She could be your secret weapon."

Walsh scoots forward in her seat, eyes sparkling.

"The trip is too expensive . . ." I begin, but Christina chimes in, brows furrowed.

"Even with the employee family discount?"

I wince at the sharp look Walsh shoots me. "Family discount? Um, how come you never mentioned that?"

"Even if we split a cabin, you'd still have to pay for food and flights. It'd probably cost fifteen hundred dollars, maybe a couple grand."

Jaw set, Walsh pulls a long gold necklace out from beneath the neckline of her shirt. A fat pearl winks at the end. "I could sell this."

"Where did you get that?" I ask.

"Keith gave it to me and I don't want it. It's real though. I bet I could get over five hundred bucks for it."

"Okay, that's enough to cover food, but what about flights?"

Walsh spreads her arms wide. "Airline miles, baby."

I open my mouth to protest, but she reaches across the table and grips both my hands in hers. "Please, Hennie. I need this. Do you ever feel like you just need to step away from your life so you can see it more clearly? I need time to think, to disconnect. And I'll be a great sounding board for ideas on the cruise, I promise."

I turn the idea over, kneading it like dough.

Walsh isn't exactly the most reliable when it comes to making promises; she's flakier than a Hot Pocket. Looking for a life-of-the-party, one-person fun machine to go to Vegas for the weekend? Walsh is your girl. Need a ride to the accountant's office to file your tax returns? She'll show up, but a half hour late and out of gas.

Pinpricks of resentment needle my spine. Of course, Walsh is making this about her. This is *my* chance, *my* opportunity. I squeeze my bottom lip between my teeth.

But then . . . what if Christina is right? What if this is exactly the sort of approach that would impress James? I want this promotion so badly my toes curl. I need to pull out all the stops, do anything I can to get a leg up on Graeme. Maybe bringing Walsh along will give me an edge. It would sure show James I'm proactive, creative in obtaining solutions, and willing to think outside the box . . .

Walsh blinks up at me with round, guileless eyes.

I blow out a long breath. "Okay."

"Okay? I can come?"

"Yes." The word settles in the space between us like an anchor dropping.

Walsh's body practically vibrates as she jogs her feet under the table and lets out an ear-splitting squeal.

"Well, maybe," I clarify. "I still have to clear it with my boss. He might say no, so don't get too excited. But if he says yes, you have to promise you'll actually debrief with me every night. I want your honest feedback, your ideas. You can't just flit around sipping mai tais the whole time. I'll need your help."

"Scout's honor."

I slurp the watery remains of my drink. "Then it looks like the Evans sisters might be going on a cruise."

5

The first thing you need to know about a Seaquest Adventures cruise: it's not a cruise. Not in the way most people think of a cruise, anyway—gargantuan ship, thousands of passengers, on-board entertainment, and rushed day trips at busy ports.

Seaquest Adventures is different. Our ships are smaller. Much smaller. Our largest ship in the fleet—*Intrepid*—accommodates a whopping 158 guests. *Discovery* hosts 91. Due to their small size, our ships can go places larger cruises can only dream of—deep into the wilderness where no docks exist.

Where we're going, we don't need ports.

Which is why I'm perched sideways along the inflatable edge of a Zodiac, a small boat designed to transport passengers between the ship and the shore. My feet are firmly planted on the hard-bottomed rubber floor as we zoom away from San Cristóbal, the easternmost island of the Galápagos archipelago while our ship, *Discovery*, gleams like a red-and-white diamond on the horizon.

"First time on a Seaquest Adventure?" asks the man next to me in an unmistakable Russian accent. He looks to be in his midthirties. He has a thatch of receding brown hair, has a long nose, and is wearing Oakley sunglasses. His tan leg is already inches from mine since there's about seven of us squished in a row along the side of the Zodiac, but he scoots closer anyway. I can feel the heat coming off him.

"Yeah, first time," I say with a forced smile, edging toward Walsh, who's sitting on my other side.

I still can't believe James okayed her coming along. Then again, when I presented him with two pages of bullet-pointed arguments for how a real-time, outside perspective would be valuable to me in assessing the strengths and weaknesses of the Galápagos itinerary, I didn't leave him much room to say no.

James had peered at me over those wire-rimmed glasses, skin wrinkling around his watery eyes, and offered an enigmatic smile that made my skin prickle. But then he'd nodded, and said, "*Don't make me regret approving this, Henley,*" and dismissed me from his office.

What's really making my insides twitch right now, apart from that questionable sandwich I ate on the plane? Graeme. He's MIA.

He wasn't at the hotel in Guayaquil last night with the rest of the cruise-goers.

He wasn't on the plane to San Cristóbal this morning.

And he's certainly not in this Zodiac with me, Walsh, and the other dozen guests about to embark the ship.

Maybe he missed one of his connecting flights and he's stuck in an airport somewhere? Wishful thinking makes my nerves crackle and I clutch the aggressively orange lifejacket looped around my neck.

"It is my first cruise as well," the man beside me says. "Where are you from?"

"Seattle. You?" I ask automatically.

"Russia, originally. Saransk. But for fourteen years I live in Austin, Texas. I'm Dr. Kozlov, but you can call me Nikolai." He reaches out a hand.

Tucking my elbow to my side, I shake it. Trying to shake hands with someone sitting right beside you is super awkward. And with the Zodiac speeding through the bay and sea spray leaping up to ping my backpack, I'm reminded that there are no seat belts, or even seats, on this craft, and I could really use my hand back now.

"Henley Evans," I say. His palm is sweaty, and he doesn't let go. I tug my hand out of his grip and surreptitiously wipe my palm on my shorts.

"Henley . . . like the shirt?"

He had to bring *that* up. In addition to being named after a drummer, my parents also inadvertently named me after a type of casual cotton wear. Hallelujah. "Um, yeah."

"Mmm. It is my favorite shirt, you know." Tipping his sunglasses down his nose, he pumps his eyebrows once.

Walsh giggles beside me.

"Nik, you're bein' rude." The older man sitting next to him pops his head forward. He's probably in his sixties, and he has a round, friendly face, neatly trimmed white hair, and an accent as deep as south Texas. "I'm Dwight Johnson. Pleased to meet you."

We exchange introductions.

"What kind of doctor are you?" Walsh asks Nikolai, leaning across me to shout above the roar of the engine. I dig my elbow into her rib cage in a clear sign of *quit encouraging him*. She elbows me back.

"Chiropractor." His accent pulls the word into "*Kai-rrro-prr-rak-toor*."

"And a darn good one. I should know. I've been a patient of his for five years," says Dwight.

Nikolai grins smugly. "And your sciatica has never been better."

"Are you guys together?" asks Walsh, motioning between them.

The older man laughs, a deep-bellied guffaw. "Lord, no. He's not my type. Too young."

"Dwight started as a patient. Now he is friend. Only friend," says Nikolai. I'm not sure if he means their relationship is strictly platonic or if Dwight is literally his one and only friend.

"So . . . buddy vacation?" Walsh asks.

Nikolai shrugs. "This was supposed to be my honeymoon. But, wedding didn't happen. I bring Dwight instead."

"I'm sorry to hear that," I say. "About your wedding, I mean. It's nice you brought a friend." Poor guy. Ending an engagement then going on your honeymoon with another dude instead of your wife? Rough.

"Is okay. I, how do you say, dodged a bullet? My girlfriend, she was too demanding. I called off wedding before making big mistake. Now I am here and free as a bird of paradise."

Dwight opens his mouth, but swallows whatever he was going to say with an exasperated shake of his head.

Pushing his sunglasses onto his forehead, Nikolai twists to face me more fully. The intense way he studies my face has me squirming in my seat. "Do you have boyfriend?" he finally asks.

I hoist a tight smile on my face. "Not at the moment."

"Have dinner with me tonight."

I suppress a groan. This guy seems nice enough, but the last thing I need is to be dealing with unwanted attention from an amorous guest. "Um, dinner is on the ship. So, we're all having dinner together . . ."

"I mean sit with me. And Dwight," he adds with a wave. "I would like to know you better, Ms. Shirt. Your friend can come too."

"Sister. I'm her sister," she wheezes through barely contained laughter.

I surreptitiously dig my elbow into her side.

Nikolai stares at me expectantly.

"Ahhh . . ." I'm saved from having to answer when the driver cuts the engine and promptly starts a lesson on how to properly exit the Zodiac with crew members' help—wrist to wrist grip, both hands. A strong breeze chafes my bare legs and I shiver.

Above us, *Discovery*'s five decks loom. It might be a smaller, expedition-style ship, but from this vantage it looks enormous, like a towering monolith of red and white metal dotted with portholes and exposed deck. Metal scaffolding containing a staircase abuts the ship. At the bottom, two crew members wearing crisp white uniforms tie off the Zodiac, anchoring it in place.

We bob like a cork in the wind-whipped waves as passengers begin climbing off the craft, sliding toward the middle to step off a stool and onto a metal platform with help from the crew. Nikolai and his friend get off before me, thank God, and then an older couple goes, so at least there's some distance between us.

Of course, the one time a guy directs his attention at me rather than Walsh, it's a passenger looking for a rebound lay. This cruise is going to be *fun*.

"You have an admirer," says Walsh with a snort.

"I noticed." Why he hasn't spared Walsh a second glance, I have no idea. Maybe he doesn't go for blondes.

It's my turn to get off. A wave catches the Zodiac just as I step and I'm propelled upward like a giant, invisible hand is giving me a lift. I swallow back a swell of nausea and stumble as my feet connect with the metal platform. The crew member on my right guides me toward the handrail and I grasp its slick surface.

"Thanks," I choke. Walsh follows, and we ascend the stairs to embark the vessel.

With every step we climb, my stomach knots tighter and

tighter. I eye the line of passengers waiting to filter into the ship through the door at the top. None of them are Graeme. After our Zodiac is emptied, another one full of passengers pulls up. I scan each face. No Graeme.

Where is he?

When it's our turn to enter and we cross the threshold, I immediately feel the pitch of the ship. I widen my stance to gain balance as a busy scene greets us. An entourage of smiling Ecuadoran crew members line what's essentially a lobby, funneling us toward a semicircular central reception desk.

We complete check-in, drop our life jackets and backpacks in our cabin—a cozy, nicely appointed space in creams and teals with a large picture window—and head upstairs to the lounge for the mandatory safety briefing scheduled to start in twenty minutes.

The swirling pattern of sapphire-stained wood inlays on the floor and the seating in shades of blues and greens make me feel like we're in an underwater grotto. Or at least it would, if the room wasn't lined with two solid walls of windows. Light bounces off the shimmering water outside and floods the room.

Guests mill around, either gazing out the windows, ordering drinks at the bar, or gathering in clumps, chatting. My palms sweat and my breath quickens as I scan each face, each form. No sweep of dark brown hair, strong jaw, or deep-set eyes.

"Open bar, right?" asks Walsh.

Unlimited drinks are included on this departure as a special booking incentive, but she shouldn't be getting slammed right out of the gate. "Moderation," I remind her.

"Yeah, yeah." She rolls her eyes. "Want anything?"

"No, thanks, I'm feeling yuck."

"I told you that roast beef sandwich on the plane wasn't a good idea. The mayo on there was fun-kay."

My gut burbles in response, and I clutch my stomach.

When I was eleven, one of our dogs, a Lab retriever mutt named Daisy, got into a box of doughnuts and wolfed down a full dozen before my dad came downstairs and discovered the explosion of powdered sugar and cardboard remains scattered across the kitchen. Daisy spent the rest of the morning outside. Feeling sorry for her, I kept her company as she toddled around our sweeping field of a backyard and chomped mournfully on mouthfuls of grass, gait shaky, eyes glassy.

Daisy, I feel you, girl. Because right now, I am totally you post-doughnuts. And the way the floor won't stay still is *not* helping.

"It's fine. I'm fine. I'll find us a seat." I should have taken some Dramamine as a precaution, and maybe some Pepto, but it's too late now. My meds are packed away in my checked luggage and our suitcases haven't been transferred to the ship yet.

Walsh bounds across the room to the bar where half a dozen guests are seated on stools, sipping fresh cocktails. My sea legs are still on backorder, so I stumble through the curved navy sofas and swivel chairs. Every piece of furniture is bolted down and forms a ring around a small, central raised platform. I sink onto an unoccupied sofa near the back and pull a small field notebook and pen from my pocket. Time to distract myself with work.

What do I observe about the guests? About the ship so far? I tap my pen against my lips.

Most of the people in the room are probably my parents' age or slightly younger. There are a few twenty- and thirtysomethings and a solid number of retirees. No kids. I know from dipping into our booking system that the ship is only two-thirds full, so roughly sixty passengers on board. There's a buzz of collective anticipation that has my nerves jittering. I begin jotting down notes.

A roll of laughter makes me pause, pen gripped in my fist. A familiar masculine voice reaches my ears. I twist, slowly, but I already know who it is. My spine tingles.

Graeme is in the lounge.

"Thanks for your time, Gustavo. This was a real pleasure," he says. I can only see the top of his head. Another man is blocking my view.

The other man claps Graeme on the shoulder. "The pleasure was all mine." I vaguely recognize him from the staff bios in my pretravel documents as Gustavo Santos, our cruise leader, aka the person responsible for planning each day's activities and making sure the entire voyage goes off without a hitch. Next to the captain, he's in charge.

"And thanks for accommodating my request. I appreciate it," Graeme adds in a conspiratorial tone. The fine hairs on the back of my neck raise in alarm. I don't like that tone at all. Like Graeme is keeping secrets with the cruise leader. Secrets that will give him an edge in our competition? I lean over the arm of the sofa, straining to hear more . . .

"Of course, of course," says Gustavo, sticking out a hand for Graeme to shake. "We will connect after the safety briefing, before this evening's shore excursion." Just as I'm about to catch my first unobstructed real-life glimpse of Graeme, a Technicolor torso sidles into view.

"We meet again, Ms. Shirt."

I jolt and drop my pen. "Oh, um, hi." I attempt to peer around Nikolai. He steps closer until he fills my entire field of vision. I nearly growl in frustration. In one smooth move, he slides next to me on the couch, body angled toward mine, thoroughly boxing me in. His cologne hits me like a sledgehammer. On a different day I might have said it was nice, if a bit strong, but today the scent drills into my nose and pummels my gag reflex like a punching bag. My throat constricts.

Under the guise of picking up my pen, I wiggle out of his orbit and quickly stand.

"You never answered my question earlier," he says, crossing his legs, seemingly unbothered by my rapid escape. Lips squeezing together in a puckered smile, he smooths the imaginary wrinkles from his Ed Hardy T-shirt. "You, me, dinner?"

I open my mouth to decline, but—

"There you are," a deep voice purrs behind me. I whip around to find myself staring into a face I've only ever seen on a screen—Graeme's.

Sunlight frames him, highlighting the subtle dimple in his chin. My heartbeat stutters. He's shaved at some point in the last two weeks. His stubble is shorter than it was before, maybe a week's worth of growth. And I notice for the first time that his nose isn't completely straight; the bridge is slightly crooked, but it doesn't detract from his looks in the least.

It's official: FaceTime Graeme has *nothing* on live-and-in-person Graeme. He's tall, for one—a shade over six feet, I'd guess, based on how his chin is at my eye level. And with his strong jaw, patrician nose, and sweep of wavy, deep brown hair that's longer on top, he cuts a striking figure. So much for my imaginings of a squat, bulbous troll-demon. This Graeme is freaking . . . majestic. Majestic edged with down-home, aww-shucks, Midwestern charm—snake charm, that is.

Sweat threatens between my shoulder blades. Did someone crank the heat in here or what? Squaring my shoulders, I flash Graeme a tight-lipped smile. "Here I am."

"Who's your friend?" he asks.

Nikolai scrambles to his feet. "Dr. Nikolai Kozlov." He extends his hand, and when Graeme steps up to take it, I catch a whiff of something delicious: an enticingly light scent of cedar, leather, and something crisp—citrusy, even. I resist the overwhelming urge to grab him by the collar, shove my nose in the crook of his neck, and snort like a politician doing a line of coke off a prostitute's cleavage.

I swallow the sudden excess of saliva that's flooded my mouth—along with a jolt of anger. This is the *competition*. We're not on the Love Boat. We're on assignment for work. And the one who uses this experience to craft the best proposal wins.

And I'm going to win. I will. I'll make sure of it.

The two men shake hands.

"Nice to meet you. Graeme Crawford-Collins." Graeme's expression is tight and unreadable.

"I'm sorry, you two are . . ." Nikolai trails off, pointing his finger back and forth between Graeme and me.

"Together," says Graeme.

My eyes nearly bug out of my head and I scratch my nose to cover my reaction. Is Graeme pretending to be my . . . boyfriend? Why, to keep Nikolai from sniffing around? There must be some ulterior motive. I just don't know what it is yet.

Catching sight of my face, Graeme shoves his hands into the pockets of his khaki shorts and his bicep muscles flex beneath the sleeve of his white polo. "I believe you were extending a dinner invitation?"

"Yes. To her. And you. Both of you," Nikolai hedges.

"We'd be delighted to—"

A gust of wind suddenly rattles the windows and the ship tilts sharply. Several guests gasp and grab furniture to steady themselves. Heat floods my cheeks. Bile rises. My head spins.

No. Not here. Not now.

I hunch, fist pressed against my lips as my stomach heaves. Graeme's there, gripping my shoulder. Saying my name.

Need to get out of here.

I shove away, take two steps, and vomit. All over a brightly colored Ed Hardy T-shirt.

6

blink in horror. Nikolai's eyes widen and his lips curl in disgust. "I go change shirt," he says stiffly, and marches to the stairs. Only one person, Nikolai's friend Dwight, pulls a double-take at the trail of vomit oozing down his chest like pulverized egg yolks. Everyone else seems either too engaged in conversation or too transfixed by the view to notice.

With my fingers clamped against my closed mouth, I swivel slowly to face Graeme. His eyebrows are so far up his forehead that they threaten to disappear into his hairline.

I puked. In public. On a guest. *In front of Graeme.*

I want to curl up in a ball and die.

What are the odds he'll tell James? I nearly choke. What are the odds he won't? We haven't even made it to our first stop of the cruise and I've already served up the perfect shot for Graeme to spike in my face.

Are people staring? Maybe no one else saw . . .

"Honey, are you okay?" a middle-aged woman asks, bustling over.

Graeme steps between us. "She's fine. Just a little seasick." He stares her down until she leaves. His hand closes around my elbow as he guides me to the far end of the sofa. My knees buckle and I collapse into a heap. "Do you need to go lie down?" he asks, voice low.

I consider it. But my stomach is dormant now, like a hyped-up toddler passed out after a sugar rush. I feel loads better, actually. I shake my head.

Without another word, Graeme turns and walks away.

Great, he's so grossed out he can't even look at me. Humiliation courses through my veins. At least I won't have to worry about him getting in my way this week. He'll probably stay far, far away for fear that Henley the Hurling Wonder might spew all over him.

I wet my lips. I need water. And a toothbrush. And to crawl into a hole and never come out.

Shoving to my feet, I pick up my notebook and pen from where I dropped them on the floor and stumble across the room. A crew member holding a spray bottle and a cleaning rag hustles to the spot where I was sick, probably to clean up the splatters. *Ughhh so embarrassing.* I wobble down the stairs, keeping my chin tucked in case anyone is looking, and escape to my cabin.

Our suitcases are here, finally, and I tip mine onto the carpeted floor and unzip it. Digging through the inside pocket, I fish out a container of Dramamine, my toothbrush, and toothpaste. In the bathroom, I brush my teeth and tongue vigorously, almost gagging in the process, and slurp water from the tap to wash down the chalky white pill.

Bracing both palms along the narrow counter, I stare into the mirror. My cheeks are a brilliant pink and my eyes are glassy. I wet a washcloth and dab it against my face to cool down. Vomiting on someone, even someone as annoyingly persistent as Nikolai, ranks as one of my all-time worst waking nightmares. And Graeme had a front-row seat.

A voice sputters from a wall speaker between the two twin beds. "Good afternoon, good afternoon. A mandatory safety briefing will begin shortly. Please make your way to the lounge."

"Shitsicles," I mutter.

I have to attend the mandatory briefing, no matter how much I want to fade into the ether.

Shaking my hair out of my face, I square my shoulders and raise my chin. Okay. I puked on someone. So what? The quickest way to draw attention to myself will be if I slink around like a piddling puppy, and I refuse to give Graeme the upper hand here. If I pretend this episode never happened, then everyone else will too, Graeme included.

He'd better.

Taking a deep breath, I stride out of my cabin and return to the lounge. Mostly everyone is seated now. I intentionally *don't* look for Graeme. If he's planning on ignoring me the rest of the trip, I'll let him.

I spot Nikolai, wearing a different, equally ugly shirt, sitting with Dwight near the central dais. He doesn't see me—*whew*. And Walsh is still perched on a barstool, happily chatting away, oblivious to everything that just went down. I could join her, but the thought of making small talk with strangers right now has me feeling queasy all over again.

I skirt through the sea of sofas and find an empty spot in the opposite corner from where I was before.

"You're back," says Graeme at my elbow. My muscles jerk. He wasn't here a second ago. Leaning over my shoulder, he places a glass of ice water, a packet of Dramamine, and a candy wrapped in blue foil on the cocktail table in front of me before sinking into the nearest teal swivel chair, unfolding like a king assuming his throne.

Graeme's . . . not avoiding me?

I blink at the water, then at him. He inclines his chin as if to say, *There you go.*

This is so unexpected. And nice. And *weird*.

I hold the glass up to the light and rotate it, looking for any sign of foul play. Then I bring it to my nose and sniff.

"It's water. Not cyanide."

"I know." Wetting my lips, I take a tentative sip.

"I mean, I spit in it, but . . ."

My first instinct is to open my mouth and spew the water back into the glass. Instead, I lift my chin, lock eyes with him, and deliberately swallow. A droplet of water clings to the corner of my lips and I brush it away with my fist.

He chortles. I glower.

Resting an elbow on his armrest, he considers me. "You know, whenever I imagined meeting you in person for the first time, I never pictured you projectile-vomiting on someone."

Don't acknowledge. "What did you picture?"

"Henley, warrior princess. Armed with the sharpest of knife collections to skewer the hearts of her enemies."

"The knives are in my cabin. They were a bitch to get through customs, especially the meat cleaver, but I can go get them if you like. You never know who might need skewering." I flash my teeth in a wide, beatific grin.

Graeme throws his head back and laughs. The sound is rich and warm like molten chocolate cake. Still chuckling, he shakes his head slowly. "You, Henley Rose, are too much."

Shifting in my seat, I cross my legs and perch an elbow on the sofa back. "So where have you been today? I didn't see you on the plane this morning."

"Why, did you miss me?"

"Like herpes."

His nostrils flare. "I flew into San Cristóbal on Wednesday to do some exploring and boarded the ship a few hours before you got here."

The fake smile slides off my face like goop. Graeme's been in the Galápagos for three days already? Damn it, I should have thought to fly out early too.

Yeah right. I'm too busy to take extra leave. Being away for ten days is going to be hard enough, let alone nearly two weeks; I'll be checking in every day as it is. How nice for Graeme that his workload is manageable enough to take the extra time off.

Anger at the fact that James thinks we're equals—even though I *clearly* work harder than him—boils to the surface.

Gustavo's voice cuts through my seething thoughts. "Good afternoon, good afternoon," his voice buzzes through the speakers. "If everyone could please take a seat, we will begin the briefing."

The remaining guests filter through the room, talking and laughing. To my surprise, Graeme stands and shuffles over to sit next to me on the sofa. His leg is a full foot away, but still close enough that it's weirding me out. There's no phone screen, no incorporeal voice floating across a phone line. He's here and he's *real*.

He leans over until we're practically shoulder to shoulder. I catch another whiff of his intoxicating scent and inhale deeply through my nose before I can give myself a mental kick.

"Look, I know we're both here because we're competing for the same position," he says. "But I want you to know—"

"Hey," says Walsh. She's standing in front of us, holding a pair of beers. Flicking a glance between me and Graeme, she curves her lips upward, slow and calculated. I've seen that look before. I furrow my brows. What does she think she's doing?

She hands me one of the beers and flounces into the chair that Graeme vacated. Setting her bottle on the table, she crosses her legs—linen espadrille bobbing—and leans forward until her cleavage peeks from the neckline of her striped boatneck shirt.

"You must be Graeme," she croons.

Yep, she's going for it: full-on flirt mode. Cold condensation slicks my palm. I set my beer next to hers without taking a sip.

"And you must be Henley's sister."

"Walsh Evans." She sticks out her hand, palm down.

He tentatively shakes it. Even though he's perfectly polite, I get the feeling he's not impressed by her guns-a-blazing approach. The strange tension between my shoulder blades eases until a new thought strikes me. I frown.

"Wait, how did you know she's my sister?"

"James told me you were bringing her along."

I roll my eyes. "Of course he did."

"What's that supposed to mean?"

"It means you're all buddy-buddy with our boss. It's the bros club, and you two are its only members."

"It's not the bros club."

"Oh really, how many women do you see him making small talk with?"

"You should be friendlier."

I bark a bitter laugh. "Right. Because James makes women feel so comfortable, as if I could just plop down and have a chat with him whenever the mood strikes. Kind of like how I can control the way he talks to me." A crease forms between Graeme's eyebrows and he opens his mouth to say something, but I plow on. "What else did he tell you? My initial thoughts on the Galápagos cruise market?"

"No, he just said your sister was traveling with you, and he asked if I'd like to bring someone along too. To make it fair, I guess. I turned him down. I told him I wanted to use the opportunity of a solo trip to focus."

I grind my teeth until my jaw pops. He's even managed to make my flash of ingenuity with Walsh as objective secret shopper look like a negative.

A mic switches on, speakers crackling to life, and Gustavo strides to the central platform in the middle of the room. Voices quiet and I force my attention to the dais.

"Welcome, everyone, to *Discovery*! I'm Gustavo, your cruise leader, and we're going to enjoy a fantastic Galápagos adventure together!" The guests applaud.

Gustavo's voice embraces the audience, his warm, energetic demeanor stoking excitement and guaranteeing engagement. He's a congenial mix of a salt-and-pepper-haired Enrique Iglesias and Richard Simmons. He takes the first few minutes of his spiel to touch on the highlights of what we'll experience—a new island each day, snorkeling, hiking, kayaking, and abundant wildlife with no inherent fear of humans, the hallmark of the Galápagos Islands.

Then he begins introducing the other staff on board: the naturalists, who will accompany us on all shore excursions to share their knowledge about the wildlife we see, and the officers and crew, the folks responsible for operating the ship.

My gaze drifts to Graeme. I try to listen, but his presence pulls my attention like a yo-yo. Swerving his chin, he glances at me and I quickly look away. My cheeks heat under his gaze. Squaring my shoulders, I tighten my jaw.

Graeme edges closer. "It's strange seeing you in person too," he whispers.

I whip my head to look at him and find his face inches from my own. At this distance, I can make out the color of his eyes. They're blue. Not cornflower blue like Walsh's, or light watery blue like a spring sky. They're a deep, bottomless blue. Like the sea.

I lick my lips, and his gaze flicks to my mouth. I grimace. He smirks.

Gustavo's voice cuts through my reverie and heat creeps up my neck. "I have one more person I'd like to introduce. She's a marketing manager from our home office . . ."

Noooo. Please don't say my name . . . please don't say my name . . .

He's going to say my name.

"Henley Evans. Where are you, Henley?"

My stomach drops like a two-ton garbage truck. I didn't want the other guests knowing I work for the cruise line—too many questions, too many headaches. So much for traveling incognito.

Hitching a smile on my face, I stand and offer the guests a halfhearted wave. Walsh punctuates the round of golf claps with an energetic *whoo-ooo*. I resume my seat.

"Now, on our ship, safety is most important . . ."

Wait. He's not introducing Graeme?

"Why isn't he introducing you?" I hiss.

"Because I asked him not to." His smug smile makes me want to dump my beer on his head.

This must have been what he was plotting with Gustavo when they came into the lounge. He's given himself yet another advantage—if the guests don't know he works for the cruise line, he can fly under the radar. He won't have to be on all the time. But I will.

Oh, hell no. If I'm out, he's out.

I leap to my feet like a popped jack-in-the-box. "Hold on, Gustavo. You forgot one."

Gustavo freezes midsentence, his mouth falling open.

Graeme's eyebrows knit together in a scowl. Tugging at his

bicep, I silently urge him to stand, and holy hell his arm is *hard*. It's like gripping granite. With a deep sigh, he heaves to his feet.

Gustavo blinks twice. "Ah, yes. How could I forget. Henley isn't our only corporate staff on board. Please welcome Graeme Crawford-Collins, the man in charge of all our social media."

Graeme lifts his hand to the room. One of the elderly ladies seated nearby elbows the woman beside her, and they both swivel to stare at him. The woman on the right pretends to lick her finger, and when she touches her wide hip, makes a sound like steam escaping. Oh Lord.

"And one more thing," I chime in, tearing my eyes away from Graeme's new groupies. "Just a quick reminder that when you post pictures from our adventures this week—and I promise, you're going to get some fantastic shots—be sure to tag us on social media at S-Q-Adventures, one word, and Graeme here will re—"

"Remind you to enter our wildlife photography contest," he blurts.

Damn it, he guessed what I was going to say—that he would retweet and like their posts. Score one for Graeme for wiggling out of the extra work I tried to land on his plate.

"The winner of the contest will receive an all-expense-paid Seaquest Adventures cruise to Antarctica," Graeme continues. "Entries will be accepted until November 1. See *Henley* for more details." He flashes me a smile that, from the outside, would appear to be nothing more than professional courtesy. Except I can see through his facade like cellophane. It's a smile full of challenge. A shark's smile.

Applause fills the room. My nostrils flare as we sit. I realize too late that we're closer than we were before, only inches away. Energy surges between us so fiery it could melt diamonds.

"Yes, the contest. Thank you, Graeme. We're pleased to have both you and Henley on board," Gustavo acknowledges. "Now, if everyone could direct their attention to the screens for a short safety video. Afterward, we will gather in our muster stations for a lifeboat drill."

Crossing my arms over my chest, I lean over until my mouth is inches from Graeme's ear. "Smooth move, making me the point person for that photography contest. Now every other guest with a fancy camera is going to be hounding me with questions."

Graeme's lips twitch. "I thought you liked being in charge."

I narrow my eyes at him. His expression is placid, but I don't miss the flush in his cheeks and the tiny beads of sweat that have gathered around his collar. Is he nervous or something?

I shake my head. It doesn't matter. "For the record, I will do anything to land this promotion. Even if I have to chat up every guest on this ship while coming up with a home-run marketing idea, I'll prove I'm the better choice. Throw all the obstacles in my way that you want. I'll still rise to the top."

Straightening, he leans so close that his shoulder brushes mine and his warm breath caresses my ear when he chuckles. "Game on."

7

"I still can't believe you puked on that Russian chiropractor and I missed it," says Walsh, her eyes obscured by a pair of reflective aviator sunglasses.

The safety briefing is over, and we're back on shore on San Cristóbal for a short evening excursion to explore Puerto Baquerizo Moreno before the ship sets sail for Española Island, the first stop on our voyage. The café's red umbrella above us casts a narrow shadow, and the strong sunlight warms my bare shins. Across the street, water laps against a concrete pier jutting into the bay.

"Is that a company record, yakking in the first fifteen minutes of a cruise?" Walsh asks.

Snatching her paper napkin from the table, I tear it into strips, lips pursed.

"I told you not to eat that sandwich."

"Knock it off, okay?"

Kicking her feet up on the empty chair across the table, Walsh slurps her chocolate milkshake through a straw.

I tip my oversized sunglasses onto my nose and take a sip of water from my Nalgene. After "the incident" earlier, no dairy for me, thanks. I check the time on my phone and a notification pops up: I have new messages from Tory and Christina in our group text.

Tory

Ahoy, stranger! Make it to the ship okay?

Christina

I'm sure she did, chill out, Mama!

Tory

Gotta make sure our girl got there safe

I grin.

Hey! I'm alive, we made it!

Christina

Told you so!

How's Galápagos so far?

Good, hot. Haven't seen much yet because we're still on San Cristobal.

Tory

Wear sunscreen and take lots of pictures

Christina

1. Sunscreen is always a good idea.

2. Have you met Graeme yet? What's he like in person?

Ugh, yes . . . and he is exactly how I thought. TERRIBLE

My neck prickles and I glance automatically over my shoulder, but Graeme's nowhere in sight. I haven't spotted many other cruise-goers in this part of town. We picked this particular café because of the free Wi-Fi (score), plus it's tucked at the far end of the main drag, away from the other tourists. If I'm lucky, Graeme won't venture this way.

In fact, I haven't seen him since the safety briefing. Good. I don't want to see him. Today or for the rest of the trip. I click off my phone and peer up and down the street one more time. Still Graeme-less. Which reminds me . . .

I nudge Walsh with my foot. "Hey, why were you flirting with Graeme earlier?"

Walsh barely looks up from her own phone. "Huh?"

I reach over and cover her screen with my hand.

"Hey!" Scowling, she jerks it away.

Something about the stiffness of her lips has me frowning. "What's wrong?"

Walsh's shoulders slump. "Remember that interview I did at the spa down the street before we left?"

"Yeah?"

"I just got an email from the interviewer. 'Thanks but no thanks.' It's the third rejection this week."

I wince. "Something will turn up soon, I know it."

"I hope so. I can't mooch off you forever," she adds in a mumble. Pursing her lips, she hammers her thumbs across the screen. "So what were you saying about Graeme?"

I should say something else to pump her up, give her hope. But I can't help but agree with her—she *can't* mooch off me forever.

Eventually she'll need to find her own place, and she definitely needs a steady income. Then there's the matter of her presence on this cruise and why she's here . . .

"Just don't flirt with him, okay? It's unprofessional. You're supposed to be my sounding board, remember?"

She huffs. "Yes, yes. Sounds galore. What do you want to hear my thoughts on first?"

"Well, what do you think of the experience so far?"

Plopping her phone on the table, she tips down her sunglasses and peeks at me over the rim. "I think you were holding out on me and your coworker is hot as balls."

"Walsh, no. Absolutely not. He's exactly like Sean, and remember how horrible he was? How he treated me—"

"I know, I know. Graeme equals villain. But I'm allowed to appreciate physical male beauty, okay?" She cranes her neck. "Oh look, there he is now."

I whip around, and sure enough, Graeme is strolling down the street, a compact black backpack hitched on his shoulders. My intestines squirm. He has a selfie stick with his phone attached to the end—he's either taking a video or FaceTiming someone because his mouth is moving.

"Graeme. Hey, Graeme!" Walsh calls.

His head jerks around in an attempt to track who yelled his name. When he spots us, Walsh motions for him to come over. He offers a tentative wave back before lowering his selfie stick and stowing it in his backpack.

"What are you doing?" I hiss at Walsh.

"What do you mean?" Her round eyes gleam with mischief. She's calling him over here to annoy me on purpose, I know it. Like how, when she was in middle school, she'd blast Miley Cyrus directly at the wall between our bedrooms whenever I was trying to study. I'd eventually lose my shit, storm over to her room, and she would giggle and shriek as I tried to wrestle the Bluetooth speaker out of her hand.

Some things never change.

Graeme's long legs eat up the sidewalk, and a few seconds later he's standing right next to our table. He motions to the chair on my left. "Anyone sitting here?"

"Yes," I say at the same time Walsh says, "No."

"Great." Flashing his teeth at me, he drops his backpack on the ground and settles into the empty chair.

Graeme must know from my frosty expression that I want him to leave, so why is he sitting with us? Oh right, because getting under my skin is one of his favorite pastimes. It looks like two people have decided to hop on the Let's Annoy Henley express.

Leaning forward, Walsh stirs her milkshake with her straw. "What have you been up to in town?"

Graeme stretches his legs out under the table and folds his hands on his stomach like he doesn't have a care in the world. I glare at him in silent disapproval.

"Let's see, I bought some souvenirs. Took pictures. Interviewed the owner of an art gallery I discovered the other day. His family's lived in the Galápagos for four generations. He has some great stories. Good material for our blog." He shoots me a pointed grin.

Pushing his sunglasses into his windswept hair, he glances at Walsh's milkshake and our phones sitting on the table. "What have you guys been doing? Enjoying a snack?"

"Working," I grate.

"All work and no play makes Henley a dull girl."

"Or it makes her your boss."

He raises an eyebrow. I incline my chin in challenge.

Walsh clears her throat in an apparent effort to cut the tension that's swelled like a balloon. "Graeme, did you see the sea lions on the boardwalk? So cute."

"I did. Amazing how they're not afraid of people. Snorkeling tomorrow is going to be killer. You're both snorkeling, right?"

Walsh's phone trills and she picks it up after glancing at the screen. "I am. Henley's probably not. She hates deep water."

"Oh yeah?" Graeme raises his eyebrows.

I glare so hard at Walsh that I'm sure laser beams are about to shoot out of my eyeballs, but she doesn't notice because she's too absorbed in responding to her latest texts.

"Yeah," she says without looking up. "I haven't seen her swim since we were teenagers. Not since—"

I aim a kick at her under the table and miss.

"What?" Graeme presses, looking entirely too eager.

"Since she almost drowned," she finishes. When Walsh finally looks up, she stiffens at the death glare I'm throwing her way. *Yeah, thanks for divulging my personal weakness to the competition, Walsh.*

Graeme squints at me. "Did you have a swimming accident or something?"

I wave him away. "Walsh is being dramatic."

"Dramatic? You weren't breathing. Dad had to give you CPR."

Graeme looks between us, elbow resting on the table, chin in hand. All he needs is a bag of popcorn. "What happened?"

"Nothing. Just a minor waterskiing incident."

"Minor," she scoffs.

"I was waterskiing without a life jacket, my leg cramped, and I went under," I explain to Graeme in my best no-big-deal voice.

"Sounds traumatic."

He has no idea. I still vividly remember the fingers of seaweed imprisoning my foot. The violation of water in my lungs, the crush of darkness. The absolute fear, the panic. I didn't venture into a large body of water after that for nearly four years, and even now I stick with the shallow end of a swimming pool or frothy ocean surf. Deep water? No, thanks.

"Nah, not really," I lie. "It was a long time ago."

"And you took a job working for a cruise line . . . with boats?"

"Yeah, we were all shocked," says Walsh.

I shrug. "I took the job because I was looking for a career change and I wanted to market something that brings people joy. And hey, I work in an office. It's not like I'm on the ships every day. But like I said, I'm over it. I'm going snorkeling tomorrow and it's going to be great. So fun."

Graeme studies me. "You don't have to snorkel, you know. There will be glass-bottomed boat rides for guests who don't want to snorkel."

"And miss out on up-close-and-personal encounters with all that endemic marine wildlife? Nice try."

Over 90 percent of our passengers opt to snorkel, so I won't get a full sense of the experience if I don't do it at least once. It's about time I faced my fears anyway. And if it gives me ideas to help me land this promotion? It's worth it.

Crossing my legs, I flip my braid over my shoulder. Time to turn this magnifying glass around and see how Graeme likes being scrutinized. "So what's the deal with you and public speaking—or is it crowds you don't like?"

Walsh sits up straighter.

Gripping an armrest, Graeme shifts in his seat. The metal chair squeaks in protest.

"Come on, don't act like you don't know what I'm talking

about. You were all red and sweaty after Gustavo introduced you at the safety briefing. Not exactly a normal reaction."

Now it's Graeme's turn to play it casual. "Remote employee, remember? There aren't many opportunities for public speaking in my living room. I'm out of practice, that's all."

I don't buy it. His voice is so tense you could pluck it like a guitar string.

The sound of a blender floats through the open door to the café's kitchen. Graeme peers over my shoulder, then jerks his chin at Walsh's milkshake just as she takes another sip. "Don't drink that."

"Why?" she blurts.

"There's a woman inside making a milkshake and I just saw her add ice to the blender." At Walsh's questioning stare, he continues. "Ice is frozen tap water, and the water in Galápagos isn't safe to drink. You might be ingesting contaminated water."

I knew not to drink the water here, but ice in a milkshake never crossed my mind. Apparently, it hadn't crossed Walsh's either.

"Come on," I scoff. "This is the main town on San Cristóbal, the political capital of the Galápagos. I'm sure they serve tourists all the time and know to make ice with purified water."

"Do you see any other tourists around here? This area is off the beaten path. All locals."

Sure enough, all the other patrons in this café—and the coffee shop next door—are Ecuadoran. Not a tube-sock-wearing tourist in sight.

Walsh gingerly places her milkshake on the table like she's handling a live grenade. A frothy slurry at the bottom is all that's left, glittering with what I now recognize are, yep, flecks of ice. My entire body goes rigid, a boatload of *oh crap* pouring though my head.

Her lips tighten and the color drains from her cheeks.

Putting on a show of bravado, I shake my head. "No worries. Walsh has an iron constitution. More than I do, anyway," I add in a mutter. "I'm sure she'll be fine."

8

Walsh is not fine.

She only nibbled her dinner last night and disappeared to our cabin when her stomach started making noises that had the women sitting next to us clutching their pearls in shock. I checked on her a few times throughout the evening, but she insisted I buzz off, so I ended up answering work emails in the lounge until well after midnight before I finally braved going to bed. Not that I blamed Walsh for wanting to be alone. Nobody likes having someone hover when they're in gastrointestinal distress.

A toilet flushes, pulling me out of my groggy half-sleep. A few moments later, Walsh opens the bathroom door, causing a beam of fluorescent light to spill into our dim cabin. I blink against the sudden brightness and push myself higher in bed. My head pounds with exhaustion—what time is it?

Before I can grab my phone, I catch sight of Walsh's face and gasp. "Oh my God, are you okay?"

"Does it look like I'm okay?" she croaks. Face pale, forehead slick with sweat, she collapses into the twin bed across from mine. Curling into the fetal position, she rolls toward the wall. Her phone buzzes on her nightstand, but she doesn't move. Wow, she must be feeling *really* bad to ignore a new text.

I lumber out of bed and open the curtains a crack. Bright sunlight streams through the window, making me squint. Holy crap, it's morning already. "Were you sick all night?"

"Ughhhhh."

Now that I think about it, I vaguely remember the bathroom door opening and closing multiple times throughout the night. No wonder I'm so tired. "What can I get you? Medicine?"

"I already took some."

I touch her shoulder. "Ginger ale?"

She groans in response and pulls the covers over her head. "Just leave me alone to *die*."

"Maybe you should see the ship's medical officer. I can come with you."

She flips the blanket away from her face. "No, no. I'll be okay. There cannot possibly be anything left in my stomach. I just need to sleep. It was a rough night."

The wall speaker crackles and Gustavo's jovial voice barrels through my ears. "Good morning, good morning. I hope everyone enjoyed a filling, delicious breakfast, because the dining room is now closed."

I grab my phone and check the time. It's after nine. How is it after nine? I set an alarm last night for seven so I could get up early and work on my proposal. I must have accidentally turned it off, and now I've missed breakfast to boot. Plopping onto my bed with a moan, I scrub both palms over my face.

"If you plan on snorkeling this afternoon or at any point during the trip," Gustavo continues, "this is your last call to pick up snorkeling equipment. Remember, please be prepared to try on your wet suit to ensure a correct fit. Guests going on the three-hour hike this morning will disembark at nine thirty. Those wishing to do the one-hour beach walk will disembark at eleven.

Thirty minutes until the long hike. Thirty minutes, long hike. Thank you."

Well, the long hike is definitely out. I need the extra time to kick-start my proposal.

"Listen, I'll see if I can get you some crackers or something—" I start, but soft, heavy breathing floats over from Walsh's bed. She's already asleep.

I quickly use the bathroom and pull on a bathing suit, T-shirt, shorts, and sandals. After popping a Dramamine, I head toward the observation deck to pick up snorkeling gear. My lungs squeeze at the thought of swimming through the ocean's murky, suffocating depths, but I'm going to have to suck it up. At least the first snorkeling excursion isn't until this afternoon, giving me a few hours' reprieve before I have to face the inevitable.

I climb the stairs to the outdoor observation deck where staff is distributing equipment. It's a swell of controlled chaos. A line of guests at least a dozen deep stretches halfway across the upper deck, leading to rows of bins and wet suits hanging on racks. Another ten guests dot the outer edges, clambering into wet suits and trying on fins.

Slipping on my sunglasses, I join the end of the line and try not to sway with the movement of the ship. A brisk breeze chafes my nose and my stomach growls noisily, reminding me how empty it is. I grumble along with it.

"Good morning," Graeme's husky voice rumbles as he steps up next to me.

I wince. Of course he found me.

He's wearing a white T-shirt and a day pack, while his eyes are hidden behind dark sunglasses. His wavy hair lifts in the wind and his skin glows with a healthy tan. My gaze travels down to his black athletic shorts and I snort.

"Is that a banana in your pocket or are you just happy to see me?" The words are out of my mouth before I can reel them in. Sleep-deprived Henley equals loopy Henley.

Graeme's lips twitch and the dimple in his chin deepens. "You're lucky I didn't record that. Human resources wouldn't approve of such innuendo."

My chest tightens for only a heartbeat before Graeme pulls a perky yellow banana from his pocket with a wink. Unpeeling it, he lifts it to his mouth, but pauses before taking a bite. "I didn't see you at breakfast this morning."

"Because I wasn't there. I slept through my alarm."

After several seconds, he sighs. "Here." He tilts the partially unpeeled banana toward me.

"I don't want it."

"Eat it. You need energy to hike."

"I'm not going on the long hike."

"You're not?"

"I'm doing the beach walk at eleven."

"That's for the elderly and people too hungover to make it off the ship by 9:30. Which one are you?"

I hit him with my iciest glare.

He nudges me with his elbow. "Come on, don't wimp out. Do the long hike. You're only in the Galápagos once. You should take advantage of every minute."

"I don't need to do the long hike to get a flavor for the guest experience, and besides, there will be hikes offered every day. Some of us have to work."

"Suit yourself." He shrugs. "Are you sure you don't want this banana?" My stomach chooses that moment to rumble like a hungry elephant. He gives my midsection a pointed look. I tap my toe against the wood deck.

"Fine. I'll take it." I reach for it, but he yanks it back. His eyebrows raise. I furrow mine. He proffers the banana again. This time, I snatch it.

Our fingers brush. A buzz of energy zings between us like a closed circuit. My insides warm and goose bumps rise along my forearms. Coughing, I jerk away. Graeme scratches his jaw and looks out over the waves toward the green and white-rimmed island beyond.

I've never had this kind of visceral reaction to mere skin contact. Not with either of my two ex-boyfriends or even with the first boy I kissed—no one. My throat tightens and I shove away any thoughts of what that could possibly mean.

Nothing. It means nothing. It's just the physical manifestation of the withering disdain I've developed for Graeme over the last year. Or perhaps it's my system experiencing residual turbulence from yesterday's stomach upset. That's probably it. I quickly take an oversized bite.

"How's Walsh?" Graeme asks.

I chew thickly and swallow. "She's been better."

"And how are *you*?" He inclines his chin meaningfully.

"Fantastic. Peachy."

"Nervous about snorkeling this afternoon?"

"No way. I got this snorkel thing locked down." I take another bite to avoid telling more lies.

"Sure you do." Diving his hands into his pockets, Graeme rocks in place in his sandals. Damn it, even his *feet* are attractive. Man feet generally aren't—the toes are always long and hairy, and nail care leaves something to be desired. But Graeme has nice feet, strong calves, and a hint of muscular thighs . . .

Stop staring.

I finish the banana in five more bites and throw away the peel in the trash can across the deck.

When I return to my spot in line, the slap-slap of flip-flops approaching co-opts my attention. I suppress a groan. Nikolai is wearing a faded shorty wetsuit unzipped and rolled down to his waist, and he's strutting, gut sucked in, arms pumping like he's on *Baywatch*. Surprise flickers through me. His stomach may be on the softer side, but his arms are relatively sculpted. Good for him.

"I see you are better today," says Nikolai. "No more—" He opens his mouth and pantomimes vomiting with his hand.

"Not yet." Not with the preventative Dramamine I've been taking.

"Good, I am glad. And you"—he wags a finger at Graeme—"you had me going for a second. You are not her boyfriend. You two work together." Nikolai punches Graeme lightly on the arm. A frown flickers across Graeme's face before he smooths it away.

"Perhaps we can get to know each other better this evening over dinner?" Nikolai asks me, pursing his lips in a puckered grin.

Really? I thought after I puked on him, I was permanently off the hook. Apparently not. I desperately want to tell this guy to bark up some other tree, but then I recall the second principle in our company's mission statement: *prioritize the passenger experience above everything except safety.* Nikolai is a guest. Politeness is required.

I force a weak smile. "Sure."

"You can't today," interjects Graeme. "Remember? We have that work thing, that *meeting*," he says meaningfully.

"Oh, right. Yes. We need to discuss—"

"Website optimization," he finishes.

"Yes, website optimization. Sorry, I completely forgot," I say to Nikolai with an apologetic shrug.

"I understand. You are career-minded woman. I like that. Some other time then." He slouches off to a chair across the deck, gut sagging.

I swivel to face Graeme. Did he just save me from unwanted male attention? This does *not* square with the Graeme I've known for a year. He's being . . . *nice*. And Graeme isn't nice. Graeme argues. He connives. He doesn't say please or thank you, and he doesn't go out of his way to be helpful.

Is this all part of the act? Some trick to get me to lower my guard?

"That was thoughtful of you," I say once Nikolai is out of earshot.

"Was it?" he drawls. "You know this means we have to sit together at dinner, right? And, *gasp*, actually have a conversation?"

"The conversation part's debatable."

"Come on, don't you think we should get to know each other at least a little? We've worked together for a year and I hardly know anything about you. Except the fact that you don't seem to like me very much. Why is that, exactly?"

"You know why."

"Can't say that I do."

I'm prepared to scoff. To laugh in his face and call him a liar. Except I don't see any trace of a lie in his guileless expression. His mouth is a thin line and his jaw could cut glass, but there's a hint of actual confusion behind his eyes.

I gape at him. Is he for real?

Viral video, constant rudeness—does that ring a bell?

I'm saved from responding when a staff member calls me forward to receive my wet suit. Thank God. If this is a new level of manipulation from Graeme, I cannot deal with it right now.

"How are you today?" the naturalist—her name tag says Xiavera—asks with a sunny smile. She's a compact young woman with dark brown hair framing an angular face. Like the rest of the crew and staff on board, she's Ecuadoran.

"Fine, thanks."

"Excited for the hike this morning?"

"I'm doing the photo walk, and yeah, it should be great."

She eyes me up and down. "Really? Why not the long hike?"

"I have to check in with the office. Work stuff."

"Too bad. The hike takes us through magnificent seabird colonies to a cliff overlooking the ocean. It is one of the most beautiful sights in the Galápagos. You will miss out."

With a tut, she riffles through a row of hanging wet suits and pulls one down that's edged in pink, size medium. After asking my shoe size, she hands me a pair of fins, a snorkel, a mask, and a long mesh bag for storage. I request a second set of everything for Walsh—she might be out of commission for the day, but I know she'll want to snorkel at some point during the trip once she's feeling better.

Beside me, a different naturalist equips Graeme. I can't help but notice his easy smile with everyone he encounters. It's just so at odds with the obnoxious coworker I've been dealing with for the last year. What's his deal?

"Take a minute to try everything on and make sure it fits," says Xiavera. "You'll be able to exchange items during lunch, but—"

"Excuse me. *Ex-c-use* me!" An elbow jabs into my side and I automatically move out of the way.

It's a red-faced passenger. She looks to be in her sixties and she's holding a pair of snorkeling fins that she plops unceremoniously on the table. "These don't fit. Just like the last pair didn't fit. I said size eight, and these are obviously not an eight. They're too small."

I notice the man behind her for the first time. He's about her age with a sizeable bald spot—probably her husband, if their matching rings and the utterly defeated look in his eyes are any indication. He sidles up next to her with his finger in the air. "Donna, dear, are you sure they don't fit? Did you—"

"Yes, I'm sure. Why don't you try on your wet suit, Charles."

Charles nods mutely and shuffles away. Clearly, he's been worn down after decades with this woman.

Xiavera picks one of the fins Donna dropped and squints at the number printed on the inside. "These are size eight, like you requested."

The woman, who is wearing a long white bathing suit cover-up, puffs until she resembles an angry cotton ball.

I step forward with a friendly smile. "Hi there." After working retail all through college, my customer service facade slips easily into place. "I couldn't help but overhear. You know, I read somewhere that fins don't necessarily go by the same sizing as regular shoes. So even though you normally wear an eight, you might be more comfortable sizing up to a nine."

The woman lets out a frosty bark of laughter. "My feet are *not* a size nine. They have never been a nine, and they never will." She looks me up and down. "You're the one who works for Seaquest's corporate office, right? What's your name again—Hester? Tell me, Hester, why is it so difficult for your staff to give me what I've asked for? Or maybe I should find out who your manager is, and ask him instead."

Graeme is beside me before I can work up an answer through my stuttering shock.

"Donna, nice to see you. Graeme. We met yesterday on the aft deck." He takes her manicured hand in both of his and graces her with a smile that could melt even the strongest of chastity belts.

The change that overtakes Donna is stark and immediate. Her mouth loses its pinched look, her forehead unfurrows, and a glowing smile spreads across her face like an angel has graced her with its presence. "Graeme, yes. Good to see you. Maybe you can help me. These people are insisting that I don't know my own shoe size."

"How about this: I'll get you a few different fins to try on and you can see what works. Some are probably more broken in than others and might fit differently. Size eight, right?"

"Yes. Finally, someone who understands what I need."

"Why don't you make yourself comfortable on that bench over there and I'll bring them over."

She pats his shoulder before walking away. As soon as she's out of earshot, the smile fades from his lips and he leans across the table to Xiavera.

"Two sets of nines, please. And if you can find ones where the size is hard to see, all the better."

Xiavera nods appreciatively. "Good idea." After some digging through a bin behind her, she hands him the fins.

All I can do is blink. "You know, for someone who doesn't like people, you sure are good with older women."

He shrugs. "I have a lot of experience."

What the heck does that mean?

With the extra fins tucked under one arm and his own equipment piled against his chest, Graeme heads over to the bench where Donna is perched, waiting in anticipation with her hands on her knees. Beside her, Charles is already wearing his wet suit and has his nose buried in what looks like a guidebook.

Gathering up my snorkeling equipment, I shuffle off to an empty spot across the deck from Graeme and Donna and drop everything onto a low bench.

I only just met Donna, but I know Donna. Because in any given group, there's always a Donna—the one who is dead-set on complaining about everything. The thing is, Donnas also love to fill out comment cards. If you're lucky enough to get on a Donna's good side, she'll sing your praises to the moon. And in this case that's Graeme, who is well on his way to snagging a glowing report that will undoubtedly make its way to James.

My gut tightens. Our marketing proposals are the most important thing when it comes to this promotion, but making a positive impression on the guests can't hurt. If this is how Graeme is going to play, I need to step up my game.

Reaching down, I thumb off my sandals, remove my sunglasses, and pull my shirt over my head. Shimmying out of my shorts, I pick up my wet suit and steal a glance at Graeme. He's down on one knee in front of Donna, helping her slip her foot into a fin, Prince Charming style.

She beams down at him, entranced. Gripping his arm for balance, she stands and nods. Graeme stands as well. When he glances up our gazes connect. He looks away, but then pulls a double-take.

All I'm wearing is a bikini. And Graeme won't stop staring. I swallow so hard my throat nearly closes.

Sweet baby Jesus, somebody save me.

9

Why, oh why did I bring a bikini instead of the matronly one-piece tucked in the back of my dresser at home? My bathing suit is teal with little red flowers and a ruffle that runs along the top's deep V, highlighting my cleavage. Each ray of sun, each lick of breeze whispering across my skin, reminds me how much of it is on display.

I fight the urge to dive for cover under my wet suit. I look away, then back. Graeme stands slowly, still staring. His eyes traverse my body; they're wide, almost unfocused.

A strange sense of power zings through me. He clearly likes what he sees, enough to throw polite convention to the wind. Is my body really that captivating?

I push my shoulders back a fraction and lift my chin.

When his gaze drifts to my face and we lock eyes, his expression transforms into pure horror.

Busted.

He takes a jerky step as though to quickly turn around, and smashes directly into the edge of the bench. Rubbing his shin, he hops to the nearest deck chair. I snort a laugh. I can't help it. Donna flaps her hands, all motherly concern, but Graeme waves her away with a pained smile. Peeking out from under his lashes, he offers me an apologetic wince.

Yeah, I caught you checking me out. Bracing a hand on my hip, I mouth the words "human resources."

His lips quirk and his eyebrows bounce upward. In one smooth move he stands, grips the back of his T-shirt, and yanks it over his head. My mouth goes dry, but I don't look away. I can't. His bare chest is strong with a smattering of dark brown hair and the perfect amount of muscle, the kind of chest that would make a nice pillow. His waist is narrow and his abs are flat and subtly defined without being so ripped that I'm self-conscious about my own lack of definition. I swallow hard.

Catching my gaze, he extends his arms. "Human resources," he mouths.

My lips threaten to smile, so I shake my head and look away. When I look back, he's stepping into his wet suit. I do the same. I don't miss his shadow of a grin.

Warmth bubbles through my chest and my breath quickens like I've run a sprint. I'm not sure what happened there, but it was unprofessional, unprovoked, and I liked it. Way. Too. Much.

But this is Graham Cracker-Collins, not some random piece of eye candy. *Enough window shopping. Time to focus.*

After adjusting the neoprene fabric where it ends around my knees and elbows and confirming that everything fits, I peel it off and put my shorts and shirt back on. The sun has disappeared behind a cloud, so I stick my sunglasses on top of my head. Gathering up both sets of snorkeling equipment, I shuffle over to the stairs.

Graeme is already standing there. When he spots me, he shifts so he's blocking the top step. I try to edge around him, but he leans so close his breath fans against my neck and I stop. He nods toward Donna, who's currently supervising her husband packing away their snorkeling gear with a scowl on her face.

"There's always one, isn't there?"

"Always."

The oddness of the moment strikes me and my stomach squirms like a trapped mouse. Here I am, having a companionable exchange with Graeme where we actually agree on something—not five minutes after we ogled each other practically naked. Something tugs at me, like a fishhook lodged in my heart, and I don't like it.

I clear my throat and take half a step back. "You don't need to wait for me, you know. It's not like we're on this trip together. You go your way, I'll go mine."

His jaw tightens and he doesn't speak for several heartbeats. "That's what you want?"

"It's for the best."

"Okay," he says.

"Great."

"Fine." He steps toward the stairs at the same time I do. We bump hips, and it's like bouncing off a wall. I press my lips into a thin line.

"After you." He motions politely.

There's so much Midwestern nice going on I want to scream. "Have fun on your hike," I toss over my shoulder as I pass him.

"Have fun working."

I nod briskly and hustle down three flights of stairs. Graeme follows. I make a left at the dining room. He's still behind me. When he turns down the carpeted hallway leading to my cabin, I shoot him a glare. "Are you following me?"

"Why would I follow you?"

"As part of a devious plot, no doubt."

"Why do you always assume I'm plotting?"

"Experience." I walk faster. He speeds up. When I reach my cabin, I whirl. "Seriously, what do you think you're doing?"

"Getting my life jacket," he says slowly, pivoting to point over his shoulder to cabin 209—the cabin *right next door*. "See, no plots." Lifting an eyebrow, he disappears inside.

The booking department put us in adjacent cabins? Oh, someone has a sense of humor.

I let out a long breath once the door is closed. I can't let Graeme distract me. I have to direct 100 percent of my focus toward nailing my proposal, and that starts now.

Walsh is still asleep, so as quietly as I can, I store our snorkeling gear in the closet and change out of my bathing suit. When I unplug my laptop from where it's been charging on the desk, the innocent beige wall that I'd barely registered before captures my attention.

Because Graeme is directly on the other side.

Having adjacent cabins feels . . . illicit. Like I'm a kid at sleepaway camp who found a secret way to sneak into the boys' bunkhouse without getting caught by the counselors. I could slip next door anytime I want . . . or vice versa . . .

I shake my head hard. Right, the only way I'm sneaking into Graeme's cabin is to boobytrap it in his sleep.

Stuffing my laptop into my bag, which is already packed from last night's shore excursion, I head for the lounge. I check my phone for new messages on the way.

I have a voice mail from my parents (*"Henley, it's Mom. Are you and Walsh alive? Call me."*), a Snapchat from Christina at her latest rec league soccer game (*"Guess who scored the game-winning goal, bitches?"*), and two texts from Tory, one of which is a grainy ultrasound photo.

Gender is a social construct, but biologically, it's a girl!

"Awwww!" I squeal.

> Congrats!!!

> How's Michelle feeling? Any names picked out yet? Miss you!

I fire off a quick text to my mom assuring her that, yes, we are alive, and will do our best to FaceTime with her and Dad later, then respond to Christina's Snap with a flame, heart, and high-five emoji. A last call for the long hike rings through the ship's speakers, but I ignore it. Once I reach the lounge, it's empty except for an elderly couple sipping tea and reading matching Kindles. I pick a cushy corner couch to set up shop for the morning.

Opening my laptop, I log on to my work email. I skim over several unread messages, including one from Barbara sharing an updated department calendar, to click open an email from Christina. She wants me to proofread some copy she drafted for an upcoming cruise guide. I fire back a reply letting her know I'll take a look ASAP.

The next email that catches my eye makes me sit up straighter. It's from Ahmed in accounting, one of Tory's direct reports—a response to an email I sent him yesterday asking for a breakdown of results from the paid digital advertising we did for our Hawaiian Islands cruises earlier this year. I scan the spreadsheet and nod slowly. The new advertisements worked. We saw decent click rates and an uptick in Hawaii bookings following the campaign.

"This could work." Our Hawaii cruises appeal to a similar demographic as the Galápagos—they're both warm weather destinations that include snorkeling, kayaking, and hiking, and they have somewhat comparable price points. If our new advertising approach worked for Hawaii, it would stand to reason that similar advertisements for the Galápagos would boost sales in the region as well.

I click over to my Galápagos digital marketing proposal document and begin typing. It might not be the most novel or fanciest idea, but it's solid and can be backed with actual numbers. Doubt threads through my gut, but I shoo it away. All I need is to make this idea pop . . .

"Ms. Evans!" Gustavo's booming voice makes me jump. He strides over to me, the door to the bridge thumping closed behind him. His red staff shirt gives his cheeks a rosy glow. "Why are you still on the ship? The last Zodiac for the long hike is leaving now."

"I'm not going on the long hike."

"No, you must. I insist. Whatever you are doing now, it can wait."

"Um . . ."

"You are healthy, yes? You can survive a three-hour walk?"

"Yes . . ."

Gustavo places his hand over his heart. "Then you have to go. Please. The beach walk is nice, yes, but Suarez Point is unforgettable. I could not live with myself knowing that you traveled all this way, to my home, and did not experience one of its most magical sites."

Jesus, Gustavo, guilt much? I force a smile. "Well, when you put it that way . . ."

"*Bueno!* You have everything you need, yes? Sunscreen, water, camera?"

"I do." Heaving a sigh, I save my proposal and shut my laptop.

"Good. I will store this for you in the staff office until you get back." He picks up my laptop and tucks it under an arm. "Hurry! Go now!"

His words are like spurs and I find myself trotting through the lounge and down the stairs to the disembarkation level. How did I get bamboozled into going on the long hike? Maybe I can multi-task . . . take some notes during breaks . . .

I'm panting by the time I reach the mudroom and a sheen of sweat coats my forehead. There's no scaffolding today, as disembarkation is taking place at the back of the ship. A harried crew member waves me through a door that leads to a sea-level outdoor deck where a single Zodiac holding three older guests is waiting. A middle-aged naturalist helps me climb in, and a minute later we're zooming through sea spray to the green shores of Española Island.

Gripping the rope running along the side of the Zodiac, I squint at the sun blazing low in the sky. At least it's early in the day—and early in our weeklong cruise. I should have plenty of time to work on my proposal. And if I don't? I'll just have to make time. My future depends on it.

10

*H*enley, you made it!" Xiavera's warm voice carries across the rocky beach.

Barely. The rest of the hikers have already set off; I'm one of the last few passengers to arrive. I hitch my backpack higher on my shoulder. "I'm here."

"You will not regret it, I promise. Okay, everyone," she calls out to all the guests. "Since the last two groups are so small, I am combining you. The ten of you will be hiking with naturalist and bird expert Juan Luis."

I turn around to take stock of my fellow hikers, and my stomach drops like an anvil.

Graeme is standing off to the side, in the shade of a short, scrubby tree. When he spots me, the corners of his mouth twitch. Can't I have even five minutes to myself on this cruise without him popping up?

Adjusting his cap, he sidles up to me. "What happened to going our separate ways? Let me guess, you can't get enough of my sparkling personality."

"I'm here against my will. Gustavo guilted me into it."

"Yeah, poor you. Forced to hike in paradise." He throws his arm out, gesturing at the scenery.

I have to admit, it *is* beautiful. A yellow-and-black lighthouse rises from the brush-covered lava rocks hugging the shore, framed by an impossibly blue sky. Farther down the beach, a mother sea lion nurses a squealing pup, and gulls circle overhead. It's otherworldly. Pure wild.

"Okay, everyone, remember to stay together as a group, don't wander from the path, and do your best to keep at least six feet away from all wildlife. Ready? Follow me." Juan Luis marches down a rocky path that winds up and away from the beach. I hang back to let the others go first, including Graeme. The sun is strong, and I'm sweating even though our pace is slow to accommodate the older passengers.

I shuffle along the gravel path, bringing up the rear. Keeping Graeme's broad shoulders and the rest of the hikers in my peripheral vision, I pull out my phone and start a pro/con chart for the advertising idea I had for my proposal.

Pfwwwth.

Water droplets sprinkle my shin and I squawk. Stumbling back, I drop my phone and it lands directly in front of a massive black lizard. Roughly three feet long from nose to tail, it's perched on a low boulder next to the path. It slowly closes its eyes, its leathery skin wrinkling as it adjusts a clawed foot. I recognize it from our marketing brochures as a marine iguana, one of the famed Galápagos species. And it *sneezed* on me.

Smacking the moisture off my leg, I reach for my phone, but it's not where I dropped it. I whip my head around. "What the . . ."

"Henley Rose."

Running my tongue along my top teeth, I straighten from my crouch. Graeme is standing not three feet away, holding my phone. I extend my hand, but he doesn't give it to me. Instead, he taps it against his palm like a disapproving schoolteacher.

I fold my arms across my chest. "Yes, Graham Cracker?"

"Get your nose out of your phone and *look around*. Work can wait for a few hours. You should enjoy this—who knows when you'll get a chance to experience the Galápagos again? Appreciate where you are. Go ahead, breathe in that salty air."

I reach for my phone again. He tilts it away from me and beckons with a lazy flick of his fingers. "Go on," he mouths.

"Fine." Throwing my arms out, I suck in an exaggerated breath through my nose . . . and immediately gag. "Oh God." I cough. "What *is* that? It smells like a snail snotted on a turd."

"That is the sublime scent of the marine iguana," says Juan Luis.

My cheeks flame as I realize that everyone, yep, *everyone*, in our group just overhead my outburst. All eyes are locked on me. Graeme's lips are pursed, but his shoulders shake with silent laughter.

Snatching my phone, I clear my throat. "I'm not sure if 'sublime' is the word I'd use," I mumble.

Juan Luis chuckles. "No, you are right. The marine iguanas are quite pungent, yes? Like a mix of saltwater, fish, and manure. But they are also incredibly special. They are the only species of iguana on earth that feeds underwater, and you can only find them here, in the Galápagos. Ahhh, look at this big guy." He strolls over to the marine iguana that sneezed on me. "He is posing so nicely for us."

The other hikers gather around to snap pictures.

One of the younger female guests wrinkles her nose. "How is it that one iguana can smell *that* bad?"

Juan Luis's deep brown eyes twinkle. "There is not only one. Come. You'll see."

He leads us around a bend, and not twenty yards away the path opens up to a wide cove along the shore. There are marine iguanas *everywhere*. Marine iguanas on rocks. Marine iguanas lying in massive piles, clumped together in the bone-strewn sand. Marine iguanas slinking into the frothy surf next to sea lions lumbering down the beach.

The smell might be overpowering, but the sight is incredible. Like something out of a nature show.

"Just remember, the wildlife may not be afraid of us, but please give them at least six feet of space so you do not disturb them. And especially watch out for tails," Juan Luis reminds us as guests begin meandering around the beach.

Pfwwwth.

Another marine iguana lets loose a sneeze not ten feet from my foot. I jolt, and nearly drop my phone again. This time, I slip it into my back pocket for safekeeping.

"It's the salt." An older passenger standing nearby nods at the marine iguana, her hands clasped on top of her metal walking stick. "They ingest a lot of saltwater when they dive down to feed on algae, and they have special glands to help them sneeze the salt out when they're back on land. Cool, huh?"

Through the chatter of guests, snapping cameras, barking sea lions, and trilling birds, I catch the sound of periodic sneezes all around the cove.

"Incredible. How did you know that?"

She gives me a kindly smile. "I was a high school biology teacher—retired now. I taught students about natural selection and the Galápagos for nearly thirty years." She heaves a contented sigh. "I can't believe I finally made it here."

Gripping her walking stick, she crouches awkwardly to take a picture of the marine iguanas. Even though I can't see her eyes behind her sunglasses, I can tell by the way her lips tremble that she's tearing up with emotion.

"Are you traveling with anyone?" I ask.

She straightens. "Nope. Flying solo."

"I'm Henley, by the way." I extend my hand and she grips it briefly.

"Henley By-the-Way, I'm Sharon." Her tone is cheerful, and I can't help but smile.

"Would you like me to take some pictures of you with the marine iguanas?" I offer. "My smartphone takes pretty decent photos, and I'd be happy to AirDrop them to you or put them on a jump drive when we get back to the ship."

"Oh!" she exclaims. "I don't want to put you out . . ."

"It's no trouble, really. I know it can be tough to get good photos of yourself when you're alone. My sister's back on the ship, so I'm flying solo at the moment too."

She tilts her chin up to assess me. "You're that Seaquest Adventures employee, right?"

I nod.

"Aren't you traveling with your coworker? Isn't that him over there?" She points to where Graeme is engaged in conversation with Juan Luis.

"Oh, well, yes. But we're not close or anything."

"Really? He's smiling at you."

I steal another glance over my shoulder, and sure enough, he's looking in my direction, and the corners of his mouth are lifted. He quickly refocuses his attention on Juan Luis, who points at a black bird with a bright red chest flying overhead—a frigate bird.

Graeme wasn't looking at *me*. Probably just taking in all the wildlife. I lick my dry lips.

Pushing up the brim of her floppy sun hat, Sharon clucks. "I hope you don't mind me saying, but that man is a whole treat. Or is it a meal? What do kids say these days?"

"Snack. He's a whole snack."

"Mm-hmm."

When it comes to looks, she's right. Graeme is, objectively speaking, a total snack. Too bad his personality is more like week-old leftovers. Although I haven't really seen as much of his bad side this trip as I expected. He's been annoying, sure. But otherwise, he's actually been pretty nice.

Still, the type of person who would commandeer credit for a massively successful video someone else created isn't the type of person whose "nice" can be trusted.

I clear my throat. "Where do you want to stand for a picture? Maybe over there so the sun isn't behind you?" I motion toward the waterline, and we amble over, careful not to step on any tails. I end up taking several dozen pictures of Sharon, who gleefully poses a few feet away from a couple of marine iguanas and a sleeping sea lion.

About twenty minutes later, we leave the cove to continue our hike.

Sharon and I chat as we walk, and a pair of middle-aged sisters traveling together migrates into our conversation. As it turns out, Sharon is from Pennsylvania, twice divorced, no kids, and she's been saving up for this trip for *years*.

Guilt crawls up my spine. Here I am, put out that I was talked into doing the long hike on a *free* cruise (thanks, work), and here's Sharon, grateful for every second of this (expensive) once-in-a-lifetime trip. I shouldn't forget that I'm damn lucky to be here. I still have work to contend with, but I can make adjustments to take advantage of the full Galápagos experience—and be grateful for it.

After a while, the path inclines and turns rocky. Conversations dwindle as we all focus on not twisting an ankle on the uneven terrain. My muscles burn and sweat trickles down my neck as we climb.

It feels . . . good. How long has it been since I've been on a real hike, not cutting through a city park or traversing a concrete sidewalk? Walsh and I grew up spending a lot of time outside. Building backyard forts. Camping with our parents. Hiking down shaded trails until the sun faded and insects sang their nighttime songs.

God, I miss it. I love Seattle, but it's been way too long since I was out in nature like this. Maybe once I finish my MBA program and land this promotion, I'll actually take some time off. Maybe head out to Mt. Rainier for some hiking.

Maybe.

We hear the seabird colony before we see it. A cacophony of honking, whistling, and screeching grows louder with every step. Most of the birds dotting the cliffs are black-and-white Nazca boobies, which are, for the record, patently ridiculous. They have beady eyes, long beaks, and clownish expressions. I make a point to snap more pictures of Sharon, who is positively gleeful when Juan Luis spots a pair of Blue-footed booby, the rarer cousin of the plentiful Nazca booby.

We all gather around to watch as a male lifts one bright blue foot, then the other, in a mating dance. He bobs his head, fans his tail feathers, and circles the female, who seems wholly uninterested in his romantic display.

"Like most males, they are willing to do anything, even look very silly, to capture a female's attention," says Juan Luis.

Isn't that the truth. The group chuckles.

Eventually, the female is won over by the male's amorous overtures and allows him to mount her. Everyone claps for him, which is only a little strange? I steal a glance at Graeme. He's kneeling several feet away, snapping photos.

We meander our way along the cliffs through the seabird colonies. In addition to the numerous boobies, Juan Luis points out swallow-tailed gulls, waved albatross, lava lizards, and even a whale in the far distance. A puff of gauzy mist hangs in the air, marking the place where it exhaled before disappearing beneath the waves.

Making the rounds with the other guests, I introduce myself and chat with everyone. Everyone except Graeme. He watches me from a distance, his expression inscrutable.

We continue. More than an hour later, Juan Luis announces that we've reached the farthest point in our hike. My breath catches as I take in the view. Dramatic, craggy cliffs overlook the azure ocean. Directly in front of us, at the bottom of the bluff, a geyser spouts saltwater in rhythmic bursts.

We fan out, each claiming our own space to soak in the view. I settle onto a low rock facing the cliff's edge. The bright sun warms my cheeks, and I close my eyes and tilt my chin toward the sky. A bird whistles softly. Another answers.

Footsteps approach and something rustles beside me. I know from the scent that floods my nose—a burst of citrus tinged with salt—that it's Graeme. I don't open my eyes. "What do you want?"

When he doesn't respond right away, I crack open one eye.

"That was nice of you. With that guest, Sharon. Taking pictures of her since she's traveling alone."

I nod uncertainly.

Staring out at the ocean, he takes a long, slow breath. "Tell me what I did."

"Huh?"

"To make you dislike me so much. I've been wracking my brain all day, and I honestly don't know. Whatever it is, I want to make it right."

I gape at him.

After several long seconds, he finally looks me in the eye. "Please."

My breathing shallows and my heart accelerates like I'm running a race. "It was the monkey video, okay?"

"The . . . what?"

"The one I made. The one that went viral last year, remember?"

"What . . . how . . ." He shakes his head twice. "Why the hell would *that* put me on your bad list?"

"Because you let James give you all the credit when *I* did all the work!" A wave of anger ignites my muscles and I shove roughly to my feet.

Before I can take a single step, Graeme stands, grabbing my wrist. Whirling, I jerk it out of his grasp.

"No. You're wrong," he says. "I would never do something like that."

11

*E*xcuse me?"

"I said you're wrong. I would never, *never* accept the credit for someone else's work. That'd be a shitty thing to do."

"Well, you did."

"When?"

"In the marketing meeting right after the video was posted. James congratulated you on it and you said, '*Thank you*.' He even went on to berate me for not coming up with the idea myself since Costa Rica is my region. And you didn't say a word to correct him."

Jerking off his baseball cap, Graeme scrubs a hand roughly through his hair. "I don't remember any of that. Was it right after I started?"

"Yeah. So?"

He expels a heavy breath. "It was my phone."

"You expect me to believe that you programmed your phone with sophisticated AI to respond for you, in your exact voice?" My tone is drier than hot sand.

"No. The first phone the company shipped me was crap. The speakers crackled and it dropped calls all the time. I probably didn't actually hear exactly what James said and only responded with 'Thank you' to cover my ass."

"That's . . . that's . . ." I make a disgusted noise in my throat. "So you pretended to listen and chimed in when it suited you?"

"Not my finest moment, okay? I should have owned up and said I didn't hear him—or probably half the meeting thanks to the shitty connection. I'm sorry. Honestly, I wasn't on my A game when I first started this job. I was going through a lot," he adds in a mumble.

What a load of BS. I'm prepared to fire back a snarky reply, but the words stick in my throat. A memory from the meeting niggles at the corner of my brain. After James spoke but before Graeme answered, there was phone static and several seconds of silence.

Could he be telling the truth?

His cheeks flush. "And why didn't *you* say anything? You should have told him you made the video. Or, if you were blindsided, you could have brought it up later. Instead, you kept quiet for a *year* and let your opinion of me fester."

"It's not that simple."

"Screw simple. I'm not the only one who messed up here, Henley. You chose not to confront me or tell James the truth. You should have stood up for yourself, but you didn't. That's on you."

My mouth opens but no words come out. Because he's right.

Shaking his head slowly, he walks away. After three steps he pauses. "I'm not the asshole you think I am."

I'm not the asshole you think I am.

Graeme's parting words ping around my brain like a pinball all the way back to the ship's dining room, where I pick up lunch to go for Walsh and me. I'm so distracted I nearly pour mayonnaise on my salad instead of ranch dressing. Balancing two plates of food, I make my way to our cabin and use my elbow to open the door.

Walsh is awake. She glances up from where she's sitting on the edge of her bed, face buried in her hands. Her phone dings from somewhere under her covers.

I set the plates on the desk. "How are you feeling?"

"Better."

"Are you sure?" Her face is pale and she still looks more zombie than human.

She wobbles to her feet and stumbles to the closet.

"What are you doing?"

"Getting dressed."

"You need to go back to bed. You're not okay."

"I'm fine. Snorkeling's up next, right? You need me."

"I'll survive." Gripping her shoulder, I firmly guide her back to bed and push her down until she's sitting. I hand her the plate I filled with bland foods: crackers, bread, pudding, and a banana.

She wrinkles her nose like I just handed her a plate of slugs. She picks up a cracker and nibbles the edge. "Did you do the beach walk this morning?"

"Gustavo talked me into the long hike."

"How was it?"

"It was good. Really good."

"Was Graeme there?"

"Yeah."

"I'm sorry I wasn't there to run interference."

I shake my head. "Not your fault."

Graeme. My intestines squirm and I slide into the desk chair and poke my salad with a fork. Have I really been wrong about him this whole time? I dig my phone out of my pocket and plug it in to charge. An email notification pops up, a reminder that registration for fall business school classes closes in a week, along with my task list.

Task #1: Defeat Graeme Crawford-Collins

I gnaw on my lower lip. Snatching my phone, I connect to Wi-Fi and open up a new text to Christina.

> Hey, can you do me a favor?

I shovel a few bites of food in my mouth while I wait for her to respond.

> Sup?

> Are you still friendly with Miriam in IT?

> Sure, why

> Can you ask her something on the down-low . . . can you find out if IT replaced Graeme's work phone about a year ago, shortly after he started his job?

> Um, of course but . . . WHY?

> Is there something juicy going on? Tell me!

> Just want to confirm something. Thanks!!

Walsh groans behind me. She gingerly places the cracker back on her plate, rolls into bed, and flings her arm over her eyes.

"Are you sure you're okay?"

She burps loudly. "I'll be fine. I'm just not ready for food yet."

The clock on my phone reminds me that I don't have much time until the beginner snorkeling excursion departs. Quickly finishing my lunch, I scoop up my bathing suit and wet suit and head toward the bathroom to change. I pause with my hand on the door handle.

"Hey, Walsh?"

"Yeah?"

"Have you ever been wrong about someone?"

"All the time."

"I mean, have you ever thought the worst of someone but it turns out they're not that bad?"

She snorts. "Not really. It usually goes the other way with me. I think everyone's great until they turn out to be dicks." She peers at me from under her arm. "Is this about Graeme?"

"Nah. Well, maybe." Graeme might not be a credit stealer, but he's still made work enormously difficult. He constantly argues with me and challenges my ideas, and his one-word emails are so, so rude.

Walsh tilts her chin at me. "Come on, Henley. What's going on?"

"It's just . . . he might not be as utterly horrible as I thought." She nods slowly. "Does it matter?"

"Yes, it matters! He's my coworker, and there might be a chicken-and-egg problem. In the chain of assholery, I thought he started it. But now, it looks like I may have been the inciting asshole all along."

"And you care if he thinks you're an asshole?"

A few days ago I would have said no way. But now . . . "I guess I do." Shock flickers through my system as the words ring true.

"So, what, you like him now?"

"I wouldn't go that far."

She shrugs. "He's still your competition though, right?"

My fingers close around the bathroom door handle. The metal is cold against my skin. "Right."

"So really, for the purposes of this trip, it doesn't matter how you feel about him or whether he's the asshole or you're the asshole. You'll have all the time in the world after you land this promotion to make nice with him—if you want. He lives in Minnesota, right?"

"Michigan," I correct.

"Exactly. So it's not like you're going to see him every day or anything. Unless he gets the promotion."

My stomach does a little flop. "You're absolutely right. Why am I even thinking about him when I have work to worry about?" I step into the bathroom but poke my head out. "When did you get so good at giving advice anyway?"

Snuggling deeper into the pillow, Walsh picks up her phone and studies the screen. "You dummy, I'm the best at giving advice. I just don't always follow it."

"Truth." Chuckling, I shut the door.

When I arrive in the mudroom several minutes later, wet suit on and snorkeling equipment slung across my back, Graeme is already there along with at least twenty other passengers waiting to disembark. His wet suit clings to him like a second skin and I swallow hard.

Walsh's advice echoes through my brain—I can ignore him. I *should* ignore him, but my conscience won't let me.

Bracing myself, I stride over to where he's waiting at the back of the room near the staff office. He gives me a long once-over when he spots me, his gaze lingering briefly on my curves. My spine tingles.

"Hey," I say.

He looks around pointedly. "Oh, are you talking to me?"

"Yes. You're not an asshole. Mostly."

"What a glowing compliment," he says, tone dry.

"I mean, your email etiquette is atrocious and you're still difficult to work with, but I'm sorry I assumed the worst about you."

Graeme blinks. "So we're friends now?"

"Whoa there, slow your roll. I never said anything about friends. We are . . . professional colleagues."

"Acquaintances."

"Friendly acquaintances," I correct.

"Competing for the same position."

"May the best person win." Nodding firmly, I stick my hand out. He gives it a brisk shake. His grip lingers . . . two seconds, three seconds . . . He doesn't let go. Neither do I. Warmth floods my cheeks and my heartbeat kicks into high gear. Graeme's nostrils flare and I swear he leans closer a fraction.

"Do we have any beginner snorkelers left?" Gustavo booms from the front of the mudroom. "Last call for beginner snorkelers. Those doing the deepwater snorkeling, sit tight. Disembarkation will begin in five minutes."

Pulling my palm out of Graeme's hand, I clear my throat. "Beginner snorkeling, that's me."

He slides me a sheepish grin. "Me too."

This is fine. Graeme and I can spend time in each other's company and act like civil adults, no problem. Lingering handshakes aside, we don't have to be buddy-buddy. Today I can focus on, you know, *not* drowning and he can focus on . . . whatever it is that Graeme thinks about.

We shuffle to the front of the room and get in line for disembarkation. We end up boarding the same Zodiac but sit on opposite sides. I steal a glance at Graeme from behind my sunglasses, but he doesn't seem to notice; he's checking settings on his camera.

Engine roaring, we zoom back toward Española Island, this time to Gardner Bay. With every wave we splash through, my stomach knots tighter and tighter. The fact that I'll be swimming in the ocean—snorkeling—in a few short minutes has my lunch churning in my gut like concrete in a mixer.

When we slide out of the Zodiac and wade through the surf onto the beach, I find a spot on the sand to drop my towel and equipment. With a little salute, Graeme claims a spot on the far side of the passengers, giving me plenty of space. A naturalist separates us into different groups for a basic snorkeling lesson, and after about ten minutes we're sent into the water to practice.

This is it. Time to face my fear. My mouth turns dry and my heartbeat kicks into a gallop as I sit to slide my feet into my fins at the surf's edge. The ocean is a clear, picturesque turquoise—vastly different from the blue-brown waters of the lakes at home.

A flurry of feathers zips across my vision. I squawk. Something small and brown lands next to me—an Española mockingbird, one of the island's famously friendly residents. It hops closer, an inch from my fingers splayed in the sand. "Hi, buddy." It tilts its head, its long curved beak twitching this way and that as it examines the silver ring on my middle finger. "Do you think I can do this?" I whisper. With a ruffle of feathers, it pecks at my ring before flying away. I take that as a yes.

Graeme comes up beside me, kicking up powdery white

sand. He stands for a heartbeat, gazing out over the ocean. "You don't have to snorkel, you know. You can still change your mind."

"I'm fine. I got this."

"All right then." With a shrug, he pulls his mask over his eyes and wades into the water.

My nerves crackle and my skin feels tight and itchy as I stand and inch my way closer to the water. Foamy blue-green waves lap at my ankles as I back into the surf so I don't trip over my fins. *Christ* it's cold. No wonder they gave us wet suits. I focus on my chattering teeth as I awkwardly shuffle through the water until it reaches my waist.

Okay. This isn't so bad. I can do this.

A handful of guests dot the shallows alongside me. Some are already floating in the water, twirling hands or paddling feet. An older woman next to me tentatively lowers her head then pops up, breathing noisily through her snorkel. Farther down, Graeme swims gracefully, facedown, perpendicular to shore. Show-off.

If he can do it, so can I. Adjusting my mask, I put the snorkel's rubbery plastic in my mouth. Slowly, I crouch. The water is murky from all the sand that's been stirred up, and I lower my face down, down, down . . .

Water rushes into my ears and my face is underwater. Past blurs with present and *oh my God my face is underwater I can't breathe, I CAN'T BREATHE!*

I jerk up and flail, water splashing. Spitting out my snorkel, I suck in deep, crisp lungfuls of oxygen. I press a hand to my aching chest and force down the panic. It's not real, this crushing suffocation. I have a tube to breathe through. I'm standing in shallow water. I'm okay. I'm not drowning.

I close my eyes and find my center—the smoldering coal inside me that fuels every ounce of ambition and drive and longing I have. I won't let my fear rule me. *I won't.*

Replacing the snorkel, I try again. But again, panic swamps me and I stand. I try again and again and again. And again.

I look around; all the other beginners are snorkeling now, paddling around the shallows, breathing easily through their tubes. Why can't I do it? It's not reasonable or even rational, this knee-jerk reaction. I can breathe through my snorkel. I'm not drowning. So what's the problem?

"You need to relax," Graeme calls from somewhere over my right shoulder.

"Easy for you to say."

I replace my snorkel and dip my chin into the water experimentally. Maybe if I submerge by degrees . . .

A wave knocks into me and I'm thrown off balance. Seawater rushes over my head and down my snorkel and I struggle to my feet, coughing and spluttering, heart jackhammering against my ribs.

Graeme's beside me in a heartbeat, mask pushed up on his forehead and his hand anchored firmly against the middle of my back. Water slicks his hair while droplets glitter on his cheeks.

Another wave slaps against my thighs, and I grab onto him to steady myself. My fingers curl around the cool flesh of his forearm. That buzzing energy surges to life between us. I snatch my hand back with a scowl.

Setting my jaw, I stuff my snorkel into my mouth and bite down hard. I taste salt.

"Wait a second," he says, placing a hand on my shoulder. His grip is gentle but firm.

I rip off my mask and give him a *yeah, what do you want* expression with an extra helping of venom.

"You can't force it."

I can force anything. I haven't met a problem yet that I couldn't solve with single-minded determination and a whole hell of a lot of effort.

"Come with me," says Graeme.

12

Against my better judgment, I follow Graeme to shore. I watch as he jogs over to talk to one of the naturalists. Several seconds later he returns, holding what looks like a bright yellow belt made of thick, padded foam.

"Come on," he says.

"Where are we going?"

"To find our own patch of ocean." Without a backward glance, he takes off down the beach at a brisk pace, fins tucked under one arm, belt hooked around his forearm.

Should I follow? He might not be the credit-stealing scoundrel I thought he was, but I'm still not sure I can trust him—we are competing for the same promotion, after all.

Then again, I do need to learn how to snorkel, and Graeme seems to have things figured out. If he has some idea how to get over this mental roadblock, it's worth the risk, right?

"You know, if you try to drown me, there will be witnesses," I shout as he jogs off.

"I'll keep that in mind," he calls over his shoulder.

Peeling off my fins, I scurry to catch up. Once I reach him, he slows down and we walk along the waterline in silence, wet sand squishing between our toes. Once we're a decent way from the other guests, visible but out of earshot, we stop. The water is clearer here and more blue than turquoise.

Dropping his fins on the sand, Graeme unbuckles the yellow belt. "This will help you float. Give you confidence."

I peer into his face, and his eyes twinkle like sunlight reflecting off waves. He swallows as he steps closer and his Adam's apple bobs above the neckline of his wet suit. When he extends the belt toward me, his knuckles brush my waist. My heart beats an erratic staccato. With scrabbling fingers, I snatch the belt from him. "Give me that."

He nods and takes half a step back as I put on the flotation device, making sure the thick, padded part is nestled at my lower back before securing the buckle in the front. He examines my handiwork with knit eyebrows. Reaching for the tail of the belt, he gives it a good tug and it cinches tighter. My breath leaves me in a whoosh.

"Good," he says with a nod, his smooth black snorkel wagging next to his stubbled jaw. "Ready?"

I position my mask over my eyes. "Like a rock star."

His lips twitch. Tugging my fins on, I wade into the ocean and he leads me farther from shore. We stop when the waves lap at my chest, sprinkling saltwater on my lips. The belt definitely adds buoyancy; I could lift my feet right now and bob in a sitting position with my head above water. The old panic rattles the bars of its cage but doesn't get out.

"The trick to snorkeling, I've found, is relaxing and breathing," says Graeme. "Don't think about anything else, okay?"

I can do that. I nod.

"Okay, now first, I want you to close your eyes and let any tension go."

Scrunching my nose, I squeeze my eyes shut, but promptly open them again. "Is this really necessary?"

"How were you doing on your own back there?"

"Point taken."

"Close your eyes. I promise I won't look at you or do anything weird." He waggles his fingers and pulls a face like a horror movie villain, and a honk of laughter escapes me before I can suppress it. His shy smile grows wider.

Clamping my lips together, I force my eyelids closed. I sway gently as the surf goes in and out. In and out. Like lungs. Like a heartbeat. I feel my own slowing and my muscles unfurling.

"Good, now put your snorkel in your mouth and breathe."

I arrange my snorkel and my lips close around rubber. My breaths bluster like wind through a tunnel, but I'm breathing. Deep in, deep out. Bob in the gentle waves. Sun warming my face.

"I'm going to help you float now, okay?"

I hesitate before nodding. This is working. I should keep going.

Graeme's hand closes on my right thigh. Even through my wet suit, his touch is electric. I tense but force my breathing to remain even as he pushes just enough so I tip forward. His other hand is firmly planted on my shoulder, guiding me.

I gasp the moment my face submerges. My muscles bunch.

"Keep breathing, easy and slow." His words are muffled and distant.

I suck in a deep, rattling breath and exhale through the snorkel. The belt around my middle keeps me suspended at the surface without any effort at all.

I blink open my eyes. My face is underwater. I can see the velvety sand beneath Graeme's fins. I'm breathing. "I did it!" I shout, but it comes out a garbled mess through my snorkel and I pop out of the water.

"Think you can do it again?"

Replacing my snorkel, I take three deep breaths. On the third, I tip forward to float. When the water rushes into my ears, my breathing hitches, but I manage to stay calm this time. In fact, I'm calmer in the water than I've ever felt. I can see what's beneath the surface and I can breathe just fine. I flash a thumbs-up above me.

Hard part's over. Now, what's out there to see?

I paddle my legs in a strong, smooth motion and shoot forward. My belt creates drag but my fins propel me with ease. Graeme's beside me now, peering through his mask. The seafloor spreads beneath us in a subtle decline.

It's gloriously quiet. Except for the whirr of my own breath and the swooshing burble of water in my ears, it's silent under the waves. The ocean is a deep, briny blue shifting to glaring white when I dip down and peer into its shining, reflective surface.

I spot my first tropical fish.

It's huge, as long as my forearm, with iridescent orange scales. I have no idea what kind of fish it is, but I still squeal in my throat, nudge Graeme, and point to it. It's wandering lazily, meandering along the ocean's sandy bottom.

We continue on. The seafloor turns rocky and the Galápagos Marine Reserve unfolds, revealing its treasures in a brightly colored, watery spectacle. Starfish that look like they're covered in chocolate chips and bigger ones in a rainbow of pinks, blues, and purples sprawl across pockets of sand. More fish pass beneath us— black and white, shimmering pink, storm-cloud gray, then a school of gleaming midnight blue with orange fins and a white stripe. They dart and weave in unison, and I'm mesmerized by how their countless bodies undulate as one.

After what feels like hours, Graeme splashes for my hand. Tugs it. My stomach tightens. He guides me around him, pointing to a shadow approaching through the murk. My heartbeat accelerates. I sweep my arms wildly, propelling myself backward. He brushes my forearm with his fingertips and motions emphatically for me to look again.

The shadow consolidates. A form comes into view. A smooth, brown head. A slick, streamlined body. It whizzes toward us, then veers at the last second, looping through the water like a graceful torpedo—a sea lion.

No, a *baby* sea lion. I squeal in delight, chest exploding with cuteness overload.

As it swirls nearer, the sea lion's big, glassy black eyes peer at us curiously while its long whiskers trail through the water. Graeme lifts a small, waterproof video camera that's looped around his wrist. It's hard to tell with a snorkel in his mouth, but I think he's smiling. Without warning, the sea lion darts toward me. I recoil reflexively before a cascade of bubbles engulfs my mask. It bounds away, swerving and somersaulting

The sea lion is playing with us. In a flash of flippers, it blows bubbles at Graeme next. A current catches us, and before I know it, a large wall of rock looms ahead. Beside its coral-dotted, jagged edges, two other baby sea lions dip and dive in a spirited dance. The current presses me forward, and I pump my arms against the push-pull of the waves.

The sun shimmers above and nature swirls all around. Time slows and I'm lost in the wildlife and waves—with Graeme.

As suddenly as the sea lions appeared, they scatter. I twist my head, trying to track where they went. I look down. And stop breathing altogether.

I'm in deep water. And beneath us, there's a shark.

I scream and flail as Graeme fumbles for my shoulder. He's not swimming away.

Is he *crazy*? There's a shark down there! And I might as well be chum!

My breaths come faster as panic trickles out of its cage.

I kick, but he holds firm. I look down.

The shark isn't coming at us; it's swimming away, its powerful gray body rippling far below us, the white tips of its dorsal fin and tail gleaming in the muted, murky light. I suck in a rattling breath through my snorkel. It's actually . . . beautiful. Scary as shit, but beautiful. I swim, cautiously, after it. I never imagined I'd see a shark in the wild, let alone from this vantage point. Like a hawk flying above a sparrow. Except in this situation, even though I'm the one above, I feel like the sparrow.

My soul recognizes what I've been feeling this entire day. First on the hike and now, swimming with Graeme. It's something I haven't experienced in a long, long time.

Wonder.

Barely daring to breathe, I watch the shark as it slices through the water and disappears from view. My heart flutters against my ribs and I feel like whooping and crying and fist-pumping all at the same time.

Fog creeps along my mask. Pulling a one-eighty, I paddle until I'm out of the current, lift my head above the waves, and push my mask onto my forehead.

Holy hell are we far from shore. We swam straight out toward a rocky outcropping at least two football fields away from the beach. One of the Zodiacs drifts several yards away, the naturalist on board keeping a close eye on us. I was so entranced I hadn't noticed how far we'd gone. Or how deep the water had become. *Huh*.

Graeme surfaces next to me and spits out his snorkel. "That was incredible!"

"Oh my God, those baby sea lions."

"And the reef shark."

"I can't believe we saw a shark!"

"You weren't afraid it was going to . . ." Something scrabbles against the side of my knee—his fingers. I shriek and kick away, accidentally splashing him in the face.

He pinches water out of his eyes. "Oh, you want to play that game?" Mischief dances in his smile.

"What, this game?" I sweep water at him again, this time intentionally. I have half a second to brace myself before he splashes me back.

My heart alights with juvenile delight even as water runs down my cheeks. Laughing and shrieking, I shovel water at him for all I'm worth, all while averting my face and squeezing my eyes shut to avoid the worst of his watery assault. His deep, rumbling laughter joins with mine and my palm connects with something firm—his chest.

Blinking open my eyes, I curl my fingers automatically against the slick neoprene of his wetsuit. He's stopped splashing me. The amusement dims from his eyes and winks out. We're close; the current from his legs swirls around my own as he pumps gracefully to keep himself afloat.

Warmth floods my veins, chasing away the chill. Graeme's nostrils flare and his eyes glint as they search my face with an unspoken question . . .

Do you feel what I'm feeling?

Oh God, I don't know what I'm feeling. Graeme's always been

larger than life, taking up an inordinate amount of space in my mind. But now his image has shifted. Instead of repelling me, it invites me to come closer.

Have a taste, just a little.

I'm Eve and he's the apple—a shiny, beckoning promise filled with the joy of delicious knowledge . . . and the threat of regret.

And I want to devour him whole.

My fingers uncoil, but instead of pulling away, I press my palm more firmly against his chest, just above his heart. His breath hitches like a rip in thick fabric and his hand finds my hip through the clear blue water. My lips part on an inhale.

"Henley?" he murmurs. His fingers squeeze, drawing me closer . . .

A loud whistle pierces the air and I hastily pull away. The naturalist on board the nearest Zodiac waves at us before extending his arm and bringing his fist to the top of his head. Graeme returns the gesture—the "I'm okay, no problems here" signal we learned about earlier.

What's the signal for "I'm losing my mind please come save me from myself"?

Gliding backward through the water, the moment broken, I tilt my head back to wet my hair and smooth the curling tendrils from my temples. "We should head back to shore." At least my voice is steady. My heart is anything but.

What is happening to me? Yes, Graeme is undoubtedly attractive, but I need to get a hold of myself before my out-of-control libido leads my career prospects into a ditch. You'd think with my bad history of romantic entanglements at work that I would have learned my lesson by now. Apparently not.

I pull my mask back over my eyes before remembering it's foggy. "Damn it," I mutter, yanking it over my waterlogged ponytail.

"I know a trick for that. Spit in it."

"Excuse me?"

"Spit in the inside of your mask and rub it around with your finger." At my incredulous stare, he adds, "Keeps it from fogging up."

"Oh." Just as I'm about to follow through on his suggestion, suspicion wells in my gut. "Wait, have you snorkeled before?"

He hesitates. "Not for a long time."

"But you're experienced."

Water swirls around his arms where he treads. "I wouldn't say that. I've snorkeled a few times, but I prefer diving. But again, it's been a while."

He's a scuba diver? That goes way past *I've snorkeled a couple times and need a refresher* to *I'm a freaking marine recreation expert*. Irritation and embarrassment burst like a Roman candle in the pit of my stomach. Pulling the mask over my eyes, I swim for the beach—fog be damned. A low curse followed by splashing tells me Graeme is behind me.

Soon my fins brush bottom, and in another dozen yards I stand. "Why did you go on this beginner excursion?" I demand over my shoulder through labored breaths. "There's a group out there right now offshore somewhere probably seeing infinitely cooler things."

Graeme splashes up next to me. "What's cooler than snorkeling with sea lions and sharks?"

I pluck off my fins and tuck them under my arm as I wade through waist-deep water. "You didn't answer my question."

"Because I was worried about you, okay?"

My cheeks flame. "I didn't need your concern. You should have worried about yourself."

"I'm still waiting for a thank-you."

"For what, teaching me how to float and breathe through a

tube at the same time? Like I couldn't have figured that out on my own."

"You know, I don't get you. I was just trying to be nice."

I thrust through the remaining tide and storm the beach like Normandy. My skin is chilled and my lungs pump from equal parts exertion and irritation. I throw my snorkeling gear down on an incline of white, powdery sand and whirl on him. I know I'm being unreasonable, but I'm past caring.

Irritation—at myself for not keeping my game face on, and at Graeme, for underestimating me—chokes off any gratitude I feel.

"You're not being nice. You're pulling the outfield in."

"What?" he splutters, standing with his feet planted in the surf, water dripping off every inch of his imposing body.

"Like in gym class."

He approaches, gear tucked under an arm, until we're face-to-face. "Explain."

"When you were a kid, did you ever play softball in gym?"

He nods.

"I don't know what it was like at your school, but at mine, whenever a girl stepped up to bat, one of the boys would smirk and say, '*Okay, bring it in*,' then all the other boys in the outfield would saunter to the infield. You know why?"

"Because boys are snots?"

"Because they assumed girls can't swing. And even if one could, they didn't think there'd be any power behind it." I take a step forward until mere inches separate us. "I. Can. Swing." I punctuate each word with a sharp tap against his chest. "I don't need your help, so stop treating me like a little girl going up to bat."

"I'm not . . . I don't . . ." Graeme scrubs a hand through his hair. Water droplets fling in every direction. "I didn't mean for you to take it like that."

Men rarely do, especially the decent ones. But still, too often their actions sting. How many times had I shown up to meetings only to be underestimated? Talked over? Snubbed by my male colleagues while they exclusively talked to one another and ignored the women in the room? Plenty. And I am *so* over it.

"What odds would you give yourself of getting this promotion? Ninety-ten? Eighty-twenty? Put a number on it."

His jaw tightens but his lips remain closed.

"You can afford to be nice because you don't see me as a threat." If I had an ounce of Walsh's wile, I would let him underestimate me and play that to my advantage, but I can't seem to keep my mouth shut.

"You have no idea how I see you." His voice is like a hammer resonating off steel and a shiver zings down my spine. "You're so wrapped up in your own preconceived notions about my motives you've never stopped to consider that maybe I'm different. You can't know what I think because you don't know me."

He takes a step closer. I hold my ground and raise my chin.

"You know what? I think you're mad because, despite your best efforts, you actually like me. And that makes your ruthless approach to this promotion harder than you thought."

"What?" I splutter. "I don't like you."

"You do, at least a little. Admit it."

"That's . . . that's . . ."

A tiny voice inside echoes in my ear. *He's right.* Letting loose a disgusted snort, I snatch up my equipment in a puff of sand and stomp down the beach.

"You can lie to yourself all you want, Henley, but you had fun hanging out with me this morning. So why try so hard to hate me?" he yells at my back.

My steps falter, but I keep walking.

I gather the rest of my things and head for one of the Zodiacs pulled up along the shore. I've had enough snorkeling for today. Climbing into the boat, I spot Graeme down the beach. He's still standing where I left him, watching me.

Even at this distance, I can tell he's shaking his head. When he sees me looking, he points directly at me, draws an enormous heart in the air with both index fingers, then thumbs his own chest.

And it's not cute at all, damn it.

Sticking my nose up, I turn my back on Graeme. But I can feel his eyes on me until the Zodiac pushes off toward the ship and the beach becomes nothing more than a blur in the distance.

13

I almost don't sit with Graeme at dinner. Almost.

But then I catch Nikolai staring at me from the dessert buffet, and I force myself to weave through the dining room until I spot Graeme sitting alone at a table for two along one of the front windows. Outside, the blazing orange sunset dips and crests with the movement of the ship.

I'm finally warm after a hot shower, but the air-conditioning chills my damp skin and I pull my sweater tighter around me. My phone vibrates in my pocket and I pull it out to see a new text from Christina.

> Miriam says Graeme got a new phone last August after his first phone went kaput.

> NOW SPILL WHAT IS THIS INTRIGUE

I blow out a shaky breath. He *was* telling the truth. He never intended to take credit for my video.

Across the dining room, Graeme scoops a bite of food into his mouth and gazes out at the shifting view of Española as the ship drifts at anchor. His jaw muscles work as he chews.

I squeeze the dinner plate I'm holding and swallow hard.

I've been unfair.

Graeme's right—I don't know him well. I've assumed a lot about him based on interactions in a single setting: work. And not even daily office interactions—mostly digital ones.

Maybe he's actually a nice guy? My calves itch to run away even as I take another step. I need to start with an apology and some sincere gratitude, since there's no getting around the fact that he did me a solid today. I've never liked the taste of crow, but I'll just have to suck it up and eat it.

Catching sight of Nikolai eyeing me with obvious interest, I kick my muscles into action and cross the final distance to Graeme. When he looks up, his flinty expression stops me in my tracks. I halt a few feet short of his table.

Forcing some iron into my spine, I lift my chin. "I'm sorry," I say before I lose my nerve. "I should have confronted you about the viral video last year instead of jumping to conclusions. And I'm sorry for blowing up at you on the beach earlier. That was uncalled for. Thank you for teaching me how to snorkel, by the way. And thanks for not being a massive dick about the whole puking thing."

I haven't received any chiding emails from James yet, so I'm assuming Graeme never told him what happened. And for all his threats to go to human resources, I haven't heard from them either.

Graeme just stares at me, jaw set. Cocking his head to the side, he taps his fingers against the arm of his chair in a slow, rhythmic pattern.

I shift my weight. "Look, I haven't treated you very well on this cruise. I've been suspicious and salty and you've been nothing but nice to me. Again, I'm sorry."

Just as I turn to walk away, he cups his hand behind his ear. "Can you speak into my good ear, please? Repeat what you just said—the last part."

"I'm sorry," I repeat in an exaggerated shout.

His full lips curl into a grin. "Words I never thought I'd hear you say."

He nods at the chair facing him in silent invitation. Sliding into the empty chair, I accept.

A waiter bustles over to fill my water glass and ask if I'd like the cocktail of the night—a mojito. I would. Graeme orders one as well.

"It's not like you're such a fountain of gratitude either," I say to Graeme once the waiter leaves.

He furrows his eyebrows. "What do you mean?"

"You never say thank you in emails. That would make your messages three words long instead of one. Practically a novel for you."

Graeme forks a bite of vegetables into his mouth. "I'm too busy to write long emails," he says thickly.

"How much longer would it take to write something halfway thoughtful?"

"Too long."

"Okay, sure."

"Do you know how many emails I get a day? *Hundreds*, no joke. From outside groups wanting to collaborate. Notifications from our social media platforms. Marketing managers hounding me to post their content." He shoots me a meaningful look. "If I answered every email like you do, with full sentences and flowery explanations, I'd never sleep."

I take a bite of fresh mahimahi to cover my bemusement, and its delicate orange and ginger flavors fill my mouth. I'd never considered there might be a legitimate reason for the curt emails. Is this more proof that I've been wrong about Graeme? My insides twist and my foot bounces under the table.

"So what brought you to Seaquest in the first place?" I ask, ignoring a new twinge of guilt.

"I was tired of working in a regular office. And I wanted a job with flexible hours."

"What were you doing before?"

"I was a marketing manager at Ford."

My eyebrows fly up. "You were a marketing manager?"

He makes a clicking sound with his tongue as he winks. "On their digital team."

My stomach clenches. Graeme was a marketing manager, and on a team dedicated solely to digital marketing. He has way more experience than I thought.

"So why take a job in social media? It was a step backward for your career."

"Not if it got my foot in the door at a great company in a city I want to live in."

He *wants* to move to Seattle?

"So working for Seaquest Adventures is your dream job?"

"Digital marketing director at Seaquest is my dream job."

We're entering dangerous territory now. My thighs tense against the upholstered chair. "What if it's my dream job too?" I challenge, curling my hand into a fist under the table.

He cocks his head to the side. "What exactly do you love about digital marketing?"

"I . . ." I shake my head and sit up straighter. "I'm inspired by working on the forefront of technology. Finding new ways to reach and engage with people. I like working in a growing field, and—"

"You sound like a Google result for 'What's great about digital marketing.'"

"No, I don't." Uh, yes, I do. Because I totally googled that exact phrase two weeks ago when I prepared talking points for James.

"But *why* do you love it? What is it about it that makes you want to wake up and devote your professional energy to it every single day?"

The truth? I have no great love of digital marketing. But securing a director position would be the precise stepping stone I need to reach where I really want to be one day: the executive suites. Plus, I could sure use the salary bump to help pay down my student loans. But Graeme doesn't need to know that.

"Because I'm good at it, okay? I'm good at crunching numbers, testing new marketing tools, and figuring out how to achieve results. And the higher up the ladder I go, the more opportunities I have to implement my vision. Now, why do *you* love it so much? You're not even on social media."

"Oh, ho, someone's been doing some light stalking."

Crap. "Not stalking. Intel. *Know your enemy.* Sun Tzu's *Art of War* and all that."

"You think I'm your enemy?"

I roll my eyes. "You know what I mean."

The waiter comes back with our mojitos and I take several long gulps of the crisp, minty drink. "So why aren't you on social media? Are you one of those privacy nuts—'the government is out to get us'?"

"No. I used to be on social media, but I deleted all my accounts over a year ago."

"Why?" Not that I'm super active on social media myself. Sure, I have Instagram and I send Snaps to my college friends every now and again, but generally I'm too busy to keep up with it. But it's strange for someone our age to have no social media presence at all, especially someone who does it for a living.

Graeme lifts and lowers one muscular shoulder. "I don't like splashing details about my life across the Internet. It's not real, what people post. It's a carefully cultivated highlight reel. Everyone is marketing their own personal brand whether they know it or not, and I'd rather keep my personal life to myself instead of trying to sell a fake version of it online. And opening up your life to others means people can comment on it," he adds, so low I barely hear.

"Seems like a lonely way to live."

"Not to me." His tone holds a harsh edge.

Flopping back in my chair, I cross my arms over my chest. "Can we ever have a conversation without arguing?"

His lips quirk. "I like arguing with you."

"You do?"

"It's fun. I like a challenge, and you give as good as you get."

"You have no idea." Instead of sounding flippant, my voice comes out in a rumbly purr.

Graeme's eyes grow hooded. "Maybe not *yet*."

My nerves sing and my heartbeat stutters. Graeme holds me captive with his glinting, raw-edged gaze. The feeling knocks me off-balance and I take a shaky sip of water. The heavy clanking of the anchor rising reverberates through the dining room.

What would it be like to *be* with Graeme?

Would he be all Midwestern polite, sweet as apple pie, holding open doors and letting me walk through first, so to speak? Or would he be the domineering Graeme I know from work—setting the pace, dictating the flow, taking the lead? I squeeze my thighs together.

"I would give anything to read your mind right now," he muses.

I take a deep breath and focus on reining in my runaway

thoughts. Time to change the subject. "I'm sure you would. Tell me something about yourself," I venture. "You said I don't know you, and you're right. Let's get to know each other."

This "meeting" has gone off the rails into territory I'm not entirely sure I'm ready to explore. But I don't want it to stop.

Graeme inclines his chin and a damp lock of hair falls across his forehead. I fight the urge to reach across the table and push it back. "What do you want to know?" he asks, voice deep and satiny.

I cast around for a topic. "What do you do for fun in Michigan? Besides walk your dog through graveyards at night."

His jaw tenses. "Oh, you know. Eat corn. Watch football. Tip cows."

"Sounds a lot like what we do for fun in Idaho." At least that's what people think.

"You're from Idaho?"

"The northern part, the panhandle. And no, I didn't grow up on a potato farm."

Graeme shrugs. "I grew up on a corn farm."

"You did?"

His face splits into a grin, showing a line of white, even teeth. "No."

I chuff a laugh. Warmth swirls in my stomach and spreads like tentacles through my limbs.

"I was born and raised in Ann Arbor. My mom was an assistant professor at the university, so most of my weekends were spent at lectures, the library, or the local park. I like to travel but haven't done much of it recently. I play pickup hockey when I can."

I can very well believe he plays hockey. He certainly has a hockey player's muscular physique.

"What about your dad?"

"Out of the picture since I was a kid."

"I'm sorry to hear that." Being raised by a single mother must have been hard. But it *would* explain why he seems to have an intuitive connection with middle-aged women.

"It is what it is. So what about you?" Bracing an elbow on the table, he rests his chin on his fist.

The way he's looking at me—like he's in a museum and I'm a particularly captivating sculpture—has my insides twisting into a bow. I run my tongue along my teeth after I swallow my last bite of salad. I hope to God there's nothing stuck in there.

"What about me?"

"What does Henley Rose do for fun?"

"Fun . . . fun?" Furrowing my eyebrows, I tap my chin and squint at the ceiling. "I think I've heard of that."

With a chuckle, he waves his hand in a tight circle, urging me on.

My eyes flit around the dining room—it's nearly empty now, and only a dozen guests remain, chatting over pushed-back plates and cups of coffee. "I played sports growing up too—mostly soccer—but not so much lately. Christina has been begging me to play on her adult rec team, but I haven't been able to fit it in my schedule. Once upon a time, I used to like camping."

"Camping? Really?"

"I grew up on the doorstep of a national forest. I practically lived outside as a kid." I tilt my head to the side. "You're surprised?"

"You're just so . . ." He brushes his shoulders off and straightens an imaginary bow tie. "And in our weekly video conferences, you wear those dresses—*very* professional. But pretty too. Colorful."

Heat floods my cheeks. "Oh, um . . ."

He laughs. "I'm saying I like them. Your style is like you—a sucker punch people don't see coming."

My lips part, but no words come out.

Wincing, Graeme scrubs a hand along the back of his neck. His tricep pops beneath the sleeve of his T-shirt. "And I've officially creeped you out."

"Only a little. Just a tiny creep. Like the size of a gremlin."

Truth? The thought of Graeme watching me during our video-conferenced weekly staff meetings, taking notice of what I'm wearing, *appreciating* how I look, has me preening.

And being compared to a sucker punch? Best. Compliment. Ever.

"Well, it was all a very ham-handed way to say I have a hard time picturing you camping," he adds, a flush creeping along his cheekbones. "Why 'once upon a time' though? You don't camp anymore?"

"Not for a few years."

"That's a shame."

"That's life, right? You get busy, your career comes first. Other things end up falling by the wayside."

"Unless you make time for those other things."

"Easier said than done."

"True. But life is what you make it. It's a balancing act. If all you do is work, you'll wake up one day—ten, twenty, fifty years from now—utterly exhausted. Then you'll be dead."

Well, that's a depressing thought. "And you're just out there living it up?"

"Me and my girl, Winnie. All day, every day."

My chest constricts, and I sprawl in my chair, casually perching an arm along the back. "And Winnie is your sister? Your girl-friend?" I hate how my voice has risen an octave.

His lips crack into a wide grin. "Smooth. No, I don't have a girlfriend."

My inner tigress rumbles its approval and I immediately recoil. Since when do I care whether Graeme has a girlfriend?

"Or a sister, for that matter. Only child. Winnie's my dog," he explains.

"Winnie like the Pooh?"

"Short for Winston."

"You named your girl dog after Winston . . . Churchill?"

With a sigh, Graeme digs his phone out of his pocket. After a few taps, he extends the screen toward me. "The underbite."

My jaw goes slack. I snatch the phone and hold it close to my face.

His dog is white with brown spots and hairless except for wispy tufts protruding from its forehead like a troll doll, and it has a lazy eye, wobbly jowls, and a severe underbite. Definitely not a purebred, like I'd assumed. It looks like a mix between one of those hairless crested breeds and an English bulldog.

"This is maybe the ugliest dog I've ever seen," I breathe.

Lips pursed, Graeme scratches his eyebrow. "I know, right? No one else wanted her, even though she's a sweet girl. She'd been at the shelter for too long and they were going to put her down, so I gave her a home."

Just like my Noodles.

Something inside me splinters and cracks like an iceberg. I tear my gaze away from the phone to stare at Graeme. At his stubble-roughened jaw, his supple lips, and his eyes. His clear, *kind* eyes. I see it now, the tenderness, the honest concern for others.

He's nothing like I thought.

"She's perfect," I murmur.

"I think so too," he says softly.

But he's not looking at the picture of his dog. He's looking at me.

Biting the inside of my cheek, I hand him his phone back and our fingers brush. Every nerve lights up like fireworks. This time, I don't pull away. Graeme brushes his thumb across my knuckles—accidentally? On purpose? He leans forward, eyes glinting.

"There are my two front office friends," a voice booms, and I nearly jump out of my seat. I drop the phone and it lands on the table between us with a thunk. Graeme gathers it up and pockets it.

"Hi, Gustavo. I didn't see you there. How are you?" I babble, trying to calm my runaway heart.

"Excellent, excellent," says the cruise leader, clapping a hand on the back of my chair. "How was the hike this morning?"

"Amazing. I'm glad you talked me into it."

"I am delighted to hear that. I will let James know."

My throat constricts and I have to clear it twice before I can speak. "You . . . you're in contact with James?"

"*Sí*, he emailed me yesterday. He asked me to keep an eye on you both while you're on board. Especially you." Laughing, he grasps my shoulders and jostles me in a friendly way, but my blood frosts.

James asked the cruise leader to keep tabs on us. I have no doubt he's looking for an excuse, *any* excuse, to trash my candidacy and promote golden-boy Graeme straight off. One inadvertently offended guest, one too many moments of distraction could spell the end of my professional dreams.

And what about *Graeme*? Gustavo just walked in on us . . .

what? Gazing longingly into each other's eyes? *Flirting?* I doubt he'll report that to James, but if we go any further . . .

I'm kidding myself if I think the impact of a shipboard fling would be equally felt by both Graeme and myself if James found out. I can already picture James, watery eyes narrowing, forehead pinching, staring down his nose at me in disapproval. But Graeme? He'd probably invite him into his office for a high-five followed by a raise just for showing up.

"Are you going on the early hike tomorrow morning?" Gustavo asks.

"Yeah," says Graeme, scratching his nose. "Are you?" he asks me.

"Uh-huh," I mutter.

"Wonderful, wonderful! You should go with Xiavera's group. She's an expert biologist, and I've asked her to be your . . . what is the word . . . *liaison* while you're on board. If you need anything at all, feel free to ask her. She'll also be keeping me informed about whether you misbehave." Hitching an exaggerated frown on his face, he wags his finger at me before his boyish features crack into a grin and he laughs genially. "I'm kidding!"

I force a weak chuckle.

"Or am I?" Serious again, he turns and strides for the door. His own booming laughter follows him out of the room.

My dinner sits like a boulder in my gut. Gustavo seems pleasant enough—certainly not malicious—but he's been roped into being James's eyes and ears on board. I can't really blame him. When an executive of the company asks you to jump, you say "to which planet?" If I don't watch myself on this cruise, the slightest misstep could spell my downfall. I curl my hands into fists and push my chair back from the table, away from Graeme. The air between us has thickened like sour milk.

"I need to go. I have to check on Walsh."

Graeme leans back, white T-shirt stretching across his broad chest. Confusion clouds his features. "Okay."

"Thanks for having dinner with me, I——" For the span of a breath, I stare into his vivid blue eyes. "Thanks."

Graeme stands. "Henley——"

"Don't. Just, don't." Turning on my heel, I quickly fill a plate for Walsh from the buffet and escape to my cabin.

I don't look back.

Walsh is in the shower when I arrive with her dinner, so I put the plate on her nightstand. The cabin is oppressively warm and stuffy. I need fresh air. I need to think.

Shucking off my sweater, I grab my phone, laptop, and backpack and head for the bridge, the glass-enclosed room on the upper deck where the captain and officers manage the ship. I don't want to accidentally run into Graeme, and while the bridge is usually open to passengers it isn't exactly a hot spot of activity—not like the lounge. Threading through hallways and up three flights of stairs, I reach the door marked Bridge: Open and knock softly.

"Come in," calls a deep voice.

I tentatively step inside. The room is narrow, with a massive control panel including the ship's wheel lining one wall. Above the controls, a row of windows overlooks the bow. Full darkness has fallen, and I feel more than see the front of the ship dip and crest as we slice through the waves.

I grab the wall to steady myself. "Hi, I'm allowed in here, right?"

"Yes, of course. Welcome to the bridge," says an older Ecuadoran gentleman with gray hair and a crisp white uniform. From his general air of command and the four gold stripes on his shoulder epaulets, I'm guessing he's the captain. "What can I do for you?"

"Nothing, I don't want to be a bother. I'm just looking for a quiet place to sit."

He offers a kindly smile. "You're no bother. Stay as long as you like."

There are two other officers in the room, both younger than the captain. They give me nods of welcome. Soon the three men are deep in murmured conversation.

I shuffle over to a round table in the corner and sit on one of its four upholstered stools. Plunking my laptop and bag down, I open my phone. Time to figure out what I'm dealing with. I type Graeme's name into the search bar of a Web browser. I googled him after our meeting with James two weeks ago, but I didn't look beyond the first page of results. I'm sure there's more out there.

To my surprise, a LinkedIn profile is one of the first results. *Huh.* This didn't come up before. He must have either recently joined or changed the privacy settings on his account since the last time I checked. Gnawing on my lower lip, I tap on the link. Graeme's profile pops up—it's his all right, complete with the same photo he uses for his work email. Bingo. I scan his résumé.

He earned his bachelor's in communications and marketing from the University of Michigan, but he attended Cornell for three years first. I frown. I've never heard of anyone transferring colleges their senior year. That's just . . . weird. Did he fail out? Drop out?

I scroll down to the employment section. His job with Ford is listed near the top. My eyes nearly bug out of my head. He worked on their digital marketing team for *four years* after spending two years as a social media specialist. And before that, he was a marketing intern for a white-water rafting company in upstate New York.

I still don't understand why he took a job with Seaquest—flexible, work-from-home hours or not. It was such a step back for him career-wise that it boggles my mind. I squint as I read the dates attached to his positions. He left Ford a full six months before he landed the Seaquest job. What was with the employment gap?

One thing is clear though. Based on his experience, Graeme's definitely qualified to be a digital marketing director—possibly even more qualified than me. I've been with Seaquest longer and I have over a year of graduate-level business classes under my belt, but I don't have the digital experience he does.

Dread fills the pit of my stomach. My proposal will need to blow Graeme's out of the water if I want to stand a chance at landing this promotion. An advertising scheme for the Galápagos based on something we've already done in Hawaii isn't going to cut it.

I need advice.

Stuffing my earbuds into my ears, I pull up Christina's contact and tap FaceTime. I slide off the stool and push through the nearest door. It takes me to an outside deck. Wind lifts my hair and I clutch the rail for support.

She answers on the fifth ring. "Hey, girl! How's the southern hemisphere?" she shouts. The image is grainy thanks to the satellite Wi-Fi, but I can see her cheeks are candy-apple red and she's breathing hard.

"Hey, Christina! It's good to see your face."

She squints at me. "Where are you? Inside a tornado?"

"Outside on the ship." I shuffle farther down the deck to stand under the ambient light flooding through the bridge's long windows. Rock music pumps through my earbuds and I notice Christina is wearing a tank top. I nearly smack my forehead. "It's Sunday. You're at boot camp class, aren't you?"

She waves me away. "No biggie. You're calling from the Galápagos. I had to answer. I need all the latest gossip. Most important, why did you want to know about Graeme's phone? Tell me everything!"

"Hey!" a male voice roars from somewhere on her end. "Is this social hour or is this boot camp?"

"Be there in a sec," she calls over her shoulder. She rolls her eyes at me. "The trainer tonight is a little intense."

"I won't hold you up. Can I just ask your advice on something?"

"Of course."

"What would you do if—" I'm about to lay out the whole business with Graeme, but the voice in the background bellows again, cutting me off.

"It's push-up time, and you're standing in the corner! Get moving!"

"Chill out, dude!" Christina roars back. "Jesus, I'm paying *you* to be here. Unbelievable." She shakes her head. "What were you saying?"

I open my mouth to speak but hesitate. I'll definitely need a long, in-person conversation with Christina to unpack everything happening on this cruise. Preferably over drinks. "Nothing, never mind. We'll talk soon, okay?"

"Wait, how's the proposal?"

I heft a sigh. "No bright ideas yet. Any suggestions for me?"

She nods thoughtfully. "I'd go back to basics. Think about what makes our cruise experience in the Galápagos special or different, then build an idea from there. You know Tory and I are standing by to help; just say the word."

"Thanks, Christina. You're the best."

"I know." She blows me an air kiss. "Talk soon. Geez, what are you standing around for? Are we doing push-ups or what?" she yells behind her before ending the call.

With a wobbly grin, I shuffle back inside. The three officers barely look up as I enter.

I resume my seat at the table and shove my feelings about Graeme aside. They're far too complicated. I can examine them later. Pulling my notebook from my bag, I open a fresh page.

Go back to basics. I consider Christina's words for several long minutes, then it hits me. Who knows the region better than the people who sail the ships?

"Excuse me, Captain?"

"¿Sí?"

"You've been to the Galápagos before, right?"

He chuckles. "Of course. Many times. I'm from Quito and my wife's family is from Santa Cruz."

"Captain Garcia is one of the most experienced cruise ship captains in Ecuador," adds one of the junior officers.

Perfect. "So, what do you love about the Galápagos?"

"Hmmm." He flashes me a wide grin. "How long were you planning to spend on the bridge?"

Clicking open my pen against the table, I poise it over my blank page. "As long as it takes," I say with a smile.

14

ix in the morning doesn't look good on anyone—except Walsh. Even fresh off the heels of a twenty-four-hour case of food poisoning, she still sparkles like a shooting star in the dim, predawn light. The color has returned to her cheeks and all traces of the milkshake debacle have vanished.

"Isn't this exciting?" Walsh croons, bouncing on her toes.

I pull my baseball cap lower down my forehead to hide the purple smudges under my eyes. I stayed up way too late chatting with Captain Garcia and the other officers.

Sinking onto a low, flat rock, I slip off my sandals and bang them together. Our Zodiac landing this morning on Floreana Island was a wet one, and damp olivine sand clings to my toes. I rub one foot on top of the other, knocking off as much sand as possible before pulling my shoes back on and tightening the waterproof straps. Farther down the shore, a handful of sea lions tumble and play in the surf. Walsh claps in delight as she watches them.

"You're in a good mood."

"Hell yes I am. I'm feeling better, it's a beautiful day, and I'm on a cruise with my sister. Let's have some fun!"

"I'll be ready for fun after coffee and breakfast." I yawn so wide my jaw pops. Waking up at the crack of dawn to watch the sunrise better be worth it. "And since when are you a morning person?"

"Since I slept fourteen hours yesterday. Oh hey, look, there's Mr. Sexy Voice. Graeme!" she calls, bounding toward him.

I frown. Graeme is helping Donna slosh from the Zodiac to the beach. Once she's clear of the waves, she gives his cheek a genial pat. I groan. At least Donna is making her way toward a different group so she won't be with us on this excursion. Less opportunity for Graeme to ingratiate himself.

When Walsh reaches him, he's crouched next to his open pack, fastening his phone to his selfie stick. A massive Nikon camera hangs around his neck. He stands, hoisting his bag. Linking her arm through his, Walsh walks him over to where I'm sitting with my elbows resting on my knees.

So this is what Graeme looks like first thing in the morning—mussed, bleary-eyed, and still ridiculously gorgeous. His army-green shorts hang off narrow hips, and his black, long-sleeved hiking shirt hugs his biceps, hinting at the knot of muscle underneath. His hair is a mess. Deep brown waves stick every which way. I clench and unclench a fist on my thigh.

"Hey, stranger," he says to me. His voice holds more gravel than usual.

"Hey."

"Stranger?" repeats Walsh. "Didn't you two go hiking yesterday? And snorkeling?"

"We did, but then Henley disappeared after dinner. You missed some A-plus entertainment in the lounge, by the way. Gustavo played the guitar and the cocktails were flowing." A wry grin graces his mouth.

I stand. "I had to get some work done." And avoid Graeme and any reminders that he and I are not operating on an even playing field.

"Wow, that's a big camera," says Walsh, fingering the DSLR around his neck. "Get any good shots yesterday?"

"Impossible not to. Not with all the Blue-footed boobies and marine iguanas everywhere."

"Sounds incredible. I hated to miss it." She pouts. "Maybe you could show me a few pics later?"

My jaw goes rigid and my eyes widen when Walsh runs her index finger down Graeme's forearm. What part of don't-flirt-with-Graeme did she *not* register?

A loud, piercing whistle cuts through the chatter. "My group, gather round please," Xiavera calls from the mouth of a trail leading away from the beach.

Graeme raises his selfie stick. "I'll meet you guys over there."

"Don't be too long," Walsh tosses over her shoulder as she strolls toward our group, hips swaying in her slate-blue yoga capris. I shoulder my daypack and follow. Twisting around to peer at Graeme, I watch as he jogs over to the sea lions, lifts his selfie stick, and turns in a tight circle like he's recording a 360-degree video. I narrow my eyes. What's he planning on doing with all this footage anyway?

With a huff, I join the group of ten or so guests crowded around Xiavera. *Of course* Nikolai is one of them. He flashes me a wide, toothy grin before puffing his chest like a frigate bird. Beside me, Walsh takes a long sip from her water bottle.

I should grab her by the elbow, drag her into a bush, and tell her in no uncertain terms that Graeme is off-limits. Period. But that might attract a wee bit too much attention. It'll have to wait.

"Can everyone hear me?" Xiavera calls out. Her voice is soft yet commanding. "*Bueno*. Now, today's hike will be much shorter than yesterday's, only forty-five minutes or so. But the rules are the same—stay on the path until we get to the beach, and don't crowd the wildlife. Today we are looking for flamingoes. There is a small population in the Galápagos, and they like to visit Floreana's lagoons in these early-morning hours . . ." She trails off, craning her neck. From somewhere in the group, smacking lips follow a noisy crunch.

"Oh, no. No, no." She presses through the crowd until she's standing in front of Nikolai. He's holding a shiny red apple, and there's a large bite missing. She plucks the apple from his grasp and holds it up for all to see.

"You must not bring food off the ship—ever. Outside food is strictly prohibited on the islands."

Nikolai's face pales as he swallows his bite. "I'm sorry."

"Why isn't food allowed?" I ask, legitimately curious.

"Good question," murmurs Graeme from directly behind me. I feel his presence like a live wire. Goose bumps dot my arms and a crackle of energy shivers down my spine. But I don't turn around.

Xiavera shrugs off her pack, pulls out a zippered bag, and stows the apple inside. "The Galápagos ecosystem is very sensitive. We are on islands that are hundreds of miles from the mainland, with many endemic plant and animal species that have evolved to be completely unique, and not equipped to deal with invaders. You will learn more about the effects of invasive species when you visit the research station in Puerto Ayora in a few days."

I raise my hand, half a dozen follow-up questions on my tongue. I'm not the only one with a hand up. I peer through the crowd—passengers are murmuring to one another, and a few are watching Xiavera, leaning forward with curious expressions.

Behind us, another Zodiac full of passengers pulls up to the beach. Xiavera flashes the naturalist on board a thumbs-up. "We need to get moving; we don't want to be the slow group. Don't worry, we won't draw and quarter you for the apple. Not this time," she says to Nikolai. He chuckles along with the other guests. "Just remember the rule: no food on the islands, yes? Everyone ready to chase that golden light? *Vamonos*."

She starts up the sandy path and the guests follow in a line. Fishing my phone out of my bag, I open the notepad in my task app and start typing furiously.

A vague idea begins to take shape. I'm just not sure what it looks like exactly. As I'm typing out the questions I want to ask Xiavera later, my toe connects with a rock.

I stumble, but a strong hand catches me by my forearm and I'm yanked backward into a hard body—Graeme's. The motion flings my daypack off my shoulder and it dangles from the crook of my elbow. My body is flush against his, ass nestled against his hips, back pressed to his chest.

His breath catches. Blood pounds in my ears. After several heartbeats too long, I step away. His fingers are the last to disconnect, slipping slowly from my arm.

I clear my throat. "Sorry," I mumble, scurrying to catch up with the rest of the group. Stealing a glance over my shoulder, I spot Graeme watching me intently, eyes hooded. I force myself to face forward.

The lagoons turn out to be a bust.

"The flamingoes were here earlier, but they must have moved on to a different part of the island," Xiavera explains. "Bad luck." She leads us farther down the path, away from the pungent, briny lakes, and pauses every few dozen yards to point out an interesting plant species or birdsong. I alternate taking pictures with taking notes, my fingers rarely at rest on my phone.

Walsh is next to Graeme again. She's saying something, a bright smile pasted on her face. His camera is raised, blocking his expression. My shoulders bunch automatically, but I force the muscles to relax.

Soon we climb over a ridge, and a pristine, empty beach spreads before the rising sun. I pause at the top of the dune, and my breath leaves me in a whoosh. The beach is bordered on three sides by green shrubs leading to brown hills dotted with white, skeletal trees. The blue of the ocean mirrors the sky above, while light dances off the glittering water like a pathway to heaven. In front of me, guests *oooh* and cameras click and whir like insects.

Farther down the beach, Xiavera waves. "Sea turtle tracks," she calls.

Most of the guests tag behind her, but a few spread out to absorb the beauty of the moment.

In front of me, Walsh drops her small pack in the sand, and, grasping the hem of her magenta wrap shirt, pulls it over her head and *completely off*. I cough in disbelief. Underneath, she's wearing a sports bra that looks more like a crop top—it's cut long and high-necked with intricate straps crisscrossing her back. But it's still tight and stretchy and shows off a lot of skin.

"What are you doing?" I demand, kicking up sand as I hustle down the ridge and over to her.

"Yoga."

"Why?"

"Because it's been days and I really need to stretch." Toeing off her sandals, she jogs over to the packed wet sand at the water's edge. Orienting herself so she's parallel with the shore, she begins a vinyasa sequence. Standing with her feet together, she stretches her arms toward the sky, folds over at the waist in a swan dive, rises halfway up then full down. Fingers anchored in the sand, she hops into a plank and then pushes her chest up into cobra and back into downward dog. She holds the pose for several long seconds, ass in the air.

The other guests are watching now. A middle-aged man raises his camera. His wife lowers it with one finger. Nikolai's mouth hangs open like a trout as he stares. Graeme is striding toward Xiavera when he stops abruptly . . . and pulls a double take at Walsh. His eyes widen—I can see it even at this distance.

Dread siphons down my throat and pools in my gut.

After a breath, Walsh rocks onto her toes and kicks off the ground, slowly raising her legs into a controlled handstand. It's so beautiful—and *powerful*—my jaw goes slack. It's like I'm watching a viral Instagram post unfold in real time: perfect backdrop, perfectly beautiful woman doing a perfect handstand on the perfect beach washed in perfect light.

A blur of movement catches my eye.

Graeme is beelining to her like a fish on a hook. He drops to his knee on the sand in front of Walsh at the same time he lifts his DSLR camera. When she scissors her legs, knees bent at ninety-degree angles, her back toes point to the rising sun. Behind her, the ocean glimmers like stardust. Graeme's camera clicks are as constant as a drumroll.

Everyone's watching now—even Xiavera. Heat explodes in my cheeks and my muscles tense to the point of cramping.

There's a splash behind Walsh and the crowd gasps. A sea lion's head bursts through the waves as it lumbers onto the beach not five feet away from her.

This seems to break the spell. Still upside down, Walsh glances at the sea lion then at Graeme with his camera pointed at her. With far less grace than before, she tumbles out of her handstand and backs several steps away. She searches the crowd. When she finds me, her eyebrows flicker into a momentary frown.

Several guests applaud. Graeme approaches her. He's smiling. Jealousy burns inside me like a fireball.

Two middle-aged ladies join them, and soon Walsh is leading the women in an impromptu set of sun salutations. Settling onto the sand, Graeme watches. His camera never stops clicking.

The rest of the morning is a blur of wildlife, people, and activity with barely a minute of downtime. Breakfast was a rushed affair since our group was late returning to the ship, followed by snorkeling and a quick buffet lunch. And now it's time for either kayaking or a Zodiac ride.

Throughout everything, I haven't been able to look at Walsh, much less speak to her. Because I have so many words I want to say I'm choking on them. And that means I haven't talked to Graeme either, because if Walsh plastered herself to him any tighter, she'd become permanently tattooed on his arm.

I make a disgusted noise in my throat. Walsh said she's kayaking, so that means a Zodiac ride for me. I've seen enough of her making a fool of herself over Graeme to last a lifetime.

Her high-pitched giggle echoes from across the mudroom, cutting through the chatter of a couple of dozen guests waiting their turn to disembark so we can all explore Floreana Island a second time today. Graeme shifts his weight beside her. I grind my molars so hard a tick starts in my jaw.

You know what? Whatever. They're consenting adults. It's not like I called dibs on Graeme. I even told Walsh I *didn't* want him. Jamming my baseball cap onto my head, I yank my ponytail through the back slot. Really, she's doing me a favor. With Graeme distracted, I can focus on my proposal. I've gone down the attraction road with a coworker before, and it led my job right over a cliff. Maybe this is just the wake-up call I needed. Maybe I should *thank* Walsh.

Three people down from me, Nikolai is talking loudly. "Dwight, you cannot kayak. Is not good for your joints. I'm your chiropractor, yes? You listen to me. You do Zodiac cruise, I kayak. We meet after."

"All right, if you insist," says Dwight with a shrug. "I just didn't want to leave you hangin', buddy."

When Nikolai claps his friend on the shoulder, he catches sight of me. Puckering his lips, he dips his chin, props one foot on a nearby bench, and leans into an exaggerated stretch. The way he's thrusting his hips, he might as well have a blinking sign pointing to his crotch proclaiming, "Hey, gurl, check out my package." Dwight rolls his eyes.

My cheeks prickle. Automatically, I glance around. Graeme is watching me. His gaze darts between me and Nikolai, his expression darkening. He makes a move as though he's going to walk toward me, but Walsh's hand lands on his shoulder. Pushing onto her toes, she leans in until her lips are an inch away from his ear. She whispers something. He jolts and blinks down at her.

My feet carry me toward Graeme of their own accord.

As I edge through the crowded mudroom, Gustavo's voice reverberates through the speakers. "Good afternoon, good afternoon. All of the single kayaks are now filled, but plenty of tandem kayaks are still available. If you would like to kayak, please find a partner and make your way to the mudroom. For those who would prefer to go on a Zodiac nature cruise instead, disembarkation will begin in fifteen minutes."

Walsh turns to Graeme. "Partners?"

Graeme hesitates, eyes flashing when they fasten on mine.

A frown flits across her face as she looks between us. "Don't worry, Henley doesn't need a partner. You said you're doing the Zodiac cruise, right, Hen? So, what do you say?" she asks him.

"Excuse me," says a familiar Russian-accented voice. Nikolai sidles up and stands at my elbow. "I do not suppose you are in need of a partner?"

Walsh was right; I hadn't planned on kayaking. But now . . .

Graeme tilts his head to the side and folds his arms across his broad chest. A single eyebrow lifts. *What are you going to do?*

It's a challenge. What the rules are, I have no idea. My heart beats a military tattoo as Graeme studies me intently.

I clear my throat and slap on a smile. Two can play at this game. "I sure am," I say to Nikolai.

"Oh, well, we can be partners then—" Walsh starts, but I cut her off.

"No, it's fine. You go with Graeme and I'll go with Nikolai. Done and done." Edging half a step closer to Nikolai, I slip my arm through his. He jerks and stares down at me like I've spontaneously started tap dancing.

The way Graeme looks away and his shoulders stiffen has my stomach folding into origami.

Because somehow, even though I'm not sure what the test was, I can't avoid the nagging feeling that I've failed.

15

This is even better than a dinner date. We are here in beautiful nature. Exercising our bodies together, working hard, sweating . . ."

This was a bad idea.

Our oars plunk through the gentle waves, and no matter how hard I paddle, I can't escape Nikolai's incessant chatter.

Because he's right behind me. In the same kayak.

"Let's go this way," I say, jabbing my oar to the left, toward where Graeme and Walsh's kayak glides parallel to shore. They paddle together in perfect synchronicity past dozens of bright red crabs skittering across a jumble of black lava rocks.

Nikolai dips his oar on the wrong side of the boat and we start drifting to the right.

"No, we have to work together. Watch me . . . left . . . right . . . left . . . right," I chant. We pick up speed. My shoulders and upper back muscles burn, but I keep up the grueling pace.

"Oof," grunts Nikolai. "You are animal. I like your effort."

We pass three other kayaks as we catch up to Graeme and Walsh. Sweat trickles down the back of my neck, causing the feathery tendrils of loose hair from my ponytail to curl and stick to my skin.

"Yes!" Nikolai crows, like we're racing in a regatta.

I'll say this much for Nikolai: he's competitive. I can respect that.

We've finally caught up with Walsh and Graeme. Walsh is still wearing her light pink crop top/sports bra, and she's sitting in the back of the kayak. In front of her, Graeme's sleeves are pushed up his muscled forearms.

As we glide past them, he offers me a two-fingered salute. I toss my head in response.

He paddles harder.

So do I.

He grins over at me, forehead glistening.

Behind me, Nikolai stops paddling.

What? Jerking around, I glare at him. He doesn't notice. He's taking a picture of a Blue-footed booby diving into the water off the opposite side of our kayak.

Graeme and Walsh pass us. I grunt in annoyance, but don't say anything.

Nikolai's a guest. He can take as many pictures as he wants.

Up ahead, a naturalist in a single kayak is paddling toward the approaching group. He waves his arm. Heads turn from every direction. "Flamingoes," he calls in a hoarse shout. "On shore, over there. But be careful not to startle them; they are migratory birds, not endemic to the Galápagos, so they are wary of people. Rarely do we see them on the beaches. Come, this is a special treat." Paddling in a circle, he takes off in the direction he indicated.

As we round a jutting edge of shoreline, the flamingoes come into view—a flock of about fifteen of them, all the brightest pink I've ever seen. Half a dozen other kayaks bob at varying intervals along the shore, along with two Zodiacs full of guests. We paddle forward slowly.

"Emily would love this." Nikolai's voice is so low I almost miss it.

Twisting around, I stare at him.

His smirk is gone. And so is the mischievous gleam from his eyes. His entire aspect has drooped, from his eyebrows to his gut. Sucking in a sniff through his nose, he straightens. "My ex-fiancée. Her favorite color is pink," he explains.

That sure doesn't sound like a man reveling in the cast-off shackles of a doomed marriage. More like a man who only has Scotch tape to hold himself together.

Seeming to snap himself out of it, he puckers his lips into his usual smirk. "She is not here. But I am glad you are."

Forcing my lips into a tight smile, I start paddling again.

We're close to the flamingoes now—maybe thirty feet away. Their cornstalk legs step through the shallow water, long necks bowed, while their curved, black-tipped beaks flutter over the surface.

Next to and a little in front of us, Walsh and Graeme's kayak floats nearby. Walsh's voice catches on the breeze. "Have you given any more thought to my offer?"

I swivel my head so fast my neck cricks. Perched on the edge of her seat, Walsh is so close to Graeme she's practically sprawled across his back.

Leaning away from her, he extends his selfie stick toward the flamingoes. "Huh?" he says, wrinkling his nose.

With an arm curled over his shoulder, she whispers something in his ear. Carefully, I lean over the side of our kayak, listening for all I'm worth.

"What are you doing?" Nikolai asks.

"Um, trying to get a better view." Sticking my oar into the

water, I attempt to swirl it in such a way that we drift closer to Graeme and Walsh . . . but no dice. Each pump of the current takes us farther away. I set the oar across the kayak in front of my knees.

Graeme rotates to say something to Walsh. His eyes are as dark as an oceanic trench.

Damn it, I *need* to hear what they're saying. Pulling my phone out of my sports bra, I wipe my sweaty screen on my tank top—thank goodness for a waterproof case—lean over the side, and extend my phone to mindlessly snap pictures of the flamingoes. The water laps higher against our kayak, but we don't tip.

"Maybe, you don't lean out so far . . ." says Nikolai.

"Shhh. Don't startle the birds," I whisper. But really, I'm straining to hear what's happening in Graeme's kayak.

Tucking my legs underneath me, I stretch over the side until half my body is suspended over the water, arm fully extended. My core screams and my fingers ache from gripping the edge, but I keep my expression neutral and my focus on the wildlife, so no one suspects I'm eavesdropping. Licking my lips, I dart a sideways glance at Graeme. He's scowling.

Behind him, Walsh's lips curl into a calculating grin. "Henley would never have to know."

And then she leans forward and runs her *tongue* along the lobe of his ear.

My muscles go slack. My palm slips. Too much of my weight is over the side. I tip . . . the water rushes toward me . . . *oh God* . . .

"Ahhhh!"

Splash!

The water is a frigid shock. The moment I submerge, my life jacket unfurls around my neck like an inflatable yellow pillow and

I bob to the surface, spluttering and coughing. With a whoosh of squawks and feathers, the flamingoes take off as one. Their long legs dangle behind them, the black undersides of their wings flashing against their pink bodies. I grip my phone to my chest, teeth chattering as I float.

"Henley!" Graeme shouts. "Are you okay?"

"Oh my God, Henley!" Walsh screams.

Obscenities dance through my brain like leprechauns as I stare at the flamingoes now winging away from the inevitably disappointed passengers.

"Yeah," I say miserably.

Who even knew birds that big could fly?

"I will save you, Miss Evans!" Nikolai bellows.

"No, no, *no!*" I screech.

But with a war cry worthy of a Viking, Nikolai leaps off our kayak, fully clothed, and cannonballs into the water beside me.

"Did you see the way he jumped in after her?"

"How romantic."

I flash the two ladies murmuring to each other a tense, tight-lipped smile. All around us, more than a dozen pairs of eyes stare at the only two people on the Zodiac who are sopping wet and wearing inflated lifejackets.

Water drips off my clothing and pools around our oars, which are lying in the middle of the hard rubber floor. I try not to shiver. Nikolai edges closer, a self-satisfied smile pasted on his face. At least our inflated lifejackets provide some barrier, preventing him from getting close enough to nuzzle me like a puppy. Rubbing my frigid arms, I let out a blustery breath.

"Are you cold? Here, I warm you . . ." He extends an arm like he's going to wrap it around my shoulders. Our life jackets squeak together. I gently, but firmly, guide his arm back to his own personal space with a pat. "I'm fine, thank you. You've done plenty."

Like make a bad situation worse. Since he jumped off our kayak, one of the Zodiacs had to come over, fish us out of the water, and then tow our kayak back to the ship. It might have been shallow enough to climb back in, but the unexpected dip in cold water put the kibosh on any more kayaking for us.

"Again, I am so sorry about this, folks," I say to the guests.

"Sorry?" the stocky, middle-aged man across from me booms. "I just got the most amazing pictures of the whole trip, thanks to you. How often do you see flamingoes *fly*?" Holding out his DSLR, he shows me the screen. On it is a close-up of one of the flamingoes taking off—a gorgeous, detailed image of feathers and movement and a beady yellow eye that any photographer would kill to capture.

"That's right," a couple of others echo.

The gray-haired woman sitting next to me pats my knee. "We're just glad you two are okay."

I murmur my thanks and steal a glance at Xiavera, sitting at the very front of the Zodiac.

She's not smiling. Instead, she murmurs a rapid string of Spanish into a walkie-talkie. Gustavo's voice buzzes back. My throat tightens.

The driver pulls the Zodiac up to the ship and two crew members untie the kayak so they can guide it along a catwalk to a netted area off to the side. Nikolai and I step off the craft onto the metal platform and up a short set of stairs into the cubby-lined mudroom.

Inside, Gustavo is there to greet us. The deep frown etched on his usually pleasant face makes anxiety slither and coil like a snake in my stomach. "Are you both all right?" he asks, looking us over.

"Yes, thank you," says Nikolai.

"What happened?"

I open my mouth to speak, but Nikolai cuts in. "Miss Evans was trying ever so hard to capture the perfect picture of the birds. She fell in. I saved her." He puffs his chest.

Saved me. I suppress a snort.

"She's lucky you were there," says Gustavo.

And *she* is standing right here. Unbuckling my life jacket, I let it fall to the floor with a wet plop and a clatter of buckles. "I'm sorry, Gustavo, it was an accident."

He narrows his eyes briefly at me before turning to Nikolai. "Why don't you get warm, get clean, and get ready for the excursion to Post Office Bay that departs in one hour. Yes?"

Nikolai inclines his chin, and before I can prevent it, he snatches my hand and delivers a kiss to my damp knuckles. "I see you later." With a small bow, he squelches to the stairs and disappears.

Gustavo's eyes widen.

"That's not what it looks like," I say quickly.

He pinches the bridge of his nose. "I hope not. There are rules about staff fraternizing with guests."

Behind us, footsteps echo up the metal stairs leading from the disembarkation platform. Walsh bounds into the mudroom, closely followed by Graeme. They're both red-faced, sweating, and breathing like they've sprinted a marathon. Or like they just paddled their kayak back to the ship at top speed.

Walsh lunges for me. "Henley, are you okay?"

I stiffen as she folds her arms around me. "I'm fine."

Graeme hangs back by the lockers but watches me intently.

Gustavo steps forward. "The problem is, Ms. Evans, your negligence disrupted an excursion for our guests today. Not to mention you scared the wildlife." He shakes his head sadly. "I will have to let James Wilcox know of these events."

"What! Why?" I demand.

"Because he asked me to report anything notable to him."

I begin to argue, but Gustavo raises his palms. "I'm sorry, but my hands are tied. And do try to be more careful in the future. As a staff member, you set an example for the rest of the guests. If you disrespect our rules, so will they."

Graeme steps forward but hesitates. His chest rises and falls twice before he speaks. "She didn't disrespect the rules. It was an accident."

Gustavo blinks at him before shrugging. "The result is the same. Now, if you will excuse me, I have an email to send." Frowning, he marches out of the mudroom toward the staff office.

My breathing hollows and my heart drums in my ears. Gustavo is going to tell James what happened. And rule breakers don't get promotions.

I've let this opportunity slip through my fingers, and all because I couldn't stay focused on what's important. Because I was too busy obsessing over a guy.

Walsh approaches me cautiously. "Don't worry, we'll—"

"I never should have brought you," I hiss under my breath. "You ruin everything. As usual."

She balks like I've slapped her. "What are you—"

"You know what I'm talking about." I shoot a veiled glance at Graeme. His expression is unreadable, but fire burns behind his eyes.

I barely make it to my cabin before the tears begin to fall.

16

As soon as I twist the knob to shut off the water, someone pounds on the door to our cabin.

Shoving the narrow shower curtain aside, I snatch a towel from the wall-mounted rack and fold it around me. Even the hottest shower I could stand wasn't enough to dispel the chill from my dip in the water earlier.

The knocking reverberates again.

"One second," I shout.

Is it Gustavo with an update from James—already? Maybe he's passing along an official withdrawal of my candidacy for the promotion. Or a two-page lecture. Or perhaps a pink slip with instructions to swim to the nearest island and hitchhike home.

My gut clenches like a fist.

I step out of the tiled shower on unsteady legs, cross into the bedroom, and yank on one of the oversized robes hanging in the closet. It reaches my ankles and the sleeves fall past my wrists, but it's soft and warm. Tying the belt around my waist, I fling open the cabin door.

Graeme is there, fist raised. His hair is damp and he's wearing a clean polo and shorts, but they're strangely rumpled, like he pulled them on in a hurry. Soap mingles with his usual cedar and citrus scent. Lowering his arm, his eyes widen as he takes in every inch of me, from my sopping wet hair to the fluffy white robe to my bare toes curling against the beige carpet. I'm suddenly hyper-aware that beneath a single layer of loosely secured terry cloth, I'm completely naked.

"Can I come in?" he asks, voice deep and urgent.

I knot my belt tighter. "Why?"

"I thought you'd like to hear about the conversation I just had with Gustavo."

Swallowing past the dry lump in my throat, I jerk my chin over my shoulder in silent invitation. He follows me inside. When the door closes behind him, the automatic lock clicking into place echoes like the gong of a bell.

Graeme is in my cabin. We're here together. Alone. And suddenly, the already cozy room feels even smaller. Like his presence takes up too much of it, filling it to the brim. I edge to the far side of the room to stand in the only place I can without being virtually on top of him: between the two beds.

Graeme approaches cautiously, the soles of his canvas loafers padding softly. He eyes the stray shoes dotting Walsh's half of the cabin and the clothes piled on top of her unmade bed. "Is your sister still at the bar?" Leaning a hip against the small desk anchored to the wall at the foot of my bed, he crosses one ankle over the other.

"I don't know."

"I take it you haven't talked to her since—"

"You were going to tell me something about Gustavo?" I brace my hands on my hips.

"Right." He nods. "I talked to him. He's not telling James what happened."

My knees buckle and I sink onto my neatly made bed. The soft sway of the ship seems to intensify, and I grip the comforter on either side of my thighs. "How . . ." I croak.

"The guests weren't upset—I have video to prove it." He pulls out his cell for emphasis. "And I warned Gustavo that James, the *chief marketing officer*, doesn't like to be bothered with nonissues."

My nerves tingle and my heart thunders. Standing, I stride across the small space, rubbing my temples. "You did it again."

"What?"

"Helped me when you had the advantage. Do you even want this promotion?"

"More than you know."

"Then why not let Gustavo tell James? You know it probably would have taken me out of the running."

"Which is exactly why I couldn't let it happen. You deserve a fair shake. And with the way James treats you . . ." He trails off and clears his throat. "Anyway, I owe you."

"What do you mean? You don't owe me anything."

His eyes flash. "What really happened on the kayak today?" he asks so quietly I barely catch it.

"I—I got startled and fell in."

"I thought you lost your balance."

"I did."

"But something startled you first?"

I nod.

He stalks toward me, but there's nowhere to go. I'm trapped between the beds. Dipping his chin, he searches my face. "What was it, Henley?"

Should I lie?

"I heard something," I hedge.

"Your sister asking me to blow off the next excursion and meet her in your cabin?"

I take a hasty step back and my calves bump into my bed. "Um, what?"

"Oh. So you didn't hear that . . ."

"No! I mean, I knew she was hitting on you. She licked your *ear*." I grimace.

Tilting his chin up, Graeme's face splits into a radiant smile. "I knew it. You *are* jealous."

"Me? Jealous?" Heat gathers at the base of my neck and I clutch the lapel of my robe. "Get real."

"You're scowling."

"You're annoying."

"I owe you an apology."

"Accepted."

"Not for this." He motions between us. "I'm sorry for not making it immediately clear to your sister that I wasn't interested. I should have set her straight, but I wanted to see how you would react. And boy, did you react."

My cheeks flame. "I did not."

"So you're telling me you *wanted* to go kayaking with that . . . that . . . chiropractor? And it had absolutely, positively nothing to do with me?"

"Not everything's about you, you know."

Graeme's nostrils flare. "Aren't you tired of this game? You can't tell me you weren't jealous. I saw your face on the beach this morning. Like you were starting fires with your mind."

This conversation is diving into dangerous waters. My legs itch to flee, but I'm boxed in between the beds with nowhere to go.

"You get a little crease, right here, when you're angry." He taps my forehead between my eyes. "I know. I've seen it in a lot of meetings. And every time your sister looked at me today, tried to show off for me, that crease might as well have been permanently tattooed."

Taking a deep breath, Graeme steps closer until he's less than an arm's length away. He's bigger than I am and his body towers over me in the cramped space, but there's a hesitancy to his posture. A vulnerability I haven't seen before. He swallows. "You gave me hope that maybe, just maybe, you might feel the same way about me as I feel about you."

"How do you feel about me?" I whisper.

"Usually? Irritation and an extreme urge to shove a whipped-cream pie in your face. But also, desperation. Desire. And, *fuck*, I want to kiss you."

Graeme Crawford-Collins wants to kiss me.

I'm dizzy with the knowledge. His face swirls in my vision.

What would the stubble on his jaw feel like against my cheek? A rough graze or a tender caress? What do his lips taste like—some strange, forbidden fruit of spice and honey, or a burst of mint as brisk and sudden as a spring snow? And how would the flavor of him pair with his heady, masculine scent?

I imagine inhaling deeply at the crook of his neck before sampling his lips. *Why yes, sommelier, you were right. Cedar with notes of grapefruit, a nice mouthfeel, and a strong, smooth finish.*

I sway, and grasp handfuls of his shirt—an anchor in this bewildering tableau. My knuckles curl against the firm muscles of his chest. His palm snakes around to the back of my neck, fingers entwining in my hair.

"May I?" he whispers. His lips ghost against mine, only the suggestion of space between us.

Pulling back a fraction, he pauses.

He's waiting for an answer.

There's heat and longing and curiosity and desire, and for once, I don't want to say no. My eyes flutter closed.

Yes.

Then the cabin door bangs open, and I launch away from

Graeme like I've stepped on a box full of mousetraps. The back of my knees jam into my bed and I tumble onto the mattress in a flail of limbs.

Walsh is standing in the doorway.

She blinks at us, pulls an about-face, and practically runs out of the room.

17

Walsh, wait."

I'm out of the cabin before I can think twice. The tie around my waist is dangerously loose and the neck of my robe has fallen open to expose more cleavage than I'm comfortable sharing with the general public. Yanking my robe together and cinching my belt, I jog after her.

Behind me, a door opens and closes followed by another—Graeme must be returning to his own cabin. Heat fills my cheeks as disappointment barrels through me like a flash flood.

I can't think about that right now.

Walsh has been flirting with Graeme since we boarded the ship, and I nearly *kissed* him. I catch Walsh by the arm just as she reaches the stairs.

She whirls around. "What are you doing?" she demands, breaking free of my grip.

"Walsh, I—"

"You get back in there right now and kiss his face off!"

"*What?*"

"You heard me. I know what you guys were about to do. Damn it, Henley, why didn't you tell me you liked him!" She punches me in the shoulder.

"Ow." I rub the spot.

"Go. Get your man." She turns to walk up the stairs and I grab her again. This time, I don't let go.

"We need to talk. Now." Gripping her by the elbow, I steer her into our cabin.

"Why didn't y—" she begins once the door closes behind us, but I cut her off.

"What is going on with you? First you throw yourself at Graeme, and now you're all 'go kiss him'?"

"Look, it's not what you think."

"Well, what is it then?"

Walsh sucks in a deep breath, like she's bracing herself. "I was trying to do you a favor. You want this promotion more than anything I've ever seen you want in your life. So I thought, maybe I could distract the competition. If Graeme's with me, he's not thinking about work or this proposal thing you guys have to do."

My jaw falls open like an unhinged door.

"I was trying to give you an edge. Pay you back for taking me in when I needed a place to stay."

"By being my jezebel?"

She shrugs. "He's hot. I've done worse. We're both adults. I figured, what's the big deal?"

Walsh has done some pretty nutso things in her life, but this one takes the cheesecake. "The *big deal* is that it's unconscionable. You're trying to sleep my way to the top. How messed up is that?"

"I know, I know. It seemed like such a good idea . . . and then I ruined everything, as usual." Her miserable expression ignites a fresh wave of guilt.

"I shouldn't have said that, Walsh. I'm so sorry."

Perching on the edge of her bed, she rakes her fingers through her loose hair. "It's true though. I can't hold down a job. I fail at every relationship I've ever had. And now you're in trouble with your boss and it's all my fault."

I march across the room and sit next to her. "That's not true. You're not a failure. You're incredibly loyal. You've had more adventures than I've ever had. And your yoga practice is on fire. I couldn't do a handstand like you did today—I'd fall on my face. And relationships—"

"Fail."

"No, you're smart. You know when to get out. Like with Keith, right? I mean, you said he turned out to be an asshole. So that was a good decision."

The skin around her mouth tightens before she blows out a blustery breath. "What about your boss? Are you going to get fired?"

"Gustavo's not going to tell James what happened."

"Oh, thank God. I was so worried. I know how much this job means to you, and—wait. Why didn't he tell James?"

"Graeme talked to him."

"He did?"

"And explained that the other passengers weren't mad, which is really the most important thing."

"Is that so?"

"Yes."

Standing, she crosses the room to lean against the closet. "So you're telling me that your competition, your ultimate adversary, went to bat—for you?"

I twist the belt of my robe around my fist. "Well, yeah."

"Girl, he has got it *bad*."

"He does not." The words aren't believable even to my own ears.

"He *so* does."

"Then why did he take all those pictures of you on the beach?" I'm grasping at straws and I know it.

"Ooo. About that." She winces as she pulls out her phone. A few taps later, she offers it to me. It's Seaquest Adventures's Instagram feed.

Graeme's face stares at me from the latest post. I tap on it to get a closer look. It's the 360-selfie video he took this morning on Floreana showing the rising sun and sea lions tumbling in the surf, and it has more than a thousand views already. Goose bumps prickle my forearms. I scroll through the comments.

> **amitakagata** Where do I sign up??
>
> **Br3nda1972** Beautiful beach, beautiful man 😍
>
> **Martinique_OP** Gorgeous
>
> **travelmumsnet** My fave destination in the whole world. Magical!
>
> **Jenniferous1** U single?
>
> **Kittykatzn** 😻 😻

I tut as I scroll. The ratio of female-to-male commenters must be at least five to one, most of whom are remarking on Graeme's insanely good looks. The second to last comment catches my eye.

> **Ryan_Collins206** Nice to see you back in the world, G.

My eyebrows pop upward. This is someone who knows Graeme personally. And based on his last name, he must be family. I tap on Ryan Collins's profile. It's listed as private, but "206" is a Seattle area code. *Interesting.*

Walsh nudges my elbow. "Check out the story." Right, I'm getting sidetracked. I go back and tap on Seaquest's ringed logo to pull it up.

My calves tense. It's a photo of Walsh doing her handstand on the beach. And damn it if it isn't breathtaking. At the bottom, there's text: *Swipe up to find wellness in the wilds of the Galápagos Islands.* Swiping takes me to the Galápagos booking page on our company's website.

Is this Graeme's plan for his proposal: use digital storytelling to sell cruises? How many swipes has the story logged? How many bookings have resulted?

And what do I have for my own proposal? Just a handful of questions and a vague idea. Closing my eyes, I drum Walsh's phone against my forehead. "Damn it," I grumble.

She winces. "I'm sorry, I wasn't trying to pose for him. The naturalist said, 'sea turtle tracks,' and I thought, 'Ooo, that sounds cool, maybe I can distract him from taking pictures.' Hence, handstands. I didn't know he'd post my picture on your company's Instagram."

I offer a conciliatory smile, but it feels more like a grimace. "I'm not mad at you. It's Graeme. If he's doing what I think he's doing for his proposal, it's going to be good."

"And I didn't help things, did I?" she moans miserably.

"You were *trying* to help, and that's all that matters."

Walsh's phone trills twice; I'm still holding it. I glance automatically at the two texts that pop up on the screen. They're both from a contact labeled Bad News Bears.

> Come on, don't leave me hanging

> I need an answer. Now.

Scrabbling, Walsh rips the phone away from me and stares at the screen. Her knuckles whiten as she grips the phone before clicking it off.

"Who are those from?"

"Nothing. Don't worry about it."

"If you're talking to someone you've labeled Bad News Bears, shouldn't you be, I don't know, *not* texting them?"

The wall speakers crackle. "Good afternoon, good afternoon. Our final excursion to Post Office Bay will be departing in fifteen minutes. As a reminder, you have the option of participating in the oldest mail delivery system in this part of the world. Postcards are provided in your cabin, so be sure to write one—to a family member, a friend, or even yourself. Disembarkation begins in fifteen minutes."

"Are we good? You're not mad at me?" Walsh asks.

"No, I'm not mad." Crossing the room, I give her a quick hug before stepping back and gripping her by the shoulders. "But you're going to tell me what those texts were about."

"Just some low-key drama. Super boring. Nothing to tell."

"Walsh."

"Oh, look at the time." She taps her bare wrist. "Got to shower, best hurry." Phone tucked in the waistband of her pants, she darts into the bathroom and closes the door.

"Brat," I shout.

"Nosy," she retorts.

I can't help but grin as the bands around my heart loosen and a warm feeling spreads through my chest. I hate fighting with Walsh. And I hate it even more when I'm the one in the wrong.

The fact is, I acted like a lunatic today, and all because I couldn't keep my mind on the job. Gnawing my lip, I brush the spot on my neck where Graeme's fingers played against my skin. I can still feel his lingering touch, as hot as midday sand.

Next door, footsteps thump faintly. It sounds like Graeme is pacing in his cabin.

I stare at the wall separating us. I could walk two steps down the hall and slip into his cabin without anyone noticing. Then we could pick up where we left off . . .

But I'm smarter than that.

I don't have the luxury of slacking off. I've already had one near miss on this cruise; I don't need another. If I want a shot at snagging this promotion, I need to be in full-on work mode. Not cat-on-the-prowl mode. And besides, I know from experience what can happen when a work romance turns sour, and it's not worth the risk. Better to keep Graeme squarely in the friend zone.

Marching to the closet, I fling it open and take out a fresh set of clothes. I pull on shorts and a long-sleeved shirt, comb out the lobster-sized knots in my hair, spritz it with salt spray, and scrunch until damp waves form—there's no time to dry it. After swiping on some lip stain and a coat of mascara, I slip into the desk chair and pluck one of the postcards from the narrow shelf bolted to the wall. It features a giant tortoise on the front. Digging out a pen from the top drawer, I click it open and hold it poised over the card.

Who should I write to? Christina? She's already been to the Galápagos. Mom and Dad?

I tap the pen against the desk and my cell phone steals my attention. I still have a few minutes . . .

I enter the Wi-Fi passcode and a cascade of notifications flickers across the screen. I have missed texts from Tory, Christina, and my parents. Some new Snapchat messages and Instagram likes. I ignore them all. But then I spot a new email in my personal account that I can't ignore.

My chest tightens as I scan the official-looking notice about my student loans. My monthly payments are increasing next month.

"Fuuuuuck."

As if I needed any more pressure to land this promotion.

My phone buzzes with a new text. It's from Graeme.

My heartbeat stutters and fuzzy warmth fills my veins. Not the reaction I need right now. I hesitate with my thumbs poised over the screen.

The wall speakers crackle with an impending announcement. "Good evening, good evening. If you would like to visit historic Post Office Bay, disembarkation begins in fifteen minutes. Post Office Bay, fifteen minutes. Please make your way to the mudroom, and don't forget your postcard. Thank you."

I lick my dry lips and type out a response.

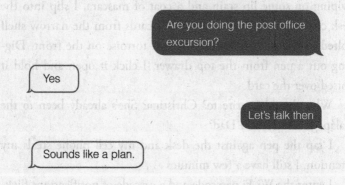

18

Walsh took her sweet time in the shower, so we ended up on the last Zodiac to shore. Graeme must have caught an earlier one because I didn't see him in the mudroom. Our boat bounces along the surface of the water, engine chugging, and I clutch my hair over one shoulder to keep the wind from whipping it in my face.

As we approach the island, I catch sight of Graeme. He's meandering down the beach, gaze down, hands stuffed into pockets, linen pants rolled up to midshin. It's sexy as hell.

I clamp my teeth together to fight the wave of attraction that swamps me. I'm doing the right thing by telling him we need to keep things platonic, I am. Definitely. No doubts whatsoever.

The driver backs the Zodiac onto the beach and we climb out.

"Want me to come with?" Walsh asks, unbuckling her life jacket and tossing it on top of the others piled in a canvas bin.

Shrugging off my own life jacket, I shake my head. "No, thanks, I got this."

"The historic post barrel is a short walk this way," a young naturalist tells our small group. Walsh flashes me a thumbs-up before following the crowd down a sandy path through the thick, scrubby trees. Pressing my shoulders back, I set off toward Graeme. My stomach trembles: not with butterflies—dainty, weak things—but with hedgehogs. Spiky, angry hedgehogs waging a battle royal in my gut. Graeme looks up as I approach. The waning sunlight catches his face and the hedgehogs pummel my rib cage.

The most genuine, soul-stirring smile forms and his entire aspect brightens when his eyes meet mine.

My steps falter. No one's ever looked at me like that before—like I'm the sunrise after a long winter's night. Or the first present on Christmas morning. It's a look you see in movies, and from Graeme, it's devastating.

Doubt creeps along my spine, but I shove it down deep. The low sigh of waves rolling in and retreating from the shore echoes in my ears as I begin walking again. Graeme lengthens his strides, and we meet in the middle.

"Hi," I say, sliding my hands into the back pockets of my shorts.

"Hey."

Awkward silence hangs between us.

He opens his mouth, but then rocks back on his heels as though he's changed his mind about whatever he was going to say. "How's Walsh?"

"Huh?"

"She seemed pretty surprised when she walked in on us earlier, and given how she's been acting toward me all day . . ." He motions vaguely, clearly embarrassed.

"Oh, *oh*. You're worried she was upset over catching us . . . together?"

He nods. I click my molars. Truth time.

"She's fine. We talked. And actually, she doesn't like you like that."

He jerks his head back in surprise. "Well, good. That's good news. But then why all the—"

"Flirting?" I say. "This is going to sound crazy, but she was trying to distract you. To help me, I guess. She figured if you were focused on her, you wouldn't be focused on the promotion." Twisting my hands together, I wince. "Sorry. I didn't know that's what she was doing."

Graeme scrubs a hand through his hair. "Well, I was trying to make you jealous, so let's call it even." The corner of his lips twitches, and he begins meandering down the beach. I fall into step beside him. Low, indistinguishable chatter hums through the trees; we're alone, but the guests aren't far away.

"Did you bring a postcard?" I ask. Not the most riveting conversation piece, but at least it's a safe topic.

He nods. "Who are you sending yours to?"

"Haven't decided yet."

"Parents?"

I chuckle. "They'd probably never get it. No one goes to Careywood, Idaho. I'm thinking Christina."

As Gustavo explained it, the way Floreana's post barrel works is you leave a postcard inside and future travelers serve as unofficial mailmen. They look through the cards and take any with an address close to their final destination for hand delivery—no stamp needed. It's apparently a tradition that started with early sailors to the Galápagos.

The catch: there's no telling when someone will come along who will be going where you want your postcard to go, so it could be weeks, months, or years before your postcard gets delivered. And bumble-bum, Idaho, is a long way from just about everywhere.

"How about you?" I ask. "Will Mom get a note from her favorite son?"

Graeme's mouth tightens and his jaw muscles twitch. "My mom passed away a year and a half ago." His voice is soft and matter-of-fact, but it still reverberates through the balmy air like a gong.

My stomach bottoms out and my mouth goes drier than the sand on my toes.

The pieces begin clicking into place. When I FaceTimed with him the other week, he was walking through a cemetery. *Probably the cemetery where his mother is buried.* His desire to move somewhere completely new and leave his old life behind suddenly makes sad, perfect sense. Even his offhand comment about not being on his A game when he first started at Seaquest was probably because he was grieving his mom.

I suck in a sharp breath. Oh God, the number of times I've made mom jokes. I want to throw up.

I stop walking. So does he.

"I'm sorry," I say, touching his arm.

After a long moment, he dips his chin in acknowledgment.

"How . . . ?"

"ALS."

Oh God, ALS is *brutal.* A tragic way to go—and a tragic condition for family to witness. To lose your mother to a degenerative disease like that . . . No wonder he took a step back in his career after a hiatus. He probably didn't need the stress.

I open my mouth, but what words could possibly be sufficient in this scenario? I lift my gaze to his, letting him see my utter sincerity. "I'm so sorry."

Inhaling deeply, he starts walking again. "Actually, I was one of the lucky ones. She was diagnosed the summer before my senior year of college, and I had another seven years with her. Most patients don't even last five."

That explains the college transfer his senior year—he was coming home to take care of his mom. On an impulse, I reach for

Graeme's hand. His palm is hot and heavy in mine and he stops walking.

I look up into his steely blue eyes. Behind the acceptance, grief hangs over him like a ghostly shadow. I squeeze his hand, putting every ounce of sympathy I can muster into the gesture. "The fact that you're standing here right now, working, thriving . . . you're the strongest person I know."

His eyes widen and his jaw goes slack, but he squeezes my hand once in silent thanks before letting go. Running a palm roughly over the back of his neck, he resumes his slow, meandering gait.

"I wrote to my cousin Ryan. He lives in Seattle. I haven't talked to him in a while, so he'll be surprised," Graeme says, patting his pants pocket where I can see the faint outline of a postcard. Ryan must be the one from Instagram. "I don't know why I brought up my mom. I don't usually like talking about her."

"Too painful?"

He shakes his head slowly. "I can't stand the pity. It's why I quit social media."

"People offer sympathy because they care," I say quietly.

The corner of his lips twitches again. "Always looking on the bright side. You're a good person, Henley."

I pluck the strap of the tote across my chest and squint at the setting sun's reflection on the water. "I'm really not."

"Trust me, you are. You're always the first to jump to a co-worker's defense whenever James goes on the attack. You organized that meal train for Barbara when she was out for chemo last year. You ask people about themselves and offer a kind word if they seem down. You're thoughtful. I've seen it over countless video conferences and here in the Galápagos too. Like how much you watch out for Walsh."

Heat flushes my cheeks. I can't believe he noticed all that. "I forgot my grandma's birthday this year," I mumble.

He lets out a hearty laugh. "You win. Rotten to the core."

The sound of his laughter dances through my body until it coils in my lungs.

We're close. But not close enough. Every cell in my body urges me to eliminate the distance between us. *No, I can't. But I want to.*

My breathing turns jagged. When I peer up at him, our gazes collide. His smile fades and his eyes grow hooded. Golden light dances across his stubbled jaw. I find myself leaning closer, closer . . .

Sucking in a breath, I stumble back. "We shouldn't do this."

"Why not?" He steps back, brow furrowed. "There aren't any rules in the employee handbook preventing consensual romantic relationships at work. I checked."

"There doesn't need to be. I already know what will happen. We do this, then Gustavo finds out. Then he tells James. And James loses the last dregs of respect he has for me and my career at Seaquest will be over."

"You don't know that."

"I do."

Confusion flickers behind his eyes and he frowns.

My stomach plummets. He'll never understand if I don't tell him the truth.

"It's—it's why I left my last job."

Shock registers across his face for a handful of heartbeats. "What happened?"

"A guy named Sean happened. It was four years ago. I was working for an insurance company, Prima Health. Sean started several months after me, and we were assigned to work on the same big project: the digital rollout of a new branding concept. There were sparks from day one, but we didn't act on it. Not right away. But then there were a lot of long nights, extra time spent together . . . one thing led to another . . ."

My thighs tense as I stare out at the blue-gray ocean. "For a few weeks, I thought he was *it*. He was funny and charming and seemed so interested in me and supportive of my ambition. Looking back, he was mostly interested in my ideas for our joint project. We spent almost every night together. I started thinking of him as my boyfriend, but it was all a sham.

"When it came time to present the project to our boss, he completely steamrolled me. He talked 90 percent of the time and made it sound like our presentation was his alone, and that I only helped even though I actually did the bulk of the work. I tried to speak up, to assert myself, but our boss just seemed annoyed by that. As if I was wasting his time by splitting hairs."

Sucking in a long breath through his nose, Graeme briefly closes his eyes. "Everything makes so much sense now. Why you thought the worst of me when it looked like I was taking credit for your work on the video. I wish you would have said something sooner, but I understand now why you didn't."

My mouth goes dry, and I nod once. "That's not the worst part though. When I confronted Sean later about how he behaved, he called me dramatic and tried to convince me that what he did was no big deal. Like he was presenting for both of us and I should be grateful."

"He was gaslighting you."

"Yeah, I figured, which is why I broke up with him on the spot . . . or at least I tried to, but he said we couldn't break up since we were never actually together. Because it was just sex."

The vehemence in Graeme's gaze makes me shiver, and I rub

my arms. "Of course, word got out at the office that we were sleeping together. Guess whose reputation took a hit? Not his. Our boss never treated me the same after that. I was passed up for plum assignments and consistently talked over in staff meetings all while Sean's star continued to rise. Six months later, he was promoted over me. He would have been my direct boss. That's when I quit.

"Not that I was a perfect employee or didn't make mistakes or that Sean wasn't talented," I babble. "It's just . . . I knew I was never going to get a fair shake, not working for him and not at that company."

"You don't have to explain. I get it." Turning to me, Graeme gathers up my hand, giving me plenty of time to pull away. When I don't, he runs his thumb along the length of my palm. "I'm not Sean."

"I mean, I don't think you are, not anymore, but getting involved with you is still a risk. One I'm not sure I'm willing to take."

"I respect you, Henley. You say you don't want to do this? Okay. I'll leave you alone. You say you want to give us a shot but keep it on the DL? I'm down. This is your decision, your choice. I would never do anything you don't want to do, including reveal personal feelings at work if that makes you uncomfortable."

Tears prickle my eyes and my throat burns with raw emotion. No one's ever said anything like that to me before.

"If you're game, I want to get to know you better, spend some time with you outside of work. Whether it's in person or long distance, I don't care. You're the first person I've had feelings for in a long time, and I want to see where this thing goes." He shrugs. "And for the record? Sean is a douchebag. If I ever meet him, I'm going to punch him in the nuts."

I laugh weakly. "Not unless I do it first."

Graeme's lips twitch, but his eyes fill with uncertainty. "What about you? What do *you* want?" The vulnerability in his tone makes my chest ache with longing.

What do I want?

I want to work hard and earn respect. I want companionship. I want to pay off my student loans. I want to help Walsh find her footing in life. I want to be the boss someday. I want to be happy.

I want Graeme. I want it all.

Taking half a step closer, I run my tongue along my lower lip. The setting sun warms my neck and Graeme's chest rises and falls as he studies me intently.

"I want . . . to try something," I whisper.

The ground seems to retreat under my feet. Like I'm suddenly standing on the edge of a cliff peering down into a mist-shrouded unknown. My heart swells until it threatens to beat out of my chest.

Closing the distance between us, I tilt my chin up and rise onto my toes. I brush my lips against his. *Bliss.* Groaning, Graeme pulls me closer, his mouth moving against mine. Energy sizzles between us as effervescent as champagne.

His scent fills my nostrils and his body is firm and warm. His tongue dips into my mouth. He tastes sweet with a hint of tart, like huckleberry pie and a fine, crisp cider—like home. My nerve endings crackle like sparklers.

I know we should stop. There's too much at risk. But I don't want to. Thrill pumps through my veins and my breathing shallows. I'm somersaulting off a high-dive. I'm chasing a shark.

Except for the pounding of the surf against the shore and my heart against my ribs, the empty beach is silent. Even the birds have quieted along with the murmur of guests through the trees behind us.

Graeme pulls back a fraction. Searching my face, he smooths his thumb roughly over my cheekbone. There's no smug satisfaction in his expression—only open, honest wonder.

"Screw it," I murmur, yanking him back down to me.

I meet every swirl of his tongue with a roll of my own. Give and take. Advance, retreat. I suck on his lower lip before nipping it with my teeth. He rumbles deep in his chest—part sigh, part growl, and the sound unleashes something between us. His lips move against mine with new urgency, his heart thundering under my palm. Heat blooms in my stomach and spreads like wildfire as his scent envelops me.

I want to savor him like a delicacy, like how you'd nibble truffles or caviar, but I can't hold back.

I devour him like a 1 a.m. pizza.

Want him. Hate him? *Need him.*

"Henley," he groans. With his hand clamped to my lower back, he rolls his hips and my eyes nearly roll back in my head. I twine my fingers through his silky hair and push onto my toes. It's like I've tried the first bite of food at a banquet only to realize I'm ravenous. And by the way Graeme is kissing me, *moving* against me, he's starving too.

There's fire in my lungs and Pop Rocks in my soul. And I never want this to end.

"Xiavera . . . Hey, Xiavera! Wait up, I have a question!" Walsh's voice cuts through the lust fogging my brain. Her shout is a clear warning—to me.

We burst apart like a seam ripping just as Xiavera appears from around a grove of trees, Walsh dogging her heels. Graeme retreats several steps down the beach. My heart stops completely before trilling in panic.

Xiavera turns around to address Walsh, but then spots us.

"Oh, there you two are. We've sorted through the existing post-cards in the barrel and now it is time to make your delivery. You have a postcard, yes?"

"Right . . . yes," I stammer. "We were just . . . admiring the view."

Graeme already has his phone out and is taking a picture of the sunset. Quick thinking. Except it'll probably mean more great photos and even more Instagram likes.

"Okay. Don't take too long. We're winding down."

"Thanks, we'll be right there," he rumbles.

Xiavera lifts a nylon backpack from the pile next to the life jackets and strides back toward the path. Walsh waits for her, bouncing on her toes. "Can you tell me more about the history of this post office barrel thing? What year did it start again?"

"We don't know for sure, but possibly as early as 1813 . . ." Xiavera trails off as they disappear back down the path, Walsh beaming at me over her shoulder.

"We should go," I say, but Graeme catches my arm in a gentle grip.

"Are you okay?"

I shake my head, mouth suddenly dry. "That was too close. Xiavera almost caught us. What if she told Gustavo, and he told James . . ."

"It's okay. She didn't see anything."

"This time." I step away from him, breaking contact. "Look, I still don't know if this is a good idea. There's a lot at stake—for both of us. And once one of us gets the promotion it will be even harder. Someone will be more senior than the other and . . . I just don't know."

"You kiss me like that, then you say you might not want to kiss me again? You're killing me, Henley Rose." My heart sinks, but then I spot his wry smile. Sauntering closer, he tucks a strand of hair behind my ear.

"I get it. You have history with this sort of thing, and you're worried. If you want, we can keep things professional until the promotion is decided."

"Yes, good." My muscles sag in relief, even though a coal of disappointment smolders in my gut. "We'll put a pin in it for now. It's only for a few weeks."

"Except . . . I bet you can't stay away. I'll give you all the space you need—platonic colleagues only, Scout's honor. But before the end of this cruise, I think you'll kiss me again. Because you *want* to."

The arrogant set of his jaw competes with the sensual curl of his lips. He squares his wide shoulders and brings his face closer to mine. My brain turns foggy. Abruptly, he pulls back, and I only realize I've been caught in the magnetic power of his lips when I stumble forward.

He smirks. "See you around, Henley Rose." Sliding his hands into his pockets, he strolls down the path. There's a bounce in his step that wasn't there before.

I don't know whether to scream in frustration or run after him and climb him like a flagpole.

I settle for kicking a mound of sand. The wind catches it, and the scattered sand pelts me in the face. "Ack," I splutter.

After taking a minute to compose myself—and shake sand out of my hair—I amble down the path to where the other passengers are congregated in a tree-ringed clearing. The "post office" is actually a whitewashed barrel with a hole cut in the middle. It's lodged in the sand next to a ruined heap of splintered wood—the remains of a much older barrel claimed by the elements.

Walsh is standing at the back of the crowd, and I make a beeline for her on trembling legs. She's staring off into the middle distance, expression clouded, but it smooths once she spots me.

"What happened?" she demands as soon as I reach her. She tucks the stack of three postcards she's been flipping through into her bag. The top one has a Seattle address; it looks like Walsh found some mail to deliver.

"I don't want to talk about it."

She pulls me to the very edge of the group. On the other side, Graeme is chatting with an elderly couple. He flashes me a knowing grin.

"You kissed him, didn't you," says Walsh.

"Shhh," I admonish, but no one's listening.

"How was it?"

How was it? Earth-shattering. Mind-blowing. Supernova central. "Fine."

"You're so full of shit."

"Walsh, I can't do this with him. The timing—"

She claps her hands on either side of my cheeks and squeezes until my lips pucker. "Stop overthinking it. He likes you. You like him. Boom goes the dynamite." She releases me with a flourish.

"You wouldn't understand."

"You're right. I reeeally don't. Nice, gainfully employed, crazy-hot guys like that are hard to find. Believe me, I know".

"Last call for postcards, last call for postcards." Gustavo's voice rumbles through the murmuring crowd.

"Be right back," I say, scuttling toward the barrel. I don't care about sending a postcard at this point, but I don't feel like subjecting myself to Walsh's inquisition either.

I pause at the rough-hewn boards serving as a writing surface next to the barrel. Rummaging through the bag at my hip, I pull out a pen and the blank postcard. I clamp my jaw and sneak a glance over my shoulder at Graeme. He's watching me. My heart flutters when our gazes connect.

Before the end of this cruise, I think you'll kiss me again. Because you want to.

Fire scorches my neck and my cheeks warm. Of course, he has to make it a challenge. Because he knows a challenge is exactly my sort of catnip. Well, too bad I never back down once a gauntlet is thrown.

There will be no kissing for the remainder of the cruise.

But after?

Maybe I'll finally give Graeme a chance.

Clicking open my pen, I scribble a note on the postcard along with my name and address. Before I can think twice, I stuff it into the barrel, inside the plastic bag filled with cards.

Maybe the postcard will take a week to find its way back to me. Or a month. Or a year.

And whenever it does, maybe Graeme will be in my life. Maybe not. Only time will tell. In the meantime?

I will not think about his lips. Or how his voice caresses my name. Or the way his forearm muscles ripple when he lifts his camera.

With only four days left on the cruise, how hard can it be?

The next two days pass in a blur of hiking, snorkeling, and pure, simmering agony. I spend every excursion with Graeme, every meal. He's polite and professional—the perfect platonic colleague. He doesn't encroach on my space and he doesn't mention our kiss.

On the surface, it seems that everything between us is back to normal.

Except it's not. It's *so* not.

His deep, rich laughter after spotting a sea turtle while we snorkeled along Isabela Island made my stomach somersault. Then yesterday, on Santa Fe Island, his hand brushed mine as we hiked beneath prickly pears down a dusty path, and it was like a burst of oxygen to a smoldering flame. I nearly combusted.

Nights aren't any better. I lay in bed, laptop open to a planning doc full of notes from my brainstorming sessions with Walsh, imagining him in his cabin on the other side of the wall . . . and how easy it would be to knock on his door.

I'm well on my way to losing the bet, and at this point, I'm not even sure I care.

When the sixth day of the cruise arrives, my jaw is stiff from clenching. It's been three days since our kiss and I'm twitchier than a thief in church. Walsh and I opt to eat breakfast outside on the covered deck. Graeme wasn't in the dining room and he's not out here either; I don't know whether to smash my plate against the wall or melt into a puddle of relief.

We spend the first fifteen minutes debriefing from the previous day. I methodically record Walsh's impressions of the cruise—what she likes, what she wishes were different, what would make her want to travel with us again.

When we're done, I pull out my notebook. The pages have filled since talking to Captain Garcia on the bridge. After picking Xiavera's brain about invasive species on the islands, I've circled words like "unique wildlife," "connecting with nature," and "wonder," but I'm still not sure how they might all fit together for a digital marketing proposal.

Walsh's phone dings. It's become so constant I barely notice it anymore. Conversations drone around us along with the hum of the ship's engine. I polish off my croissant and wash it down with a gulp of orange juice before returning to my notebook. A stiff breeze lifts the corner of the top page and I smooth it down.

Walsh nudges my forearm. "So what do you think?"

"About what?"

"You weren't listening, were you?"

"Sorry. I was thinking about work. Maybe we should add more interactive content to the website? Or maybe we could find a way to tap into influencer networks better . . ."

Walsh tips her chin and folds her arms across her chest.

I close my notebook and brace my elbows on the table. "Go on. You have my full attention."

"What are you going to do when we get back to Seattle?" she asks.

That's a weird question. "Same old. Work. Classes. What about you? Have you heard any more about those jobs you applied for before we left?"

"Nothing promising." Pursing her lips, she peers over the ship's railing to Santa Cruz in the distance. Several dozen boats bob in the bay between us and the shore, clogging access to Puerto Ayora, the largest town in the Galápagos. She taps her cell phone against one open palm.

I narrow my eyes at her. "Walsh, what is going on with you? You've been acting weird this whole trip. You're constantly on your phone and you're more scattered than usual. Talk to me."

She sets down her coffee. "Okay, fine. I—I'm not sure I want to be a massage therapist full time."

"What else would you do?"

"I was thinking of doing something that combines yoga and massage. Like a wellness coach." She frowns. "You're making a face."

"I'm not making a face."

"Wellness coach is a thing, you know."

"So is balloon artist."

Walsh pushes her chair away from the table. Its heavy wood legs screech across the deck. "Forget it."

I reach out and grasp her wrist. She jerks, and I quickly let go. "Wait, I'm sorry. I'm just not in your world of massages and wellness coaches and stuff. But if that's what you want to do, then we'll figure something out. I'm sure there are plenty of resources online. When we get back to Seattle, I'll help you. We'll come up with a plan, you'll see."

"That's what you said before." The words are so quiet I'm sure I misheard her. She turns to walk away.

"Hey, where are you going?"

Glancing at her phone, she stuffs it into the back pocket of her shorts. "Back to the cabin. We only have twenty minutes before the Zodiacs are going to shore, and I have to get ready."

I push my chair back, intending to follow her, when my phone pings with a new email. It's from James. I tap it open with a grimace.

To: HenleyE@sqadventures.com
From: JamesW@sqadventures.com
Subject: Update

Where are you with your digital proposal? Send me an update on your ideas asap.

James P. Wilcox
Chief Marketing Officer
Seaquest Adventures | www.seaquestadventures.com

"Damn it," I hiss. My thumbs hover over the screen.

I have ideas, sure. Lots of mediocre ideas. But nothing exceptional has coalesced yet. The answer is like fog—hanging resolutely on the horizon, but when I try to snatch it, it slips through my fingers.

Meanwhile, Graeme's digital storytelling efforts are racking up likes and, according to Christina, extra bookings. The passengers on board love him; Donna is practically his new best friend. I saw them sitting together in the lounge last night, and she laughed—laughed!—at something he said.

If we were on a track, he'd be so far ahead he'd be lapping me by now.

I click off my phone and toss it onto the table. If James gets cranky that I don't respond right away, I can blame it on the spotty Wi-Fi.

One thing's for sure: I have to figure out what I'm pitching for this proposal. Today. And it needs to be stratosphere-level amazing.

When we disembark at Puerto Ayora half an hour later, it's a shock to the system after spending so many days surrounded by nature. People are talking and shouting in Spanish, cars chug down the oceanfront road, and hungry gulls make a beautiful cacophony.

I step off the Zodiac and my hiking shoes thud against the pier. It's our first dry landing since the day we embarked the ship. I wiggle my toes in my cotton socks, relishing not having wet sand stuck between them.

Graeme has already disembarked; he's meandered several yards down the boardwalk and is taking another selfie video. His crisp white T-shirt contrasts with his tan, and his calf muscles flex as he walks.

I grind my teeth in equal parts frustration and desire.

"Giant tortoises today, huh?" Walsh asks, slipping her phone out of her pocket and checking the screen.

I tear my eyes away from Graeme. "Yep. Wild tortoise spotting in the highlands, then a visit to the breeding center in the afternoon. But remember, I'm going to be gone for a bit after lunch. I reached out a couple of weeks ago to our liaison in the region, a woman who lives in Puerto Ayora. We have a meeting scheduled."

"Yeah, yeah, no problem." She waves me off. "Do you think there's Wi-Fi in town?" She raises her phone in the air and takes a few steps. "Never mind. I found an open network."

I narrow my eyes at her. "You're not still talking to that Bad News Bears person, are you?"

She gives me her *none of your business* face.

My phone dings insistently in my pocket and I automatically check the notifications.

Christina

GUYS, you will not believe what happened

Tory

What??

Christina

Rick sent me a bottle of lotion

I wrinkle my nose.

Who's Rick?

Christina

The guy I went on a date with last week. The programmer. He mailed me a bottle of LOTION. To my apartment.

WTF

What kind of lotion?

Christina

Super nice actually. High end from Saks. But LOTION. TO MY APARTMENT. HALP.

Tory

How does he know where you live?

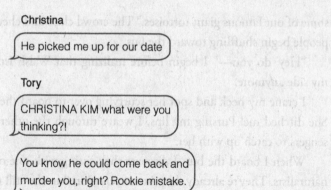

Christina

He picked me up for our date

Tory

CHRISTINA KIM what were you thinking?!

You know he could come back and murder you, right? Rookie mistake.

I find a *Silence of the Lambs* "it rubs the lotion on its skin" GIF and send it to them.

Christina

Nope. Didn't need that. Way too creeped out already

Tory

Send it back and block him

And maybe get a Ring camera for your door because *yikes*

"Attention, everyone!" Gustavo's voice soars over the crowd and I look up. He's perched on a low railing along the boardwalk, arm raised. "Our coach bus is here. I hope you are ready to meet some of our famous giant tortoises." The crowd claps and cheers as people begin shuffling toward the bus.

"Hey, do you—" I begin before realizing that Walsh isn't by my side anymore.

I crane my neck and spot her scurrying over to board the bus. She ditched me! Pursing my lips, I weave through the other passengers to catch up with her.

When I board the bus, I discover she's sitting with one of the naturalists. They're already deep in conversation, but she still manages to shoot me a smug look. I counter it with a *don't-think-you've-avoided-talking-about-Bad-News-Bears* glare. Bumping her shoulder as I pass, I find an empty row in the back and shuffle into a blue-and-orange window seat.

Outside, a handful of fishermen are selling their morning catch at a table set up near the water. I take a picture of a massive sea lion resting its head on the table next to a fisherman's elbow like a dog begging for a treat.

The chatter on the bus grows louder as it fills with passengers.

Without warning, Nikolai pops his head over the seats in front of me. I jolt. "Good morning," he purrs, but the effect is ruined when he bumps his head on the low overhead storage rack. Wincing, he rubs the spot.

"Good morning," I say politely.

"I have not seen much of you these last few days. You have not been avoiding me, have you?"

I force a strained smile. "Just busy." And avoiding him whenever possible.

Dwight is sitting next to Nikolai; I can't see him since his seat is blocking my view, but I catch his low voice, murmuring an unintelligible admonishment. Nikolai mutters something back then refocuses his attention on me.

"I wonder, is this seat taken?" He nods to the empty seat beside me, already inching out of his row.

"Actually . . ." I quickly look for an escape. Several rows up, Graeme is making his way down the aisle. I exhale in relief. "Graeme!" I call. "There you are. I saved you a seat . . . like you asked," I enunciate with a meaningful flick of my eyes at Nikolai.

"Super, thanks." The smile Graeme gives me makes my stomach muscles quiver involuntarily. "Nikolai," he acknowledges as he passes the other man.

Nikolai's lips pucker like he's just swallowed a lemon. "I hope you enjoy the turtles."

"Tortoises," Graeme corrects.

"You too," I say to Nikolai.

Swinging his backpack off, Graeme lowers himself into the seat next to me. A buzz of electricity surges between us when his knee brushes mine—warm skin on skin. I pretend not to notice.

"Thank you," I whisper.

"You're welcome." His voice is low and as smooth as melted chocolate. He shifts subtly, causing more contact. The air between us crackles with undeniable energy.

With a mischievous grin, he reaches down as though to adjust his backpack at his feet but grazes my knee with his fingertips instead. I shiver as heat pools low in my body. Since when are knees erogenous zones?

"You're cheating," I croak.

"Am I?" he drawls.

With a crooked smile, he pulls away, just enough to break our minuscule contact.

I suck in a trembling breath to steady myself before yanking my water bottle out of my bag and taking a sip. I glance at him out of the corner of my eye—he's studying me intently. Inclining his chin, he takes a Galápagos field guide from his pack and begins reading.

It's a clear reminder: the bet is still mine to win. Or lose. I can't keep track anymore which is which.

Gustavo lumbers up the aisle, counting guests. When he reaches the end, he shouts an "okay to go" to the driver. I bounce as the bus rumbles over the curb and onto the street.

It's barely nine in the morning, I've spent approximately four minutes in Graeme's company, and I'm ready to rip off our clothes and set this bus on fire.

How in the world am I going to survive the day?

20

Xiavera halts our group of a dozen passengers. Around us, the lush tropical highlands are a stark contrast to the windy beaches and arid lowlands of the rest of the archipelago. Towering scalesia trees form a canopy over the grass-covered, red-clay ground, and the air carries the fecund scent of rot and growth—the smell of a healthy forest.

Behind Xiavera, four giant tortoises loiter in the undergrowth. None of them are particularly big—the largest is the size of a cocker spaniel—but they're still incredible. Wizened heads poke out of slick, patterned shells. Cameras click all around, including Graeme's. He's standing several feet away, while I've ensconced myself between a pair of elderly women, but I don't need to look to know where he is. My body already does.

"Decades ago, this sight was not possible," explains Xiavera. "When Charles Darwin came to the Galápagos Islands, giant tortoises were plentiful, but then they were hunted to near-extinction by sailors. It is only because of intensive breeding programs that we see tortoises in the highlands today. People are the problem. But they can also be the solution."

Rolling up the sleeve of her red hiking shirt, she checks her watch. "Okay, you have an hour to explore the highlands on your own. We will reconvene at the welcome center at half past eleven."

Guests immediately peel off. Five head for the nearby tortoises, cameras poised. Two more, a husband and wife, take off at a brisk pace back toward the welcome center. Walsh is already gone, having joined a different group as soon as we got off the bus. And Xiavera accompanies two couples as they meander through the undergrowth.

And just like that, Graeme and I are alone.

I shift my weight and adjust my day pack. I could make an excuse and head to the welcome center too. Maybe find a hammer, crack open my brain, and poke around for a proposal idea, since a good one refuses to come out.

But then Graeme smiles, and I feel it down to the very tips of my toes. He sweeps his arm in a gesture of invitation.

Who am I kidding? I want Graeme's company like a drowning man wants oxygen. Even if I can't admit it out loud.

Inclining my chin, I begin walking. Graeme falls into step beside me. There are no real paths through this highland farm, so we amble between tree trunks and over roots. Soon the camera clicks and exclamations of delight from the guests fade away, and the only sounds are the soft shuffle of our shoes and the flutter of leaves on branches.

"Say 'tortoise,'" says Graeme.

Huh? I whip around to look at him, eyebrows raised, and he takes my picture. "You didn't."

His smile widens. "I did."

"You're not posting that on the company's Instagram, are you?"

He scrubs a hand across his stubbled jaw. "Hey, I'm sorry for posting a picture of Walsh. It was just so compelling—"

"Don't worry about it. All's fair in love and war."

His lips tip into a mischievous grin. I swallow thickly.

A rustle in the underbrush steals our attention and we stop walking. I gasp as a giant tortoise emerges from behind a grove of bushes not twenty yards away.

And it's not just any tortoise. It's a massive mamma jamma, nearly as big as the armchair back in my apartment. It must weigh hundreds of pounds and is probably older than the Second World War. When it stretches out its long, wrinkly neck to tear up mouthfuls of grass, the claws on the tips of its paddlelike feet leave deep gouges in the dirt.

"Holy crap," I breathe.

We venture closer, making sure to keep a respectful distance away so as not to startle it. I lift my phone and take a video. When we're about fifteen feet away, Graeme sinks to the ground.

"What are you doing?" I ask.

"Absorbing the moment."

Tugging down the hem of my shorts, I follow suit, kneeling onto the dry earth next to him. We sit there for several long minutes in companionable silence, observing the grazing tortoise, which is either blissfully unaware of or indifferent to our presence.

Graeme raises his camera. "You never told me about your parents. What's their story?" *Click.*

"A very boring one."

He casts me a sidelong look.

I crisscross my legs beneath me. Grass tickles my thighs. "My folks moved to Idaho for my dad's job when I was two. He's an engineer for the navy."

"There's a naval base in Idaho?"

"I know, shocks the hell out of most people. It's on Lake Pend Oreille. They test submarine sonar and whatnot. Pretty high-level, secretive stuff." I zoom in on the tortoise and take a picture.

"And your mom?"

"She works for the post office and runs an Etsy business on the side. Music-themed wood carvings."

"They sound like hardworking people."

"They are."

"Makes sense." When I raise my eyebrows at him, he continues. "I figured you learned your work ethic from somewhere."

Graeme draws a knee up to steady his camera and silence falls between us again.

Curiosity nibbles at me. "What was your mom like?"

His eyes flick to me and away.

"If you'd rather not talk about her, I understand—"

"She loved ABBA."

"ABBA?"

"ABBA. She knew all their songs. When I was a kid, she'd blast her ABBA CDs in the kitchen while she cooked dinner and we'd sing along at the top of our lungs. She was a terrible singer though. Really, really awful." He laughs at some private memory. "She hated the color yellow. She loved teaching, but she didn't like the politics of being a professor. She wanted to travel to Petra in Jordan more than anywhere else on earth, but she never made it there. And . . . she would have liked you."

Warmth creeps across my collarbone. "You think so?"

"Definitely. And I'm not just saying that. She met my ex years ago, and she did *not* like her. At all."

"What was the deal with your ex?"

"We dated through college. We met freshman year at Cornell and even stayed together long-distance for a while after I transferred to Michigan."

"What happened?"

Graeme unzips his backpack and stows his camera. "My mom got sick. Avery couldn't handle it. I went from carefree, doting boyfriend to caretaker. Weekends away turned into endless doctor's appointments. Months of experimental therapy. Drained bank accounts. We lasted a semester after Mom's diagnosis before it got to be too much for her to handle."

"If she really cared, she would have stuck with you."

"That's what my mom said. But it didn't make it any less hard at the time."

"What about your girlfriends after Avery?"

"There haven't been any after Avery. No one serious, at least. Women don't like to date a sob story, and I didn't really have time for a girlfriend until . . ."

Until his mom wasn't sick anymore.

"You must have been lonely."

He doesn't answer, but he doesn't need to. His deep sigh says it all. Graeme pushes to his feet. I stand too and he faces me. "I—" He swallows. "You have to understand, I was a mess after my mom died. I quit my job and shut everyone out. I barely talked to people. Barely left the house. It was bad."

Sympathy curls around my heart and I want to reach for him, gather him in my arms, but I hold myself still.

"The only reason I took the job with Seaquest was because the life insurance money ran out, and I could work from home and wouldn't have to be around people. At that point, I was completely numb. I tried to shut out the grief over my mom by closing myself off from the world. Do you want to know what finally changed things for me?"

"What?" My voice is barely above a whisper.

Dappled sunlight falls across his face, highlighting his flushed cheeks. "I met someone. She's about five-six, golden brown hair, devastating smile. The kind that warms you from the inside out. And she made me so *mad*. Not two weeks after I started the job, she called to grill me about a story I posted on Facebook. She insisted I edit it because I didn't get the wording right."

He adopts a mock falsetto voice. "'It isn't the "Panama Canal" cruise. It's "Panama Canal and the Wonders of Azuero." Fix it, please.'"

My muscles go limp and my knees nearly buckle.

Because he's talking about me.

"Finally, someone who wasn't walking on eggshells. She actually snapped at me, and it was like she snapped me out of my fog. I may have been unnecessarily combative after that, just to get a rise out of her, but I started to feel again. Irritation, at first, but then more. After a while, I began getting out of the house. Seeing a therapist. Playing hockey. I adopted Winnie—best decision ever. I actually started looking forward to waking up in the morning."

Graeme steps closer, but I'm glued to the spot. Heat sizzles through my veins when he reaches up to run his knuckles along my cheek.

"And staff meeting Thursdays? They became my favorite day of the week. Because I got to see her face."

My heart is hammering and my lungs seize. The sound of guests approaching rumbles closer, but I don't look away.

I swallow past the lump that's lodged in my throat. "After this cruise, they're my favorite day of the week too." Reaching up, I run my fingers lightly along the hand that's cupping my cheek. Graeme's eyes widen and his lips part.

Gathering every ounce of resolve I can muster, I step away just as Nikolai and Dwight crest a nearby hill. We continue through the highlands, fastening our platonic coworker facades into place. But an unspoken understanding hangs in the space between us, heavy and undeniable . . .

This just went way past any bet.

When I step off our coach bus at the Tortoise Breeding Center back in downtown Puerto Ayora, the afternoon sun sears my eyes, making me squint.

Graeme's earlier confession swirls in my brain alongside the jumbled feelings of my own heart. Since the highlands this morning, we haven't exchanged much more than loaded glances. At lunch I got roped into a conversation with some of the passengers, and he was already sitting with Gustavo on the bus when we all boarded at the restaurant.

I need to focus on my proposal, but I can't. I need to talk to someone. I need to talk to Walsh. I look around—she's standing by the bus, texting.

"Hey." I nudge her, and she nearly jumps out of her skin. I frown. "Are you okay?"

Slipping her phone into her back pocket, she waves me off. "Of course."

"You're not. What's going on?"

"Nothing."

I brace my hands on my hips. "Who is Bad News Bears? Is it Miles, that bartender who gave you his number a couple weeks ago?"

She makes an exasperated sound. "You're like a dog with a bone. No, he's just some guy I met. Super hot."

"But?"

She rolls her eyes. "You know the type. Emotionally unavailable. Flaky. But did I mention super hot?"

I'm not buying it. The way she's looking away and shifting her weight—it's like that time she borrowed Mom's car and brought it back with "just a scratch." And the scratch ended up being the bumper dangling half off.

"Walsh—"

"Excuse me, Henley Evans?" A petite woman wearing a red Seaquest Adventures polo taps me on the shoulder.

"Oh, Analisa, hi." After the highlands, I'd completely forgotten about our appointment. "Thanks for meeting with me."

"Of course, it is my pleasure." Her Spanish-accented voice is as warm as a sunbeam. Her dark hair swishes around her chin and she stretches up to give me an air kiss on the cheek. "I was delighted to hear that one of our marketing managers is visiting." She peers behind me. "And you must be Graeme. I received your email last night."

My mouth falls open as Graeme steps even with me.

"It's nice to meet you," he says. Analisa air kisses him on the cheek, too.

Wait a second. It was *my* idea to contact Analisa. *My* meeting. A tick starts in my jaw and I curl and uncurl my toes inside my shoes.

Graeme's smile falters when he catches my expression.

Analisa spreads her arms wide. "Well, this is exciting! Two office staff here on the same day. Are you ready for a private tour of the breeding center? My husband works there and I volunteer for their outreach events—"

"I'm sorry to interrupt," says Graeme. "But was this tour already scheduled for Henley?"

"Yes, is that okay?" says Analisa. "I thought it would be easiest to combine our meetings and give you both a tour at the same time. Then we can talk more about our operations in the region and I can answer any questions you may have."

My muscles relax a fraction. Graeme didn't know about my meeting and reached out to Analisa independently. It looks like great minds think alike.

Graeme shifts his weight. "I don't know. I don't want to intrude . . ."

"It's fine," I chime in. "No problem."

Analisa looks between me and Graeme and then to Walsh, who's edging away. I grab her arm and tug her back over. "Analisa, I'd like you to meet my sister. Walsh, this is Analisa Mendoza. She's our regional liaison for the Galápagos."

"A pleasure to meet you. Would you like to join us as well?" she asks Walsh.

Walsh shrugs one shoulder, shaking her head as she looks between me and Graeme. "I—I don't want to interrupt . . ."

"Come on, you're not interrupting," I say.

"Please," Graeme offers.

My sister's cornflower eyes meet mine, and her perky facade cracks. For an instant, I see uncertainty—vulnerability, even— swimming beneath the surface. I furrow my eyebrows.

One of the younger guests jogs over. She's about our age and is traveling with her parents, if I remember correctly. "Ready, Walsh?" She nods toward a group that's already started walking toward the breeding center.

"Yeah, I'll be right there."

Grinning, the young woman rejoins her family.

"I'm good, thanks anyway," Walsh says to Analisa before inclining her chin toward me. "Meet you after?"

"Definitely." We have at least two free hours this evening to explore the town. It'll be the perfect chance for us to talk.

Walsh flashes me a thumbs-up before she scurries over to join the departing group.

Analisa claps her hands. "Okay then, let's start the tour."

We begin walking down the paved sidewalk toward the breeding center. Hitching his bag higher on his shoulder, Graeme leans over to murmur in my ear. "Are you *sure* you don't mind that I'm tagging along?"

My phone weighs heavy in my pocket, the first task on my to-do app blazing in my mind.

Task #1: Defeat Graeme Crawford-Collins.

Even now, he's scuttling my shot at gaining an advantage. I scheduled this meeting with Analisa two weeks ago, while he only thought of it at the last second. I wanted to get an insider's look at the breeding center and pick her brain in private about the region. I needed this boost.

But excluding Graeme would be a shitty thing to do. He has every right to meet with Analisa, same as me.

"No," I say. "It's fine."

His eyebrows shoot up his forehead.

"Really."

After searching my face for several heartbeats, he spreads his supple lips in a grin—lips that only three short days ago were pressed against mine. "Okay then."

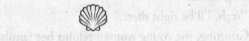

Analisa's tour is a whirlwind. After the outdoor enclosures, which are full of adult tortoises of various species and surrounded by throngs of visitors, she leads us through quieter areas closed to the general public: juvenile rearing pens (baby tortoises, squee!) and research buildings.

Through it all, Graeme and I engage in a silent dance of nearness and retreat. I touch his forearm to point out a bright yellow warbler hopping on a stone wall behind us. He grasps my elbow to lead me around a mud puddle obscuring the path. But each time, we pull away before the proximity can pull us under.

I listen intently to Analisa, and we both pepper her with questions. She leads us through lab after lab, and we stop in one that's filled to the brim with cases of creeping, crawling insects.

"*Hola, mi querido*," she calls to a lanky man with gray-streaked blond hair who's hunched over a microscope.

When he spots Analisa, his craggy face splits into a grin. "G'day, love. This is a nice surprise." He tugs her into his lap and gives her a lingering kiss on the cheek.

My own cheeks warm. Not that I'm opposed to a bit of light PDA, but these two are so clearly to-the-moon-and-back in love with each other that their mutual affection is blinding.

"Friends of yours?" He nods at us.

"No, these are my colleagues. I told you I was giving a tour today, remember? It's why I asked for this." She lifts the dangling access badge from around her neck.

Smacking his forehead, the man stands and sets Analisa on her feet again. I notice his T-shirt for the first time: it's distressed gray and reads Entomologists Fear No Weevil. I suppress a snort. "Right. I'd forget my own head if Analisa didn't remind me. I'm Doug, her husband."

He extends his hand and we make our introductions.

"Dr. Douglas Shaw," she corrects, lifting her chin with pride. "One of the preeminent entomologists in the Galápagos."

"I take it you're not from here," says Graeme.

"You think?" Doug barks a laugh as he motions at his own ruddy complexion. "I'm an Australian import, mate."

"What brought you to the Galápagos?" I ask, leaning against the table behind me. Something buzzes near my ear and I peer over my shoulder. A case full of flittering ladybugs is sitting on a shelf directly behind my head.

He flashes a wide, bucktoothed grin. "Love and bugs."

Analisa chuckles. "Mostly bugs."

"All love," he says softly, wrapping an arm around his wife's shoulders and tucking her into his side. "I never thought I'd leave Australia, but it turns out I'd follow this woman anywhere."

My throat tightens reflexively and I cough to clear it. I don't look at Graeme. "Why the ladybugs?" I ask. "They're not native to the Galápagos, are they?"

Graeme meanders over to Analisa and they begin chatting.

"Ahh, no, they're not. Excellent observation." Doug taps a finger against the side of his wide nose and strides over to the container of ladybugs. "These beauties helped us fight a nasty invader a few years back called the cottony cushion scale. But don't be fooled by the name, the destruction those buggers caused was anything but cute and fluffy."

Reaching to a higher shelf, he pulls down a clear container the size of a shoebox. Inside, an insect that looks like a white, fuzzy squirt of toothpaste clings to a leafy twig.

"They attach themselves to woody plants and suck the sap, draining their vitality. They hitched a ride to the Galápagos years ago, and it was a disaster. So many of the plants here are endemic, found nowhere else on earth, and species on entire islands were in decline. So we brought in a secret weapon: the cottony cushion scale's greatest enemy."

With a flourish, he flips the lid on the ladybug enclosure, reaches in, and scoops up a single ladybug with his finger.

I lift my eyebrows. "Ladybugs?"

He holds it out to me, and I let it crawl onto my knuckles. I giggle at the ticklish sensation of tiny legs scurrying over my skin.

"Right-o. Ladybugs naturally attack cottony cushion scales. After we released them in quantity on the affected islands, the scales weren't a problem anymore and endemic plant populations recovered."

Grinning, I gently brush the ladybug off my wrist back into its plastic home. As Doug shuts the lid and returns the case to its spot on the shelf, I stroll over to the microscope he was looking through when we came in. "What are you working on now?"

"Ahh," he says, his voice dropping. "A problem we haven't found a solution for, I'm afraid." Pulling a tray toward me, he lifts the cover off. I recoil reflexively.

A featherless baby bird with gray sightless eyes is lying on the tray—dead. Next to it, a petri dish contains what looks like half a dozen fat brown grubs.

"What happened to it?"

"An invasive parasitic fly called *Philornis downsi*. It lays eggs in the finches' nests and when the larvae hatch, they suck the blood from the baby birds, killing them. The finches, many of which are highly endangered, have no defense." He shakes his head sadly. "We're currently studying the best methods to eradicate the flies."

"Any promising results?"

"Some. But the funding isn't there yet."

"So you're looking for donations?"

He nods heavily. "Always." He flashes a sideways smile at me and a dimple appears on his rough cheek. "It's too bad we can't solicit donations from your cruise-goers. After experiencing the natural treasures the Galápagos have to offer, they might like to support our conservation work."

Every muscle in my body freezes. I don't even breathe.

That's it.

The hazy kernel of an idea that had formed during Xiavera's

early-morning hike on Floreana pops into existence like a flood of hot, buttery kettle corn. Her words from earlier today echo through my brain like a bell.

People are the problem. But they can also be the solution.

I suddenly know exactly what I'm pitching for my proposal. Except it's more than a marketing scheme. So much more. It's a total realignment. My heartbeat ticks upward like an accelerating metronome and I whip off my daypack and dig for my notepad.

"Ready to go?" chirps Analisa. "You still have a few hours left to explore Puerto Ayora. There's a fantastic recycled art gallery in town, and of course you must visit the fish market—"

"Can I talk to you for a minute?" I pull Analisa into the hallway.

Less than ten minutes later, I have a plan. A wonderful, crazy, pie-in-the-sky plan. But there's no time to waste. I'll need every available second between now and when the last Zodiac returns to the ship to get the initial details ironed out.

"Ready?" Graeme asks, hooking his thumbs under the straps of his backpack.

"I'm going to stay here. I have some things I need to talk over with Analisa. Doug too. You go on ahead."

"I know that gleam in your eye. You're onto something, aren't you?"

"Maybe."

"Should I be worried?"

"Ehh. Maybe just a little bit."

Concern flashes across Graeme's features before it melts into resignation. He offers me a small but genuine smile. "Good luck. Not that you need it."

"Graeme, I need all the luck I can get."

My lungs tighten as I watch him murmur his goodbyes to Doug and Analisa and push through the lab's swinging door and out of sight, but I shove any longing I feel deep down and lock it away.

It's go time.

Turning to Analisa, I square my shoulders. "First things first. Can I borrow your office?"

21

"Where have you been?" Walsh appears beside me holding a half-empty cocktail when I emerge on the observation deck. Tables and chairs have been brought up and spaced at intervals, while a buffet dinner is being set up in the middle. The ship rocks gently in the evening breeze.

I tuck a lock of hair behind my ear. "Working."

"I thought we were going to meet up after the breeding center?" Hurt flashes across her features, but it's gone in a blink.

Groaning, I close my eyes. "Crap. Walsh, I'm so sorry. I completely forgot."

Pursing her lips, she waves me away. "It's fine. I figured you got busy or whatever. I bought you these." Tilting her cheek, she fingers a pretty blue bead dangling from her ear. "The beads are made by a local artisan out of recycled paper. But because you ditched me, I'm keeping them."

My gut twists. "Sounds fair." Snatching Walsh's drink, I take a long gulp. It's a watery gin and tonic. She tries to take it back, but I polish it off in two more swallows, ice cubes rattling.

She smacks my arm. "You just drank my backwash, you twat."

I shrug and set the empty glass on a tray full of discarded glasses a few steps away.

Walsh leans against the metal railing behind her, the hem of her flowered maxidress floating around her ankles. "I saw you with Graeme today. Did you guys talk?"

Clasping my hands, I lean against the railing next to her. "Not exactly." Automatically, I search for him in the crowd. My nerves hum and I lick my lips. I wonder what he'll think of what I'm about to offer the guests. It'll give away the direction of my proposal, but it can't be helped. I need the trial run.

"Are you really still worried about this promotion?"

"Not as much as I was before. I had a brainwave at the breeding center."

"Good! See? I knew everything would work out. Now quit worrying so much and ask that man very politely if you can sit on his face."

I roll my eyes. Face sitting aside, I *do* still need to tell him what I want. It's been three days since we kissed. Three days of professional veneer slapped over simmering, bubbling attraction. And it's not fair for me to keep him dangling.

Do I want him?

The answer flashes in brilliant Broadway neon. *Yes!*

But the practical angel on my shoulder tuts and pushes the Coke-bottle glasses up her nose. *Okay, smart girl. What happens if you two get hot and heavy and then you get the promotion?*

He'll stay in Michigan. I blow out a long breath. Long distance can work though . . .

Ha! You barely have time to date a guy in your own city. Like you could make long distance happen. And if he gets the promotion, he'll move to Seattle, but your career dreams will be dead.

At least I'd get a consolation prize.

Scrunching my nose, I let out an irritated huff.

Why can't anything ever be easy?

At least the weight on my chest that was the gaping void of

solid ideas for this proposal has lifted. My throat is scratchy from all the talking I've done today, and I haven't even fully fleshed out this idea yet.

"Hello, earth to Henley!" Walsh snaps her fingers under my nose.

"Huh?"

"I said you'll have a chance to talk to Graeme tonight."

"Why? What's tonight?"

"I've arranged for some very special after-dinner entertainment."

I cut her a sideways look. "What?"

Walsh's crystal nose piercing twinkles in the waning light along with her eyes. "It's a surprise."

Oh God. I can only imagine. "Did you clear it with Gustavo?"

"He gave me the green light. He thinks it'll be fun for whoever wants to join."

"As long as it doesn't conflict with what I already have planned."

"What do you have planned?"

Doug and Analisa emerge onto the observation deck wearing khakis and matching T-shirts with stylized giant tortoises emblazoned on the front.

"You're about to find out," I mutter to Walsh before striding over to them. "Hi! Thanks for coming." I graze my cheek against Analisa's as I give her an air kiss.

"Thank *you*," says Doug, shaking my hand enthusiastically. "You don't know what this means to us."

I nod in acknowledgment. "I think Gustavo wants us over there." I point to the benches set along the bow of the ship. My thighs quiver as we weave through the crowd. Unlike Graeme, I don't mind getting up and talking in front of people, but my nerves still tingle with anticipation.

When we arrive at the designated spot, Gustavo is there to greet us. After a flurry of hellos and last-minute logistics, he picks up a microphone and steps onto a bench so he towers above the crowd.

"Good evening, good evening," he says, his voice booming through the outdoor speakers set beneath the bridge. Voices quiet and heads turn.

"Before we enjoy our outdoor dinner on this second-to-last night of our cruise, marketing manager Henley Evans has a special offer to share with you. Here she is to give you the details."

He helps me climb onto the bench before passing the microphone over and stepping down. At this height, the pitch of the ship makes my head swim, and I steady myself on the pole to my left. I wish I wouldn't have worn heels; even these platform wedges are making me dizzy. My pale pink sundress flutters around my knees and I smooth it down.

"Hello. How's everyone doing tonight?" I say into the mic.

A smattering of cheers answers me. A few guests raise half-filled wineglasses. Walsh whoops enthusiastically.

"How many of you enjoyed the giant tortoises today?"

More whoops and whistles.

"And who here spotted a Darwin's finch?"

Hands go up all over the deck.

A familiar face bobs through the crowd, drawing my attention like a homing beacon. Graeme edges toward the front until he's standing not ten feet away. He's wearing slim navy pants and canvas loafers, and his short-sleeved white shirt is unbuttoned at the top. Grinning, he lifts two fingers in a sexy salute before tucking his hands into his back pockets.

My mouth goes dry. I swallow thickly. "Wildlife like the giant tortoises and Darwin's finches are what make the Galápagos Islands special, and we want to keep it that way. Scientists are working hard to preserve these unique species to ensure they survive and thrive for generations to come.

"For those of you who may feel moved to support such conservation efforts, Seaquest Adventures would like to extend a special offer. For every hundred dollars you donate to the research station, we will enter you into a monthly drawing to win a free cruise. So if you donate two hundred dollars, you will receive two entries. Five hundred dollars, five entries, and so on. And anyone who donates five hundred dollars or more today will become an inaugural member of our Conservationist Club, which includes benefits such as advanced sales on new cruise itineraries and access to special discounted travel."

Guests murmur to one another. Graeme's muscles go lax and his arms fall to his sides. Lips curving upward in wry understanding, he drops his chin in a heavy nod.

He gets it. What I'm proposing is a substantial shift toward ecotourism. A philanthropic initiative like this can become a cornerstone of our marketing in the region, including digital. It can help us stand out as a company that cares about giving back, not to mention entice people to support a good cause and potentially travel on a future cruise with us as a result.

When Graeme looks up at me, his eyes blaze, but not with anger or jealousy.

With pride.

Warmth seeps through every cell of my body, down to my bones.

"Donations can be made through your shipboard account; no checkbook needed. Just fill out one of the cards located on the dining tables and give it to any staff member. We also have two special guests joining us for dinner tonight: Dr. Douglas Shaw, a scientist with the research station, and his wife, Analisa Mendoza. Analisa is one of our staff members and an outreach volunteer. They're here to answer any questions you may have about how your donation dollars can make a positive difference."

Hoisting himself up onto the bench next to me, Doug waves to the crowd before hopping down. Analisa twirls her arm in the air.

"Thank you for letting us share the wonders of the Galápagos with you, and for considering supporting conservation efforts in the region. And with that"—I look to Gustavo, who gives me a thumbs-up—"dinner is served."

Excited murmurs break out through the crowd as staff carries the last of the hot serving dishes to the buffet. The spicy aroma of barbecue permeates the air and my mouth waters. Switching off the mic, I twist sideways to step carefully off the bench, but between the pitch of the ship and my platform heels, I stumble as my feet hit the deck.

A firm hand catches me by the waist and warmth expands from the spot. "Brilliant," murmurs Graeme, taking the mic from me and returning it to its case.

"You think?"

Something wistful flashes behind his eyes, a hint of worry, and then it's gone in a blink. He nods. "I see the marketing potential. But more than that, you're doing something good for this place, and that's priceless."

"We'll see," I mutter, rubbing the goose bumps from my forearms.

"What did James say? I assume you had to get permission from him before making an official offer to the guests."

A waiter comes by with a tray of filled wineglasses. I pick out a white wine and Graeme snags a red. I take a noisy gulp. I did indeed call James today from Analisa's office. That had been a fun conversation. After a lengthy inquisition about my big-picture plan, James was silent for so long I thought my heart would implode. But then he spoke.

"If you really feel this is your best idea, fine. Try it."

At least he threw me a bone by offering to loop in all the necessary office staff on his end so I could focus on immediate logistics with Gustavo and the ship's accountant. I take another sip of wine to cover my ambivalence over how much to tell Graeme.

"Now, now," I say, wagging my finger. "I won't give away my secrets to the competition." I force a weak chuckle.

Graeme steps closer, eyebrows furrowing. "Is that still how you see me?"

"Yes . . . and no," I whisper. I lift my chin and our gazes lock. The chattering noise and movement around us fades away and we're the only two people on the ship.

All I see is Graeme's face—the stubble dotting his jaw, his soft, angular lips, his ever-so-slightly crooked nose, and the fan of dark lashes framing his ocean-blue eyes. All I feel is the overwhelming pull to eliminate the distance between us. All I hear is the beating of my own heart.

A plate shatters somewhere across the deck and reality comes careening back. I shake my head to clear it.

"No more work talk." My voice wobbles but my grip is sure when I raise my wineglass.

Eyeing me, Graeme clinks his glass against mine, the sound clear and piercing as a bell. "Agreed. What do you want to talk about?"

I glance around for inspiration. "How delicious dinner smells?"

"Buffet time?"

"Let's hit it."

We each fill a plate with food. Graeme gets held up at the far end of the buffet when a couple of guests begin chatting with him. He lifts his chin toward the tables in a *go on ahead* gesture.

I make it all the way to the table where Walsh is sitting before realizing that I forgot to put dressing on my salad. Pulling an about-face, I weave back through the throng of guests toward the buffet but get stuck behind a particularly stocky, slow-moving passenger. He digs a serving spoon into the tray of barbecued pork, scooping and rescooping until he has the perfect mound. Donna's voice cuts through my irritation.

"Graeme, there you are."

"Good evening, Donna. You're looking lovely tonight."

I peek around the edge of the guest, who is now resolutely poking around a plate of potatoes. Donna and Graeme are at the end of the buffet. They don't see me. I jerk my head back and listen.

Donna *harrumphs*. "I have something I want to say to you. This request for donations . . ." she begins.

I brace myself for impact.

"I think it's wonderful."

My fingers go slack and I nearly drop my plate.

"Charles and I are so happy to have the chance to do something good for this place. Thank you for giving us the opportunity."

"You're welcome, although you really should thank my colleague, Henley. This was all her idea. She set all the wheels in motion."

"Oh. Well. Be sure to tell her thank you from us."

I'm almost at the end of the buffet now, and I slink away through the crowd before Graeme and Donna can spot me.

Tears burn behind my eyes and I have to take a deep, steadying breath. The fussiest passenger on the cruise loved having the chance to support conservation in the Galápagos. And Graeme made sure she knew it was *my* idea.

I'm still fighting back a wave of emotion when he joins me at the table not a minute later.

"What?" he asks, when he catches the look on my face. His expression is one of honest puzzlement; he doesn't know I overheard him.

"Nothing." I pick up my fork, but put it down a heartbeat later. "Thank you," I add.

"For what?"

"For what you said to Donna just now. I overheard you talking."

Reaching under the table, he gathers my hand in his and squeezes it. I don't want him to ever let go. "You're welcome."

After several long seconds he pulls away. We tuck into dinner. Crew members come around with bottles of wine, topping off glasses, and the volume of happy chatter rises. At the next table over, Doug and Analisa are sitting with a handful of the oldest guests. Doug's hand covers hers on the table, his thumb stroking her knuckles. What easy tenderness. Why can't things be easy with Graeme?

I swallow a bite of pork.

Why *can't* things be easy with Graeme?

Maybe I need to do what Walsh suggested and simply focus on the now. So what if I don't know how things will turn out tomorrow or the next day? It doesn't change the way I feel about Graeme right now, in this moment. And he said he's willing to keep any relationship between us quiet. It comes down to . . . do I trust him?

Yes. Undeniably.

As plates empty and glasses are refilled, the ocean swallows the sun in a wash of hazy purples and pinks. Another glass of wine later, someone taps my shoulder.

"It is time for us to leave," says Analisa from directly behind me. "Thank you again for everything." She brushes her cheek against mine.

Standing, I edge around my chair and lower my voice. "How did it go?"

"Astounding. Absolutely astounding," Doug chimes in. He hands me a stack of donation cards. His eyes are wide and almost dazed, and I don't think it's from the wine.

I flip through the cards, scanning the checked-off amounts.

$100
$500
$200

I gasp. *A thousand dollars.* From Donna and Charles Taylor. My heart is so full it nearly bursts.

"Oh my God," I murmur.

"And those are just the responses from our table," says Doug.

How much money did we raise? If the other tables were half as engaged as this one, tonight proves my idea is *gold*. Wild laughter edges up my esophagus, but I shove it down. Cackling like a madwoman and jigging on the spot isn't exactly the most professional response. A tendril of guilt creeps into my heart then. If this lands me the promotion, Graeme stays in Michigan. Alone.

I can't think about that right now. I won't.

"I'm so happy your conservation work resonated with our guests," I say.

"You have no idea how much this means to me—to us. And to the finches. Thank you." Doug shakes my hand with both of his. "Maybe we can do it again on some other cruise?"

"I hope so." If everything works out according to plan, we'll be doing it on every cruise.

Doug and Analisa depart with a final wave. Before I can turn around, however, Nikolai appears in front of me.

"Good evening, my—"

"It's time!" Walsh launches from her chair.

"Time for what?" I ask.

Walsh flashes me an enigmatic smile as she picks up her fork and taps it against her water glass. "Can I have everyone's attention, please?" she calls out.

The guests on deck quiet.

"For anyone who's looking for a little after-dinner entertainment, make your way to the lounge. We're having a lip-sync battle."

22

My jaw nearly crashes through the floor and sinks the ship. "I'm sorry, what?"

"Lip. Sync. Battle," she enunciates. "I originally wanted karaoke, but Gustavo didn't want us to use the mics. Lip-sync battle is the next best thing."

"And why exactly do you think this is a good idea?"

"Look around," she says.

The response is overwhelmingly positive. Lots of wide smiles and enthusiastic nods—from the under-forty set at least. Some of the older guests chuckle and wave a no-thanks, but they still beam indulgently as they make their way to the stairs and presumably back to their cabins. Even Donna is smiling. The mood is one of revelry, and I find my muscles loosening and nerves buzzing.

Graeme pushes back from the table and stands as well. "Will you lip-sync?"

"Nah, I'll probably watch," I admit. "But it sounds fun. You're not going to do it, are you?"

He flashes a self-deprecating grin. "Crowds still aren't my thing."

Nikolai sticks his finger in the air. "What is this 'lip-sing' battle?"

Walsh steps between Nikolai and me and loops her arm through his, leading him toward the stairs. "Lip-*sync*. It's where a song is played and you have to mouth along to the words, but you don't actually sing. Dancing is optional. Dramatic flair is required." Her voice drifts off as they descend the stairs toward the lounge. God bless Walsh for running interference.

"Shall we?" Graeme offers his arm.

I hesitate for only a heartbeat before taking it. His skin is warm to the touch and his glorious scent makes me want to nuzzle my face in the crook of his neck. I edge closer, but not too close. We still have to keep up professional appearances.

The lounge is crackling with anticipation when we arrive. Roughly three dozen guests are sprinkled throughout the room—mostly women, but a few men too. Boozy, happy conversations punctuate the space. Graeme steers me to one of the curved navy sofas that ring the central dais and we sit. Across the room, Xiavera is directing Walsh on how to plug her cell phone into a set of speakers concealed in an AV cabinet.

"She really has a knack for this," says Graeme, jerking his chin in Walsh's direction.

"A knack for what?"

"Connecting people and bringing out the fun, like how she led yoga on the beach the other day. The guests love her. What does she do again?"

"She's a masseuse and soon-to-be yoga instructor."

"She'd make a good shipboard spa coordinator."

Huh. "She would."

Nikolai's friend Dwight ambles over and sits next to me on the sofa. We all exchange pleasantries.

"Anybody want anything from the bar?" Graeme asks.

Dwight shakes his head with a murmured thanks. Graeme looks to me.

Oh, what the hell. "Pinot grigio."

"You got it." The smile he flashes as he stands has my toes curling and my stomach tumbling.

Dwight leans over as soon as Graeme's gone. "He's not a bad guy, you know," he drawls.

I whip my head in Dwight's direction. "Who now?"

He nods at Nikolai. "He tries too hard." Across the room, Nikolai edges closer to Xiavera and casually attempts to rest his elbow against the wall of cabinets. He slips, nearly stumbling into her before nailing the pose. "Way too hard." Dwight chuckles. "But he's a good egg. Some people simply insist on learnin' their lessons the hard way."

Hooking an elbow over the sofa back, I twist to face Dwight more fully. "You two are good friends, aren't you?"

"I know it's hard to believe, but we actually have more in common than you might think."

There's something disarming about Dwight. Like a favorite uncle who always has a smile in his pocket and a story to share. I find myself grinning. "Like what?"

"Well, we both love classic horror movies. And the ferocious purr of a muscle car. Nik comes over every Sunday to help me work on my '69 Mustang, even though I know he has better things to do." He chuckles softly. "I think he likes to distract me. You see, I haven't talked to my son in over five years . . . not since I came out with what he likes to call my 'lifestyle.' He's a pastor at the fastest-growing Baptist church in Odessa. Having an old queen like me for a father would scandalize the church, you see."

Scrunching my eyebrows together, I squeeze Dwight's leathery hand. He gives me a genial pat. "And with Nikolai's parents still in Russia, and immigration being what it is, he hasn't been able to get the necessary approval to bring his family over. I guess you could say we're just two lonely souls looking for completion."

With a wry shake of his head, he crosses one slim leg over the other. "It's amazin' how a first impression of someone can completely change once you get to know them."

Isn't that the truth.

Licking my lips, I peer over my shoulder to find Graeme. He's thanking the bartender, a glass of wine in each hand.

Somehow, in the course of a few short days, Graham Cracker-Collins has become simply Graeme: the person who makes my heart rap-a-tap-tap whenever I even think about seeing him, and the biggest surprise of my life.

Walsh bounds onto the platform in the middle of the room. "Who's ready for a lip-sync battle?" she croons like an announcer on WWE.

Cheers erupt throughout the room. The sofa cushion next to me sinks as Graeme returns and extends a wineglass toward me. When I take it, our fingers brush. Holding my breath, I slide my index finger over his thumb in a slow caress. It's a small gesture, something no one else would notice. But it's like I've snuck a sip of brandy from my dad's liquor cabinet. It's illicit, fiery, and delicious. Graeme's chest visibly expands and the heat in his gaze could melt icebergs.

"Now . . ." Walsh continues. Graeme lets go of the glass and I take a shaky drink of wine. My head is pleasantly fuzzy, and the crisp alcohol slides down my throat like silk. "How this will work is contestants will battle in pairs—best lip-sync performance, as judged by the audience, wins. Judging criteria shall include enthusiasm, lyrical accuracy, and, if you've got 'em, sweet-ass dance moves." Raising her arms above her head, she swings her hips side to side to a chorus of whoops from the crowd.

Something niggles at the corner of my brain. Walsh is certainly basking in her element as ringmaster, but there's something . . . not quite right . . . with her. Like her energy is more manic, more frenetic than usual. Maybe it's the gin and tonics.

Walsh spreads her arms. "Who wants to go first?"

The room quiets for a heartbeat before Nikolai leaps forward. "Me. I am first."

I suppress a groan.

Nikolai jogs up to Walsh. After a brief murmured conversation, he turns and walks straight out of the room. I exchange a puzzled glance with Dwight.

"Buckle up, people," says Walsh with a wry shake of her head as she taps her phone.

The opening line to Right Said Fred's "I'm Too Sexy" blasts through the lounge. And Nikolai makes his entrance in full hip-thrusting glory.

He struts around the room, mouthing the words to the song, and runs his hands through his thinning hair. When he hops onto the dais and turns in a circle, light glitters off the metallic threads in his T-shirt. He swaggers and sways and shakes his moneymaker with enough enthusiasm to power a merry-go-round.

I want to squeeze my eyes shut but I can't look away. My gut is somersaulting in secondhand embarrassment, but he's not embarrassed at all. Not with the look of utter glee on his face.

Pointing his finger, he scans the crowd until he stops . . . on me.

Dread settles in my stomach like a stone and I barely keep myself from bolting.

Sure enough, he dance-skips over to our couch until he's gyrating on the other side of the cocktail table. Thank God for that little round table.

Except then he props his sneakered foot on the table. And pumps his hips.

In my face.

Graeme's face too, because he's sitting right next to me in the direct line of fire.

I flatten myself into the sofa, but sadly, it doesn't swallow me up. I push back, back, back as Nikolai's hips sway forward, forward, forward like a wrecking ball inching toward destruction. To my right, Graeme is watching Nikolai with a clamped jaw. On my left, Dwight chortles and shakes his head.

The middle-aged women behind us scream—not cheer, *scream*—as he air-humps along with the beat.

Finally, *finally*, Nikolai lowers his foot.

I exhale in relief, but then he shimmies even closer, fingers clawing the air like a cat, his lips moving in sync with the lyrics. When he's standing inches away from my knees, he lifts the hem of his shirt . . .

No.

"Yes!" someone screeches. "Take it off!"

Just as he lifts his shirt to reveal his marshmallow abs, the music fades out.

"Okaaaay, that was quite something. Let's give it up for Dr. Kozlov," Walsh shouts over the smattering of applause. A quick glance around the room confirms what I suspected: most of the audience is as shell-shocked as I am, with the group of rowdy women behind me forming Nikolai's fan club.

Nikolai raises both arms like a conquering hero. He reaches for me—presumably to grab my hand—but Graeme blocks him by clamping his own hand over mine. I flash him a small, grateful smile.

With a half shrug, Nikolai blows me a kiss as he sashays around the cocktail table and collapses onto the sofa on the other side of Dwight.

Walsh steps forward. "That's a tough act to follow. Who wants to take that on?"

Heads swivel, scanning the room.

Graeme shifts beside me . . . and stands. "Me."

I stare at him, mouth open. But he hates getting up in front of people . . . and this isn't like saying a few words at the safety briefing. It's a whole other level.

He takes three long gulps of wine, sets his glass on the table, and winks at me from over his shoulder. The ladies in the lounge grin and elbow one another.

Walking over to Walsh, he whispers something in her ear. She beams and scrolls through her phone. When she nods, he strides to the dais and stands in the very center, facing me. Spreading his legs shoulder width apart, he forms a circle with his fingers and thumb and brings it to his mouth as though he's holding a microphone. Walsh scurries over to fill his vacated seat and plops down next to me.

I lock eyes with Graeme. The lounge speakers crackle. With a grin that makes me tingle all the way to my toes, he drops his chin to his chest.

The opening refrain to ABBA's "Take a Chance on Me" pumps through the speakers. And my heart bursts like a piñata.

Graeme holds completely still, only his lips moving in time with the lyrics. Then as the backup vocals join, he lifts his chin to meet my eyes. His heel bounces in time to the rhythm. The instruments surge. His eyes gleam. And his movements swell with the music.

Whereas Nikolai was all shimmying shoulders and gyrating hips, Graeme's dancing is understated, subtle.

And sexy as *fuck*.

Heat rises through my body like steam escaping a vent.

A stained glass window doesn't need fancy curtains. And a perfect male specimen like Graeme doesn't need *look-at-me* dance moves to ooze sensuality. A swirl of his hips does the trick.

Graeme rocks rhythmically back and forth and thumbs his chest during the refrain. When he rolls his hips in time to the music, my mouth goes dry and a shiver zings down my spine. He channels the enthusiasm of Tom Cruise and the carnality of Patrick Swayze. He's Jake Ryan, Patrick Verona, and Clark Kent rolled into one. An Adonis mouthing the soprano words to the iconic 1970s disco pop musical group.

And through it all, his eyes never leave my face.

Walsh clutches my forearm in a *holy shit* grip.

Guests murmur to one another, shooting me covert glances.

I don't care.

Because my inner thirteen-year-old is squealing so hard right now I could rip a pillow. He's putting himself out there, sacrificing his pride—for me. I barely notice when Walsh lifts the tilting wineglass from my slack grip and places it on the table.

The second verse arrives, and Graeme falters. His smile wavers as he seems to register the bevy of enraptured guests for the first time. A flush spreads across his cheekbones.

I stand.

My mouth automatically forms the lyrics I know by heart. I extend an arm toward him . . .

His chest rises and falls for a breath before he smiles, eyes shining. He takes my hand and pulls me onto the dais and straight into a twirl.

And then we're alone. The lights go black except for the spotlight above us. The crowd fades away. There's only the sway of the ship, the swell of the music, and the energy rising between us.

Take a chance on me.

We begin to move, only our palms touching. We're in perfect sync, mirror images of one another. I let the music fill me and I channel every ounce of giddy joy filling my lungs.

He slides me in front of him, my back to his front, allowing me to take the lead. I cartwheel my arms from hip to hip, fluttering my fingers in a thoroughly cheesy move. Graeme mirrors a beat behind me. I dip and shimmy side to side and mouth the lyrics, peering at him over my shoulder as he sways opposite me.

Strong fingers grasp my hip and Graeme spins me to face him. We move together in time to the music.

I devour every angle and curve of his face. I bask in the ecstasy seeping through my veins and the pull between us and even the apprehension tugging at the threads of my heart—I bask in it all. Because I'm here and I'm ready to take a chance . . . on Graeme.

I lose the flow of the lyrics and my mouth stops moving. His lips still as well and his eyes blaze. I slide my hands up to his shoulders. I'm swaying in his arms. We're close, his lips inches from mine, but it's still too far . . . I rise up on my toes . . .

The music changes abruptly. Bass notes strum a different disco beat.

Walsh leaps to the center of the platform. "Dance party interlude!"

Several guests cheer as they stand, already dancing their way toward the center of the room. I blink rapidly, realizing that, no, the lounge lights haven't dimmed, and we've been dancing together on brightly lit display for a third of the ship this entire time. Nikolai frowns with crossed arms, but Walsh shimmies over to him and pulls him up and into the dancing crowd. From behind his back, she mouths "Go."

I look up at Graeme. Nibbling my lower lip, I tilt my head toward the door. "Want to get out of here?" I murmur.

His eyes flash like sparks as his fingers tighten around mine. An audible sigh laced with a growl radiates from his chest. "Hell yes."

23

We're not three steps from the lounge when Graeme pushes me against the wall, crushing his lips against mine. The song Walsh chose to cover our getaway filters into the hall: "Don't Stop 'Til You Get Enough." My lips curl into a smile against Graeme's.

"I win," he breathes.

"Technically," I murmur between kisses. "You kissed me. So I win."

"It's a tie."

"Deal."

His fingers tangle in my hair and I moan as his tongue dips into my mouth. We're all teeth and lips, hunger and heat. It takes me several breaths to realize a metal handrail is digging into my lower back.

Pushing at his chest, I disconnect. We're alone here in the hall-way at the top of the stairs, but that could change at any second. The last thing I want is Gustavo catching us making out like a couple of horny teenagers. He's still James's eyes and ears, and I can't afford to forget that.

"Cabin?" My words come out in a raspy pant.

Swallowing thickly, he nods.

We fly down the stairs, and I can't repress the giggle of pure

joy that bubbles up in my throat. He doesn't ask the question—
your cabin or mine?—because the answer is obvious.

Mine is closer.

We barely make it through the door before we're on each other
like duct tape. I reach behind me to flip the lock. My back careens
off the wall as he presses his body against mine. Moaning, I run
my fingers underneath the hem of his shirt and up his corded abs.
His muscles quiver under my touch.

"We have to keep this quiet," I murmur against his lips.

I feel him nod.

"I don't want anyone to know. Not until after the promotion
is decided."

"You got it." He kisses me again and alternates thrusts of his
tongue and hips with a soft, sensual slide. A hint of sweet with
the strong. His soft lips are a stark contrast to the firmness of his
body and the abrasion of his stubble. Heat swamps me and I roll
my hips forward, urging him for more, faster, but he doesn't re-
lent.

"I've wanted this for so long," he murmurs, trailing kisses
down my neck. Every glide of his lips sends a jolt of lust straight to
my core.

I can't lie anymore. "Me too." Pressing my face against his
chest, I kiss the exposed skin above the top button of his shirt. A
sparse smattering of hair tickles my cheek as I nuzzle him.

His chest expands. "Really? Since when?"

Taking a step back until my hips are anchored to the wall, I
reach behind me to unzip my dress. Without looking away, I tug it
down until it pools on the floor at my feet. All I'm wearing are
heels and a pair of white lace panties. His gaze devours me whole. I
shiver.

"Since the first time you said my name on the phone. I almost spontaneously combusted." Taking his hand, I bring it up to cup one of my breasts.

He moans deep in his chest. Curling over me, he drags his thumb across my pebbled nipple.

I gasp.

"Ever think about me naked?" he murmurs.

"Every night since we boarded the ship."

"Good enough for me."

He's on me again, and there's nothing gentle or tentative about it. We are pure, unbridled need.

My fingers tremble as I work the buttons down his chest. Partway through he becomes impatient and jerks his shirt over his head. Threads pop and something pings against the closet door. He drops his shirt and I nearly trip on it as we stumble over to my bed.

He lands on the mattress first, with me tumbling on top of him. Shooting out a hand to brace against the wall, I straddle his lap.

Skin. So much glorious skin. Diverting from his lips, I suck in a noisy, snuffling breath at the crook of his neck. I'm about as graceful as a truffle-sniffing pig. "God you smell good. I want to eat you up."

"Right back at you." His voice is raw, molten promise. Scooping me up, he flips me over so I'm underneath him. The ship rocks us in a gentle embrace, but the heat between us is an inferno. He thumbs the strap of my shoes over my heels and flips them off. One lands with a resounding *thunk* on the floor. The other clatters onto the desk at the foot of my bed.

I want to feel more of him. *Need* to. Reaching for his pants, I unbuckle the top button. My knuckles brush his arousal and he rolls his hips with a groan. His lips descend down my rib cage as his fingers edge along the lace trim of my underwear. I shudder when his fingers hook the elastic.

A knock from somewhere over Graeme's shoulders startles us both to stillness. We look at each other, Graeme peering at me from where he's hovering over my belly.

Someone knocks on my door again, more insistent this time.

I fling my head back into the pillow. "Are you serious?"

Graeme groans like he's been punched in the gut.

Scrambling out from under him, I kick my dress under the bed, dive for the robe in the closet, and yank it on. I glance back at Graeme. What if someone sees him? We still need to keep this—us—under wraps.

Holding open the door to the bathroom, I motion toward its crisp, cold interior. "Please?"

With a nod, Graeme lumbers off the bed and in the general direction of the bathroom. "Don't take too long," he murmurs as he slides past me.

Before he can turn away, I place both palms on either side of his face and bring my lips to his in a burst of a kiss. My body screams not to stop, but I force myself away.

"Two minutes," I mouth as I quietly shut the door.

Cursing all the gods in the heavens, I tromp to the main door and open it a crack.

Nikolai Kozlov is standing on the other side.

His smile falters when he catches sight of my expression. I imagine it's thunderous. My nether-kitty yowls and hisses at this interruption. "Can I help you?" My tone is curt, but I can't help it.

"Yes." He nods like a bobblehead. Sweat gathers along his receding hairline. "Since I met you five days ago, I have developed strong feelings for you. You are beautiful and charming and I want to know if maybe you would—"

"Stop. Please, stop." I pinch the bridge of my nose. "Look, I'm sorry if I've given you the wrong impression. I don't have those kinds of feelings for you."

Hurt flicks across Nikolai's face, but he smooths it away. He braces his forearm against the wall next to my door. "Are you sure? I am like vodka. It is, on first taste, not everyone's favorite. But after a few sips, you may find you like it." Waggling his eyebrows, he leans closer.

"No!" I explode. "I really don't know how to say this any more clearly. I'm not interested. Please leave me alone." I enunciate each word so it's sharper than a dagger.

Nikolai takes two stumbling steps back. "Oh, I . . ." He sniffs. His shoulders quiver.

"Are you okay?"

"Yes, yes I'm——" A wet snuffle escapes him. Tears slip from the corners of his eyes and trickle along the side of his long nose.

"Are you *crying*?"

He answers me with a noisy sob.

Great. I made a guest cry. "Here. Just, get in here." I yank him by the arm into my cabin. Every ingrained instinct screams, "*Don't let a strange man into your cabin!*" and not only because staff aren't allowed to have guests in their cabins. But this is Nikolai. I believed Dwight when he told me he's not inherently terrible. Misguided and a wee bit goofy? Yes. A dangerous predator? Well, you never really know about people (men), but in this case, I'm willing to wager a no.

Besides, Graeme is hiding in the bathroom merely a few feet away. All it'd take is one scream and he'd come running.

Graeme. My thighs clench together and my heartbeat stutters. I need to get Nikolai calmed down and out of here. Stat.

I steer Nikolai, who is trying—and failing—to hold back his

flood of tears, toward the two beds. I intend to sit him down on my bed, but Graeme's shirt is lying conspicuously in front of it, so I turn Nikolai at the last minute and push him down onto the edge of Walsh's unmade bed instead.

With my back to Nikolai, I snag Graeme's shirt and stuff it under the desk before picking up a box of tissues and offering it to him. He plucks one out with a wobbly nod and blows his nose. The sound reverberates through the cabin like a tuba.

"I am so sorry," he says, crumpling up his tissue. "I know my personality can be strong. Perhaps I have bothered you on this cruise."

"Well?" Yeah. You have.

"It is only . . . you look like her."

I sink onto the bed opposite him. "Who?"

"My ex-fiancée, Emily." Dragging his wrist across his nose, he digs in his back pocket and pulls out his phone. A swipe and a few taps later, he holds it up so I can see the screen.

My mouth falls open. An image of a smiling woman stares back at me—and holy Moses does she look like me. Her cheeks are a little rounder and she's built a little stockier, but we have the same long, layered haircut, the same light brown eyes, similar noses (hers has a more pronounced bump in the bridge), and the same thick, dark eyebrows.

He certainly has a type. No wonder he never gave Walsh a second look.

Nikolai lowers the phone with a last longing gaze at the picture.

"What really happened between you two?" I ask.

His shoulders sag. "I broke off our engagement, it is true. But not because she did something wrong." He swallows hard and a tear spills down his flushed cheek. "She's too good for me. I knew it was only a matter of time before she would wake up one day, realize the truth, and leave me. So, I left her first."

"Let me get this straight. You dumped her because you don't think you deserve her?"

"She is the perfect woman. She likes riding horses and singing carols on Christmas and she is the kindest person you will ever meet. Her smile could cure the world of sickness and her laugh sounds like angels." He heaves a sigh of pure misery. "How could I ever deserve her?"

"Why wouldn't you deserve her? You're a smart, successful chiropractor. You didn't hesitate to jump in and save me when I fell out of the kayak. You're like a son to Dwight. And your dance moves . . ."

He tilts his chin up, eyes wide. "Yes?"

"Well, I've never seen anything like them." Puffing my cheeks, I exhale. "Clearly, you're still hung up on her. Why all this with me then?"

Bracing his elbows on his spread knees, he hangs his head. "I think, if I could only make myself be with another woman, then maybe I forget her. If you and I—" He forms a circle with one hand and halfheartedly pumps his index finger through it. "Then perhaps I can finally break this hold she has over my heart."

With a deep sigh, he shakes his head sadly. "But now, sitting here, I realize that will never happen, because there is no other woman in the world for me except her. I've been so stupid." He lumbers to his feet and edges toward the door. "I leave you alone now. My sincere apologies."

Running my tongue along the edges of my teeth, I stand. "You need to call her."

"Why? What is the point?"

"Tell her everything you just told me. Everything that's happened."

"Everything?"

"Everything."

"Even the . . ." He pistons his arms like he's kayaking.

"Yep."

"And the . . ." He shimmies his shoulders.

"Uh-huh. I mean, you don't need to tell her you were hitting on another woman. Just be honest about your feelings."

"What if she hates me? What if she wants me to be shot by firing squad and my limbs dragged to the four corners of the earth by wild horses?"

I wince. "She might." His face falls. On an impulse, I grip his shoulder. "But you love her. That's obvious. And if you love her, you need to tell her. You don't want to spend the rest of your life wondering 'what if.' If you're honest with her about your feelings, even if she says it's over for good, at least you'll know you tried."

A spark of hope lights behind his brown eyes.

"Here," I say, twisting around to open the drawer to my nightstand. "Take my staff Wi-Fi card—I get them for free. Use it to call her."

He takes the card from my outstretched hand like I'm offering him the keys to redemption. Bringing the card to his lips, he kisses it. "Thank you, Miss Evans. I will never forget your kindness."

I cast a glance at the bathroom where Graeme is still hiding—waiting. Impatience wells in my gut and I steer Nikolai across the cabin with a friendly, but firm, pat on the back. "Don't mention it." I pause, looking him in the eye. "Really, please don't tell anyone you were here. Let's keep this between us."

Nikolai places a hand over his heart. "I promise."

Just as my fingers close around the door handle, a knock reverberates through the thick metal.

I jump, and bump into Nikolai, who stumbles.

The knock sounds again. "Miss Evans?"

It's Gustavo.

24

"Shit," I whisper, backing deeper into my cabin.

"Is there a problem?" Nikolai asks.

My heartbeat quickens and I can't seem to catch a breath through the boatload of *mayday, mayday* barreling through my system.

Gustavo can't find Nikolai in here, he just can't. Staff isn't allowed to have guests in their cabins, and he already has the wrong idea about Nikolai and me. Maybe if we stay very quiet, he'll go away . . .

Fanning my fingers, I hold perfectly still and stare at Nikolai, who stares back with wide, confused eyes.

Silence.

I begin to exhale, when . . .

Knock, knock, knock.

"Miss Evans? Are you there?"

"Are you going to answer?" Nikolai asks in a low voice.

I shake my head so rapidly I swear I can feel my brain bouncing around my skull. I swallow. "No," I whisper. "See, I'm up for a promotion, and if my boss finds out I had a guest in my cabin, that's it for me. Game over."

"But it is innocent. We are not doing anything untoward," he says.

"It doesn't matter. The appearance of impropriety is enough, believe me."

Based on the insistent pace of knocking, Gustavo's not going away. I pace the cabin. *What to do, what to do . . .*

I gnaw the inside of my cheek. "Can you keep a secret?"

He nods solemnly. "Yes, of course."

"Good."

I open the bathroom door. Graeme is sitting on the closed toilet lid, chin propped on his fist. His look of anticipation fizzles into pure *what-the-flying-fuck* when he spots Nikolai, who hops back, fists raised.

"He was here whole time?" Nikolai asks.

I steer Nikolai inside the bathroom. "Yeah, clearly."

Graeme springs up and steps into the open shower to make room for him. The snug bathroom is barely big enough for one person, let alone two full-grown men. Graeme's eyebrows knit together. "What's going on? Why is he here?"

I put my finger to my lips, then pump my hands toward the floor. "It's Gustavo. He's at the door. He wants to talk."

"Now?" Graeme whispers.

Nikolai looks between me and Graeme like he's putting together a puzzle. "Everything makes so much more sense now. You two *are* together. Felicitations."

Gustavo's fist pounds my door.

"We'll talk about it later. Sit tight, okay? And try not to kill each other," I add in a mumble before flicking off the bathroom light and shutting the door.

Rubbing the tension from the center of my chest, I take a deep, steadying breath before hitching a smile on my face and cracking open the door.

Gustavo is standing on the other side. "There you are, Miss Evans."

"I'm sorry, but you caught me at a bad time. I was just getting ready for bed." I pull the lapel of my robe tighter at my collarbone. "What's up?"

Gustavo steps forward and I have no choice but to step backward. Edging into my cabin, he peers around the empty space. Sweat gathers between my shoulder blades when his gaze lingers on the bathroom, but with no light seeping from under the door, his attention quickly moves on.

"I wanted to give you the good news myself. I have tallied all the donation cards. You raised over sixteen thousand dollars for conservation in the Galápagos." His lips crack into a beaming grin as he extends his hand to shake mine. "Congratulations."

My jaw slackens and I stumble backward with the pitch of the ship. Sixteen *thousand*?

Victory barrels through my chest. I'm so happy I could hug Gustavo . . . whoop with joy . . . I could . . .

Crash! A shattering noise reverberates from the bathroom.

My heart stops and my eyes widen in horror.

Gustavo casts a sharp look at the bathroom door. "Is there someone else here?"

"What?" My voice is about an octave too high to be sincere. "No one here but me," I add in a deeper register, except now my voice is so low I sound like the herald of Satan. Get it together, Evans. I clench my jaw so tight I could splinter steel.

Gustavo's eyebrows raise.

"I mean, no one besides Walsh. She's taking a shower," I lie.

He frowns. "That is . . . not possible. She is still in the lounge doing her lip-sync battle. I saw her not a minute ago, on my way down from the bridge."

"Ahhhh," I croak. Words have left me. I try to swallow, but all moisture has been zapped from my mouth.

A toilet flushes and the bathroom door opens. Graeme walks out—still shirtless. He quickly closes the door behind him.

"Good evening, Gustavo. Can we help you with something?" Strolling over to me, he puts his arm around my shoulders.

Gustavo blinks. "Oh. *Oh*. No. I had no idea . . ."

Graeme tightens his hold on me. "Well, now you do. Although if you could keep it to yourself, we'd appreciate it."

Every muscle tenses and my jaw quakes.

"No rules against two staff members . . ." He clears his throat and laughs uncomfortably. "I will leave you to your evening then. Congratulations again on your achievement, Miss Evans."

I nod mutely and watch as Gustavo leaves.

Grinning, Graeme turns to me, but his smile slides off his face like sap when he catches my expression. He reaches for me, but I step back.

"What did you do?" I growl.

He frowns at me. "I salvaged the situation."

"By outing our . . . our . . . whatever this is to the cruise leader?"

"Henley, I just didn't want you to get in trouble for bringing *him* into your cabin. What were you even thinking?"

Nikolai chooses that moment to shuffle out of the bathroom. He winces. "I made the noise. I'm sorry, it is my fault."

A floral bouquet of pear, lime, and lemongrass wafts through the room. I sniff the air. "Did you spray my *perfume*?"

He raises both palms. "Not for me. I remember your perfume is very nice. I thought Emily might like it as well, for an apology gift. I spray a small squirt, to remind me of the smell. Then *he* tried to take it from me and I dropped it in the sink."

"And that was the noise you heard," Graeme finishes.

Marching to the opposite side of the cabin until I'm standing between the two beds, I crush my fists to my temples and squeeze my eyes shut. I've reached my limit. "Please leave."

Nikolai doesn't have to be told twice. With a murmured "Good night," he retreats. The door closes quietly behind him.

As soon as he's gone, I storm over to the desk and yank Graeme's shirt out from under its murky depths. I shove it at him, right in his bare chest. "You too."

He blinks at me. "Are you honestly mad at me right now?"

"I didn't want Gustavo to know about us. You knew that. And you just announced it like it was nothing."

Graeme yanks on his shirt. "He won't tell James."

"Do you know that for sure?"

"We're not breaking any rules."

"And when has that stopped gossip from happening? James will find out, and everything will be ruined. I know it." I'm so angry I'm shaking.

Graeme paces the cabin. "Why are you so afraid?" he explodes.

"Because this is my career, my life." I wrap my arms around my stomach to keep the nausea at bay. "I was wrong about us. This was a mistake. It's like Sean all over again." My words are barely above a whisper, but they slice a gaping hole in my chest. I can't move. Every breath is a knife in my breaking heart.

"I'm not Sean!" Graeme roars. "Yes, I told the cruise leader about us. But not because I'm an asshole. I did it to *save* you, Henley. Because it was the only one of two options that didn't involve you breaking any company rules."

A tiny voice recognizes the truth in his words, but it doesn't matter. Because my career at Seaquest is over. I know it.

Nostrils flaring, Graeme closes the distance between us in three strides and grips my upper arms. His movements are jerky but his touch is gentle. Inhaling deeply through his nose, he closes his eyes briefly. "This is sad. I'm sad for you, Henley. You deserve to be happy, and you're never going to be happy working like a draft horse with nothing and no one else in your life."

A fissure forms somewhere deep down inside me. A web of cracks creep and spread. Anger bubbles up—a thick, viscous mortar. I rip my arms out of his grasp.

"Like you're one to talk." My thighs tremble as I stagger to the far side of the room. "How are all your friends, huh? Oh wait, you probably wouldn't know because you've walled yourself off from everyone. I saw the Instagram comment from your cousin about 'nice to see you back in the world.' And you want to lecture me about isolation? You've been hiding under a rock."

He jerks like I've slapped him. A dark cloud settles over the room. The ship groans as it crests a wave and dips into a trough. I grab Walsh's headboard to steady myself. We're both breathing hard. Any desire between us has burned up like a shooting star crashing to earth.

Graeme's voice is flat when he finally speaks. "You act like you're the only one with a stake in this game. You're not. I understand how this"—he motions between us—"complicates everything. But I was willing to give it a try. Because I care about you, Henley. But maybe I was wrong to."

His words hang in the air, waiting for me to bat them down, to argue. I don't. Chin trembling, I suck in a deep breath and harden my heart. "Maybe you were."

Graeme's shoulders slump as his chin falls into a heavy nod. "Okay then." He walks out.

And I'm alone.

I'm still awake when Walsh stumbles into our cabin two hours later.

The tears have dried on my cheeks, leaving salty tracks in their wake. I roll over when she clicks on the desk lamp.

"Why are you here?" she asks. "Scratch that—why are you here *alone*? Where's Graeme?"

"He left." My voice is rougher than a nettle patch.

"Trouble in paradise?"

"It was never paradise. It was a mistake."

"Please. Any straight man who can sing ABBA is a keeper," she slurs. Something rattles in her hand—a glass filled with ice and clear liquid. Lurching as the ship pitches, she takes a swig before setting it on the edge of the desk along with her cell phone, which she fishes out of her cleavage. Fumbling with the cord, she plugs it in to charge.

"Don't worry, you'll have plenty of time to work it out when we get back." Grasping handfuls of her dress, she pulls it up and over her head and lets it fall on the floor on her way to the closet.

"How do you figure that?"

She exhales, her shoulders sinking. "I'm not going to live with you."

I sit up higher in bed. "Where will you go?"

"Back to Boulder," she says, pulling on an oversized T-shirt.

"I thought you were done with Boulder."

"It's like a velvet-lined pit. I try to climb out, but I slide back in."

A warning buzzes in my brain, cutting through the tumbling grief. "What's this about?"

She doesn't answer me. Instead, she disappears into the bathroom.

I swing my legs out of bed. "Walsh," I call. When I pass the desk, I pause. I can smell the booze from here. Lifting the glass, I sniff and take a tiny sip. Fire burns my throat and my face scrunches. "Holy shit." It's straight-up gin with maybe a splash of tonic. How much did she drink tonight?

Her phone lights up with a new text. Two more pop up in quick succession. All of them are from Bad News Bears. I pick up her phone with unsteady fingers.

> Come on, baby. You know I'm the only one who appreciates you. I'll always take care of you.

> You just have to be nice to me. No more talking back and no more sneaking off to Seattle.

> Come back and all will be forgiven. I promise.

I reread the texts three times, my stomach hollowing out. I try to swipe open her phone, but there's a pass code. I tap out the code she set years ago, but it doesn't work. She's changed it.

Unplugging her phone and grasping it in my trembling fist, I swing open the bathroom door. Walsh jolts as she wipes her mouth with a towel, her toothbrush and open tube of toothpaste sprawled on the vanity next to the sink.

"You lied to me. Bad News Bears is Keith, isn't it? You're still together."

She spots her phone and tries to snatch it from me. I hold it away from her.

"That's none of your business."

"Tell me."

"Give it back."

"Walsh," I plead.

"Yes, it's Keith, okay?" She grabs her phone from my slack grip. Swiping it open, she shoulders past me into the cabin as she reads the new texts. Her flushed cheeks pale. "It—it's not what it looks like."

I hug my arms to my chest. "Oh no? So what is it then?"

"You wouldn't understand."

"What wouldn't I understand?"

"I'm hard to live with."

"You don't think I get that?"

"I—I don't have anything going for me. I dropped out of college. I can't keep a job or even get one now, and I'm broke. Keith . . . he doesn't care about all that. He's there for me."

"He condescends to you. '*Don't talk back to me*'? '*Don't sneak off to Seattle*'? Who the hell does he think he is? He acts like he owns you. Is that how he talks to you all the time?"

Sinking onto the bed, Walsh pulls her knees up to her chest. "He doesn't mean it. He's not a bad guy, he just gets angry sometimes . . ."

Ice fills my veins. "What does he do when he gets angry?"

She turns her face away.

I sink onto the floor in front of her and grip her knees. "What did he do, Walsh?"

She lifts and lowers one shoulder. "He threw something at

me. It was the first time he lost control like that. Usually, he just yells."

"What did he throw?"

"A dinner plate. It smashed against the wall," she mumbles.

My chest tightens and I can barely breathe. "Walsh, that is a very big deal."

She shifts as though she's going to stand, but I duck my face, forcing myself into her field of vision.

"Talk to me. Please. What happened?"

"I cut my hair." A tear spills down her cheek and she dashes it away. "He doesn't like it when I make big changes and don't consult him first. I knew that, and I still got the haircut anyway. And when I got home, he got mad. Honestly, I should have known better."

Rocking back on my heels, I stare at her in openmouthed horror. I thought maybe he'd cheated on her, or vice-versa, and that's why they broke up.

I didn't think it was anything like this.

"He apologized right away. In fact, he's been sending me apology texts every day since. But it scared the crap out of me, and that's why I left."

I pull myself up to sit next to her on the bed. "Look at me." She doesn't move. I grab her arm and shake it. "Look at me." Her head pivots and her wide blue eyes meet mine. "Keith is an abusive, controlling asshole. He thinks *he* gets to decide when and how you cut your hair? No. He doesn't. And I bet he also has strong opinions about your clothes, friends, and the way you spend your free time, doesn't he?"

Snuffling, she nods.

"Walsh, that's *abuse*. And he was escalating. If you stayed with him, he wouldn't have missed next time. He would have hurt you."

"I don't know . . . he's been so apologetic. Like what he did scared him too . . ."

I gather her hand in both of mine and squeeze. "No." I shake my head. "He's not sorry. He's only sorry you got wise to him and left. Abusers don't stop. If you go back to him now, he *will* hurt you, I promise." My voice cracks and I swallow a wave of emotion.

Her face scrunches and her eyes dart wildly. "But what if I fail and can't hack it on my own? What if I can't get a job or help you pay rent or—"

"Walsh, you have *me*. I will always be there for you, no matter what. You don't need him."

A sob escapes her in a hiccup.

"You're right," she croaks. "You know deep down, I think I knew what Keith was all along. What does that say about me?"

"No, no you couldn't have known," I say, but she keeps going.

"I mean, he was just so charming. Taking me to expensive restaurants all the time. Helping me pay my rent. He made me feel special. But on the other hand, nothing I ever did was good enough. He always found a way to tear me down. But then he'd do something so over the top, like invite me to move into his penthouse apartment or buy me a thousand-dollar pearl necklace and I'd think I was crazy for ever feeling like he wasn't such a nice guy."

"Because he's a master manipulator. You are so brave for leaving him and I am so proud of you for recognizing the danger you were in. Don't ever talk to him again. Never, okay? In fact, here." Gently, I pry the phone from her bloodless fist. Working slowly so she can see exactly what I'm doing, I tap through the necessary set of commands.

With my thumb hovering over the screen, we lock eyes. After three shaky breaths, she nods. I tap block, and Bad News Bears disappears. Hopefully forever.

"There." I drop her phone onto the bed beside me. "That man is poison. And you deserve so much better."

Walsh's chin quivers as tears cascade down her pink cheeks. "Henley . . . you have no idea how much I needed to hear you say that."

We both completely dissolve. Gathering her in my arms, I rub slow circles up and down her back as she sobs against my shoulder. My own tears fall, trickling into my hair.

"How did I not know about any of this?" I whisper.

Walsh swipes a wrist across her nose. "Because it's hard to get a hold of you. And sometimes, even when I do . . ." She trails off.

"What?" I urge.

"Well, I feel like I'm talking to a robot. Like you're only half there because you're thinking about the next thing to check off your list. 'Talked to Walsh—check. Now time to feed the cat.'"

My jaw loosens and guilt floods me like a tsunami.

Because it's true.

I can't remember the last time I talked to Walsh where I've been 100 percent focused on her and not folding laundry or skimming emails or, literally, feeding the cat.

"I wanted to talk to you about Keith so many times. I just . . . didn't know how."

The anger and anxiety that has been holding me together since my fight with Graeme melts away, and the fissure inside me bursts open down to my soul.

Visions from our shared childhood cycle through my memory like a slideshow.

Walsh, a chubby three-year-old, crying because she fell and scraped her knee. I press a lopsided rainbow Band-Aid onto the spot along with a kiss.

Walsh, throwing her textbook across the room in frustration. She's in seventh grade and failing math. I pick up the book and carry it back to the kitchen table. I open it in front of her and pull up a chair.

Walsh, getting into a screaming match with her high school boyfriend at a New Year's Eve party. I'm visiting from college, and I tell him to get lost.

Walsh . . . fading into the background of my life. I graduate from college and move to Seattle. I find a job. I stop visiting as often. She calls, but I'm busy. Our talks are brief. She texts. I text a few words back. The years roll by and the distance between us grows. I start an accelerated evening MBA program. I work long hours. I hardly text her back at all.

Walsh is my baby sister. And I haven't been there for her. Not for a very long time.

And she's not the only person I've pushed away. How many times have I blown off Christina when she's invited me to lunch? And now Graeme . . .

"I've been a bad sister." My voice cracks. Walsh shakes her head, but I nod, my lips straining to form words through the tears. "No, I have. I'm so sorry I haven't been there for you, Walsh. That's going to change, okay? We're family, and there's nothing more important than family. I'm going to do better. I promise."

Wrapping her arm around me, she leans her head on my shoulder. "You already are."

25

The final morning of the cruise dawns as stark and heavy as a hangover.

Clouds blanket the sky as we disembark on Bartolomé, the youngest island in the archipelago and nothing more than a lifeless spit of rock. Walsh walks beside me as we climb the 372 wooden stairs leading to the top of the island.

The skin under her eyes is purplish-blue from our late-night heart-to-heart, but there's a lightness to her that wasn't there before. There's hope.

Too bad any hope for my own love life has extinguished like a bottle rocket. Three flights in front of us, Graeme climbs, his stride sure and even. My heart thunders, and not just from exertion.

"Talk to him," says Walsh. She wouldn't let me go to sleep last night until I filled her in on what happened with Graeme, so she's up to speed.

Pulling up short on a platform, I walk to the edge and grip the wooden railing. Below me, a tumble of red and black volcanic rocks leads to the sea. "It's over. I pretty much carpet-bombed any chance we had of being together."

"I have a hard time believing that."

"Believe it. I've been so caught up with this promotion that I completely lost sight of everything else. Maybe I should drop out.

Withdraw my name from the running. I need to focus on you right now."

Walsh grabs me by the forearm and whirls me around to look at her. "Don't you dare. You're Henley Fucking Evans. When the going gets tough, you pack that mother with TNT and raze it to the ground. Obstacles? No such thing."

"I need to be there for you."

"Hen, I'm not your responsibility. I appreciate you wanting to help me, and honestly right now I'll take all the help I can get. But you shouldn't give up everything for me. I won't let you. First step? Talk to that man. I've never seen you so happy as when you're with him. You practically glow. If you're in the wrong, apologize. Make it better."

Walsh is right. I owe Graeme an apology. It's the right thing to do—even if it doesn't change a damn thing.

Please let it change things. Graeme has turned out to be the most thoughtful, kind, supportive man I've ever met, and I threw him out of my life like garbage. My gut seizes and I force down a sudden swell of nausea.

I like him so much it scares me.

But then there's Walsh . . . and the promotion . . .

How can I choose? Do I have to choose? Can I really be there to support Walsh, give my career my all, *and* somehow be with the man of my dreams?

It doesn't seem possible. Especially after last night.

I swallow hard. I have to at least try to make things right with Graeme, even if it's too late. I owe it to him, and I owe it to myself.

With a stiff breeze pushing tendrils of hair from my face, I climb the final flight of steps to the dirt incline leading to the top of the island. Taking a deep breath, I shuffle over to stand next to Graeme. Wind whips my cheeks and I tuck a stray lock of hair behind my ear.

"Hey," I say, wiping my sweaty palms on my hiking shorts.

He doesn't look at me. "Hey."

"The view up here is really something," I say lamely. An untold expanse of ocean embraces the rolling green hills of neighboring Santiago Island, spreading out before us.

He cuts me a sideways look as he raises his camera.

I deflate. "Okay, scratch the small talk. I'm sorry—for what I said last night and how I acted. You didn't deserve any of that."

Nostrils flaring, he nods once. His camera clicks.

"The truth is . . . I don't know what I want right now. I learned something last night, after you left . . ." I steal a glance at Walsh, who's pointedly not looking our way. She's leaning against the railing on the stairs, gazing out at the view.

"It made me realize something. You were right about me. I am scared—of everything. I'm scared I'll lose this promotion, and I'm scared of what will happen if I don't. I'm scared of trying new things and of failure. I need to make some changes in my life. Big changes."

Something skitters under the railing to my left. It's a little black lizard with a splotch of red on its muzzle. Apparently, the island isn't devoid of life after all.

I swallow the dry lump coalescing in my throat. Graeme still won't look at me. "I—I understand if you don't want anything to do with me. I wouldn't either, if I were you . . ."

Graeme's shoulders stiffen. Behind his camera, his face is an impassive mask.

Heart crumbling into dust, I rest my hand on his forearm. "So I just want to say thank you. For everything. No matter what happens with the promotion or us or any of it, know that I'll always cherish this time with you. You are the kindest, most caring man I've ever had the privilege to know. Your resilience inspires me. I'm in awe of you."

I slide my fingers from his arm and stuff my trembling hands into my pockets. He still hasn't put the camera down. "Good luck on the promotion. For what it's worth, I think you'd make a great digital marketing director. See you around."

I turn my back just as the sun creeps out from behind the clouds, illuminating the landscape in dazzling color. At the base of the island, Pinnacle Rock, a jagged, ruddy peak, points toward the blue sky like an arrowhead.

Graeme doesn't say a word.

It's been two full weeks since the cruise.

Two weeks of meetings and the fall term starting and sliding back into the daily grind of existence. I've caught up on all my work emails, my current projects are up to date, and I'm ahead of schedule on next month's Alaska mailing.

So why do I feel so empty?

My phone pulses like a beacon from where it's tucked inside my purse. On it, hundreds of pictures from the Galápagos hover in the cloud. At least three dozen include Graeme. I run my index finger along the purse strap peeking out from under my desk. I could swipe through the photos again . . . it'd only be the fourth time today . . .

I ball my hand into a fist on my lap, forcing it to stillness.

No. I said my piece two weeks ago, and Graeme hasn't called or texted since—nothing except obligatory work communications.

His silence is perfectly clear. My chest aches and I grind the heel of my palm against the physical pain.

No more crying over what might have been. I need to face forward, especially now that I've taken stock of my life. Nearly losing my sister to an abusive relationship and falling for a guy only to drive him away changed everything. It made me realize I've been so singularly focused on my career that I've sacrificed too much—missed out on too much with the people I love.

Not anymore.

I can be career minded *and* make room for meaningful experiences in my life. Even if it doesn't include Graeme.

Shaking my head with an exasperated moan, I open the PowerPoint presentation of my digital marketing proposal: thirty-two slides of persuasive data laid out in rich, numbers-supported glory.

"Girl, are you still tinkering with that?" Christina's voice rings out from behind me. She's standing in my cubicle, a light jacket pulled tight around her to chase away the hint of autumn hanging in the air. "I thought you already shared it with Barb."

"I did, this morning. Well, I sent it to James. He wanted to see it before I formally presented it to him. I'm just proofreading," I hedge.

"I told you, this promotion is in the bag. Your idea to start a conservation initiative in the Galápagos is killer. James is going to love it, you'll see."

I force my lips into the semblance of a smile. "Yeah." At least Gustavo never told James about finding Graeme in my cabin—that's one less roadblock to this promotion. My jaw tenses at the reminder that Graeme had been right.

Christina leans a hip against my desk. "Tory and I are headed to lunch in a few. Want to come?"

"I'd love to, but I'm already booked. Lunch with Walsh. How about a rain check? What are you doing after our soccer game on Saturday?" I finally let Christina talk me into joining her rec league. Even after two weeks, my muscles are still stiff from the new level of exercise.

She drops her chin and her dark eyes twinkle. "Can't. Date night with the new man."

"Ooo, is this Nerd Glasses or Man Bun?"

"Nerd Glasses. Now I know what you're going to say. His Bumble profile was sooooo dorky, but I don't know, he just seems . . . nice."

I suppress a sigh. There is *so* much to be said for "nice." "Brunch on Sunday to debrief?"

"Only if I'm not up too late the night before." She clicks her tongue twice and points her index finger at me like she's shooting a pistol. "I'll text you."

"Sounds like a plan."

When she leaves, I check the time on my phone. Half an hour until lunch with Walsh. The photos folder beckons, but I text her instead.

> How was therapy today?

Not twenty seconds later, my phone buzzes.

> Super. I had a breakthrough . . . I think I finally hate Keith!

> YES!

I text her a meme of a kitten gleefully firing a machine gun, Rambo-style.

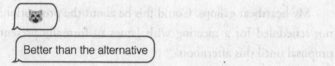

Better than the alternative

A chill creeps down my spine and I pull my sweater tighter around myself at the prospect of what could have happened.

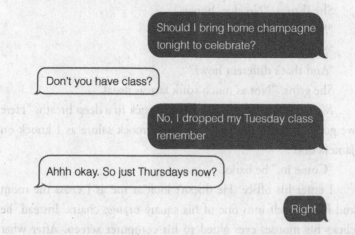

Should I bring home champagne tonight to celebrate?

Don't you have class?

No, I dropped my Tuesday class remember

Ahhh okay. So just Thursdays now?

Right

Reducing my course load meant I'd extend my degree program by a couple of semesters, but what would I get in return? Sanity. Balance. And sweet, sweet free time to spend with the people most important to me—like Walsh. My phone buzzes again.

Let's pop the bubbly then! Except make it sparkling cider because I have an early morning yoga class tomorrow.

Atta girl.

"Evans," a voice barks behind me, and I nearly drop my phone. James is scowling at me from over my cubicle wall, his ruddy cheeks barely clearing it. "My office, ten minutes."

My heartbeat gallops. Could this be about the promotion? I'm not scheduled for a meeting with James to formally present my proposal until this afternoon.

Eight minutes later I'm standing at Barbara's desk, a notepad, phone, and pen tucked against my chest. "Do you know what this is about?" I murmur.

She shrugs. "No clue, honey."

"Mood?"

"Smug."

"And that's different how?"

She grins. "Not as much stink face as usual."

My shoulders relax a fraction as I suck in a deep breath. "Here we go," I mouth. Barbara gives me a mock salute as I knock on James's door.

"Come in," he barks.

I enter his office. He doesn't look at me as I cross the room and fold myself into one of his square orange chairs. Instead, he clicks his mouse, eyes glued to his computer screen. After what feels like an eternity, but is probably only ten seconds, he removes his wire-framed glasses and tosses them onto the desk.

"I've reviewed your and Graeme's proposals—" he begins, but a familiar voice from the phone on his desk cuts him off. My breath catches.

"Excuse me, James. Henley, I'm on the line too. Just wanted to let you know."

"Graeme," I acknowledge. My voice cracks and I clear my throat.

James squeezes his pale lips into a thin line. With deliberate slowness, he picks up his glasses, wipes the lens with a cloth he pulls from his shirt pocket, and settles deeper into his leather office chair.

"As I was saying, I've reviewed your written proposals and I've reached a decision. Graeme, congratulations. You're our new director of digital marketing."

"What?" I splutter. "I thought I'd have a chance to present—"

"That was before I read your proposal. Henley, what was your assignment?"

I swallow the bile rising in my throat. "To come up with a way to use digital marketing to increase sales for cruises in the Galápagos."

"When you called me with your harebrained idea to solicit shipboard donations for a local nonprofit, I was skeptical, to say the least. I failed to see how supporting philanthropic efforts related to increasing sales. I didn't say anything at the time because I wanted to give you a chance to prove yourself. But your proposal has done nothing to convince me that this is the best use of our company's resources. It's a cute idea, nothing more."

"Are you serious? Her idea is *fantastic*, and if you can't see that—" Graeme cuts in, but I talk over him before he can say something he'll regret.

"James, shifting to ecotourism in the Galápagos would be a strong move for us. As you can see from the proposal, I've run the numbers, and—"

James smacks the desk, startling me into silence.

"You are *not* the chief marketing officer here. I am. And the last thing I want in a director, someone who reports to *me*, is insubordination. You did not follow the parameters of the assignment. Therefore, you will not get the promotion. End of discussion."

"Now, wait just a minute—" Graeme begins.

"No, it's fine, Graeme." My throat tightens, choking on the flood of disappointment. I have to cough twice before I can speak again. "I'm sorry to have disappointed you, James. Thank you for considering me. Graeme, congratulations."

I rise on unsteady legs and cross to the door.

"Don't worry, Henley," James simpers behind me. "Maybe another opportunity will arise. In the meantime, you keep that nose to the grindstone and do your job. And if you keep working like the busy little bee you are, who knows what can happen for you."

I don't look at him as I shove through the door. Barbara stands when she sees me, her smile fading into a frown of concern. "Hey, what happened?"

"I didn't get it." My voice hitches. The words echo in my brain like the gong of a mourning bell.

"Oh, honey. I'm sorry."

"It's fine. I'm fine." I'm so not fine. Oh God, the tears. They're coming. I wave off Barbara as I fight back a sob and make a dash for the bathroom.

I'm crying at work. This day could not get any worse.

Hustling down the hall, I shoulder my way into the ladies' room, which is, thankfully, empty. My heels click against the white-and-black marble as I pace the length of the room. I can't seem to get enough air. Disappointment clogs my lungs like coal dust. I take a deep, shuddering breath.

My phone vibrates from where it's pressed against my chest. Through my tears, I catch the name on my screen. Graeme is calling. A sliver of happiness threads through the pain in my heart. He won the promotion. He wanted it as badly as I did, and he got it. Shock flickers through me. I can't believe I'm legitimately happy for him.

And now he'll be moving to Seattle.

My emotions churn and froth like a whirlpool, but beneath it all, longing bobs to the surface. To hear his voice . . .

The bathroom door opens and Christina enters. I send the call to voice mail and dash the tears from my cheek. "What are you doing here? Why aren't you at lunch?" My voice is as wobbly as my knees.

Christina launches herself at me in a bone-crushing hug. "Barbara told me."

Bad news sure travels fast. Tory bustles into the bathroom behind Christina. Barbara is hot on her heels.

"Henley, I'm so sorry," Tory says, platinum eyebrows pinched. Her voice echoes in the empty bathroom.

It takes me two heartbeats to register that Christina is actually *hugging* me, a veritable first, before I squeeze her back. My tear ducts decide to swell like we're watching a Hallmark movie, and a big, fat tear rolls down my nose.

"Thanks, guys." Disconnecting, I grab a paper towel at the dispenser near my elbow and dab it under my eyes.

"This is some grade-A bullshit," says Christina.

I shrug. "James didn't like my proposal. What can you do?"

"You don't have to take it lying down," Barbara offers from beside the sink.

"How so?"

"Go over his head," she says.

"What, to Marlen?"

"Yes," Tory chimes in. "He always says at our all-company meetings that he welcomes fresh ideas from any of the staff—even though he's the CEO. What if you took your proposal to him directly? Maybe he would overrule James and give you the promotion?"

A month ago, I would have jumped at the slightest possibility of a second chance for a director role. But now . . .

"No. Screw the promotion."

Tory and Christina exchange openmouthed expressions of shock.

"Um, Henley, is that you? Or is that a brain-eating amoeba talking?" Christina asks, eyeing me like a doctor examining a terminal patient.

"Screw it," I enunciate. "This goes way past the promotion. I did something in the Galápagos, something good."

The vision of the dead baby finch, Doug and Analisa's gratitude, and the enthusiastic faces of the guests when they had the chance to give back flash through my mind and I stand a little straighter. "I'm going to Marlen, but it's not about the promotion anymore. It's about taking a stand for something that can make an actual difference in the world."

Tory nods, her cheeks bunching in a wide grin.

"How can we help?" asks Barbara.

"Well, to start, what's the best way to get a meeting with Marlen?"

"Let me work my executive assistant magic."

Barbara turns to leave but I catch her by the arm. "Barb, why are you helping me? Not that I don't appreciate it, just—why?" Barbara and I get along, but we're not exactly friends. We've never spent time together outside of work, and besides our snarky exchanges about James, we haven't really spoken all that much.

Her full lips quirk. "You remind me of me when I was younger. Before life threw me some babies and an ex-husband and my hopes for college and a fulfilling career went out the window. It wasn't my dream to be a secretary, you know. But now I get to live vicariously through you."

"It's not too late. You can always go back to school, get a degree . . ."

She shakes her head. "Don't worry about me. This is your time. Just don't give up without a fight." She strides out of the bathroom.

Christina steps forward. "What can we do to help?"

I rub my jaw as I begin pacing. "If I'm going to present this idea to Marlen, I'm not limiting myself to the Galápagos. I'm scaling up. What if I proposed the creation of a company-wide conservation initiative that touches all of the regions we operate in? A major pivot toward ecotourism?"

"Like a company-wide rebranding campaign?" says Christina.

I nod.

Tory blows out a long breath. "That's complicated. You'd need to identify organizations that we could partner with in every region, preferably nonprofits that overlap with our itineraries. Then there's the cost of handling guest donations, and the legal framework to protect us from liability. We'd have to update the website, all of our printed materials . . ."

My shoulders slump.

Tory pulls out her cell and taps the screen. "One second, let me make a call. Hey, babe," she says into her phone, and walks over to the far side of the bathroom, murmuring quietly.

My own phone dings. A notification has popped up. *Lunch w/ Walsh in 10 minutes.* I shoot her a quick text, letting her know lunch may be off and to stand by.

Tory returns and slips her phone into her back pocket. "I told Michelle about your idea, and she says she'll help. She can advise on some of the legal aspects and I'll work the numbers."

The bathroom door opens again and Barbara reappears. "I talked to Rose, Marlen's executive assistant. I got you a meeting with Marlen this Thursday morning at ten. Sorry it's so soon, but it was the only opening he had for the next two weeks."

My heartbeat accelerates. That's less than forty-eight hours from now. "Thanks, Barbara. You're the best."

"Planning meeting at your place tonight?" says Christina, pushing off from the counter and brushing her hands together. "Tory, does that work for you and Michelle?"

"Of course."

"Barb, you in?" she adds.

Barbara nods. "Wouldn't miss it."

Three pairs of eyes study me expectantly, and I find my own misting. "You don't know how much this means to me." Lips quirking, Tory wraps an arm around me just as Christina does the same. I return the hugs. How did I get so lucky to have such good friends? "Tonight it is."

My phone buzzes from my pocket. Walsh is calling. I answer. "Hey—"

"Hey yourself! What's going on? What happened to lunch?"

"I found out about the promotion. I didn't get it, but I'm moving to plan B. Christina, Tory, and some others are coming over later to help me prepare a presentation for our CEO."

"Are you okay?"

With my sister by my side and my friends at my back . . .

"You know what? I am."

26

My tiny apartment has never been so full of people. Noodles has claimed a spot on Michelle's lap, snuggling against her adorable little baby bump as she points over Tory's shoulder at something on her laptop. Walsh is in the kitchen refilling water glasses, Christina is sprawled in my armchair, flipping through a legal pad, and Barbara is sitting at the bistro table in my kitchen, entering notes into my PowerPoint presentation. Her phone rings, and she answers it.

Pressing my fists into my lower back, I arch my spine from where I'm sitting on the floor. In front of me, a notebook filled with highlighted scribbles fans across the coffee table next to two mostly empty pizza boxes. We've been at it for three hours, but I feel like we've barely scratched the surface of my idea. Panic threatens to claw up my throat, but I shove it down.

I got this. *We* got this.

Barbara pushes back from the kitchen table, chair legs screeching against linoleum, and stands. She hitches her tote bag over one shoulder. "I've got to run."

I furrow my eyebrows at her harried expression. "Is everything okay?"

She rolls her eyes. "It's Maya, my youngest. She was supposed to catch a ride home with another player after her volleyball game tonight, but she forgot to tell me that her ride was out sick so now I have to pick her up."

Standing, I force the tension from my shoulders and give her a quick hug. "Thanks so much for your help."

"No problem. This is what you have to look forward to with teenagers, by the way," she adds to Tory and Michelle. "Enjoy those baby years while you can."

"Oh, we will," says Tory, gazing lovingly at her wife as she caresses her rounded tummy.

Barbara's footsteps retreat from my apartment and the door closes with a click behind her.

"So, these numbers look good," says Tory, returning her attention to her computer. "Especially if you propose piloting your program in the Galápagos, British Columbia, and Hawaii first, then scaling up over the course of two years."

Christina flips her head upside down, and when she rights herself, gathers her long sheet of hair into a high ponytail. "This could be revolutionary, you know. There aren't many other cruise companies our size doing anything like this."

"Not to mention it has the potential to make a wide-scale impact. If even half of our travelers choose to contribute modest amounts, that can make a big difference," Tory adds.

A knock reverberates from my front door. Frowning, I stride down the short hallway to answer it. It's Barb.

"I forgot my phone," she croons, squeezing past me to bustle into my kitchen.

"So why didn't Henley's gremlin of a boss go for her idea?" Walsh asks. She carries two glasses of ice water into the living room, setting one on the trunk beside Christina and handing the other to Michelle.

I shrug. That's the million-dollar question.

"Because he didn't think of it first," Barbara calls before hustling out of my apartment again.

"He's definitely threatened by Henley," says Tory, her normally cheery voice flattening.

Christina nods emphatically.

"When it comes to smart, ambitious women, mediocre men usually are," says Michelle.

Before I can sit, someone knocks on my door again. Barbara.

"Coat," she says, smacking her palm against her forehead. I scramble into the kitchen, pluck her navy trench coat off the back of the chair, and hand it to her. With a thanks and another round of goodbyes, she leaves.

I carry my laptop over to the coffee table and resume my seat on the floor. My phone buzzes from somewhere by my slippered feet. Patting around, I find it and swipe it open. Three missed calls from Graeme. I sigh. Nothing new—those are from earlier. He and I have been playing phone tag today, and the last time I tried him a few hours ago it went straight to voice mail. I wince, remembering the bumbling message I left him full of "congratulations" and "I'm happy for you."

And I am happy for him. My stomach fills with warmth at the thought of working alongside him, hearing his voice, seeing him every day . . .

Too bad he wants nothing to do with me. At least not in the way I want.

I scan my apps to find a new notification—it's from Instagram. One new follower. I gasp when I open it.

Graeme Cracker_Collins has followed me. *Graham Cracker.* My own private nickname for him. My heart gallops and my chest aches.

I click on the tiny photo of Graeme, his face smiling at me

from underneath his windswept hair. He's posted three photos from the Galápagos, and one of them is of *me*, although you can't exactly tell. It's the one he snapped in the highlands. A sunburst obscures most of my face, casting it in shadow, but the outline of my profile cuts a dramatic figure against the trees. I tap on the photo to read the caption.

> **Graeme Cracker_Collins:** To the woman who inspired me to rejoin the world, "thank you" will never be enough.

Graeme already has more than two hundred followers, many of whom have left messages of love and welcome. Clearly, friends and extended family. Ryan_Collins206 commented on the photo of me: "Who is this woman? I need to give her a kiss."

I swallow past the painful lump in my throat. Graeme has officially returned to the world.

Heart cracking, I follow him back.

A knock sounds from my front door. "Barbara," I murmur. What did she forget now?

The knock comes again, less tentative this time. "Coming," I yell. Standing, I rub feeling back into my prickling thighs as I edge through the living room. The thin fabric of my yoga pants is slick against my palms.

I open the front door. And nearly faint.

It's not Barbara.

Graeme is standing in my hallway. It's him. Here. In person.

His scent breaks through my shock first, that citrusy cedar bouquet, followed by the vaguely rumpled state of his appearance. He's wearing jeans and a faded blue polo and his customary black backpack. His cheeks are scruffy and his eyes widen when they meet mine.

"Thanks for following me back," he says. And for one insane moment, I wonder if following him back on Instagram summoned him here through a magic portal in the ether.

"You're welcome."

He scrubs a hand across the nape of his neck. "I came to see you. I hope you don't mind I let myself up. There was a woman running out of your building and I caught the door before it closed."

Probably Barbara.

"How . . . do you even know where I live?"

The wood floor creaks behind me, and just as I turn around, Walsh scurries into the living room. "Ah." Walsh.

"When I couldn't reach you, I messaged Walsh to make sure you were okay. She told me, very emphatically, that I should hop the first flight to Seattle. So here I am. And, well, I thought I'd give you this."

Reaching into his bag, he pulls something out—a postcard.

My postcard.

The one I wrote to myself on Floreana Island. Graeme must have fished it out of the historic post office barrel when I wasn't looking. A bark of incredulous laughter escapes me. When I take it, our fingers brush and I can't stop a shiver of energy from zinging through my veins.

"I was intending on delivering it later, but today seemed like the right time."

Lifting the card, I read the three words I penned to myself in an oversized scrawl.

Keep chasing sharks.

Letting out a breathy laugh, I tap the card against my palm. I've been chasing a shark all evening, and with Graeme here . . .

I might chase the biggest shark of all.

"I'm turning down the promotion," he says.

My eyes snap to his. "What? You can't."

He shakes his head, a wry smile gracing his angular lips. "It's for the best. I don't believe in getting ahead at the expense of someone else. You weren't given a fair shake, and that's not okay. I'm turning it down and—"

I grab his biceps. "I don't want the promotion anymore."

He blinks at me like I've sprouted another head. "You don't?"

"You were right about me and digital marketing . . . I don't love it. Not the way you do. I think I'd be happier, more fulfilled, in a role that spans multiple departments, not only marketing. I'm not sure what that looks like or whether I'll find it at Seaquest, but I can finally admit something: being a director for the sake of the title isn't worth it. I need to find a position that will actually make me happy. You're a better fit for the job."

His forehead creases. "So you're giving up?"

"Oh, definitely not." Leaning against the doorframe, I cross my arms to keep my heart from beating out of my chest. "Since James won't take me seriously, I'm pitching my idea to Marlen. This conservation proposal is the right path for the company—I feel it in my bones. Now I just have to make my voice heard."

Graeme laughs. It starts out a soft chuckle and balloons into a full-throated belly laugh. "You know, I thought by delivering this postcard I'd be the one riding in on a white horse, giving you a boost when you needed it most. I should have known you had it in you all along."

Sucking in a deep breath, he steps closer. "I'm so sorry, Henley. I'm sorry for not saying anything on Bartolomé and I'm sorry for the distance between us since the cruise. What you said got to me—it was harsh, but I needed to hear it. Because you were right.

I've come a long way in the last year, but I've still been hiding. I decided to change that."

"You have?" My voice is barely above a whisper.

"I can't wait for the stars to align to start living the life I want. That's another reason why you haven't heard from me in the last couple weeks. I finally cleared out the last of my mom's belongings, put her house on the market, and I've been applying for jobs in Seattle. It's where my remaining family lives, and it's where you are. It's where I want to be. Now. I don't want to wait anymore for a company to relocate me on their timeline and under their conditions." His jaw tenses and his nostrils flare. "Can you forgive me for how I treated you?"

"Only if you can forgive me."

"Deal."

The weight that's been pressing on my chest for the last two weeks evaporates like a puff of smoke. I groan low in my throat. "Now get over here and kiss me."

Grinning, he reaches for me.

Someone coughs behind us. We have an audience. I pull back.

"We're gonna go now," says Tory, wincing. Christina and Michelle crowd behind her wearing matching expressions of gleeful surprise. "Unless you feel like we should get more done tonight on your proposal?"

My proposal for Marlen definitely needs more work, but there's always tomorrow. Right now, there's something—*someone*—more important. "No, it's fine. You've been a huge help. I'm way further along than I would have been at this point without you. Thank you, all of you."

Christina, Tory, and Michelle file out of my apartment one by one.

"Hey, Graeme." Christina waves as she passes. "Great to finally meet you."

"Likewise," he says, dipping his chin.

"We need to talk," she mouths at me from behind her hand, shooting a meaningful glance at Graeme.

I chew on my lip to suppress a grin. "Later. Promise," I mouth back.

Tory and Michelle step out and Walsh brings up the rear. She's wearing my gray hoodie and has a gym bag slung across her chest.

"Where are you going?" I ask her, pushing off from the wall.

"To Christina's. The latest season of *Nailed It!* just dropped on Netflix, so we're going to binge. Have fun, you two. Don't wait up. Good to see you, Graeme," she says before jogging to catch up with everyone else. She flings an arm around Christina's neck and they all disappear around the corner.

It's just Graeme and me now in the green-carpeted hallway. The air between us charges.

"Do you want to come in?" I say at the same time he says, "Well, I should probably get an Uber to Ryan's."

He chuckles. "I'd love to."

I feel Graeme's presence at my back all the way into my apartment. When we reach the living room, the mess of paper plates, pizza boxes, and cups has me frowning. "One second." I begin bustling around, stacking paper plates and stuffing them into pizza boxes.

When I carry them to the kitchen, footsteps follow. Graeme is behind me, his front to my back. Warm. Solid. My breath catches when his fingers curl around my waist. I still.

"Don't worry about it. We can clean up later," he murmurs in my ear. Reaching around me, he takes the boxes from my slackening grip and places them on the counter. In a caress as gentle as a summer breeze, he brushes my hair from my neck until it's gathered over one shoulder.

Pure electricity zips through me as he kisses the sensitive skin at the nape of my neck, directly above the loose neckline of my slouchy sweater. I shiver when his tongue touches my skin and he trails kisses up the side of my throat. Pulling me closer, he reaches around to cup my face. I twist to look at him over my shoulder.

His eyes are hooded and his gaze consumes me.

Like he's afraid I'll disappear.

His lips descend to mine.

Bliss.

I close my eyes as I turn within his embrace to face him, not breaking the kiss, which is like no kiss I've ever experienced. It's an apology. An affirmation. And a promise of what's yet to come.

Graeme hauls me closer until our bodies are flush. I dive a hand into the soft strands of his rumpled hair. I'm on my toes. Then I'm off the floor completely as he lifts me to sit on the counter. I shove the pizza boxes away and they land with a *fwap* on the floor, crusts scattering across linoleum.

I don't care.

His tongue dips into my mouth, and he tastes as crisp and bright as peppermint. Like a warm, sunny day on a white-sand beach. Like a lifetime full of promise. I hitch my legs around his waist, pulling him closer.

A yowl like a woodchipper full of rocks echoes through the kitchen.

Graeme pulls back, frowning. "What the . . ."

"Noodles," I groan.

Noodles the cat is sitting in front of his empty food bowl, snaggletooth jutting, feigning starvation—even though I fed him three hours ago. One eye stares at us like a disapproving chaperone, while the other ogles the refrigerator. His fur is especially wild today, a fluffy, ruffled mop.

Graeme's eyebrows fly up his forehead. "That's your cat?"

"Mm-hmm."

"That's *your* cat."

"That's my Noodles."

His expression softens, his lips curving into an exultant grin. "And I thought Winnie was ugly," he murmurs. Sliding his fingers into my hair, he palms my cheek. His blue eyes blaze like stars. "You know, I think I could fall in love with you."

Warmth floods my chest. "Ditto."

27

*Y*ou've seriously never taken a personal day before?" Graeme asks. Dull, hazy sunlight peeks through my curtains and fans across his face from where he lies sprawled next to me in bed.

"Not like this."

Except for a bout of pneumonia two years ago, this is the first time I've ever called off work last minute. I text Walsh a heads-up that I'm staying home today with Graeme, replace my cell phone on the nightstand, and snuggle back into the warm depths of my bed. My bare legs tangle with Graeme's under the sheets. "Won't James think it's weird that we both called off today?"

Graeme props himself up on one elbow. "I doubt it. He doesn't know I'm in town."

My floral watercolor comforter pools low around his waist, revealing his strong chest, sculpted arms, and acres of glorious skin. My cheeks warm. Having a naked man in my bed has been a rarity in recent years. And having that naked man be someone who makes me want to sing and laugh and cry big, fat happy tears all at once is an absolute first. I run a palm over his whiskery face.

From God knows where, he pulls out his cell phone and snuggles onto the pillow next to me before lifting it high above us. "Morning selfie."

"Ugh, no, I look terrible," I say, diving for cover. My hair is a veritable squirrel's nest and I'm pretty sure I have mascara smudges under my eyes.

"You're beautiful."

I purse my lips but can't prevent the smile that rises from the depths of my soul. With his lips pressed against my temple, he snaps a picture. We both look at it. My breath catches at the casual intimacy displayed on the screen.

"You're not posting that on Instagram, are you?" I ask.

"No way. This one's all for me."

"What made you finally join anyway?"

He kisses the tip of my nose. "You did."

"And your handle, Graeme Cracker_Collins. Is that because of me?"

"Partly. It was my mom's nickname for me too. But I like hearing you say it."

I roll over until I'm on top of him. The sheet falls away, and goose bumps form along my exposed skin. "Graham Cracker," I drawl.

His chest expands as he growls, and I brush my lips against his. I jerk back a fraction. "When are you heading back to Michigan?" *Please don't say today.*

"Tomorrow."

I exhale.

"But I'll be back next week. I have a job interview with a local company and they're flying me out—"

I edge off him, clutching the comforter to my chest. "No. You can't."

He pushes himself up to sit higher against the pillows. "Why not?"

"Because you have to take the digital director job at Seaquest."

"Why?"

"Because you're perfect for it! Your digital storytelling ideas are amazing and you love to travel, and this job can give you that."

"But what about you?"

I shrug and flop back on my pillow. "Let's just see what Marlen says about my idea. If he approves it, maybe I'll have a chance to work out of a different department. Maybe with Renata." Renata is the chief itinerary officer, the only woman on the executive board, and my personal hero. She worked her way up in the company after starting as a deckhand on one of the ships in the nineties. Talk about a self-made success story.

"In that case we should get our day started. Because you need to polish your pitch for Marlen." Even as he says it, a wicked gleam lights his eye.

"We should get up. We definitely should." But right now, no part of me wants to. Releasing the blanket, I crawl on top of him. His body is warm and all too inviting. "How about in fifteen minutes?"

"Thirty, at least. I need to taste every inch of that delectable skin," he rumbles.

My stomach does backflips at the pure, molten lust in his gaze. "Forty-five," I counter.

"Now you're just being greedy," he murmurs into the crook of my neck before nipping me with his teeth. "Deal."

He's right, I am greedy. Because I want it all. And I'm going to have it.

"There's still so much to do," I say four hours later, bare fleet slapping against wood as I stride across my living room and snag the notepad from the coffee table. "I don't know how I'm going to have everything polished by tomorrow morning."

"You don't need to," says Graeme from where he's sprawled on the couch, laptop perched on his lap. "You just need to have your main talking points, the basic framework for implementation, and a few examples fleshed out. I don't think Marlen will expect you to launch the entire program by the end of the meeting."

I grind my molars. "I hate feeling unprepared."

Setting his laptop aside, Graeme rises to his feet. His jeans hang low on his hips, and his Red Wings T-shirt hugs his biceps. Gripping me by the shoulders, he stops my frantic pacing. "You got this. It's barely noon. We have all day and night to make your proposal perfect before your meeting tomorrow."

Taking a deep breath, I nod. "I'm happy you're here."

"Me too." He rests his forehead against mine for a breath before stealing a kiss. "Now, what do you think of this?" Plucking his laptop off the coffee table, he rotates it so I can see the screen. On it is a mock Facebook post with a photo of a Darwin's finch and a story of the conservation work supported by donations from our guests.

I grin. "Fantastic. Now what if we—"

My cell phone buzzes against my hip. Probably Walsh, since I haven't seen her since last night. When I catch the name on the screen, I frown and hastily tap the green accept call icon.

"Hello?"

"Oh, Henley, thank God I caught you." Barbara's words are a breathless jumble. "You need to come into the office. As soon as you can, right now."

I wedge an arm across my chest and stride to the other side of the room. "Why? What's going on?'

"It's James." Her breath hitches, and I catch a jangle of earrings against the phone that sounds like she's walking somewhere quickly. "He called a meeting of the executive board for one o'clock today. He's presenting *your* fund-raising proposal."

My jaw falls open. "Oh. That's a one eighty. Well, that's . . . that's great. I can be in before then, for sure. Would he like me to present or does he want to—"

"No," she blurts. "You're not getting it. He emailed me the PowerPoint for *your* Galápagos proposal. I thought it looked familiar, so I double-checked the metadata, and sure enough, you're listed as the author. Except when I opened the file, your name was nowhere on it, but his was. Right there on the title slide: James P. Wilcox. Henley, he doesn't want you to come to the board meeting. *He's stealing your idea.*"

My heart thunders in my ears like the roar of the ocean. "He's what?" My voice is low and deadly and reaches me as though it's echoing through a long tunnel.

"He's passing it off as his own; he's stealing it. And that's not even the worst part."

What in ever-loving hell could be worse than that?

"It's not the first time he's done it."

28

All the blood rushes to my head and I sink onto the couch. "What?"

"He's been stealing your ideas for two years, maybe longer," says Barbara. "I had no idea until today. I'm so sorry."

My gaze connects with Graeme's.

"What's going on?" he mouths.

Covering the microphone with my palm, I quickly fill him in. Fire explodes behind his eyes and he balls his hands into fists. "James," he breathes, his tone pure venom.

I return my attention to the call. "How do you know all this?"

"I wasn't sure at first, but after he sent me the PowerPoint I started going back through his files, comparing metadata. I've found proof that he's taken documents you created, removed your name, and then passed them off to Marlen like they were his. Emails between them confirm it."

"Like what? What documents?"

"Oh God, where to begin . . . The most recent was a memo copied and pasted from a Google Doc, something about Snapchat."

"Expanding our marketing strategy to Snapchat?"

"Bingo."

"Motherfucker," I breathe. "That was my idea. He shot it down at a staff meeting last spring and made feel like I was stupid for even bringing it up. He told me—" I gasp, and lock eyes with Graeme. "He told me to come to him first before adding any new ideas to our shared marketing department planning doc in the future."

"Because he wants to keep your ideas to himself," Graeme growls through gritted teeth.

The realization hits me like an ocean liner.

James never had any intention of promoting me—ever. If it weren't for Marlen suggesting me for the position, James never would have put my name forward as a director. Because he wants me right where I am: his workaholic underling feeding him a pipeline of ideas he can pass off as his own to boost his career.

I see red. I literally see red—every shade from magenta to scarlet overlays my apartment. War drums beat through every corner of my mind.

The front door opens and closes and Walsh's voice rings through the apartment. "Honey, I'm home! I hope you two are decent!"

"Barbara, can you hold on a sec?"

"Sure."

I press my cell to my shoulder.

Walsh lopes into the living room and stops dead, taking in the scene. "Who died?"

"No one yet," I growl.

Graeme kneels in front of me. "Henley, you need to get in there and pitch your idea to Marlen. Now. Before James takes it to the executive board."

I stop grinding my molars and take a deep, bracing breath. "You're right. The longer I wait, the harder it'll be to convince him I came up with it first." I lift the phone to my ear again. "Barbara, can you get me in to see Marlen today before one?"

"I'll make it happen. Rose owes me a favor. Just get here as soon as you can, okay?"

"Thanks. I'll be there in fifteen minutes." I tap the end call button and stare at my phone for three hectic heartbeats before springing from my seat. "I'm pitching it now. *I'm pitching it now.*"

"Wait, your ecotourism proposal? I thought that was tomorrow." Walsh's eyes are wide.

"I'll get us an Uber," says Graeme, whipping his cell out of his back pocket.

I dash for the bedroom, peeling my shirt over my head as I go and shimmying out of my yoga pants. Walsh follows me. "Wait, what's going on?"

"My boss has been screwing me over, that's what. I just found out from Barbara that he's been stealing credit for my ideas behind the scenes to help himself get ahead."

"That asshole. Where is he? I'm going to gut him like a toad."

My lips quiver at the razor blades in her tone. "Just help me get dressed."

I run to the bathroom to wash my face and brush my teeth. Mascara. Lip stain. Hair thrown in a bun. No time for anything else. Walsh scurries in holding a bundle of hangers containing my best suit coat, a matching pencil skirt, and a silk blouse. I pull them on in record time. I'm still zipping my skirt when I dash into the living room and nearly bump into Graeme. He's wearing the same polo and jeans from yesterday and he's scooping my notepad and laptop into my work tote.

"Uber's here," he says.

Walsh tosses me one shoe, then another—black four-inch stilettos. My power shoes. Hopping toward the door, I slide them on. "I'm coming too," she says. Her tone brooks no disagreement.

She's wearing yoga pants, slip-on sneakers, and a hoodie . . . to my office. And I couldn't care less.

Two minutes later, the three of us are in the back seat of a Toyota Corolla zipping through downtown Seattle. I dial Christina's number. She answers on the first ring.

"Hey, Hen—"

"Christina, I need a favor. If I send you a file, can you print it out and put it in a binder for me? Like, right now?"

"Of course, but what's going on?"

I give her the bullet-pointed version. A string of expletives follows.

"I'll have it ready when you get here."

"Thanks a million."

My phone dings as I hang up—an email from Graeme.

"The mock Facebook post I put together. In case you need extra ammunition," he says.

Leaning over, I brush my lips against his cheekbone in a quick kiss. "Thanks."

I forward Christina my roughly scaled-up proposal so at least I have something for Marlen to look at. Stowing my phone, I smooth my coat over my blouse. "Okay. It's okay. I'm doing this." My breathing accelerates along with the car. Panic claws at the edges of my mind.

What if Marlen doesn't like my idea? What if I blow it? What if he doesn't believe me about James and I come across looking like a vindictive employee with an ax to grind and . . .

Graeme's hand lands on my thigh, warm and reassuring. "Take a deep breath," he says.

"I'm not ready." Diving into my bag, I pull out my notepad and begin flipping through pages. "I don't have my presentation finished or the details ironed out or—"

A biting pain explodes in my side. "Ow! Hey!" I jerk around to glare at Walsh. "Why'd you pinch me?"

"Snap out of it!"

I blink at her.

"This is what you've been preparing for your whole freaking life. Right here, your chance to take your ideas to the big boss and shine. You might not have the perfect report lined up or the perfect talking points or whatever, but damn it, you're Henley Fucking Evans. And this is your moment."

"She's right," says Graeme. "You don't need a fancy presentation or a script. You're smart, successful, and passionate, and knowing you, you've already mulled over every angle of this idea. You'll sell him on it. I know it."

I loop my arms through Walsh's and Graeme's and hug them tight. "You have no idea how much I needed that."

The car lurches to a stop. "We're here," says the Uber driver.

I check the time: 12:41. Less than twenty minutes until the executive board meets and my career at Seaquest gets permanently neutered.

My chest tightens. "We need to hurry."

I rush into the building, moving as quickly as my legs, constricted as they are in my pencil skirt, will carry me. Skidding to a stop at the elevator, I jam the up button half a dozen times. The elevator indicator flashes 4 . . . then 5 . . .

"Damn it," I spit. "I don't have time for this."

"Stairs?" offers Graeme, looking around.

"This way." I burst into a jog toward a back hallway and push open the metal door to the stairs.

Up, up, up we climb. By the third flight, I'm huffing. By the fifth, I'm sweating.

Crack.

My ankle rolls on the sixth-floor landing and I stumble into Graeme, who catches me.

"Shit," I breathe. The heel of my right shoe has broken clean off. Anxiety siphons down my throat and pools in my chest. I can't present to Marlen looking like this.

"Here, swap," says Walsh, toeing off her slip-on sneakers.

Kicking off my ruined heels, I put on her shoes. "You're a lifesaver." They pinch—her feet are half a size smaller than mine—but they're all I've got. At least they're black like my suit. I take off up the stairs with Walsh dashing behind me, barefoot and clutching my ruined heels.

We burst into the lobby, startling Sadie, the receptionist, and fast-walk through the serpentine hallways until we reach Marlen's corner office suite. Barbara, Christina, and Tory are already there.

"Thank God, you made it," says Christina.

Bracing my hands on my waist, I suck in oxygen and attempt to calm my roiling nerves.

"Are you ready?" Tory asks.

My stomach churns and I'm grateful it's empty. I offer a twitchy smile. "Not remotely."

"It's now or never," says Barbara. "You have fifteen minutes."

I nod frantically. "Okay. I can do this."

Christina hands me the binder. "Just remember your main points."

"And let the numbers back you up," adds Tory.

"And don't forget," says Graeme, tucking a loose strand of hair back into my bun. "You're Henley Evans. And you're a rock star."

"Damn straight." Walsh nods as she brushes lint off my suit coat and straightens my skirt.

"Is he ready for me?" I ask Rose, Marlen's secretary, who's watching our exchange with a curious expression.

Picking up her phone, she pushes a button. "Henley Evans is here to see you . . . Yes, Mr. Jones." She hangs up the phone and peers up at me. "Go on in."

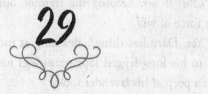

29

When I open the door, Marlen looks up from where he's reading a spiral-bound report from his sleek gray sofa. "Miss Evans, come in." His jaunty voice beckons me out of the threshold and into his expansive corner office.

Marlen Jones is the last person you'd expect to be a CEO of a major corporation. He's young as far as CEOs go—midforties—with a full head of wavy black hair, an ever-present grin, and a twinkle in his eye.

But looks are deceiving. In fact, he's a former venture capitalist with a reputation as a shark in the finance world. He purchased Seaquest when the travel industry took a wallop during the last recession, and he's managed to grow it from a regional operation to an international corporation. In fact, Seaquest's growth has been the largest of any company in the cruise industry over the past ten years.

I'd be naive to buy into Marlen's laid-back charm. Sustained success at his level requires a hefty dose of determination and hard work, with a dash of ruthlessness for flavor. He's the man in charge, the one holding my future in his hands. I can't forget that.

He smiles warmly at me. "You know, your ears must be ringing. Because I just received a letter about you."

"Oh?" I say, keeping the tremble out of my voice through sheer force of will.

"Yes. Darndest thing." Beaming at me, he strides over to his desk in his long-legged lope, pant legs just a hair too high, so I catch a peep at his lavender socks.

Lifting stacks of paper until he finds a pair of slim tortoiseshell glasses, he slides them on. "From a guest. By the name of"—he squints at the letter—"Nikolai Kozlov. Ring a bell?"

I nearly choke. "I think so."

He motions to one of the black leather chairs in front of his desk and I take a seat.

"Well, Mr. Kozlov certainly remembers you. Apparently, you went above and beyond in making his experience with us a memorable one. He had a lot to say . . ." Marlen flips over not one, not two, but three stapled sheets of paper. "A lot. But what stuck out to me most is how you made him feel like more than a customer. You made him feel like a friend, and now he says he's a Seaquest Adventurer for life." Dropping the letter onto his desk, he flashes me a wide, approving smile. "Well done."

If my insides weren't frozen with sheer nerves, I might just cry. That sweet, silly Russian did me a solid.

"Thank you, sir."

"And it looks like he'll be traveling with us again soon for his honeymoon—to Mexico this time. Let's arrange something special for him, yes? An upgraded cabin and first-class flights, perhaps. I'll let you take care of the details."

He then picks up a three-by-four photo and flashes it in my direction. It's of Nikolai and his Emily, and they're wearing matching goofy-in-love grins. I smile to myself. So he got the girl after all. Marlen glances at the photo, then me, then the photo again. "She kind of looks like you." He shrugs as he settles into his low-backed office chair. "So, Miss Evans. Enough chitchat. What can I do for you today?"

I allow myself a single, calming breath before I push my shoulders back and inject every ounce of confidence I can muster into my voice. "It's not what you can do for me, sir. Traveling to the Galápagos last month inspired me, and I have an idea for how we, as a company, can make a difference in the world by inspiring others."

I launch into my proposal. It's not perfect or polished, but I dig into every ounce of the expertise I've developed since I've been back from the Galápagos—my late nights researching at the office, last night's planning meeting, and sheer instinct. When I'm done, I hand him the binder containing the hard copy of the scaled-up proposal.

"This will give you an idea of how the initiative would work company-wide."

Marlen purses his lips as he flips open the binder. His expression is opaque as he thumbs through the pages. I swallow thickly.

"You have a daughter, right, Mr. Jones?" I blurt.

"Please, call me Marlen. And yes. One daughter, Arianna. She's a sophomore at Wellesley." He twists a framed photo on his desk toward me so I can see the lanky young beauty.

"Good school," I murmur. "Can I ask you—what kind of world do you want to leave her with? Climate change. Plastics pollution. Mass extinction. All problems facing our planet today. And we're in a position to do something about it. You and your family have a rich philanthropic history. You're a board member of two different organizations dedicated to wildlife conservation, isn't that right?"

"Yes," he says.

"If we bring those efforts into the heart of the company, weave it into its very essence, what can we accomplish? And when given the choice between traveling with a company that cares about our world, and one that's merely out for profit, which will consumers choose? Experience has proven that the conscientious consumer chooses the conscientious company. I believe we can be that kind of company in the adventure cruise industry."

Marlen rocks in his office chair, lips pursed, eyes never leaving my face. "Tell me, Miss Evans. Can you read minds?"

I blink, unsure how to respond. Marlen saves me the trouble.

"Because I have been thinking along these same lines for quite some time. You're absolutely right. The world is facing challenges like never before, and a better future is only possible if we take action. It's like you pulled a thread right out of my brain and wove something tangible with it."

Fireworks explode in my chest as vindication washes through me.

Marlen flashes me the ghost of a grin. "Did you—"

His desk phone rings and he answers. "Yes. Yes, I know. Push the meeting to two. Something came up." Hanging up the phone, he leans forward and rests his forearms on his desk. "Did you come up with this idea all on your own?"

The answer is on the tip of my tongue when I stop. I won't be like James. Not today, not ever.

I wet my lips. "The initial idea was mine, but I had help pulling it together. May I call in my team? They're right outside."

Marlen nods once, expression inscrutable.

Smoothing my jacket, I stride to the door and poke my head out. Christina is chewing her thumbnail, Tory is scrolling through her phone, Walsh is perched next to her, twisting a bracelet around her wrist, and Graeme is standing at the window behind Rose's desk. "Tory, Christina, Graeme. I need you." Three pairs of eyes jerk to me.

"What, in there?" blurts Christina.

"Yeah. Rose, can you call Barbara for me and ask her to come here?"

Rose wobbles her chin and picks up her phone.

Walsh flashes me a thumbs-up as the rest of us file into Marlen's office.

"These are the staff members I collaborated with on the idea. Christina researched regional nonprofits with ties to the areas we sail; Tory calculated costs, and her spouse, an attorney for Brickle, Boone & Davis, informally advised on the legal framework that we'd need to launch a charitable conservation initiative."

The door opens and closes, and Barbara walks in, buckles jangling on her knee-high boots. "Barbara assisted with logistics and presentation prep, and Graeme created some mock-ups for a digital marketing rebranding campaign." Pulling my phone from the inside of my jacket, I tap in several commands. "They're in your in-box now."

Clicking open the email, Marlen scans his screen. His eyebrows rise and the corner of his lips wavers. "This is good stuff. But why didn't you take this idea to James? He's your direct supervisor."

I clear my throat. "I did. For the Galápagos, anyway. It was the proposal I crafted for the director of digital marketing position before he disqualified me."

Marlen knits his arched eyebrows together. "I don't understand. When I asked him what was happening with that this morning, he said your proposal was so subpar that we shouldn't even consider it. But there's nothing subpar about this idea. It's bold, well researched, and brilliant."

Graeme's fist tightens at his side. "That's because James intends to steal Henley's idea." His eyes flick to me and he offers a small, encouraging nod. I step forward.

"Graeme's right. Less than an hour ago I learned that James is going to present this idea at today's board meeting, but he's going to say he came up with it."

Marlen frowns. "That's quite a claim."

"I have proof." Barbara's voice cracks but she lifts her chin. "Proof that he never intended on giving Henley the credit she deserves, and, in fact, that he's been taking her ideas and passing them off as his own for years. The direct call campaign for British Columbia, the monthly wildlife spotlight on our blog, and the Snapchat marketing plan from the last board meeting—all originally Henley's ideas."

Marlen's deep brown eyes nearly pop out of his head.

"And Henley's not the only one. Do you remember Samantha Charles, the marketing manager for North and Central America before Henley? The one who left after four years to take a position with Wild Wonders, our biggest competitor?"

"I do," says Marlen.

"I haven't had time to investigate thoroughly, but I began digging through some old emails, and there's evidence James co-opted her ideas as well. Both smart, hardworking young women with big ideas and even bigger dreams. I just wish I would have realized it sooner. But I never had reason to suspect . . ." Her voice cracks.

"It's not your fault," I murmur.

She flashes me a small, heartfelt smile before handing Marlen a black thumb drive. "It's all here."

Marlen takes the thumb drive with a curt nod, plugs it into his computer, and begins clicking.

I stand there, not looking at the others, barely daring to breathe. The clock on the wall ticks. Tory's leather loafers squeak as she shifts her weight. Graeme goes very still beside me. A bead of sweat forms between my shoulder blades. I swallow.

With every click, Marlen's expression grows darker, more thunderous. Finally, with a heavy sigh, he shoves to his feet and strides to the massive bank of windows that make up an entire wall of his office.

"James has worked for this company for nearly two decades," he says, clasping his hands behind his back. "He started under the previous owner as the print marketing director. I promoted him to chief marketing officer eight years ago because his ideas were on point and cutting-edge, and he seemed to be taking the company's marketing program in the right direction. I had no idea he was stepping on other people's backs to do it." Dipping his chin, he shakes his head slowly and returns to his desk.

Picking up the framed photo of his daughter, he runs his thumb over the glass. When he sets it down, he splays his palms on the desk and looks me dead in the eye.

"I know exactly how to handle this."

"re you nervous?" asks Walsh nearly an hour later. She's wearing a pair of neon-green flip-flops she's procured from God knows where.

I snap my laptop shut and rub my temples. "Ask me after."

"We got your back," she says.

I bump her with my shoulder. "I know you do."

Even with Tory and Christina roped into other meetings (it is a Wednesday and the workday chugs on, despite my drama), the usually empty lobby feels congested with Graeme, Walsh, and me filling the small seating area next to the conference room. Sadie, the front desk receptionist, frowns. She's probably used to a bit more peace and quiet.

Two executive board members stride through the lobby toward the largest conference room, and one of them is Renata. Her gray-streaked hair gleams under the lights, her soft yet commanding voice trailing her as she disappears into the conference room. Three more executives follow.

I bounce my heel. A minute later, James enters the lobby. Every muscle in my body tenses and I glare at the squat, self-satisfied snake of a man.

When he catches sight of me, a frown flickers across his face but quickly vanishes. He detours over to us, lip curling. "Henley." He sniffs, giving me a once-over, gaze lingering on my incongruous shoes. "I thought you were taking a personal day."

"I am. I'm just giving my sister a tour," I lie smoothly.

Walsh hops up, a fake smile plastered on her face. "Hi, I'm Walsh. You must be Henley's boss. I've heard so much about you." She titters. "My, that's an interesting tie. My grandpa has one just like it."

I suppress a savage bark of laughter. Walsh is the queen of insulting people without them quite catching on that they were insulted.

His gaze flicks to Graeme and he pulls a double-take. "Graeme, is that you?"

Graeme surveys him coolly.

"Graeme Crawford-Collins, you didn't tell me you were in town." He extends his hand and Graeme takes it, jaw as hard as marble. His knuckles turn white and James twists his much smaller hand out of Graeme's grip. He shakes it with a nervous chuckle. "Quite a handshake. Why are you sitting here with Henley?"

"She's giving me a tour too."

"Good work, Henley. That's the kind of attitude I like to see." He swivels to address Graeme again. "Are you around tomorrow? If so, have Barbara schedule a meeting. I'd like to discuss the next steps for your promotion—relocation and finding you administrative support. Maybe Henley here can help you out in the meantime. You wouldn't mind, would you, Henley?"

I use every ounce of restraint not to throw myself at him like a jaguar attacking a mouse. Instead, I force myself to smile. I show all my teeth. "Whatever you say, boss."

"That's the spirit," he says, squeezing my shoulder. My gut churns at the contact and I nearly hurl when his touch lingers several seconds too long. Finally, he slips his hand down my arm. I imagine his fingers leaving a trail of slime like a slug.

He walks into the conference room, smirking.

Graeme stares after him, every muscle tense. "That dirtbag."

I grunt in agreement.

"Oh, he's getting his," says Walsh, folding her arms across her chest.

At two o'clock on the nose, Marlen strides into the lobby, footsteps echoing off marble. He inclines his chin at me as he passes, and I nod in return.

When the door closes behind him, he starts the meeting.

Graeme and I barely speak as we listen, ears straining. Words float in and out like a badly tuned radio. The AC is humming from a vent directly above us and all we can see are indistinct blobs through the conference room's frosted glass wall. Sadie, the receptionist, pops her bubblegum, and I'm tempted to shush her like a Catholic school nun.

A pair of heels clicks across the foyer. "Sorry, that meeting with the itinerary manager took longer than I expected. How's it going?" Christina asks.

"The board meeting just started. I think James is about to speak," I say.

With absolutely no decorum, Christina flops into the chair next to me and presses her ear to the opaque glass wall. All pretext abandoned, Graeme, Walsh, and I follow suit.

James is talking, all right. He's giving *my* presentation. Or rather, a dumbed-down rendition of it. He's limiting himself to the Galápagos Islands, unlike my scaled-up version, and he flubs some of the numbers. And it's clear from his money-driven talk that he doesn't get it. Not really. For him, it's all about sales, when really, it's about inspiring people, adopting stronger corporate responsibility, and making a difference.

After ten minutes of impressive-sounding bluster, a general murmur sounds from the rest of the executive board.

Marlen's voice rings loud and clear. "That is a very interesting idea. How did you come up with it?"

A chair groans. I can just imagine James leaning back, hands behind his head. "As you know, I recently sent two of our marketing staff down to the Galápagos for familiarization trips, and their experience inspired me. I thought: Why not solicit donations for conservation efforts and use that as a cornerstone of our marketing in the region?"

I grind my molars like an industrial sander. Graeme's nostrils flare and his face flushes.

"So, this is your idea?"

James coughs. "That's what I said."

"You're lying."

"Excuse me?"

"I have irrefutable evidence that what you just presented is, in fact, work that belongs to Henley Evans."

"What evidence?"

"Time-stamped emails and metadata."

Chairs inside the conference creak and James lets out a disapproving snort. "What does it matter? She's my staff, my subordinate. Her idea, our idea. It's a win for the marketing team."

"It's a win for *you*," Marlen booms.

The conference room falls silent. Even Sadie in the lobby stops chewing her gum at the shouting.

"It's recently come to my attention that you've been taking credit for work that doesn't belong to you. Even this presentation—you didn't create it, did you? Not a single slide."

"Well . . . I . . . didn't exactly . . ."

"Why is your name on it then?"

James laughs, a nervous, braying sound. "Come now, Marlen. There are those of us at the top who have to make the tough decisions, and then there are the people at the bottom, the drones who keep the hive going. As long as we're making the company more marketable and turning a profit, that's all that really matters. This idea is coming from the department I happen to manage, so all ideas that come through it belong to me—to us. All of us."

I imagine the temperature dropping ten degrees in the conference room as silence swells. When Marlen finally speaks, his voice is low and deadly.

"I don't know what kind of company you think you work for, but we're not only about making a profit here. I will not tolerate anyone, whether it's an executive or a mail clerk, taking credit for work that isn't their own—*lying* to get ahead. That's not the kind of company I run, and those aren't the kind of people I want leading my team. You're fired."

"I'm *what*?"

"Fired."

"But . . . I have obligations. A mortgage, my son's college to pay for, alimony . . ."

"You'll have a chance to formally resign, if you go quietly—today. But if I have to call security, you get nothing."

For a heartbeat, I think James is going to argue. The silence feels charged with malice, and I can practically see the foam that must be dripping from his pale lips. Finally, a chair squeals as it rolls across marble. Cloth snaps, like James is straightening his suit coat.

"Gentlemen," he says, voice dripping with venom.

The conference room door whooshes open.

James emerges in the lobby, hands balled into fists. When he catches sight of me, his eyes narrow. I scramble to my feet. He stops inches short of me and jams his stubby index finger in my face.

"You did this to me. You little—"

"Back off," hisses Graeme, who's suddenly between us. He towers over the much shorter, paunchy man, and James stumbles back a step. Walsh and Christina scurry to my side, flanking me.

James's nostrils flare as he glares at me. "I helped build this company, goddamn it. Who the hell are you? You're nobody. Just a mousy little girl who thinks she's ready to play in the big leagues, when really you're barely out of the kiddie pool."

In the past, his words would have stung like wasps. Now?

Lifting my chin, I stare down my nose at the man who would have suffocated my career until it withered.

"Who am I? I'm Henley Evans. And don't you forget it."

For a heart-stopping moment, I think James is going to slap me. The muscles in his neck spasm and Graeme tenses, ready to intervene.

But instead, with a sneer, James turns on his heel and marches out of the lobby. It looks like he'll be getting severance after all. As soon as the elevator doors close with a ding, a knot of anxiety loosens in my chest and floats away. I feel lighter than I have in three years. I'm almost giddy.

Marlen pokes his head out of the conference room. "Miss Evans, if you will?"

Tucking my laptop against my chest, I square my shoulders and step through the door into a future full of possibility.

've invited Miss Evans here this afternoon to share the *real* con-servation proposal. What you heard from James only covered the Galápagos, and was a poor imitation of the real thing. Henley's idea would be implemented company-wide and involve a top-to-bottom rebranding effort. It aligns with the direction I've been thinking we should take for quite a while. Whenever you're ready, Henley." Settling into the chair at the head of the table, Marlen motions for me to join the executives.

Swallowing hard, I cross the room on quivering legs to the conference table. One of my rubber soles catches on the tile and a deafening squeal fills the silent room. I wince.

Calm. I need to be calm.

Six pairs of eyes stare at me as I open my laptop and cast my PowerPoint to the large screen on the opposite wall. It's not pretty or my best work—there are only photos on the first couple of slides, and the graphs I included later on are sadly basic—but at least I had some time to clean it up after I left Marlen's office. It'll have to do.

Meeting each executive's gaze in turn, I begin. The words flow, and after a minute, I begin to relax. I have no idea what time it is when I finish, but I'm greeted with nods of approval.

"Excellent," murmurs Renata.

Marlen raps his knuckles against the table. "Brilliant."

The chief financial officer, a white-haired man named Mark, leans forward. "I'm not convinced."

He pelts me with questions, which I answer haltingly at first, but with each follow-up, my confidence grows. Renata pitches a new angle I hadn't considered. The executives discuss it. And I'm part of the discussion. *Me.* They look to me for additional information, for ideas. Marlen specifically asks for my input more than once.

My stomach growls, thankfully quiet enough so I don't think anyone can hear it. I check the time on my laptop and my eyes bug. I've been in the meeting for nearly two hours.

Marlen flops back in his leather office chair. "Now, there's the question of Henley's promotion."

I jerk my chin at him so fast my neck cricks. My what now?

"It's clear she's being underutilized as a marketing manager. She has vision, drive, and leadership. You know she assembled her own team of staff to help her with this proposal? She actually called them into my office earlier to give them credit." Marlen chuckles to himself. "She has a keen eye for strategy and a dynamite résumé, including significant graduate-level coursework."

Marlen pulled my résumé?

"Digital director?" offers Mark.

I'm poised to interject, but Renata beats me to the punch. "Digital director doesn't seem like the right fit. Too narrow."

"I agree," says Marlen. "James pegged Graeme Crawford-Collins for that position, and I like him for it."

Renata taps a manicured fingernail on the table. "As of two hours ago, there's an opening on the executive board. We could use fresh blood."

My heartbeat accelerates like a runaway train.

"Indeed," says Marlen, contemplating me. "Miss Evans, how would you like to serve as the chief strategy officer for Seaquest Adventures? It would be on an interim basis to start. But if you prove yourself, after a set amount of time—eighteen months, let's say—it could become permanent."

I'm dizzy. It's so far beyond my wildest imaginings that I can barely process.

Me. On the executive board.

I lick my dry lips. "I—I would need to consider the particulars."

Marlen's rich laughter shakes the ceiling tiles. "See? She's perfect for a chief strategist role."

Renata rests her forearm on the table. "What are your concerns, Henley?"

"Well, responsibilities of the position. Workload. Staff support. Long-term goals. Compensation package."

"All valid questions," she assures me. The skin around her brown eyes crinkles when she speaks, and I can't help but feel like I've found an ally today.

"Marketing can stand on its own with a digital and print director calling the shots. I'm thinking you'd have a small team working under you to focus on implementing our ecotourism vision, plus developing the company's other strategic initiatives," says Marlen. "It's a big undertaking, and you'll need your own department."

I nod. "I'd want to handpick my team. Barbara Jenkins as my executive assistant, but with room for her to grow into a more substantial role. Christina Kim for her marketing and communications skills. I know Tory Hageman can't be spared from accounting, but someone else with a detail-oriented mindset, preferably with a background in conservation or nonprofit management."

Grinning, Marlen smacks the arm of his chair. "Done. I'll have Rose schedule a meeting for Monday so you and I can hash out the details. Shall we reconvene next week?" He puts the question to the board.

A murmur of ascent follows, and the meeting is adjourned. I stand on shaking legs. Before I can dash out of the room, Renata touches me lightly on the shoulder. "Congratulations," she murmurs, offering her hand. Her grip is firm but not overpowering. A diamond-studded wedding band sparkles on her ring finger.

"Thank you," I say, a bit breathless.

She leans in and drops her voice to a conspiratorial whisper. "You'd better say yes to this promotion, you know. It's high time we had another woman on the board, especially one as intelligent and determined as yourself."

I offer an apologetic smile. "I still need more information before I can make a decision."

"I don't blame you. It can be difficult, working your way to the top in a man's world. You'll have plenty of naysayers, and imposter syndrome can be a constant struggle. But Seaquest is a good place to be. Marlen is an outstanding boss. He values hard work and honesty, and he appreciates work-life balance. Not that it's a cakewalk, you understand. There will be long hours at times, and high stakes. But it's better than at a lot of other companies, and here, you'll have a chance to make a difference."

Sucking in a deep breath, I nod slowly.

"Tell you what," she says. "Before you talk to Marlen on Monday, you come see me. I'll give you my two cents about working at the executive level and share some negotiating pointers."

"Thank you, that would be wonderful."

She inclines her chin. "Life doesn't give you many of these opportunities. My advice? Seize it, mold it, and make it everything you want it to be." With a final encouraging smile, she breezes from the room.

"Holy shitballs, *chief strategy officer*?" Christina screeches after I fill her in on the news.

Walsh squeals at a decibel high enough to shatter glass as Graeme lifts me in his arms, twirling me on the spot. My heart soars while Walsh giggles.

"I knew you could do it," he murmurs, and sets me on my feet.

"Hey, do you mind?" Sadie grouses.

"Sorry, Sadie," I call, and begin edging across the lobby toward the elevator. The rest of the executive board has left the conference room, so besides Sadie, we're alone in the lobby.

"Do you know how much money you'll make as a chief strategy officer?" Christina croons. "You could pay off your student loans in, like, three years instead of thirty. You could move into a nicer apartment. Get another cat . . . one that doesn't eat its own hairballs."

"What about workload?"

"Dude, you already work the hours of an executive."

"Yeah, but I don't want to. I want balance in my life."

"So make sure you have it," says Graeme. Pride shines from the depths of his gaze. "Establish your boundaries going into this job negotiation. You're the one with the power right now. They want *you*. Make sure you're coming at this thing from a position of strength. Ask for what you want and don't budge on the nonnegotiables."

I gaze up at him. "If I take the job, I guess this means we won't be working together. Not in the same department, anyway."

"No issues with human resources then." He wraps his arms around my waist and hauls me close. "Hold up—'if'?"

"I told them I'd think about it. I'm meeting with Marlen on Monday to discuss the details."

Christina pats Graeme's forearm. "Don't worry. I'll make sure she takes it."

I bump her with my hip. "I told them I want you on my team. You interested?"

"In working for you?" She nods so fast her hair bounces around her shoulders. "Um, yes. Definitely. But don't think I'm going to call you *ma'am*. I prefer Badass Boss Lady."

I can't hold back a burst of laughter. "Works for me."

"Is it time to celebrate yet?" Walsh chimes in.

"Abso-freakin-lutely," says Christina. But then she catches sight of the clock above the front desk and groans. "Ugh, it's only four thirty. I have another half an hour on the clock."

"Dinner and drinks at my apartment tonight?"

"And dancing," adds Walsh.

"And dancing," I echo.

Christina grins. "Sounds perfect. I'll tell Tory. Catch you at your place at six?"

"See you then."

Ten minutes later, Walsh, Graeme, and I are in the back of another Uber—an impeccably maintained Prius. Energetic house music filters through the back seat, and the driver's head bobs to the rhythm.

My phone dings with a new email—it's an all-company notice announcing James's unexpected departure. I'm about to pocket my phone when the subject line of a different email catches my eye:

Launch of the Kodiak scheduled for April.

The *Kodiak* is a new ship currently being built that's set to double our offerings in my region, North and Central America. I smile to myself. My former region, if I take this promotion.

I skim the email out of sheer force of habit. It's mostly logistical details, but at the bottom there's a list of positions the company will need to fill. A new ship requires all new crew and staff. I forward the email to Walsh.

I nudge her with my elbow. "Hey, check your email."

Frowning, she pulls out her phone and opens it. "I don't get it."

"Keep scrolling . . . farther . . . there, the job listings."

"Sanitation expert?"

"Spa coordinator. Aboard our newest ship that's launching next spring. It involves giving massages, teaching Pilates and yoga, leading meditation sessions, that sort of thing. You'd be perfect for it."

"Henley," she breathes as her eyes dart across the screen. "Meeting new people every week . . . traveling on a ship that sails around the world? This is my dream job." Then the excitement ballooning in her expression deflates. "You really want me to move out that badly?"

I scoot closer to her. "No! God, no. In fact, I was thinking I need to find a bigger place when my lease is up in November. Maybe a two-bedroom apartment? Even if you take a job on one of our ships, it won't be year-round. You'll have certain months off, so you'll need a home base somewhere. And I want you to know you can stay with me—always. What do you say?"

Her eyes twinkle. "I say it's a dream come true."

Wrapping my arm around my sister, I give her a hearty squeeze. "I love you, Walshers."

"Love you too, Hennie-Bennie."

"So, uh, do you ladies live around here?" The Uber driver

swivels around, beard braid swishing as he eyes Walsh with obvious interest.

She leans forward. "We do."

As they chat, I snuggle closer to Graeme and lean my head on his shoulder. The car edges to a stop at a red light, the windows of the buildings outside winking in the early-evening light. He presses a tender kiss to my temple. "I'm so proud of you."

I sit up to look at him. "Are you sure you're not bothered by my promotion?"

He snorts. "I'm not Sean, remember?"

"But me working above you . . . you, director. Me, e-level . . ."

Tipping my chin up with his forefinger, he brushes his lips against mine in a slow kiss that has my libido blinking awake and my nerve-endings crackling. "You know I like a woman on top." When he pulls back, he pumps his eyebrows once.

I can't help but laugh. "What are you doing a month from today?"

"Hanging out with my girlfriend."

I blink. "Excuse me, what?"

"You. I'm hanging out with you."

"Girlfriend?" I repeat.

"Is that okay?"

"Definitely."

His lips descend to my neck and he presses a kiss directly under my ear, making me shudder. "What did you have in mind?"

"Hmmm." I glance at the car's smooth gray ceiling. "How about camping? I hear Mt. Rainier is beautiful this time of year."

Graeme's blue eyes sparkle and his shoulders relax in a contented sigh. "I thought you'd never ask."

The Uber pulls up outside my building, and Graeme and I clamber out.

"I'll be up soon," says Walsh through the open door, still engrossed in conversation with the driver.

Graeme opens the heavy front door at the same time my neighbor Sophie walks out. I remember it's Sophie this time, not Sophia, because Sophie has a longer nose. She flashes me a small smile as she passes.

I step through the threshold, then pause. "Hey, Sophie?"

She plucks an earbud from one ear. "Yeah?"

"What are you up to tonight?"

"No plans."

"I'm having a party, a celebration of sorts. Do you and Sophia want to come?"

She shrugs, eyes crinkling. "Sure, sounds fun."

"People are coming at six, but feel free to swing by whenever."

"Sounds good. Catch you later." Replacing her ear bud, she waves at me over her shoulder.

"That was nice," says Graeme.

"It's about time I made friendly with the neighbors."

"You know, we have over an hour until your party. Maybe *we* could get friendly." His voice drops to a register of pure mischief.

I tilt my head. "But you didn't say please."

"You want me to beg?"

I flash him a wide, innocent grin. "Only if you're on your knees."

"Henley Rose." With a growl, he lifts me up and carries me across the lobby. I giggle uncontrollably, even as heat floods my cheeks. An elderly man collecting his mail shoots us a disapproving look, and I sweep an air kiss in his direction. His bushy eyebrows jerk upward.

When we reach the elevator, my heart is hammering and my fingers itch to run over every inch of Graeme's skin. He pushes the up button before wrapping me in a tight embrace. Diving a hand under his shirt, I let my fingers play along the waistband of his jeans. When my knuckles brush against his stomach, he sucks in a breath.

My phone dings with my daily 5 p.m. task list reminders. Reaching into my pocket, I pull it out.

Task #1: Defeat Graeme Crawford-Collins.

I don't cross it off the list.

I delete it.

The battles have been waged—some lost, some forfeited, some won. New allies were revealed, an old enemy became a friend and then a lover, and I strengthened the precious bonds of family. A wave of gratitude washes over me that's so powerful tears threaten behind my eyes.

The elevator doors rattle open and Graeme pulls me inside and captures my lips in a searing kiss. My bones turn to liquid and I sink into his heart-melting touch.

A rush of excitement fills my lungs and my head fills with pure, unbridled bliss. I'm soaring like a sparrow above an eagle. I'm swimming with the sharks. For the first time in my life, I feel like I've lived up to my namesake.

I feel like a rock star.

Author's Note

Dear Reader,

Thank you for reading *Shipped*! I hope you enjoyed Henley and Graeme's story as much as I loved writing it. Although *Shipped* is a work of fiction, most of the island settings described in the novel are based on real locations in the Galápagos. There are indeed cafés along the waterfront in Puerto Baquerizo Moreno, San Cristóbal Island, albeit without Walsh's bad milkshake (still, don't drink the water—ice cubes included). You can hike to Suarez Point and snorkel in Gardner Bay on Española Island and drop off a postcard in the historic post barrel on Floreana Island. On Santa Cruz Island, there are wild tortoise–spotting opportunities in the highlands and a wonderful recycled glass art gallery in the main town of Puerto Ayora. And the stairs leading to the top of Bartolomé Island gifts you one heck of a stunning view.

And while Seaquest Adventures is a fictional cruise line, there are small ship adventure cruises that operate in the Galápagos and all over the world. If you're fortunate enough to have the means and opportunity to travel and you're considering booking a cruise, I encourage you to research your options. Lindblad Expeditions, for example, is a longtime leader in sustainability and responsible, eco-friendly travel (and my personal favorite).

As for other locales, the research station and tortoise breeding center that Henley and Graeme visit is fictional, but was inspired by the Charles Darwin Research Station and the Galápagos National Park Directorate's tortoise breeding center in Puerto Ayora, Santa Cruz Island.

But fun facts aside, one of the most important elements I included in *Shipped* is not at all fictional, although I wish it were. The parasitic fly *Philornis downsi* is quite real, and so is the impact that it and other human-brought invasive species are having on the islands. I first learned about invasive species like *Philornis* in the course of my day job working in the realm of corporate philanthropy, but it wasn't until I had the opportunity to travel to the Galápagos in 2016 that I truly understood the importance of managing invasive species to protect native wildlife.

Part of the wonder of Galápagos is the chance it offers to deeply connect with nature in a way that's not often available. Because the Galápagos Islands have so few natural predators and people didn't arrive until 1535, the wildlife there evolved with no inherent fear of humans. When is the last time you approached a bird and it didn't fly away? Walked by an iguana and it only turned its face into the sun instead of scurrying under a bush? Snorkeled alongside inquisitive—not frightened—sea lions or penguins (penguins!)? These are some of the special wildlife encounters I experienced in the Galápagos, and they took root in my heart and touched my soul.

Exploring Galápagos helped me understand that we're all connected—humans, plants, animals, ocean, ecosystems. The wild places of the world are shrinking, so it's all too easy to picture ourselves as existing separately from the natural world, but humans play a critical role in the health of the planet. Our actions can have negative consequences (climate change, pollution, mass extinction, etc.), but what I found most inspiring in the Galápagos was proof that people are capable of catalyzing positive changes as well. It all comes down to which you choose.

The people of Galápagos, for example, are choosing to take action to protect the UNESCO World Heritage Site that is their home. During my travels, I met local artisans who are using recycled materials like paper and glass to create beautiful works of art and, at the same time, reduce the amount of waste on the islands. I saw giant tortoises in person—reptiles that not fifty years ago were on the brink of extinction—and met the scientists who are working hard to preserve them and other endemic species. I learned about the Galápagos National Park Directorate's efforts to monitor the Galápagos Marine Reserve and prevent illegal fishing. And I spoke with children at a school in the highlands of Santa Cruz who are passionate about their role as environmental stewards.

Researchers, scientists, nonprofits, government organizations, local leaders, and community members in the Galápagos are working together to reduce plastic pollution, control invasive species, and restore natural habitats. And their efforts are making a tangible difference. Which makes me wonder: What can *we*, each of us, do to positively impact the world?

In writing *Shipped*, it was important to me to craft a character who felt as inspired by her experience in the Galápagos as I did, and for her to promote conservation within her own spheres. But we don't necessarily all have to be Henley and launch a corporate-sponsored global conservation initiative in order to create real change. We all make choices every day, and even small choices can add up to making a big difference if enough people join in.

We can choose reusable straws, utensils, grocery bags, and water bottles over single-use plastic varieties. We can eat fewer servings of meat each week, especially beef and pork, and opt for sustainably caught seafood to lessen our impact on the ocean. We can choose to shop at eco-friendly businesses and support local producers. We can recycle, and we can take public transportation, bike, or walk whenever feasible instead of driving a car.

For those with the financial means and inclination, you might choose to make a monetary donation to your favorite charity or nonprofit. If after reading *Shipped* you happen to feel inspired to contribute to conservation efforts in the Galápagos, two organizations doing vital work are the Charles Darwin Foundation (www.darwinfoundation.org) and Galapagos Conservancy (www.galapagos.org), among others.

On a personal level, we can make a difference by choosing empathy over division. Listening over shouting. Thoughtfulness over self-interest. We can choose to look outside ourselves and act in ways that positively impact our neighbors, our communities, our environment, and the wider world.

My wish for you, reader, is that you find your own spark of inspiration that leads to a deeper connection with the planet. For me, it was traveling to the Galápagos. For you, it might be stepping outside, exploring your own backyard or local park, and letting the miracles of nature seep into your soul.

The world is a big, beautiful, complicated place, and I hope you discover your own slice of wonder in it.

Love to all,
Angie

Acknowledgments

Shipped is the book of my heart, but it never would have set sail without the help and support of many wonderful people.

My mentor, Sarah Andre, magically appeared in my life at a point when I needed her most. Thank you for believing in me when imposter syndrome came knocking. For that, and your advice on many fronts, I am eternally grateful.

To my critique partner, Amanda Uhl: thank you for keeping me on track and letting me test out all my bad ideas on you. You're a talented writer and I feel lucky to count you as a friend. Gratitude to beta reader Danielle Haas for the superb feedback on an early draft of *Shipped* and to friend and travel partner Lindsey Davis for cheering me on and being willing to read whatever I send your way. Also, thanks to members of the Northeast Ohio chapter of RWA, Wellesley Writers, and the Omegas—I feel fortunate to be a part of so many supportive writing communities.

To my twelfth grade English teacher, Mrs. Hogan: thank you for introducing me to women's fiction by assigning *Like Water for Chocolate,* and for teaching me that writing is a skill you can improve through effort over time.

To my agent extraordinaire, Jessica Watterson: you are, simply, the best. Thank you for championing *Shipped* and making a long-standing dream come true. I'm so fortunate to have you and the entire Sandra Dijkstra Literary Agency team in my corner.

Many, many thanks to my brilliant editor, Molly Gregory. You helped elevate this story in ways I couldn't have imagined, and your enthusiasm for *Shipped* has meant the world to me. Working with you is a joy and a privilege and I'm beyond grateful for the experience.

Sincere, bottom-of-my-heart thanks to the entire Gallery team as well for their work on *Shipped* and their tremendous support. Thank you, Jen Bergstrom, Connie Gabbert, Jen Long, Aimée Bell, Christine Masters, Faren Bachelis, Sally Marvin, Abby Zidle, Anabel Jimenez, Lisa Litwack, Caroline Pallotta, Rachel Brenner, and Anne Jaconette. And to Kate Byrne and my UK publisher, Headline Eternal, thank you for bringing *Shipped* to readers overseas.

To my Wellesley tribe—you know who you are—you are the most brilliant, driven, empowering women I know. Your friendship is the most uplifting force in my life, and you inspire me every day with your empathy, humor, and trailblazing spirit. Thank you for setting the standard for how I write female friendships.

To all of the people working in—and supporting—conservation in Galápagos, and all over the world: I'm inspired by your dedication to not only preserving the planet but creating a better, more sustainable future. Thank you for the critically important work you do.

Finally, to my family: I truly could not have written this book without you.

Mom: thank you for sparking my imagination at a young age, opening my eyes to the world through travel, and always encouraging me to follow my dreams. You're my rock and my springboard. I wouldn't be here without you (literally, but also at this stage in my writing career).

Jimmy: every day with you is an adventure (in the best possible way). You keep me laughing and inspire me with your tenacious approach to life. Your support means more to me than you'll ever know—I love you.

Cooper: I didn't believe I could actually finish writing an entire novel until you came into the world. You catalyzed my inner determination to overcome challenges and keep moving forward. I'm so lucky to be your mom.

Grandma: thank you for your unconditional love and lifelong support. You and Grandpa have made an indelible mark on my soul and will be in my heart forever. Also sincere thanks to Don, Chris, and Jim—thank you for supporting my writing journey through all its ups and downs.

Finally, a huge, heartfelt thanks to you, reader! With the ocean of books out there, I very much appreciate that you chose to read mine. Also, much gratitude to the librarians, booksellers, reviewers, teachers, bloggers, and all the other folks who connect readers with books. I get to do what I love because of you, and I'm grateful. Thank you all!

HEADLINE
ETERNAL

FIND YOUR HEART'S DESIRE...